THE 7TH CANON

THE 7TH CANON

CANON

A THRILLER

BESTSELLING AUTHOR OF *MY SISTER'S GRAVE*

ROBERT DUGONI

THOMAS & MERCER

Text copyright © 2016 by Robert Dugoni
All rights reserved.

Published by Thomas & Mercer, Seattle
www.apub.com

Amazon, the Amazon logo, and Thomas & Mercer are trademarks of Amazon.com, Inc., or its affiliates.

ISBN-13: 9781503939424
ISBN-10: 1503939421

Cover design by Rex Bonomelli

Printed in the United States of America

To Sam Goldman. People always said you were a character, and I'd hoped to make you one before you passed, but I know you're up there in Heaven still calling everyone hero, chief, and friend. You were one of a kind—a teacher, a mentor, a friend. I'll miss you. And no dedication to you, Sam, would be complete without mentioning your bride, Adele. She was always there with you for all those many adventures of the Wildest Journalism Teacher in the West! Keep smiling, hero.

Chapter 1

December 21, 1987

Peter Donley had run out of time. Behind the elevated bench at the front of the courtroom, San Francisco Superior Court Judge Franklin Jefferson Barnes peered at Donley over the top of his reading glasses.

"If counsel is prepared to submit this matter, I am prepared to issue my ruling," Barnes said, adjusting his considerable girth hidden beneath the pleated black robe.

Opposing counsel Rebecca Rattigan shot from her chair, its legs screeching on the worn tiles, though the sound was still not nearly as grating as her voice. "Submitted, Your Honor."

And why wouldn't she? Possession being nine-tenths of the law, and her client being the possessor, Rattigan figured she'd won, and rightfully so.

Judge Barnes shifted his gaze to Donley. "Mr. Donley, is the plaintiff prepared to submit?"

Donley looked down at his seventy-eight-year-old client. Victor Russo sat slumped beside him at counsel table, as forlorn as a man who had just lost his best friend. In some respects, Russo had. Since the death of his wife, Russo had shared an apartment above Victor's, Russo's North Beach restaurant, with Albert, an African gray parrot. That is, until Russo's cleaning lady opened Albert's cage without closing the apartment window. Russo spent two weeks calling animal shelters and pet shops. A store on Divisadero said they'd sold an African gray that matched Albert's description, but when Russo offered the twenty-four-year-old, tattooed, punk-rock drummer twice what he'd paid the pet store, the man had refused. Russo called Donley's Uncle Lou for help.

Donley gently scooted back his chair and slowly stood, prepared to submit the matter, but when he opened his mouth to speak, he just couldn't bring himself to do so. Instead, he heard one of his Uncle Lou's favorite adages.

You only go around once in life, kid. You might as well have some fun.

At twenty-eight, just three years out of law school, Donley already felt like he'd gone around in life more than once. He looked at his client. The tears that had pooled in Russo's eyes throughout the afternoon began to slide down the man's cheeks.

"Mr. Donley?" Judge Barnes asked, now sounding impatient.

What the hell, Donley thought. He straightened and faced Barnes. "Your Honor, the plaintiff wishes to call one more witness."

Rattigan's smug expression turned to exasperation. Throughout the trial, her inexperience had been on display like a bad actress overacting her scenes. "Your Honor, the defense objects. Mr. Donley has called every witness disclosed on his witness list."

Donley tried to sound conciliatory. "I apologize to Ms. Rattigan and to the court, but this witness's possible testimony just recently came to my attention, and it is germane to the issue of ownership."

Rattigan shook the witness list Donley had submitted to the court. "If this *surprise* witness is not on the list, he cannot testify. Code of Civil Procedure, Section—"

Judge Barnes held up a hand as thick as a catcher's mitt. "Ms. Rattigan, why don't you concentrate on making the objections and allow me to worry about ruling on them," he said, a hint of his Louisiana dialect slipping into his baritone voice.

"I apologize," Rattigan replied, "but this is highly prejudicial—"

Barnes again raised his hand, this time with the index finger extended. "Unless you're going to tell me that your client has transformed himself into Rosa Parks and been asked to sit in the back of an Alabama bus, I don't think it's possible for him to have suffered any further *prejudice* than you've already opined during this three-hour trial."

Rattigan's face flushed, but for once she had the good sense to remain silent.

"Now," Barnes said, slowly turning his attention to Donley, "who is this *surprise* witness, Mr. Donley?"

Donley steeled himself. "The plaintiff wishes to call Albert to the stand."

The reading glasses that had been perched on the bridge of Judge Barnes's nose fell, dangling by a chain. "Say what?" Barnes asked.

"I know this request is unusual—"

"Unusual?" Barnes drew out the word like a worked-up Southern Baptist preacher. "Unusual? Mr. Donley, you just asked me to call a *bird* to the witness stand."

"Actually, Judge, Alfred is an African gray parrot."

"I know what he is, Mr. Donley. And if I recall from my simple southern education, I do believe a parrot is a *bird*."

"What I mean," Donley continued, "is that, well, being a parrot, Albert is . . . for lack of a better word, he is able to 'parrot' back certain phrases he's been taught or has learned on his own."

Though Barnes's brow remained furrowed, his expression of disgust softened, and his eyebrows rose. Was it curiosity? At least he hadn't rejected the idea outright, or directed the bailiff to put Donley in handcuffs for contempt. "And you intend to put him . . . it . . . you intend to put the bird on *my* witness stand and have it mimic a phrase it has been taught?"

"Every day when Mr. Russo left his apartment, he turned on the television to keep Albert company." Russo nodded like a bobblehead doll. "And it seems that Albert picked up an ability to mimic something he heard."

Rattigan furiously flipped the pages of her Code of Civil Procedure book. "Your Honor, we object. This is a bird. Only people can testify."

"You found that in the code, did you?" Barnes asked.

Rattigan lifted her head. "Well . . . no. But I mean, it has to be in here . . . somewhere. I mean, this . . . this is a bird!"

"Actually there is precedent for introducing animals as evidence." Donley snapped open his black binder and pulled out a short brief he'd typed up late the previous evening but had hoped to never use. He handed one copy to Rattigan and a second to Judge Barnes's clerk, who provided it to the judge. "The court will take particular note of the Connecticut case *Adams v. Martin*, in which Barney, the dancing terrier, was allowed to demonstrate a unique ability to juggle red rubber balls."

"Your Honor, that is not the same thing," Rattigan whined. "We're talking about letting a bird testify, not demonstrate a trick."

Donley lowered the brief. "I mean no disrespect to this court, but the most important thing here, the equitable thing, is to determine Albert's rightful owner. Allowing Albert to take the witness stand will conclusively prove either he is, or is not, the same bird that has lived with Victor Russo for more than five years."

Barnes sighed. "What exactly is the phrase you contend this bird will mimic, Mr. Donley?"

"It's not exactly a phrase, Judge."

"Then, what is it?"

"It's . . . well, it's a show tune."

Barnes leaned forward, now considering Donley out of one squinted eye. "A show tune?"

"Apparently, Albert is particularly fond of *The Andy Griffith Show*, and—"

"Andy Griffith?"

"Yes, Your Honor. You know . . . Mayberry RFD. Andy and Barney, Opie, Aunt Bea—"

"I know the show, Mr. Donley; I raised three kids of my own and have seven grandchildren."

"Right. Well, apparently Albert picked up the ability to whistle the show's opening tune." And with that, Donley put aside what little dignity he retained and whistled the tune to *The Andy Griffith Show*.

Barnes sat back, lips pursed, running a hand over his bald head for what seemed an eternity but was just a few seconds. Then, without uttering a word, he looked to his bailiff and swept his hand toward the large birdcage on the table between the two counsel tables. When she hesitated, Barnes repeated the gesture and widened his eyes to encourage her. The bailiff lifted the cage by the ring and placed Albert on the witness chair.

Now it was the clerk's turn to look perplexed. "Should I . . . swear in the witness?"

Barnes closed his eyes and gently shook his head. Opening his eyes, he gestured for Donley to proceed.

"Your Honor, if it is acceptable to the court, Mr. Russo would like to handle this witness himself."

Barnes clasped his hands. "Of course he would. Why not?"

Donley whispered in Russo's ear. "OK, Victor. He's all yours."

Russo pushed back his chair and walked to the open space between the judge's bench and the witness stand. He bowed with great deference to Barnes and turned to the cage.

"Albert? Over here, Albert. That's a good boy. Albert, do you want to watch Andy Griffith? Andy Griffith?"

The bird began to prance along the bar and bob its head.

"Andy Griffin, Albert. You know." Russo whistled.

"Objection!" Rattigan shouted so loud, Russo flinched as if she'd snuck up and goosed him.

Barnes looked dumbfounded. "Excuse me, Ms. Rattigan?"

"He's leading the witness, Your Honor."

Barnes bit his lower lip and closed his eyes. "Overruled."

"But, Your Honor—"

The catcher's mitt hand reached out again. "Sit . . . down, Ms. Rattigan."

"But—"

Barnes moved his hand as if placing it on Rattigan's head and forcibly lowering her into her chair. "Sit . . . down." He looked to Russo. "Continue, Mr. Russo."

"I think he's distracted, Your Honor," Russo said.

"Just do your best, Mr. Russo," Barnes said.

Russo bowed again and resumed. "Andy Griffith, Albert. Andy Griffith." His voice became desperate. He whistled, but Albert remained silent.

Russo coaxed the bird a third time, also without success. Tears had again pooled in his eyes, and he dropped his head in resignation.

Barnes sat forward, speaking gently. "Thank you, Mr. Russo. I think that will be all."

Donley stepped out from counsel table and touched Victor Russo's elbow, leading him back to his seat.

"Madame Bailiff, you may take Albert from the witness stand," Barnes said.

As the bailiff carried Albert back to the table, Barnes said, "I assume you are prepared to submit this matter, Mr. Donley?"

Resigned, Donley nodded. "Yes."

"Very well, then. Mr. Russo, I'm deeply sorry, but the burden in this case was upon you, as the plaintiff, to convince me the parrot belonged to you, and I'm afraid I can't conclude that is the case. Therefore, it is the decision of this court—"

"Andy Griffith. Andy Griffith."

The court reporter, taking down every word spoken in the courtroom, lifted his head, uncertain who had interrupted the judge. Everyone else, however, had turned to the table behind Donley, where Albert, head bobbing, pranced along the bar.

"Andy Griffith," he squawked.

"I'll be damned," Barnes said.

And with that, Albert began to whistle.

At nearly six in the evening, Donley had expected Ruth-Bell to have left the office and gone home, but when he stepped into the cramped reception area, she remained at her desk, the telephone pressed to her ear. Lou's voice spilled from his office, a one-sided conversation indicating he, too, was on the telephone.

Ruth-Bell handed Donley a stack of pink message slips without any further acknowledgment, and he stepped past the file cabinets and small table with the stained coffeepot into his office.

He draped his jacket over the back of a chair and set his briefcase beside his desk. Outside, he heard two of San Francisco's homeless arguing. The Law Offices of Lou Giantelli were located on the first floor of a historic building in San Francisco's Tenderloin District. The building's proximity to the courthouse had prompted Lou to buy it three decades earlier, when the neighborhood had been a relatively safe area. The intervening years had not been kind to the Tenderloin. What remained were run-down apartment houses and commercial buildings, and corner liquor stores and peep shows that attracted drug dealers and addicts, prostitutes and their pimps and johns, and the homeless and mentally unstable. Sometimes getting to work meant stepping across bodies—not all still alive.

Donley's desk phone rang, and he was surprised to see from the console that it was Ruth-Bell. Usually, she just shouted from reception that Donley or Lou had a call.

"You have a call," Ruth-Bell said.

When Ruth-Bell didn't elaborate, Donley said, "Did they give you a name?"

"Someone named Polly."

"Polly? Polly who?" he said, and immediately regretted it.

"Polly want a cracker," Ruth-Bell cackled, and with that Lou, who had obviously been waiting just outside the door, stepped into Donley's office flapping his elbows and squawking. "Andy Griffith. Andy Griffith."

Ruth-Bell hurried in behind him. "I heard you almost got yourself in trouble because your star witness was a little *fowl mouthed*," she said.

"Very funny," Donley said, letting them have their moment. "You two should go on the road together." He checked his watch. "How about now?"

Lou paused, laughing so hard he was having trouble catching his breath. When he did, he said, "I would have given anything to have seen it."

"Can't believe it worked," Donley said. "And it cost me only my dignity and my career."

Lou's voice rose. "Are you kidding? You're the talk of the courthouse. My phone has been ringing off the hook. Three judges called to ask if it was true; apparently, they're having their Christmas party, and Barnes is telling everyone and anyone who will listen."

"And that's a good thing?" Donley asked.

"The papers seem to think so." Ruth-Bell handed him a pink message slip. "Bill Main called from the *Chronicle*."

"And I just got off the phone with Victor," Lou said. "Three television trucks are parked outside his restaurant. He and Albert are going to be on the six o'clock news. It's the best publicity his restaurant has had in twenty years." Lou turned for the door. "Come on. Let's watch it on the television in my office."

"I'd rather not," Donley said. "I had to live it."

Ruth-Bell started for the door. "And much as I'd like to, I'm already late, and if I don't get home and make husband number three something to eat, I'll be looking for husband number four. That man can't boil water."

After Ruth-Bell had left, Lou leaned on the edge of the round table in the corner of Donley's office, nearly toppling the stack of case files.

"Come on, give me the details."

Donley explained how he knew he had not proved the bird belonged to Russo and how he'd come up with the idea the night before and performed research to support the argument. "I just couldn't bear the thought of Victor watching that guy carry Albert out of that courtroom. To be honest, I was surprised Barnes let me do it."

"Please," Lou said. "Franklin Jefferson Barnes lives for stuff like this. He's got an ego as big as his gut, and you made him the star attraction at the party. Trust me, no matter what he looked or sounded like in court, the only thing Barnes likes better than telling a good story is when he's in it. And he'll be telling this one long into his retirement. He won't forget it. Neither will you."

Lou straightened and started for the door, but he paused at the threshold and turned back. His shirtsleeves were rolled up, revealing meaty forearms. Though nearing seventy, Lou had maintained much of the stocky build that made him an All-City high school football player back in the day when running backs were still called wing backs. The notable exception was an expanded waistline from a healthy love of Italian food. "I know this hasn't been exactly the practice you had in mind—"

"Lou, I've told you before, I'm grateful for the job."

Not to be deterred, Lou continued. "Your day will come, Peter. And when it does, you'll be ready because of days like today. There's no experience like standing up in court before a judge or a jury and letting your ass hang in the wind. You don't get that experience sitting in a law firm library performing research and drafting interrogatories for six years."

"Let's hope I don't die from overexposure," Donley said. Just three years out of law school, he'd already had seventeen jury trials and numerous bench trials.

Lou laughed. "Your Aunt Sarah made calzone. You want to join us?"

"Thanks, but Kim usually needs a break from Benny about this time," he said, referring to his wife and two-year-old son.

Lou left the office with a skip in his step, whistling a tune Donley also knew he'd not soon forget.

Chapter 2

Father Thomas Martin prayed for bad weather the way some people prayed to win the lottery. Tonight it looked as though his prayers would be answered. Dark clouds advanced across an indigo night sky, and gusts of wind rattled the glass panes in his office and whistled through the putty-filled cracks in the hundred-year-old wood sash.

Bad weather was good for business at his Tenderloin boys' shelter. He had no empirical data to support his theory, but in the few months since he'd opened for business, he'd noticed a definite correlation between bad weather and the number of boys who chose his shelter over sleeping on San Francisco's streets.

He counted eight entries on the log-in sheet, then drew a line through the name of Andrew Bennet, who'd checked in but left unexpectedly. Seven boys. Father Thomas always hoped for more, but he tried not to get discouraged. He knew it would take time to build the boys' trust. They considered anyone over thirty either an agent of the police department or associated with social services. With that thought, Father Martin placed the log-in sheet within the pages of his Bible, shoved it into the top right-hand drawer of his army-green metal desk, and locked the drawer. He quickly pushed back his chair and checked his watch.

He was late locking the front door. He could stall only so long. Rules were important at the shelter. He didn't want it to become a midnight crash house. The goal was to get the boys off the street before they sold themselves or did drugs.

He stepped into the hall. The front door was at the bottom of a flight of stairs. Halfway down the hall, however, he turned 180 degrees, like a pitcher lifting his leg and spinning to fake a pickoff move to second base. He walked instead to the dormitory at the other end of the hall. He'd check on the new boy. Then he'd lock the door.

You're stalling.

Just hoping for one more.

The dormitory looked like an army bunkhouse with metal-framed beds perpendicular to the wall, but it was the best use of the space. Several boys lay watching grainy images on the television mounted to the ceiling. The shelter received only four channels, none clearly. Cable was not in the budget, which explained the cardboard box of well-used videocassettes.

The new arrival sat on the edge of the bed nearest the window. Father Tom had never seen him before. Sadly, the faces in the Tenderloin changed too often. Getting a boy to come to the shelter was difficult, and establishing trust that first night, critical.

The boy had been unwilling to provide a name. This being his first night, Father Martin decided not to push it. The boy said everyone called him Red. With bright-red hair, it wasn't difficult to figure out why. Father Martin watched Red take a quick drag on a previously concealed cigarette and flick the burning butt through the grate covering the window. He prohibited smoking in the shelter, as well as drugs, alcohol, and fighting.

Father Tom stepped lightly; he liked to make the boys think he could materialize out of thin air, everywhere and nowhere. "How's it going?" he asked.

Red's head snapped as if on a string. Strands of red hair fell across his face. He'd shaved the other half of his head nub short. Silver loop earrings pierced his left nostril and right eyebrow on a face pockmarked by acne. Father Tom estimated him to be fifteen, though in the Polk Gulch, age was often difficult to determine. The boys grew up fast. Red's problem at the moment was he had not exhaled his last drag.

Father Tom looked out the window as if to consider the darkening sky. "Looks like a storm," he said. "Why don't we close the window so we're not heating the neighborhood, as my mother liked to say."

Red's face contorted. His brow furrowed.

"Do you smell smoke?" Father Tom asked. He turned to Danny Simeon. The young man sat in a corner of the room working with an array of circuit boards and computer parts. "Danny, do you smell smoke?"

Simeon lifted his head and sniffed the air like a dog detecting an odor on the wind, all part of their routine. "You know, Father T, I think I do smell smoke."

"I hope it's not a fire, could burn the whole building down."

Unable to hold out any longer, Red coughed a gray cloud. When he'd stopped hacking, Father Tom smiled and pointed to the sign on the wall—a cigarette outlined in a red circle with a slash through it. "You have any more?"

Red shook his head.

At check-in, each boy stored his valuables in a locker in Father Tom's office. Cigarettes fell into that category. It prevented bartering and intimidation. Everybody at the shelter was equal. Each had nothing.

"OK. Any questions?"

Red shook his head. Then he blurted, "Yeah. Are you really a priest?"

"Don't I look like a priest?"

Red shook his head. "No."

Father Tom wore blue jeans with holes in the knees and a white T-shirt stretched tight across sinewy muscles. His shaved head, diamond-stud earring, and tattoo had caused considerable alarm in the upper-middle-class parish to which the Archdiocese of San Francisco had first assigned him. Those parishioners' rejection had given him the opportunity to pitch the archdiocese his idea to open a shelter for troubled young men. When the shelter finally opened—after a long detour around roadblocks, red tape, and vocal opposition—an article in the *San Francisco Examiner* had dubbed Father Tom "The Priest of Polk Street."

Father Tom smiled. "Yes, I'm really a priest." He pulled out a large ring with multiple keys. "Though sometimes I feel more like a janitor. At the moment, I need to go lock the front door. Then I'll come back, and we can talk."

He walked to where Simeon sat, deep in concentration. Once a street kid himself, Simeon had been Father T's first real success. They'd met at a homeless shelter. Simeon had an affinity for computers, and Father Tom eventually convinced him to enroll in technical classes at a local junior college. To get Simeon off the street, Father Tom had him supervise the dormitory at night. With Simeon's class load increasing, however, he needed more privacy to study and kept a room at the back of a restaurant where he worked as a busboy.

"One kick-ass computer, Father T," Simeon said. He fit two pieces onto a circuit board. "Though this is like putting parts of a sixty-five Chevy into a new Cadillac."

"Sorry, Danny, right now we need lights and heat more than a computer."

"Yeah, yeah, I know." Simeon put down the stubborn pieces. "Lockdown?"

"We're a shelter, Danny, not a penitentiary."

"Tell me about it." Simeon stood. "If we were a pen, we'd get a lot more money from the state, and better food."

Father Tom couldn't argue the logic.

Simeon faced the bunks and spoke in an uncanny Sylvester Stallone impersonation. "All right, convicts, lockdown. Warden here is taking the keys. Anyone leaves, better hope to find a stairwell smells like urine to sleep in."

Father Tom smiled and shook his head. He walked out the door, checking his watch. He was really late. He hurried down the hall, sandals slapping the worn linoleum. A streak of lightning flashed overhead. He looked up to the chicken-wire-reinforced skylight. It shone blue. Seconds later, thunder rumbled. Music to his ears.

Then the lights cut out.

"Damn," he said, stopping. He hoped it was the weather and not PG&E cutting power to the building. He was late paying his bills again, though he'd called and they'd said they'd work with him. He hoped it was just a blown fuse. The building was old and still on a breaker system, and fuses were cheap.

From down the hall, he heard the dormitory door open. "What's going on?" Danny Simeon asked.

"Could be the storm," Father Martin said. "I'm going to check the fuse box. Get the flashlights out of the closet, and keep everyone inside the room."

The fuse box to the building was in a closet located at the back of the recreation room, which was situated across the hall from Father Tom's office. Father Tom kept a flashlight in the closet. He sorted through his key ring in the limited ambient light from the skylight, found the key, and unlocked the double-wide doors. Stepping in, he hurried across the room. In the dark, the life-size ceramic Nativity scene at the front of the room looked like a group of San Francisco's homeless huddled against the cold.

He'd made it halfway across the linoleum when his sandal slid out from under him and he fell backward. Instinctively, he put out his hand to brace his fall, catching his left wrist at an odd angle. He heard it snap.

An electric bolt of pain shot up his arm, momentarily sapping the world of color. On the tile floor he writhed in agony, fighting the nausea and urge to vomit. When he was finally able to sit up, he cradled his arm to his body. A cold sweat broke out across his forehead. He'd broken his arm, no question about it, and he'd need to get to the hospital, which meant calling an ambulance and leaving Danny in charge. He looked to the spot where his foot had slid; he needed another leak in the roof like he needed a hole in the head.

Instead of a puddle, however, he noticed a series of spots, a linear pattern that didn't fit with a leak. Neither did the dark color, too dark to be water, even with the lights out. He touched a spot with the tip of his finger and held it up to the dim light. Still uncertain, he touched his finger to his tongue and recognized the bitter, iron taste.

"Blood."

He checked his hands and elbows but found no cuts.

In pain, and with his nausea worsening, he managed to get to his feet. Clutching his arm, he followed the trail of blood to where the three Magi knelt shoulder to shoulder alongside a lamb and cow, all in adoration of the child in the manger.

"Oh, no."

Father Martin stopped. Though his brain urged him forward, his feet remained anchored to the floor. He dropped to his knees and reached out, hoping to touch porcelain but instead feeling flesh.

Andrew Bennet's body lay in the manger, arms draped over the sides, knuckles dragging in the puddle of blood beneath the straw.

Lightning crackled overhead, a strobe of sharp, blue light. A second later, thunder rocked the building, and the first drops of rain splattered on the glass roof.

The storm had arrived.

Chapter 3

Donley shut the door on his way out of Benny's room and stepped over Bo, their Rhodesian ridgeback. Bo lay in the middle of the hallway, trying to get as close to the heater vent as possible. The lights glowed in their bedroom, but Kim had rolled onto her side, with her back to him, covers pulled tight. He picked up the legal file from the filing cabinet doubling as a nightstand, slid into bed, and adjusted the flexible lamp clipped to the headboard. No rest for the wicked. He needed an argument to explain why another of Lou's clients, Vincenzo Anitolli, was of sound mind at the time he executed a codicil to his will, re-inheriting his three sons.

It would not be easy. Witnesses for the stepmother, thirty years Anitolli's junior, would testify that Anitolli claimed to be Elvis Presley the day before he executed the document and had broken into a spontaneous rendition of "Jailhouse Rock" in the retirement-home cafeteria—still apparently nimble enough to get up on a table, arms and hips swinging until his pajama pants slid to his knees and the orderlies corralled him.

Where Lou found all these people, and how he had managed to run a law firm for forty-plus years without charging them, were two of the great mysteries of his practice. Lou's clients knew him from every walk of his life, and every one of them professed to know and love Lou like a brother. Thank God one of those was Archbishop Donatello Parnisi, who had grown up with Lou in North Beach, and whose friendship explained why the Catholic Archdiocese had rejected the downtown law firms for the solo practitioner with the crazy clientele to handle its legal matters.

Too tired to concentrate, Donley set aside the file and reached to turn off the light. He hesitated when he saw Max Seager's business card on his nightstand.

Seager was a highly regarded and successful plaintiff's attorney who had approached Donley in the Superior Court halls after one of Donley's trials. Seager offered him a job on the spot at a salary three times what Lou could afford to pay him. He told Donley to set up an appointment with Seager's assistant after the holidays.

Donley turned out the light. Lightning flashed outside the bedroom window, coloring the cloud layer a purplish hue. He counted, as his mother had taught—a way to calm a frightened child.

One thousand one, one thousand two, one thousand . . .

Thunder rumbled, finishing with a boom. Donley listened down the hall but did not hear Benny call out.

When another streak of light pulsed, Donley reached only "one thousand one" before the boom rattled the windows and rain tapped a ticker-tape beat on the roof shingles. Again, he listened but did not hear Benny. Mother Nature was putting on a show, but Kim, a sleep-deprived medical resident, looked intent on proving she could literally sleep through a storm. He pulled back the covers to check on Benny when Kim said, "Let him sleep."

"You're awake?" Donley slid over and spooned her, feeling the radiating warmth.

"Who could sleep through this noise?" She rolled toward him. "He'll be three in a month. You have to let him go to sleep alone; at this rate, you'll be sleeping in his college dorm."

He rested his chin on her shoulder. "I just don't want him to be afraid," he said.

She found his hand under the covers. "You had something to fear, Peter. He doesn't. And if you don't start getting to bed earlier, we may never have sex again."

The magic word.

"Is that an invitation?" When Kim didn't respond, he brushed strands of dark hair from her face, tracing the contours of her Korean features with his finger. "You were quiet when you got home."

"Two of my students got into a fight." Despite her schedule at the hospital, Kim continued to teach tae kwon do classes at a local YMCA. "It's the stuff they watch on television. Teenage mutant turtles. What the hell are those things, anyway?"

"Well, it is martial arts," he said, tweaking her.

She inched close, as if to kiss him. "Tae kwon do is taught up here," she whispered, gently touching his temple. "It has nothing to do with this." Her hand beneath the covers grabbed his groin.

"Ow. Hey, OK, OK, I'm sorry."

She laughed. "Two can play at that game, Mr. Donley."

He rolled on top of her, pinning her arms. "I tease you only because it makes you horny."

"It does not."

She halfheartedly struggled but was physically no match for him. At six feet two inches and 215 pounds, he outweighed her by nearly a hundred pounds. He kissed her.

The telephone rang.

Kim groaned.

"Let it ring." He ran his fingers along the curves of her body.

"It could be the hospital," she said.

"You're not on call tonight."

"It could still be the hospital." She reached for the phone, but he grabbed her arm.

"Not tonight," he said.

Chapter 4

They treated him as if he were something to be placed in a plastic evidence bag, zipped closed and tagged. Father Martin sat in a folding chair, the events continuing to swirl around him, the pain and nausea causing the room to tilt and whirl, everything black and gray.

Uniformed officers, plainclothes detectives, and crime-scene technicians came and went, stepping around yellow sticky notes marking the drops of blood on the floor. They took photographs, dusted for fingerprints, and drew sketches. A doctor from the medical examiner's office and his assistants attended to Andrew Bennet's body. Static echoed from radios, and flashes of red, white, and blue lit up the windows from the lights atop the patrol cars parked in the street.

Father Martin cradled his arm, now immobilized in a splint and elastic wrap but still painful. His wrist had swollen to the size of a lemon, and he remained so light-headed, he thought he might lift from the chair. He pressed the soles of his sandals to the floor, desperately trying to keep the room from spinning.

The African-American detective who had introduced himself as John Begley held out a pack of cigarettes, but Father Martin declined.

Begley returned the pack to his jacket pocket and started again with his questions.

"Did you know this boy?"

"Not really, no."

"He's never come to the shelter before?"

"No. Tonight was the first time." Andrew Bennet's body remained in the manger, a pool of blood beneath the straw.

"And you say he left?"

"Yes."

"But you don't know when."

"No." His head pounded.

"Your procedure is to lock the front door at ten, but tonight you didn't do so. Why not?"

"I didn't get around to it."

"What were you doing?"

"Stalling, hoping for one more." The cracks in his hands looked like red rivers from the dried blood. He'd pulled Andrew Bennet to him, clutching the boy, disbelieving. His white T-shirt had become a rose-colored mix of blood and perspiration.

"Why did you come into this room?"

Father Martin's stomach gripped, then lurched. "I think I'm going to be—"

He bent forward and threw up his dinner, splattering the detective's black wingtip shoes.

After the dry heaves and waves of nausea had passed, Father Martin sat up, fighting to catch his breath. He watched Detective Dixon Connor duck beneath the police tape strung across the doorway. Stocky, with a square jaw and well-trimmed crew cut, Connor strode toward them looking like he'd walked off a Marine Corps recruiting poster. Father Martin had crossed paths with Dixon Connor more than once. On the most recent occasion, Connor had come to the shelter looking for a particular boy. When Father Martin refused to provide him any information, Connor accused him of harboring prostitutes and drug dealers and threatened to shut him down. Father Martin told Connor he could arrest the boys from now to eternity, and each time they'd be back on the streets before Connor finished the paperwork. He was offering an alternative.

Connor didn't see it that way.

Connor spun a folding chair and straddled it. His right hand held two plastic bags.

"Found it," Connor said holding up a bag with what looked to be Father Martin's letter opener, a gift from a South American missionary. The teak handle, carved with the image of Christ on the cross, appeared stained with blood.

"Along with these." Connor handed Begley a second plastic bag, this one containing a brown nine-by-twelve-inch envelope.

Begley, already wearing blue latex gloves, unzipped the bag and folded open the envelope tab. He pulled out what appeared to be photographs. His face contorted in disgust. "Where?"

"Office across the hall," Connor said. "Inside a file drawer."

Begley looked from the photographs to Connor, about to say something, but his cheeks puffed as if swallowing his words. He turned, raincoat splaying like a cape. "Listen up, people." Everyone in the room came to a sudden stop—the patrol lights swirling and the radios crackling. "We're going to freeze the building," Begley said. "Right now! Bag everything and catalogue it. Do not leave this room. Do not open doors."

After a beat the room started up again, the men and women quickly going about their business.

Connor grabbed Father Martin by his shoulder and pulled him to his feet. A sharp pain radiated from his wrist, buckling his knees and bringing another wave of nausea.

"Connor," Begley said.

"You have the right to remain silent," Connor said. "Anything you say can and will be used against you in a court of law. You have a right to an attorney . . ."

◆   ◆   ◆

Danny Simeon stood in the hallway behind a uniformed officer stationed at the recreation-room door. Simeon had heard the sirens, which were not unusual in the Tenderloin. He'd paid little attention to them until the windows of the dormitory lit up in strobes of flickering color. Looking out the window, he saw police officers exiting patrol cars and hurrying up the building steps to the front door. The boys, well versed in police procedure, scattered from the dormitory like billiard balls.

Simeon hurried into the hallway in time to see beams of light bouncing off the staircase walls, the officers' boots pounding up the stairs. He did not see Father Martin in the hallway and quickly checked the office. The door was locked, but Simeon had a key and quietly slipped inside.

The first wave of officers came up the stairs and entered the recreation room across the hall. Those who followed fanned out throughout the building. Simeon stepped from the office and got as far as the double-wide doors when an officer stopped him. Inside the recreation room he caught a brief glimpse of Father Tom kneeling on the floor with his back to the door. Another officer shoved him down the hall and started asking him questions.

Now he watched as two uniformed officers stepped into the hall, Father Tom between. His arm was immobilized in a sling and his T-shirt covered in blood. Simeon stepped quickly toward him. "Father T? What happened? Where are you taking him?"

But just as Simeon neared the priest, Dixon Connor exited the room. Before Simeon could react, Connor had grabbed an officer's nightstick, jabbed the end into Simeon's stomach, and whipped the other end across his jaw.

Chapter 5

December 22, 1987

Donley drummed his fingers on his desk and dismissed another case summary as not helpful. Frustration had set in. He'd come into the office early to search for legal precedent on which to base an argument that a man who'd professed to be Elvis Presley could somehow also be sane enough to decide how to dispose of his estate. The stack of books on his desk grew, but so far, Donley had nothing to show for it.

He drained cold coffee from his mug, grimacing at the taste. He rarely drank coffee, which was likely part of the reason he felt on edge, but he needed the caffeine after working three late nights in a row. He wanted to clear his desk so he could enjoy the Christmas holiday but was quickly learning the truth of another of Lou's adages. "The law," Lou liked to say, "is a jealous mistress, and she will take all of your time if you let her."

In need of a mental break, Donley stood from his desk to stretch. When he did, he sensed something out of the ordinary. The accordion-style radiator beneath the window hissed and spit, but otherwise, the office was quiet. Too quiet. Eerily quiet. He checked his watch. Lou was late.

Lou was never late. Lou was as regular as the spit and hiss of the radiator. He'd stormed through the office door at precisely seven thirty every morning for better than forty years. Within minutes, he had his jacket off, shirtsleeves rolled up, and the phone pressed to his ear. Once Lou arrived at the office, quiet went out the window. His volume dial was loud, louder, and loudest. If Lou wasn't talking on the telephone, he was shouting for Ruth-Bell to get him another file, lunch, or more coffee. No shrinking violet, Ruth-Bell gave as good as she got, usually yelling back something like, "I have two arms. If you wanted a receptionist with eight, you should have hired an octopus!"

How the two of them had worked decades together without killing each other was one of life's great mysteries. Donley just tried to avoid the cross fire.

Donley walked into the reception area and refilled his mug from the well-stained coffeepot, figuring edgy was better than sleepy in court. He again considered his watch, confirming the time with the German cuckoo clock on the wall to the right of the door. This was getting downright unnerving.

The door opened, nearly hitting him. Lou burst in, briefcase and brown-bag lunch in hand, a raincoat over his arm.

"Where in the love of Christ were you last night?" Lou didn't stop for an answer, walking into his office. He tossed his raincoat at a cigar-store Indian, one of the many knickknacks he'd accumulated from appreciative clients. The coat hit the wooden figure and slid to the throw rug.

Donley followed him, picking up the coat. "What are you talking about? I was at home."

Lou removed his sport coat and rolled up the sleeves of his shirt. He'd already pulled down the knot of his tie and unbuttoned the collar. "I called."

"When?"

"Late."

Donley recalled the phone ringing and not allowing Kim to answer it. He draped the coat over a chair. "I must have missed it. Why? What's going on?"

"Did you watch the news?"

"Please don't tell me Albert flew off on the six o'clock news."

Lou didn't smile. The good lawyers, like Lou, had short memories. Albert was already a distant memory.

"I got a priest at SF General," Lou said.

"What do you mean? What happened?"

Lou handed him the folded newspaper. "Page one. I've been on the phone with Don for an hour already this morning. They took him to the hospital."

"The archbishop?"

Lou looked at him like he was nuts. "What? No, the priest." Lou pulled open the door behind his desk, revealing a water closet with a sink and medicine cabinet. He shot a plug of shaving cream into his palm and began to lather his face. "Three hours to put a cast on his wrist. What were they doing, grinding the plaster? I got the Martinez trial this morning. Don is going to call to find out what I know, which is jack at this point. Tell him I'm in trial, but tell him I'll try to call him when we break." Donley cringed as Lou swiped the old-fashioned double-edged razor down his cheek, the blades scraping the coarse stubble. "I called a friend of mine last night, a private investigator named Frank Ross. Ruth-Bell has his number, if she graces us with an appearance this morning. I asked him to run some things down for me. Call him this afternoon, and find out what he knows. In the interim, I need you to get a hold of the district attorney, and find out what they have and when I can have it. They'll jerk you around, but just get the five *w*'s," he said, meaning *who*, *what*, *when*, *where*, and *why*. "Then get down there and talk to him."

"The archbishop."

"The priest. He's at the county jail, Hall of Justice, sixth floor. Ruth-Bell can help. And have her cancel everything on my calendar for the rest of the week. What she can't cancel, you'll have to handle."

Donley saw his Christmas break evaporating.

Lou tapped the razor on the porcelain sink, making a metallic clinking. He started on the other cheek. "Your aunt isn't going to like this; she had her heart set on Christmas in Florida with her sister. Me? I'd just as soon do without the heat and her sister, but you know your aunt."

Donley rushed to get in a sentence when Lou ran the blade under the stream of water. "What happened? What did the priest do?"

"Read the paper, and you'll know as much as I do at this point. Can you handle it? Good." Lou grabbed the white towel hanging on the bar inside the door and wiped the remaining foam from his face. Then he unrolled his shirtsleeves, buttoned his cuffs, and grabbed his brown blazer. "I'll be back sometime after five. We can go over it then. I'll try to call during a break, but I cross Dr. Kinzerman today, and I'll be lucky to get one straight answer out of that SOB."

"OK, I'll—" Donley started, but Lou had already picked up his briefcase and stepped into the lobby, nearly colliding with Ruth-Bell.

"Talk to Peter. He knows everything."

Ruth-Bell stepped in. The office door slammed shut, the fogged glass with the stenciled letters rattling. Ruth-Bell turned to Donley. "You don't know anything, do you?"

"Not a damn thing," Donley said.

◆ ◆ ◆

"Everything *was* in plain sight," Dixon Connor said, not surprised his partner was not supporting him.

"Then you must have X-ray vision," John Begley said. "You must be Superman, Connor." Begley turned to Lieutenant Aileen O'Malley and continued to stab Connor in the back. "The office was across a hall.

That door was locked. I know. I checked it when I came up the stairs. He should not have gone in there without a warrant."

"It was a fucking crime scene," Connor said.

"We came upon a crime scene after the crime was committed. We needed a warrant to search that office."

Connor wanted to bust the black son of a bitch in the mouth, and just being in O'Malley's cramped, glass-enclosed office made him want to puke. There had been a time when room 450 of the Hall of Justice had felt like his living room. San Francisco's homicide detectives, men like him who'd spent years paying their dues, sat at cramped desks amid battered file cabinets solving San Francisco's murders. Now Connor felt like an unwanted guest, and Begley and O'Malley represented the poster children for what had gone wrong with the department: quotas. Blacks like Begley and women like O'Malley got promoted so the department could meet its quotas while more-deserving white male candidates got early retirement packages or the pleasure of humping their asses on the street, knowing they were entitled to the next promotion but wouldn't get it.

"I've been doing this job for better than twenty-five years. I got a dead body in a building, *not* a private residence; that makes the whole operation subject to search."

Begley continued to direct his comments to O'Malley. "The crime took place in the recreation room across the hall. The priest keeps a bed in his office."

"We don't know where the crime took place," Connor countered. "We found the body in the recreation room, but we also found drops of blood."

"Not in the office, we didn't," Begley said.

Connor shifted in the chair. The thin fabric cushion offered little comfort for the deteriorating disc in his back, the pain a lingering reminder of a bullet still lodged near his spine. His back bothered him when he sat too long, lay too long, or stood too long. It always bothered him. Some mornings he couldn't open his eyes without feeling as if someone had jolted him with five thousand volts of electricity. The Vicodin helped, but not enough. The Vicodin and Jameson's, a lot of it, usually did the trick.

O'Malley rubbed her forehead as if fighting a headache. Dressed in blue jeans and a T-shirt, her red hair pulled back in a ponytail, she looked more like a Pacific Heights PTA mom than a cop. Thanks to a husband pulling in several hundred grand as an investment banker, that's exactly the role she played. She spoke to Connor. "Were you concerned there was an imminent chance of evidence being destroyed?"

She sounded like a goddamn police manual. "When I enter a building and find a dead body, *everything* is possible evidence, and everyone present a suspect, a witness, or a problem. Who knows what they could have destroyed while we were getting a warrant?"

"Is that why you busted that kid's jaw?" Begley said.

Connor glared at him. "He isn't a kid. He's eighteen. And he attacked a police officer."

"Rambo here hit one of the residents with a nightstick. The kid's at SF General."

Connor shook his head. "I thought he was going for the gun. And he isn't a resident. He works there."

O'Malley put up a hand and nodded to the door. "You can go, John. Get started on the paperwork. Keep me apprised. The press is already calling. So is the brass."

Begley left the office without looking back.

"Where's the priest now?" O'Malley asked.

Connor fingered his father's Marine Corps ring, spinning it on his finger. "Bryant Street," he said, referring to the jail.

"Why'd they take him in to General?"

"He broke his wrist."

"How?"

"Unknown."

"Who was the first officer on scene?" she asked.

"Cameron."

"Scott? How'd the call come in?"

"Anonymous source. Likely a pay phone on Polk. Don't have the tape yet, but the operator said it was short. 'There's a dead body in the shelter.' Something like that."

O'Malley paused. "I take it the kid in the hospital isn't talking?"

Connor shrugged. "Ain't a kid."

"Is he talking, or isn't he?"

"His jaw's busted, and they won't let us near him."

"Any other witnesses?"

He couldn't hide a smile. She really didn't know shit. "They scatter like ghosts, those kids; I wouldn't get your hopes up."

O'Malley shook her head. "You've testified a hundred times."

"Seventy-eight."

"Then tell me why you would go in a locked office if we had a secure building? Why give the defense attorney something to argue? Why not wait for the warrant?"

"I told you why."

She pushed back her chair and stood. "I'm trying to work with you here. If the door was locked, you should have waited for a warrant. I don't need to tell you that."

"No . . . you don't."

O'Malley stared at him. "Internal Affairs needs to look into the kid with the broken jaw and sort this out."

"Are you suspending me, Aileen?"

"Enjoy the holiday."

"I'm not using my personal days. You want me gone, suspend me."

"Fine," she said. "Leave your badge and gun on your desk."

Connor stood. His back ached like it was on fire. He thought of a number of things to say, but none were as good as what he wanted to do. He wanted to grab Aileen O'Malley right between the legs. The look on her face would be the final Kodak moment in a scrapbook spanning twenty-five years, but he wasn't going to make it that easy for them. She'd suspended him, his prelude to retirement, and that little bullet would be his gold mine. A full pension and disability, unlike his father, whom they'd kicked to the curb. That was the only reason he didn't grab her. His father.

"You have a Merry Christmas, Lieutenant," he said.

◆ ◆ ◆

Donley stepped from the cab onto Bryant Street and looked up at the heavy gray clouds cloaking the city. The chilled morning air seeped through his suit jacket. "Here we go again," he said.

For the past three years, Donley had felt like he'd stepped onto a treadmill operating at high speed. It had started the day he'd taken the oath to be a lawyer at city hall. Lou shook his hand, handed him a file, and told him he had his first trial in municipal court. It had been only a traffic-crash dispute, and the trial lasted all of an hour, but Donley had not had a clue what he was doing. Still, he'd managed to get through it and prevail. When he'd returned to the office that afternoon, Lou had family and friends waiting and a spread of food.

"That trial was your baptism by fire," Lou had said. "You'll never be less prepared, but you did it. Now, you know you can handle anything. There's nothing like standing in front of twelve people with your ass hanging in the wind."

When the pace in the office seemed out of control, Lou just worked harder. "You'll have time to rest when you're at Crosby-N. Gray," he'd say, referring to a well-known local funeral parlor. Donley just hoped he didn't get there sooner than he wanted. The long hours were killing him, especially with Benny now old enough to do more than eat and poop. Benny and Kim were the reasons Donley had kept Max Seager's business card, and why it was now burning a hole in his pocket. He intended to call Seager's assistant and set up a meeting for after the holidays. He owed it to his family. They needed the money. They could buy a home on the peninsula, and Benny could go to a better school.

Donley hurried up the steps of the Hall of Justice, a concrete monolith as long as a city block and as gray as the sky, with small cubed windows and absolutely no architecturally redeeming qualities. The building housed the offices of the San Francisco Chief of Police, the Homicide Division, the District Attorney's Office, the County Medical Examiner, and the criminal courts.

According to the article in the *Chronicle* Donley had read on the cab ride from the office, Father Thomas Martin had opened a shelter for teenage prostitutes and runaways who sold themselves in an area of the Tenderloin referred to as The Polk Gulch. Police had not released details of Father Martin's arrest, but the reporter cited anonymous sources and reported that the body of a young, white male had been found in a bloodied manger at the shelter.

Donley had shuddered at the image that description conjured, and thinking about it made him shiver again as he entered the building. *Just get the five w's. Get in and get out,* he told himself.

Ruth-Bell instructed Donley to ride the elevator to the sixth floor and cross a catwalk connecting the Hall of Justice to the county jail. She explained that once jailed, a suspect never left the building prior to being arraigned and making bail. Father Martin wouldn't be given that option. No judge in San Francisco who wanted to be reelected would grant bail to someone suspected of the brutal slaying of a youth.

After finding the right department and identifying himself, Donley followed a beefy sheriff's deputy, everything coordinated so no two doors remained open at the same time. A sterile corridor led to an interior catwalk above an open pavilion. Below, men walked about freely in bright-orange jumpsuits, the noise echoing up at Donley like engines humming inside a metal drum. With it came an odor that reminded him of the smell he'd once endured wedged up against a homeless man on a crammed Muni bus.

As they approached the end of the hall, another deputy stood from a plastic chair and peered inside a narrow, wire-mesh window, then scribbled a note on a log posted to the door.

"What's that for?" Donley asked.

"Suicide watch," the deputy said. "Your boy is out of it; hasn't said a word since he was brought in."

The officer put a hand on the doorknob and signaled a guard in the tower to disengage the lock. The deputy who'd escorted Donley said, "I need to go through your briefcase."

Donley handed over his briefcase. His mouth had become dry, and he felt nauseated and light-headed, likely from too much coffee on an empty stomach. The officer removed all of his pens, except one.

"Make sure you come out with it," he said, without the need to elaborate.

The door lock buzzed. The deputy pulled it open and slid the blue plastic chair into the room. Donley stepped in but abruptly stopped. The man sitting with his feet folded beneath him on a thin mattress of a metal-framed bed didn't look like any priest he'd ever seen. He looked like a comic-book villain. He had his head tilted back against the cinder-block wall, eyes closed, and he'd lowered the orange, jail-issued coveralls to his waist, revealing a white tank top. A fresh cast on his left arm extended to his elbow, stopping inches below the tattoo of a bird of prey.

Donley looked back to the door, thinking this had been some sort of mistake, but he did not see the deputies through the glass. He slid the chair across the floor, hoping the noise would get a response, but the priest's eyes remained closed. Donley didn't know if the man was sleeping, sedated, deliberately ignoring him, or preparing to jump off the bed and rip his throat out.

"Father Martin?"

Donley heard the hush of the ventilation system circulating air through a ceiling grate, though the air in the room felt stifling. He wiped trickles of sweat from his temples. "Father Martin, can you hear me?"

Father Martin opened his eyes, two black pools of ink, but it was brief. He closed them again.

A tiny movement caught Donley's attention. Father Martin had pressed the index finger of his right hand to his thumb. After several moments, the thumb moved to the ring finger. Donley reconsidered the priest's face and noticed his lips moving, ever so slightly. Had Donley not seen his mother's lips do the same thing for so many years, he might not have recognized the act. The priest was praying the rosary, keeping track of the prayers on his fingers: one Our Father, ten Hail Mary's, one Glory Be. Five decades.

Donley knew each prayer by heart. His mother had recited those prayers every night, her voice drifting down the hall to his room as a faint whisper.

"Hail Mary, full of grace, the Lord is with thee. Blessed art thou among women, and blessed is the fruit of thy womb, Jesus . . ."

A chill ran down his spine. He hadn't thought of that in years.

He shook the recollection. "Father Martin, I'm Peter Donley." His voice sounded like it was coming from somewhere outside his body.

The priest moved his thumb to the next finger.

The car engine sputtered and died at the curb. Donley, still a child, heard it and slid quickly from the mattress and scurried beneath his bed. His mother's voice grew louder, the rhythm of her prayers intensifying.

"Hail Mary, full of grace . . ."

Donley tried again to shake the recollection. "Father Martin, I need to ask you a few questions."

"The Lord is with thee . . ."

The front door to the house opened and slammed shut.

A bad night.

Just get the five w's. "Father Martin?"

"Blessed art thou among women . . ."

His father's heavy work boots thundered up the stairs. Donley slid to the farthest corner, pressing his palms tight against his ears.

"And blessed is the fruit of thy womb . . ."

The first hit sounded like a sharp snap, the crack of a whip.

His mother cried out in pain, pleading.

Sweat trickled down Donley's face. The scar on his cheek, the one the plastic surgeons had turned into a thin white line, burned numb. His chest heaved, but it brought no air. He couldn't catch his breath. Couldn't breathe. The walls began to close in. The floor tilted and turned.

Panic attack.

Donley stood, toppling the plastic chair.

The priest's eyes opened—dark, inhuman.

Donley moved unsteadily to the door, pounding on the glass. When the door didn't immediately open, he felt his face flush and his legs weaken. About to knock again, Donley pulled back his hand when the guard appeared and motioned to the tower. Donley heard the lock disengage. The door swung open. He stepped past the guard into the hall, sucking in air, ripping loose the knot of his tie, and undoing the button of his collar.

The deputy looked confused. "You done already?"

"Yeah," Donley managed to say, still struggling to catch his breath.

The deputy stepped into the room and retrieved the chair. Exiting, he said, "Creeps me out, too."

Donley took back the contents of his briefcase. About to leave, he glanced at the narrow, wire-mesh window.

The priest had shut his eyes.

Chapter 6

Lieutenant Aileen O'Malley massaged her eyelids, careful not to dislodge her contact lenses. At 10:00 a.m., the damn things already burned, and the pounding in her temples maintained a steady beat that two Tylenol hadn't come close to silencing.

Gil Ramsey, San Francisco's district attorney, stood with his back to her, staring out the glass wall into the homicide room, where detectives sat at cluttered desks. In the middle of the room, someone had set the traffic-signal light to red, but O'Malley knew that was wishful thinking. There would be no stopping this day. O'Malley had been going since getting the call at four thirty in the morning.

Linda St. Claire, Ramsey's chief prosecutor, sat across O'Malley's desk, her bare legs crossed, foot tapping. John Begley stood in the corner, trying to avoid the wandering leaves of a philodendron plant.

"Without a search warrant?" St. Claire shook her head. "I say we let the priest go and try Connor."

O'Malley buried her chin in her hand. On first blush, she and St. Claire had much in common. Both had succeeded in traditionally male-dominated professions by being smart and resolute. Tall, both of them kept in good physical condition. But the similarities ended there.

O'Malley exercised because her job required she be in shape, her figure an athletic cut with swimmer's shoulders and narrow hips. Growing up, she'd been the girl next door the boys wanted to play with. St. Claire worked out to further her significant social life, her curves defined under the tutelage of a personal trainer and augmented by a plastic surgeon. Growing up, she'd been the girl next door every boy wanted.

"There's no sense trying to make it better than it is," St. Claire said. "Connor screwed up. How did he find out about the kid at the shelter? Anything we can use?"

O'Malley shook her head. "Anonymous caller. Connor and John were on standby. Connor was in the office when the call came in."

Ramsey turned from the window, impeccably dressed in a navy-blue suit, white shirt, and silver tie that matched the color of the salt in his salt-and-pepper hair. He directed his attention to Begley. "What did the caller say?"

"'There's a dead body at the shelter,'" Begley said.

"Anything else?"

Begley shook his head. "You can hear background noise, cars on the street, people talking. It was a pay phone."

St. Claire spoke to Ramsey. "What evidence we'll be able to get in will depend a lot on Connor's state of mind."

"Then pack your bags," Begley said. "'Cause we're going down if that's the case."

St. Claire continued as if she hadn't heard him. "We need to know whether, when Connor got to the building, he thought there could be more than one body, or if he had probable cause to believe there was something or someone in the locked office."

Begley shook his head. "Not likely."

St. Claire persisted. "There has to be something to justify his knocking down a locked door."

Ramsey jingled the change in his pockets, a habit. "The crime scene was the recreation room. It's a stretch to extend that to a locked office across a hall. John's right. It's a building, not a home, but let's have someone do some research and see if there is some precedent when the building is for a single purpose, like a boys' club . . . something like that. It could be a stretch, though, since the priest keeps a room in the office, and the boys sleep there."

"He lives there?" St. Claire asked.

"He has a bed and a sink in a closet at the back of his office." Ramsey sat in the chair next to St. Claire, crossed his Ferragamo loafers, and pressed his fingertips together, creating a pyramid beneath his chin. "I had a tour."

Ramsey would not be district attorney long. Every significant poll predicted he would be California's next attorney general. His father, Augustus, had taken the same career path to become a two-term governor, an office from which he had launched an unsuccessful bid for the Republican presidential nomination.

Ramsey said what everyone in the room had been thinking. "We all know this is a political hornet's nest. A lot of people in city hall supported Father Martin and his project, including me. If we mishandle this, there will be enough mud to cover us all."

"What about the letter opener? Where did Connor find it?" St. Claire asked.

"Also in the office," Begley said.

"Also a problem," Ramsey said. "How bad are the photographs?"

"Bad," St. Claire said. "Hard core, prepubescent. Enough to shock any juror."

The softness of St. Claire's blonde hair and blue eyes belied her reputation and her résumé. Her ten capital-murder convictions numbered more than any other prosecutor in the state and had earned her a nickname she publicly rebuffed, but which many of her colleagues believed she privately relished: "St. Claire, the Chair." This was the type of high-profile, winnable case Ramsey seemed to always assign her, which had led to other, less-flattering nicknames from her colleagues, names like "Cherry Picker" and "Glory Hound." It had also raised suspicions about the nature of their relationship.

"How old is the victim?" Ramsey asked.

"Undetermined," O'Malley said. "Sixteen, according to his juvenile records."

"Any theories on a possible motive?"

Begley shook his head. "Father Martin has no history of violence or sexual misconduct."

"He has a juvenile record in New York," St. Claire said.

That got everyone's attention, which O'Malley suspected had been St. Claire's intent. Out-of-state records had to come from the FBI through the National Crime Information Center. Getting them was difficult, getting them so quickly, usually impossible.

"I made a call to a law-school friend this morning," she said coyly. "Father Martin was arrested for vandalism and malicious mischief. He stole a car when he was thirteen and did some time in a juvenile facility."

Ramsey dismissed it. "I could have saved you the call. He offered that information when he was stumping for his shelter. He made it a positive, said it helped him to relate to the boys—kids with problems, without role models; kids in need of a break."

"Maybe not so positive," St. Claire said.

"The point is, he isn't hiding it." Ramsey stood and stretched his back, then resumed jiggling the change in his pockets.

O'Malley turned to Begley. "What do we know about the victim?"

Begley pulled out a notebook. "Andrew Bennet. Goes by the nickname 'Alphabet.' Multiple arrests for prostitution, lewd behavior, drugs, possession with intent to distribute, a couple of B and E's. He's a regular in the Gulch."

"Not a choirboy," Ramsey said.

"Far from it," Begley agreed.

"We need to get back inside the building, find something that gets us closer to a motive. You froze it?" Ramsey asked.

"I had no choice after Connor went Rambo."

"Does the priest have a lawyer?" Ramsey asked.

Begley shrugged. "I don't know."

"Has he asked for one?"

"No, but I don't think we can question him again without the defense making a stink later."

"I'm more curious whether the archdiocese will get involved," Ramsey said.

St. Claire shook her head. "Not if they're smart, they won't. Isn't this the reason why it did not affiliate itself with the shelter in the first place?"

"Don't be so sure," Ramsey said. "The archbishop's a stubborn SOB when he wants to be."

St. Claire stood and poured herself a glass of water from the pitcher on the edge of O'Malley's desk. "Who's handling the arraignment?"

"Trimble," Ramsey said, referring to Judge Milt Trimble.

St. Claire stopped in mid-pour. "Maximum Milt?"

"With the consolidation of the municipal and superior courts, he's on the rotation," Ramsey said, though O'Malley detected a tone to Ramsey's voice she inferred meant he had something to do with the assignment. Ramsey changed gears. "I want to move quickly. My phone's ringing off the hook. Be prepared to go day after tomorrow."

"Christmas Eve?" St. Claire asked.

"The courts are open a half day," he said. His tone again suggested he'd played a part in expediting the matter.

St. Claire set down the pitcher. "Maximum Milt on Christmas Eve—he should be in a good mood."

Ramsey looked to O'Malley. "We'll need to be prepared to meet a Riverside standard," he said, referencing the US Supreme Court case requiring a prompt judicial hearing to determine whether sufficient evidence existed to establish probable cause to hold a defendant arrested without a warrant.

"You'll have my statement this afternoon," Begley said.

"What about a statement from Connor?" St. Claire asked.

O'Malley shook her head. "I put him on the beach. Hopefully, he stays there. John can handle the specifics." She stood, eager to end the meeting so she could deal with a dozen other matters, finish her Christmas shopping, and try to find at least a spark of holiday spirit. "Anything else?"

"That should do it," Ramsey said. "Except for determining who'll be representing Father Martin."

◆　◆　◆

Ruth-Bell was not at her desk, and Donley was glad he wouldn't have to answer her questions about what he'd learned from the priest, which was jack. Too early for lunch; she was likely in the bathroom down the hall. Donley went into his office and shut the door. He removed his tie and jacket and draped them over a chair, trying to make sense of what had just happened. His legs and arms felt weak, like he was coming down with the flu. He had the onset of a headache and felt like he'd just woken from a deep sleep.

It had been years since he'd suffered a panic attack, and even longer since he'd had an attack brought on by the memory of his father. Donley opened his desk drawer, shook free two aspirin, and downed them with water. Past experience had taught him the best thing to do to get past the attack was to keep busy, occupy his mind, bury the memories under an avalanche of legalese and critical thinking. It had worked before. It had worked for years.

He made a to-do list of things to accomplish before the Christmas holiday and began checking them off as he went, pouring through one file after the next, making phone calls, dictating letters. An hour passed. He heard the telephone on Ruth-Bell's desk ring in the reception area. Simultaneously, the red light on his desk phone console lit up, indicating an outside caller. When Ruth-Bell failed to answer on the third ring, Donley answered the phone himself.

"Law Offices of Lou Giantelli." No one spoke. "Hello?"

"Peter."

He hardly recognized the voice.

Twenty minutes later, Donley was racing down a linoleum floor, turning corners and following signs.

In between sobs, Ruth-Bell had managed to tell Donley she was calling from a pay phone at San Francisco General. The court clerk in Judge Kaplan's courtroom had called that afternoon. Lou had collapsed during his cross-examination of Dr. Kinzerman and been taken from the courtroom on a stretcher.

When he reached the waiting room, Donley paused to take a few deep breaths before entering. His aunt Sarah sat beside Ruth-Bell, both pale, their eyes swollen and red. Sarah stood and hugged him.

"Have they told you anything?" he asked.

Sarah opened her mouth to speak, but the words choked in her throat.

"The clerk said it was a heart attack," Ruth-Bell said. "We haven't talked to anyone since we got here."

"I'll go see what I can find out," Donley said.

He stepped past an empty nurse's station to glass doors that opened automatically. Continuing, he peered behind curtain partitions. He found Lou behind the second partition from the end, though he had to look twice to confirm it was his uncle. The old man in the bed looked nothing like the robust drill sergeant who'd been barking out orders that morning. A morass of tubes and wires pierced his body and connected to humming machines with blinking, colored lights. Donley gently rested a hand on Lou's arm.

"It's OK, Lou," he whispered. "I'm here. It's going to be OK."

A woman in blue scrubs with a stethoscope wrapped around her neck stepped around the partition. "You can't be in here."

"I want to talk to his doctor."

"I'm his doctor. You need to wait outside."

"I'm his nephew. His wife hasn't been told anything, and she's very worried."

The doctor folded her arms. She looked exhausted. "Come with me." She walked Donley back outside the glass doors into the hall. "Do you want your aunt to be a part of this conversation?"

Something in the doctor's tone convinced Donley he did not. "No."

"Your uncle has had a stroke."

"I thought he had a heart attack?"

"His stroke was most likely associated with the heart attack, which was likely because he's overweight, probably works too much, has high blood pressure, and doesn't watch what he eats. At present, he has partial paralysis on his left side."

"He's paralyzed?"

"We don't know to what extent his nervous system has been affected. Until we do, we have no way of providing a prognosis. He may recover full movement; he may not. He's resting, but the shock to his system has been severe. On the positive side, he's strong and relatively young. The next twenty-four to forty-eight hours will be the most critical. His wife indicated he has no history of heart trouble?"

"He's never had any problems. He swims twice a week." Donley ran a hand through his hair. Lou had always seemed indestructible. "How bad is it?"

"It's bad," she said matter-of-factly. "Your uncle is intubated; he's not breathing on his own."

Gil Ramsey sat at his desk feeling as though he were being pulled in ten different directions. The press clamored for details on the arrest of the priest of Polk Street and on his apparent victim. His staff was prosecuting a highly publicized capital-murder case in the shooting of a police officer, and a speech he was to deliver that evening at a San Francisco firefighters' annual toy drive sat unfinished on his desk. The toy drive would be a significant photo opportunity. Everyone loved firefighters. Everyone loved underprivileged kids. Together, they were gold to a candidate on the campaign trail.

The last thing Ramsey needed was for his door to open without a knock or a phone call from his secretary advising him he had a visitor. Only one person could get away with such a breach of protocol.

Augustus Ramsey stepped into the office resplendent in his three-piece, navy-blue Brioni suit, hand-tailored white shirt with black onyx cuff links, and Italian silk tie.

"Hello, Dad," Gil Ramsey said.

"Good morning."

Ramsey stood. "What are you doing here?" He tried to sound more pleased than annoyed.

"I was in the neighborhood and thought I'd drop in."

Not likely. His father had never "dropped in" anywhere in his life. Every one of his days was carefully orchestrated. Though retired, the former governor continued to wake each morning at five thirty, slip into his silver-blue Jaguar, and drive from his Pacific Heights home to the Bohemian Club on Taylor Street, where club members followed Augustus Ramsey like pilot fish. He swam laps, pulled on a rowing machine, and usually finished with a twenty-minute steam. After working out, his father ate breakfast with a CEO of a Fortune 400 company, a managing partner of a law firm, or some government official.

His father removed his raincoat and placed it and his umbrella on the stand-alone valet, a further indication this was not a quick drop-by.

"Unfortunately, I have a lot going on this morning," the younger Ramsey said. "Can I call you later tonight?"

His father sat. "I read the paper. I know all about the priest. An unfortunate situation."

Gil Ramsey thought that could be the understatement of the year. "Yes, it is."

"So, how are you handling the press?" Augustus Ramsey crossed his legs. His shoes reflected the overhead lights. His political career had been as carefully groomed as his appearance. Having failed to achieve the ultimate prize, he had become determined that his son would not suffer the same fate. The attorney general's office was the next step in his son's ascent.

"For the moment I'm having my press secretary handle all inquiries. Once I know more clearly what I'm dealing with, I'll hold a press conference, likely late this afternoon."

"You're being cautious."

"I thought it prudent."

"In light of the screw-up by your police, so do I."

Ramsey didn't bother to ask how his father knew about Dixon Connor's unauthorized search. His father kept walnut boxes in his study filled with thousands of alphabetized three-by-five-inch cards containing the vitals of every significant person he'd ever met. Augustus Ramsey didn't go to lunch or dinner with friends or family or share tickets to sporting events with them. That was a wasted opportunity. He invited contacts and potential contacts and learned everything he could, because he might need to call on them for a financial commitment or a political favor somewhere down the road.

"That's one reason, certainly," the younger Ramsey said.

"And would the other reason be the same reason that you're still standing—because you're trying to pull your foot out of your ass?"

That didn't take long, Gil Ramsey thought. But then, the "I told you so" comments never did.

"If you had listened to me in the first place, you wouldn't be back-pedaling now. I told you not to jump on the bandwagon and support that man or his shelter. I told you it was a disaster waiting to happen and an unnecessary political liability for anyone who supported it."

Ramsey bit his tongue, in no mood to be lectured. "Times have changed, Dad. In this city, at this time, if you don't support the special-interest groups you don't get the support of the gay and lesbian community. If you don't get the support of the gay and lesbian community, you don't stand a chance in hell of getting elected."

"Is that who you're pandering to now?"

"It's not pandering. It's reality."

"Reality?" His father paused as if considering the word. "The last time I checked, the gay population represented less than eight percent of the vote, and—"

Gil Ramsey turned his back and started for his desk. "I've heard this speech before," he told his father.

Augustus Ramsey shot from his chair faster than a seventy-two-year-old man should have been able to move. He grabbed his son's shoulder and spun him, then wrapped his meaty fist around the Windsor knot of Gil's tie.

"Do not turn your back on me," he said. "I will not be disrespected in an office that I prepared for you. And if you don't fuck up this campaign, you'll be sitting in Sacramento because of me. Do you understand?"

Gil Ramsey clenched his jaw. "Perfectly."

His father released his grip and stepped back. "Good. Let's discuss how you intend to handle this."

Ramsey tried not to sound exasperated. "Handle what?"

Augustus Ramsey sat. "The priest."

"He'll be arraigned day after tomorrow."

"What about the problems with the evidence?"

"We're working on it."

"Working on it?"

Gil Ramsey sat, resigned. "One of the lead detectives froze the building. The crime unit has obtained a warrant and will be returning to perform a further search and additional forensic work. I'm confident we can get the photographs and the murder weapon in under the Nix decision, along with whatever else forensics is able to gather."

"And while a trial takes place, you give the press a daily opportunity to dig up every photograph out there of you shaking hands with a kid-killer."

"I can't go back and change history, Dad."

"No, you can't," Augustus Ramsey agreed. "But you can mold the future."

Crap, another of his mantras.

"Have you thought through what happens if you're wrong, if you don't get the evidence in? What if the police don't find anything else?"

"They will."

"You can guarantee that?" His father paused. "You just talked about the liberal special-interest groups running this city. Those same people are also likely to be your jurors. If you can't get the evidence in, you'll look like a jackass when you appear on television trying to explain why a guilty man just walked out of your justice system."

Ramsey massaged his forehead. It would be a massive headache. "What is it you would have me do, Dad?"

Augustus Ramsey sat back with a contented smile. He folded his hands in his lap. "Get rid of the problem," he said. "As quickly and quietly as possible."

Chapter 7

December 23, 1987

Back in his office, Donley had the telephone resting on his shoulder, suffering to elevator music. A secretary had placed him on hold. He'd slept little, maintaining a vigil at the hospital through the night, then driving home to change clothes and get to work.

Donley had tasked Ruth-Bell with calling the courts to request continuances of hearings and pending motions. It was a sizeable chore. Lou appeared in court for one reason or another almost every day, sometimes two and three times. At least with Lou having suffered his heart attack in court, just about everyone at the San Francisco courthouse already knew about it. Donley had spent his morning calling opposing counsel to seek extensions to respond to discovery requests and continuances of depositions, mediations, and an arbitration. With the holiday, and a planned respite in Florida, Lou had no trials pending until after the first of the year. Thank God for small favors.

The elevator music ended. The secretary returned and advised Donley the lawyer apparently couldn't be bothered to get on the phone.

Donley suspected it was intended to avoid agreeing to continue the deposition of Lou's client. Donley's temper flared.

"No, I do not have time to wait for him to call me back," he said. "During the five minutes I've been on hold, I could have finished the conversation with him three times." Then, not wanting to take out his anger on the secretary, he said, "Tell him if I have to bring a motion to continue, I intend to put in my declaration his unwillingness to get on the phone, and I don't think Judge McGrath will be happy about it. He and Lou worked together in the district attorney's office. That's right. So tell your boss that maybe he would like to rethink his position. If he does, have him call *my* secretary."

He ended the call and picked up the next file. No time to suffer fools, idiots, or assholes, as Lou liked to say.

The file had a sticky note indicating Ruth-Bell had already confirmed an extension. He set it aside and stood. He'd meant to use the bathroom six calls earlier and could no longer put it off.

Ruth-Bell met him at the threshold looking and sounding harried, a wadded tissue in her hand. Her mascara had clumped her eyelashes, and the tissue had reddened the area beneath her nose. Wisps of hair shot off at odd angles from the massive bun on the back of her head. "The archbishop is on the phone. He asked about Lou. I didn't know what to say. I'm sorry."

Donley's bladder wouldn't make it through an extended telephone conversation, be it the archbishop or the Pope. "Tell him I'll call him right back."

"He said it was urgent."

"So is not wetting my pants."

Donley shot out the door and down the hall, thankful to find the single-stall bathroom vacant. In the grout of the tile above the urinal, someone had neatly printed:

Why are you looking up here? The joke is in your hand.

"Don't die on me, Lou," Donley said. "Don't you do it."

It had been Lou who convinced the San Francisco district attorney to drop the investigation into Donley's father's death. And it had been Lou who arranged for Donley's mother, Aunt Sarah's sister, to get a job as a clerk at the municipal court. Lou had also helped them move into an apartment in North Beach. Over the past three years, in between discussing legal theories and case strategy, Lou had provided Donley lessons on life. Donley had been reluctant to have children, uncertain what type of father he would make given the role model his father had been, but Lou had taught him that being a good father had nothing to do with the odd-shaped organ between his legs and more to do with the muscle between his ears.

Donley scrubbed his hands at the sink, splashed water on his face, and blotted it with a coarse paper towel before taking a deep breath and plunging back into his office.

"Ruth-Bell, get the arch—"

"His secretary is holding on line two."

Donley picked up the phone and hit the second line. After a moment, Archbishop Donatello Parnisi greeted him with a baritone voice a bass drum would envy. Donley tried not to sound rushed but still cut corners as he explained Lou's condition. "It will be some time before he's out of the hospital. He's also going to likely need rehab. But you know Lou; he'll probably move the intensive care unit over here." He hoped that would end the conversation. It didn't. As the archbishop explained the second purpose for his call, a dozen thoughts rushed through Donley's head.

"What time were you and Lou supposed to meet?" Donley asked, checking his watch. "No. Don't do that. I'll come. Don't do anything until after we've spoken. I appreciate it, Archbishop. Thank you."

He hung up and called out, "Ruth-Bell!" She stood beside his desk, another of her unnerving habits.

"Lou keeps razors in his office closet. I'll get a fresh one for you," she said, regaining some measure of vinegar. When he didn't immediately respond, she said, "Get moving. I've called a cab. It will be close."

"Slow down. The meeting isn't until this afternoon."

"I'm not talking about the meeting with the archbishop." She handed him a file. "You have Mr. Anitolli's competency hearing in probate court."

Vincenzo Anitolli's competency hearing lasted longer than Donley thought necessary. As a result, he had less time than he needed to get to the archdiocese's offices on Church Street in the Mission District, which he thought a fitting address. He had never been to the building, and he was surprised when the cab dropped him in front of a rectangular structure with aluminum-framed windows and patches of discolored stucco where paint had been rolled to cover graffiti. He wasn't sure what he'd been expecting, perhaps Gothic grandeur with gargoyles and turrets and stained glass. Instead, a simple silver cross atop the roof was the only indication the tenant was a religious organization. The inside décor was just as understated, without any of the dark-stained wood, red-velvet curtains, or fresco paintings Donley associated with eighteenth-century Roman Catholic excess.

As the archbishop's secretary led Donley to Parnisi's office, the building shook, and it took Donley a moment to realize it was the Church Street trolley rumbling past the front of the building and not an earthquake. Don Parnisi stood behind his desk, his extra-large body blocking the light from a window like the moon causing a near eclipse of the sun. Parnisi carried his weight on a six-foot-seven-inch frame like a Midwestern farmer—barrel chest, huge shoulders, and beefy arms and legs. Donley doubted the man had ever lifted a weight in his life. His was a body genetically engineered. Dressed in all black but for the white clerical collar, Parnisi crossed the office, causing the floor to shake nearly as much as when the trolley had rolled by. Donley noticed dark circles under the archbishop's eyes, a chink in his suit of otherwise-substantial armor.

The archbishop's hand swallowed Donley's. "How's Lou doing?"

"Not much change in his condition, I'm afraid," Donley said.

"He's tough. Always has been. I'll get to the hospital later today."

"I know my aunt would appreciate it."

Donley declined the secretary's offer of a glass of water, and the woman departed. As Parnisi returned to his desk, Donley took the opportunity to consider photographs and football memorabilia lining shelves and hanging on the walls. The collage chronicled the life of a tall young man from his days in a Saint James High School football uniform to priesthood. On the east wall hung a picture of Parnisi about to kiss Pope Paul VI's ring, the Pope smiling, his eyes and face expressing amazement at Parnisi's sheer size. Beside it, framed behind glass, hung Parnisi's Notre Dame football jersey. Lou said Notre Dame had won a national championship Parnisi's senior year.

"I guess the last time we saw each other was your mother's funeral," Parnisi said, turning as he reached his desk.

"That day is a bit of a blur," Donley said. Six years earlier, at Lou's request, Parnisi had presided over Donley's mother's funeral, an ornate affair for a very simple woman.

"I buried my mother two years ago. She was ninety-four. It's never easy. Your mother died too young; she had a lot of life left to live."

Given that she'd had no life when his father had been alive, Donley thought his mother's cancer had been a particularly cruel fate. He hadn't set foot in a church since her funeral.

"You look more like your father with each year." When Donley didn't respond, Parnisi said, "I meant it as a compliment, Peter. For all his faults, your father was a good-looking man."

That was like saying Idi Amin had faults but a nice smile. Even so, Donley couldn't deny he'd inherited his father's sandy-brown hair and blue eyes.

"The girls used to flock to the gas station on Divisadero where he worked, but not your mother. Your grandmother forbade her; she said it looked cheap. Your father had to find her at a dance." Parnisi smiled. "She was a sight to behold, your mother."

Donley wondered if Parnisi also knew his father got his mother pregnant on her eighteenth birthday and married her only after she refused to get an abortion, or whether he knew that his father never forgave either of them for ruining his ambition to move to Hollywood to become the next James Dean.

As Parnisi lowered himself into the leather chair behind his desk, Donley unbuttoned his suit jacket and sat in one of two chairs on the opposite side. Hopefully, the stroll down memory lane was over. The archbishop directed his gaze out a window with a view of the salmon-colored spire of the Mission Dolores church. "I've leaned on Lou so many times over the years, I feel lost without him. I practically have to force him to bill me for his time, and even then, he grossly under-charges me."

Terrific. No wonder Donley was underpaid. "He speaks highly of you," Donley said.

"He'd better," Parnisi said, refocusing his attention on Donley. "I saved his butt more than a few times. Did he tell you we were born three houses apart, three months apart?"

A hundred times, Donley thought, but sensing Parnisi needed to reminisce, he shook his head and said, "No."

"He's been following me ever since. I darn near convinced him to go into the seminary with me until he met your aunt. God was no match for her. Probably for the better; your uncle's always had a mouth like a sailor."

"It would have made for some colorful sermons," Donley said.

Parnisi smiled. "Indeed, it would have." Parnisi opened a desk drawer and removed a pipe and a bag of tobacco, placing it on his desk. "You've read the *Chronicle*?"

"I have," Donley said.

"Father Martin's arrest is getting national exposure. One of the afternoon talk shows called." Parnisi nimbly packed the pipe with a pinch of tobacco, flicked a lighter, and sucked the flame into the bowl. The room soon filled with a sweet aroma that reminded Donley of the smell of maple syrup.

Parnisi clenched the pipe between his teeth, looking like something out of Scotland Yard. "I was the one who approved Father Martin's shelter; I gave it my blessing and approved his mission."

"It was a good mission," Donley said. "A lot of kids out there need help."

Parnisi took a long pull on the pipe before placing the bowl in a tray on his desk. Smoke escaped his nostrils as he spoke. "I received a telephone call from the district attorney. He called it a courtesy call. He wanted me to know the evidence against Father Martin is substantial. Between the lines, I think he's fishing."

"For what?"

"He's trying to find out if I intend to get involved or to stay out of the matter."

"You'll want to consider the likelihood of an eventual civil action by the family of the victim," Donley said. "They'll look for the deepest pocket."

"Your uncle would have said exactly the same thing. I won't run, Peter . . . and I can't hide. I'm a reflection of this church—I'm too damn big to hide. If someone is going to sue the archdiocese, they'll know where to find us. Ramsey wants to meet. He says it's to discuss the evidence, but again, I think he wants to find out if I intend to help Father Martin with legal counsel."

"I assume that's why you called," Donley said.

"I won't abandon Father Martin, Peter." Parnisi took a deep breath and sat back in his chair. "I want you to know that after I learned of Lou's heart attack, I spoke with Larry Carr at Easton, Miller, and Carr. I've asked him to meet with Gil Ramsey."

Donley sat forward. On those rare occasions when Lou had a conflict of interest, the archdiocese sent its work to Larry Carr. "Archbishop, I know you're concerned because Lou is in the hospital, but I can assure you, I can handle the meeting with the district attorney. I've already met with Father Martin at Lou's request." Donley left out the specifics of that meeting, since there were none. "So I'm familiar with the charges, and I've handled several criminal matters." Again, he didn't elaborate. "These things move slowly, Archbishop. I can evaluate the evidence and give you my assessment. With the upcoming holidays, nothing is going to happen quickly. That gives us time to determine the severity of Lou's condition and when he will be returning to work."

The archbishop looked unconvinced. "Lou speaks very highly of you and your abilities, Peter. Please don't misunderstand. But I know Lou handles the criminal work, and I suspect a murder charge is well beyond your experience or expertise."

Donley knew it had taken Lou forty years to build his practice and felt an obligation not to let Lou lose his biggest client on his watch. "I understand, but that's not something you need to decide at this moment. If I have to, I can bring in co-counsel." Donley put a hand on the edge of the big desk. "I'm not your typical third-year lawyer, Archbishop. I've had more than forty trials. Let me meet with the DA and hear what he has to say. What is it you're looking for right at this moment?"

Parnisi sighed. "I need someone who will cut through the political crap and legal rhetoric and tell me what is in Father Martin's best interest. I'd prefer not to take advice from Gil Ramsey. I'd look out the window if he called to tell me it was raining."

Donley looked to the window and smiled. "It's not raining, Archbishop."

Parnisi smiled.

"I can handle it," Donley said. "I'll talk to Ramsey, and I'll evaluate the evidence. I'll be as straight with you as I know Lou has always been."

"I'm not sure that's a positive. Lou's roughed me up a bit over the years." Parnisi sat back, the pipe again clenched between his teeth, considering Donley through the blue-gray haze.

Chapter 8

Gil Ramsey watched Linda St. Claire literally come out of her chair. "You're going to LWOP a murderer?" she asked, using the acronym for a plea of *life without parole.*

"I didn't say we're going to offer anything."

Ramsey had politicked on a tough-on-crime platform, and it was well known he did not plea-bargain a first-degree-murder charge. "But given the potential problems with the evidence, it would be irresponsible not to consider alternatives."

"The press will crucify us," St. Claire said, now pacing his office.

"No, they'll crucify us if *you* don't get a conviction."

She bristled. "I'll convict the son of a bitch. Just get me twelve jurors and a courtroom."

"Are you going to guarantee that?" He raised a hand to stop her before she could respond. "You better think before you answer that question, because there's a hell of a lot riding on this . . . for both of us."

St. Claire turned her back like a chastised nine-year-old. Her desire was to succeed Ramsey as district attorney.

"If the defense accepts life without the possibility of parole, the matter will be over before it—or the press—finds out about the problems with the evidence," Ramsey said, hating the fact that he was parroting his father's admonition from earlier that morning. "We'll all have a Merry Christmas and a Happy New Year, and Father Martin goes away for life, where he can never hurt anyone again."

St. Claire shook her head. "I can't even fathom you'd consider making such an offer."

Ramsey sat forward. "That's because your ego is clogging your ears. You're not hearing me. I'm not suggesting *we offer* anything. That's exactly why I assigned you to handle this. Your reputation will confirm we intend to seek the death penalty. I've just issued a statement to the media hinting that the evidence against Father Martin is substantial. The press won't crucify us; they'll help us. Whoever represents Father Martin will get an immediate and strong dose of reality. Father Martin is going to the gas chamber if they don't do something to prevent it."

St. Claire stopped pacing and considered him. "You want his attorney to *request* a deal in exchange for a guilty plea."

Ramsey shrugged. "One would hope a good lawyer would see the wisdom of it."

"So, how do we do that? How do we get his attorney to think we'd consider a deal without hinting at it? Nobody in the public defender's office would think it a possibility."

"I put in a call to the archbishop this morning and requested a meeting."

St. Claire sat. "I would have assumed the church would run from this as fast and far as possible."

"And ordinarily that assumption would be accurate, but as I said, you don't know Donatello Parnisi."

"I heard he's a tough old bird; I didn't hear he was stupid."

"Oh, he's not stupid," Ramsey said. "But he's also not your typical church bureaucrat, either. He's his own man. He'll see honor in standing behind Father Martin, damn what the eventual financial and political ramifications might be."

"When is he coming?"

"He's not. He's sending Larry Carr." Ramsey checked his wristwatch. "Within the next twenty minutes."

"Carr's not bad," St. Claire conceded. "I've tried a few cases against him before he went into private practice. I thought he handles only white-collar stuff now?"

"He does, but if one of the wealthiest institutions in the world calls, do you turn them down?" Ramsey asked.

"So, how do we play this?"

"We advise Larry the evidence against Father Martin is substantial, but we might be open to considering something so as not to embarrass the church. Carr will be duty bound to bring the information to the archbishop. With all the recent press about priest indiscretions, the archbishop won't be able to ignore such an opening. He'll also be duty bound to talk to those in power above him."

"And if the archbishop doesn't see the wisdom of it?"

Ramsey turned his gaze to the window. In a few years, there would be a new county jail there, but at the moment, he had a view of the 101 Freeway and, beyond it, the San Francisco skyline. Farther to the east awaited the capitol in Sacramento. "Then you'll get your shot at Father Martin."

Donley walked down a light-green marble floor and stepped through double-wide oak doors, the words **DISTRICT ATTORNEY** stenciled in black block letters on the smoked glass. He asked to speak with Gil Ramsey and provided the woman behind the counter with his name and a business card. The woman made a phone call, repeated Donley's name twice, and hung up. After a few minutes, a second woman, this one identifying herself as Ramsey's assistant, met Donley in the lobby and led him through a maze of narrow hallways lined with metal filing cabinets to a corner office.

Ramsey looked very much like the man whose face was bombarding voters on television and plastered around the city on large billboards, sometimes alone and sometimes with his father, the former governor. A pronounced shadow extended from just under Ramsey's cheekbones to a point somewhere below the collar of his starched white shirt. Ramsey sat with both feet propped on the edge of a large mahogany desk, a document in hand, reading glasses resting on the bridge of his nose. In a chair across the desk sat an attractive blonde woman who also looked familiar, though Donley could not place her. From their surprised expressions, he could tell they'd been expecting Larry Carr. Ramsey finally removed his feet and stood, motioning for Donley to enter with a wave of his hand. "Please, come in."

The assistant took Donley's umbrella and placed it in a container near the door.

Ramsey introduced himself. He was taller than Donley had expected, over six feet, with a marathon runner's physique. Ramsey gestured to the empty chair beside the blonde with the sour face. She'd also stood and now thrust out her hand like she was going to remove Donley's kidney.

"Linda St. Claire."

The name and the staccato voice clicked. St. Claire had been a television commentator during a recent high-profile trial of a man accused of kidnapping, raping, and murdering a twelve-year-old girl from a northern county. The trial had attracted national headlines.

"You'll have to excuse us if we appear a bit caught off guard. We were expecting Larry Carr," Ramsey said.

Donley smiled. "Sorry to disappoint."

"Do you work with Larry?"

"No, I don't." Donley removed two business cards and handed one to each. Ramsey lifted the bifocals dangling from the string around his neck onto the bridge of his nose and held up the card. The eyebrows inched closer together. "You work for Lou Giantelli?" he asked.

"Yes, I do."

Ramsey lowered the card. "I've known Lou for many years. We tried a few cases against each other back in the day. He's a very capable lawyer."

Six cases, Donley knew from Lou. *And Lou beat you every time.*

Lou had once related to Donley how Gil Ramsey had been a young deputy district attorney when Lou did criminal-defense work on a regular basis. Lou described Ramsey as competent but arrogant, a lawyer who failed to learn from his mistakes and repeated them, making him predictable.

"I understand Lou had a heart attack in court yesterday."

"Yes, he did."

"I'm sorry to hear that. Is there any word on his condition?"

"The doctors are optimistic he'll make a full recovery," Donley said, not about to tell Ramsey anything different.

"I hope that's true."

"The archbishop indicated you called to discuss Father Martin."

Ramsey offered Donley a seat. Donley set his briefcase down and lowered into a chair beside St. Claire. Diplomas and certificates of achievement from various law-enforcement organizations littered the walls, the flow of paper disrupted only by the drooping leaves of a potted plant. A table behind Ramsey displayed what Donley presumed to be family photographs. Ramsey was married to a brunette and had two daughters and a golden retriever. He apparently lived in a Victorian-style house with a view of the Golden Gate Bridge, probably somewhere in Pacific Heights.

Ramsey spun an uncurled paper clip between his thumb and finger like a helicopter blade. "I want to be as up-front as possible with the archbishop, Mr. Peters."

"It's Donley. Peter Donley."

Ramsey stopped twirling the paper clip and sat forward. "We intend to charge Father Martin with first-degree murder." His tufted caterpillar eyebrows drew together, stray black hairs peeking through the silver. "As you may or may not know, I adamantly support the death penalty, and seek it where I believe appropriate. And I believe it appropriate in this instance. That's why I've assigned Ms. St. Claire to handle this matter. She has a dozen capital-murder convictions."

Ramsey paused as if expecting Donley to respond. He didn't. He'd learned from Lou that often the best response was no response. People did not like silence and usually filled it with their own voices.

Free information. Take it when you can get it, Lou liked to say.

Donley also was beginning to understand why neither the archbishop nor Lou cared for Gil Ramsey. The man had an arrogance about him that permeated the entire office. Whereas the archbishop's framing of his Notre Dame paraphernalia seemed to be for his benefit—to recall a special time in his life—Ramsey's framed tribute to himself seemed intended for others. Donley also quickly deduced the purpose of the meeting was not so much to share information but to intimidate. Older civil lawyers had tried to take the same tactic. They equated his youth with inexperience and assumed he had never tried a case in his life. They usually ended up regretting that assumption. Here, however, Donley was in uncharted waters when it came to a criminal charge, particularly one this significant. He wasn't looking to impress. He was hoping only to survive the meeting without embarrassing himself, Lou, or the archbishop.

Ramsey sat back. "As a courtesy to the archbishop—and to Lou— we will provide his counsel with the evidence against Father Martin, and let me tell you, it is significant."

Donley recognized it to be a hollow gesture. Though he was, to a degree, winging it, he knew the defense was entitled to all of the prosecution's evidence in a criminal case. "I appreciate that. Is there a time when I might view that evidence and get copies?"

"They'll be provided to Father Martin's defense counsel," St. Claire said. "Are you his defense counsel?"

Something in her tone struck a nerve. "At present, I am," he said.

Ramsey cut in. "In addition to finding the victim in Father Martin's shelter and his blood on Father Martin's clothing as well as on a six-inch, hand-carved letter opener in Father Martin's office, the technicians recovered blood samples from the priest's office and the recreation room, and positive shoe imprints and fingerprints. We are confident forensics will confirm the blood on the blade and handle belong to the victim."

Donley took it all in. "And motive? Do you have a theory about what might have caused a man who devoted his life to helping teenage runaways to suddenly decide to kill one of them?"

Like a magician's assistant, St. Claire produced a manila envelope encased in a police evidence bag and handed it to Ramsey. Ramsey opened the package without speaking, removed several photographs, also encased in plastic, and, like a poker player laying down a full house, spread them on the edge of the desk. "These were found in Father Martin's office."

Donley leaned forward. The photographs bore the black-powder residue used to dust for fingerprints and depicted young boys in various stages of undress. One had been blindfolded and manacled about the wrists and ankles. Donley fought to hide his revulsion, knowing Ramsey and St. Claire sat gauging his reaction.

Ramsey held up the stack. "There are more."

Donley cleared his throat. "I get the gist."

St. Claire furrowed her brow. "To secure a death penalty, one must shock the conscience of the jurors. A pedophile priest who murders a boy who came to him for help certainly would meet that criteria . . . in my experience."

"And are any of these photographs of the victim?"

"That has not yet been determined," St. Claire said.

"And they are not of Father Martin," he said.

"No," she said. "They don't appear to be."

"Do you have reason to believe Father Martin took these photographs?"

"Again," she said, becoming agitated, "it's too early to know, but I don't really care. The fact they were in his possession is more than enough."

"So, you don't know," Donley said.

"We do know they were found in Father Martin's office," Ramsey said.

"Is there evidence the victim was abused in this manner?"

Ramsey put a finger to his lips as if contemplating his response. "That's an interesting choice of words."

Again, St. Claire turned to Donley, and he was now convinced this had all been rehearsed. "Beaten and tortured would be a more accurate way to describe it," she said. "The victim had burn marks on his body, likely from a cigarette, as well as several cuts and bruises. Under the circumstances, Mr. Donley, this might be the easiest death penalty I have ever asked a jury to render, given the severe breach of the public's trust."

Donley knew he should just remain quiet and bring the information back to Parnisi, but his mouth opened and before he could stop himself, he said, "What is it you want, Mr. Ramsey?"

"What do *we* want?"

Donley looked to St. Claire but found her face equally blank. "Yes, why did you ask to meet with the archbishop?"

"As I said, I felt a sense of obligation to let the archbishop know about the evidence," Ramsey said. "This is not the kind of thing one likes to first read about in the newspaper or hear for the first time on the six o'clock news, especially given all the adverse press the church has received lately." Ramsey leaned forward. His voice took on a hardened edge. "But make no mistake. My number-one concern is to prevent this from ever happening again. The court of public opinion will demand that we pursue the death penalty. If this goes to trial, that decision will be out of my hands."

Whether Ramsey had intended to emphasize the word or not, Donley heard *If.* "Are you suggesting some type of plea deal?"

Ramsey smiled. "This office does not offer pleas to first-degree-murder suspects, Mr. Donley. We are duty bound, however, to consider a plea if one is suggested on Father Martin's behalf."

"You mean if he pleads guilty."

"That would be a necessity," Ramsey said.

They sat in silence. This time, Ramsey did not fill it. After a moment, he stood. The meeting was apparently over. Donley rose from his chair and picked up his briefcase.

"Perhaps we'll see you again tomorrow," St. Claire said.

Donley turned to her. "I'm sorry?"

"At Father Martin's arraignment."

"Tomorrow's Christmas Eve."

St. Claire looked to Ramsey. "It's not a court holiday, is it?"

"No, it's not," Ramsey said. "And in light of the abundance of evidence, we don't believe there is any reason to seek a grand jury. We're prepared to move this matter forward expeditiously, Mr. Donley, and Judge Trimble has accorded us a place at the top of his calendar. Now that we have your business card, we'll provide you fax notice, or will you waive it?"

They had played him, and Donley wanted nothing more than to knock the smug smiles off their faces. He wanted to say something snappy—or at least semi-intelligent—in response, but, his mind a blank, he could do nothing but walk silently from the room.

A raindrop brushed Donley's cheek as he stepped from the revolving glass doors onto the concrete steps outside the Hall of Justice building, and he realized he'd left his umbrella in Gil Ramsey's office. He wasn't about to go back for it after leaving like a dog with his tail tucked between his legs. He'd have Ruth-Bell call.

He also didn't bother to look for a cab. He started the walk back to his office, eager to get away from Gil Ramsey and Linda St. Claire, and equally eager to get away from Father Thomas Martin.

A pedophile priest.

What had he gotten himself into?

He'd let his ego get the better of him. The archbishop had let him off the hook. He'd hired Larry Carr. Donley could have simply said he understood the decision not to go with a twenty-eight-year-old, third-year lawyer. If he had, he'd be spending tomorrow with Kim and Benny, preparing for their annual Christmas Eve party. After the new year, he'd be in a downtown office with a view attorneys killed for, making enough money to move Kim and Benny to the peninsula. Instead, he would be up half the night preparing for an arraignment sure to be front-page news. Hell, he had only a vague idea from television shows what happened at an arraignment.

He trudged on, periodically looking to hail a cab, but it was a fleeting thought. Late in the afternoon before a holiday weekend, cab drivers would not want to get entangled in the surface-street mess south of Market. They'd be looking for larger fares to and from the airport. The rain started as a light mist, progressed to intermittent drops by the third block, became showers at block six, and culminated in a downpour the final block to the office. Knowing it would be a futile act, Donley didn't bother to cover his head or dash for shelter. He didn't wipe the water dripping into his eyes or try to avoid the puddles overwhelming the sewer system and flooding the intersections. He just kept walking.

Morton Salt, he thought. *When it rains, it pours.*

By the time he reached his office building, Donley looked and felt like he had stepped into a shower fully dressed, hair matted to his head, the collar of his suit jacket and shirt wringing wet. His Cole

Haan leather shoes squished on the terrazzo tile as he made his way up the stairs. If they weren't ruined, they were close to it. The office door was locked. Ruth-Bell had left for the hospital. Donley unlocked the deadbolt and stepped inside. Entering his office, he removed his coat, tie, and shirt and left them in a pile. He struggled to pull his wet T-shirt over his head, threw it onto the pile, and leaned against the desk, slipping off his shoes and suit pants. He retrieved his gym bag from beneath his desk, about to slip on sweatpants when a noise at the door surprised him. Ruth-Bell stood in his office doorway in her raincoat and scarf, holding a brown paper bag.

"Your hair is soaking wet," she said, ever the master of the obvious.

"Can you give me a minute?"

She walked in anyway. "You've got nothing I want to see and haven't seen before. Give me those wet clothes. You'll catch your death of a cold. That's just what I need—both you and your uncle in the hospital."

She had obviously recovered her fire, if not yet the brimstone.

Donley pulled on his sweatpants and wrapped a towel around his shoulders like a prizefighter. "If I'm lucky, I'll get the flu and not some twenty-four-hour bug. I need something that would last about a week. Hong Kong, King Kong, whatever they call it. What are you doing here, anyway? I thought you'd gone to the hospital."

She gathered his clothes as he struggled to pull a sweatshirt over his head. "This office doesn't run on its own, you know." She gestured to his desk, which was cluttered with open legal books and newspapers. "I pulled every article I could find from the library. I think I'm on information overload."

"What are you talking about? What articles?"

"Articles on Father Martin and the shelter; they're on your desk."

Donley picked up a small stack of articles and thumbed the pages.

"They're arranged in chronological order, most recent first," she said. "Oh, and the arraignment is tomorrow morning. We received fax notice this afternoon."

"I know."

"They're holding it in the ceremonial courtroom, Department Thirteen. Apparently, His Highness, Gil Ramsey, is expecting a large crowd and wants to play to the cameras, the pretentious shit."

She found hangers behind Donley's door and started to untangle his wet clothes. "They're not doing you any favors. Milton Trimble and Lou sparred more than once during their careers. Keep your mouth shut, your temper under control, and speak only when spoken to. His courtroom is a tight ship."

"How's Lou?"

"Not much change, according to his doctors." She hung his clothes from the window frame. A drop of water hissed when it hit the radiator, and the radiator emitted a small puff of steam. "If anyone at the hospital asks, Lou has a younger sister. That was the only way I could get in to see him. But I couldn't stay. It made me jumpy seeing him lying there like that. Where did you go after your meeting with the archbishop? That should have been over hours ago."

Donley sat and rested his elbows on his knees. "I had a pleasant chat with Mr. Ramsey himself."

"Lucky you."

"For laughs, he brought Linda St. Claire along."

"Who?"

"You know, the blonde who's always on the television commenting on those high-profile criminal cases."

"Another pretentious shit."

"Yeah, well, she's been anointed to crucify Father Martin."

"What did they want?"

Donley sat up. "According to the archbishop, they wanted to discuss the evidence against Father Martin. Now, I'm not so sure."

"What do you mean?"

"It was something Ramsey said; I think they're looking for Father Martin to confess in exchange for a plea of life."

"A plea?" Ruth-Bell said. "Where did you get that idea? The DA doesn't plea murderers. I even know that."

"Where were you an hour ago when I was making a fool of myself?" He shook his head. "It sure seemed like Ramsey was hinting at it, though." He focused on a spot on the hardwood floor. "Why would he do that, Ruth-Bell?"

It was a question Donley had pondered the entire miserable walk back to his office. It was a question he wished he'd asked Gil Ramsey. It didn't make any sense.

He continued. "If the case is as strong as they say, they could get a conviction and worry about the penalty phase after they'd soaked up the media attention. The trial will be high profile, which Ramsey should want with the upcoming election."

"It could have something to do with these." She picked up the articles from the desk and tossed them in his lap. "A year ago everyone was falling all over themselves to get on the Father Martin bandwagon, including Mr. Tough on Crime."

Donley read through the first couple of headlines and opening sentences. He wasn't convinced. "These people thrive on these types of high-profile crimes, and according to the archbishop, Ramsey is as slick as oil. I'm sure he could talk himself out of any perceived alliance with Father Martin's shelter."

"Then trust your instincts. That man doesn't do anything unless there's something in it for him. He's just like his father."

"The archbishop said something similar." Donley dried his hair with the towel. "Whatever their motivation, they've managed to ruin my night. I'll be preparing for an arraignment. I barely know what an arraignment is. I can't believe I talked the archbishop into thinking I'm competent to handle this case."

"Quit complaining." She'd found the brimstone. Ruth-Bell was a pistol, but he also knew she could have been home, or holiday shopping, or otherwise taking advantage of the situation. Instead, she was at the office, working as hard as if not harder than Donley. "You're in a hell of a lot better position than your uncle. Besides, I already pulled all the legal treatises. It doesn't appear too difficult."

Donley smiled. "Do you want to handle the arraignment?"

"I'll need a substantial increase in pay, if I do." She took his towel and rolled it into a tube, placing it on the window frame to catch the water dripping from his suit. "Just keep your mouth shut as far as I can tell, and ask for a continuance. Nothing happens at arraignments; they read the charges and you say, 'We are not prepared to enter a plea at this time.' Then you waive your right to a speedy trial to get as much time as possible to figure things out. What you don't know, you fake."

"In this instance, that will be a lot."

Either his wish was coming true and Donley was coming down with the flu, or the stress was making his joints ache. The onset of a headache pulsed at his temples. Before he could say a word, Ruth-Bell walked out of his office and returned with a bottle of Advil and a glass of water. She shook out two capsules and handed them to him, then moved the brown bag across the desk.

"I bought you a sandwich and some chips. You'll feel better after you've eaten. Drink water. Coke will just make you edgy, and for God's sake, stay far away from the coffee."

"Thanks."

"You can thank me with a Jackson. We're low on petty cash, and I couldn't get to the bank."

Donley washed down the Advil and drained the glass, setting it on the desk. "They say he tortured that boy, Ruth-Bell. They say the priest is a pedophile."

She crossed her arms. "Maybe he is," she said. "Maybe he isn't. That's not your concern."

"How can it not be my concern?"

She put on her raincoat, speaking as she wrapped the scarf around her hair and retrieved her umbrella. "Quite a few years ago, when I was still thin and Lou was about your age, we got a call from the public defender's office to represent a twenty-year-old kid who had murdered four people, including two young boys. It made all the newspapers, just like this. The kid was guilty, but just the same, Lou fought like hell to save his life. I didn't understand it. I'd find him here at his desk every night working late, preparing motions and cross-examinations, whatever it took. I hated to see him working so hard for a lost cause. 'Why are you killing yourself for this kid?' I asked one night."

"What did he say?"

"He said, 'It's my job, Ruth-Bell. It's my job to defend my client to the best of my ability, regardless of his guilt or innocence. If I don't do my job, then the system doesn't work, and if the system doesn't work, we all suffer for it.'"

"The seventh canon."

"Come again?"

"'A lawyer should represent a client zealously within the bounds of the law,'" Donley said, recalling what he could from the American Bar Association code.

"Something like that," she said. "Some years later, with all his appeals exhausted, they put that man to death. I've never told anyone this, but I cried that day. Not for him. For Lou. I knew how hard he fought to save that man's life." She nodded to Donley. "You two are a lot alike. But he can't do it anymore. We both know that. It's your time now."

"I know," he said. "I know. I just hope two years from now, you're not crying again because they put Father Thomas Martin to death."

Chapter 9

In need of a break, Donley stood and massaged the kink he'd developed in his neck from being bent over the stack of legal treatise. He picked up the late edition of the *Examiner*. The afternoon articles included a photograph of Father Martin in his black shirt and clerical collar, smiling at the grand opening of the Tenderloin boys' shelter. But for the shaved head and earring, the picture looked nothing like the man Donley had met in jail. The article repeated much of the information in the earlier editions, but a sidebar quoted members of the community using words like *tragedy* and *unbelievable* in response to the allegations. In fact, the overall tenor of the article was disbelief.

Donley wasn't so disbelieving. He couldn't count the number of times he'd discovered something about someone that he had never suspected. He drank. She gambled. He had an affair. He molested a patient. He beat his wife. But of course, that was the point. People got away with those things because they didn't fit the stereotypes. Donley knew better. Everyone had a dark side. Everyone had skeletons in their closet, what the psychiatrist who treated him after his father's death called hidden dragons. In hindsight, there were always signs; everyone just missed them, or chose to ignore them.

To others, his father had been just a hardworking mechanic, a blue-collar guy who liked to drink Jack Daniel's at the Wishing Well in the Sunset District after work. He had even owned his own gas station for a few years. Jack Donley held down a job, and his son, Peter, was considered a well-adjusted kid who did OK in school and excelled on the football field. No one suspected Jack Donley beat his wife and son. There were signs, for sure—bruises and missing teeth—but nobody wanted to see them. If they did, they'd have to act. So they ignored them. And the beatings continued. Nobody wanted to get involved in other people's business, especially their business behind closed doors.

Donley sat back. So, what were the signs Father Thomas Martin was a pedophile and a killer? For some, the fact that he was a priest was sufficient. As the archbishop had said, the press printed every indiscretion in the newspaper and broadcast it on television. People loved to bash the Roman Catholic Church as an archaic system that fostered homosexuality and pedophiles by forbidding grown men from satisfying their most primal biological urge.

Donley had his own beefs with religion, but intellectually, he knew every priest was no more a child molester than every lawyer was an unethical, ambulance-chasing scumbag. Archbishop Parnisi was right: You couldn't condemn an entire institution because of the acts of indiscretion by a few. But the indiscretions made good news stories. Murder made front-page headlines.

He sat and adjusted his desk lamp, flipping through the series of articles Ruth-Bell had copied. The process of opening the shelter had been long and arduous for Father Martin. The politicians and police started out firmly opposed to the idea of using abandoned buildings to shelter teenage runaways and prostitutes—or the homeless, for that matter, which were becoming a major problem. In an election year, none of the candidates for mayor or city supervisor wanted to take a position on such a controversial subject. But Father Martin had been dogged in his efforts to open his shelter. He ignored his critics and lobbied the city's politically powerful special-interest groups, including San Francisco's large and active gay community, which was tired of being wrongly associated with the street prostitutes. The issue gave them a forum to educate the public about the clientele filtering into the Gulch and parking in the dark alleys, the seemingly heterosexual men from every walk of life preying on young boys. The sex trade was a lot like the drug trade; everyone wanted to raze the low-income housing where the drugs were sold but ignored the BMWs and Mercedes driving down the streets with $100 bills hanging out the windows.

Father Martin had also done a number on the San Francisco Police Department, disseminating information on the amount of resources spent each year trying to police the problem. He pitched the shelter as an alternative investment that would allow the police to concentrate their efforts on violent crime. After he made those numbers public, mayoral candidate Alice Herman, a long shot with nothing to lose and everything to gain, pledged her support for Father Martin's project. When she did, the rest of the politicians could no longer ignore the issue, including Gil Ramsey, who begrudgingly jumped on the bandwagon. One article included a picture of Ramsey touring the shelter.

Maybe Ruth-Bell was right. Maybe Ramsey was trying to jump from a burning ship before it sank. But something about that just didn't sit right with Donley. As only a skilled politician could, Ramsey had straddled the fence, arguing his support for the shelter did not conflict with his rigid "tough on crime" posture. He said if the shelter could prevent solicitation, he favored it. If it could not, then it was the district attorney's job to prosecute, and the legal system's job to punish.

There had to be something more.

The article in the afternoon edition jumped to an interior page, where the paper had run an article on the victim. Though the police continued to withhold much information until the next of kin had been notified, the reporter had found a source who knew Andrew Bennet. Bennet went by the street nickname Alphabet, presumably because of his initials, AB. The source said Bennet had been living on the Tenderloin streets after running away from a single-parent home in a lower-middle-class neighborhood outside of Green Bay, Wisconsin, at age thirteen. He'd taken a bus to Hollywood with dreams of becoming an actor, developed a drug problem that included heroin, and soon thereafter developed a police problem. The reporter recovered records from the West Hollywood and San Francisco police departments indicating Bennet had been picked up multiple times on charges of possession, petty theft, and solicitation.

Donley set the paper down and dialed a number committed to memory. The officer at the duty desk put him on hold. When he returned, Donley asked to speak to Mike Harris.

"Harris is already out. I can reach him in the car if it's an emergency, or you can leave a message."

"No, that's all right."

Donley started to hang up, then reconsidered. "Wait. You still there?"

"I'm not going anywhere."

"Tell him Donley called."

"Any last name?"

"Peter Donley. Tell him Peter Donley called," he said and hung up.

Two drunks on the sidewalk outside Donley's window yelled something unintelligible at each other. A bottle shattered. Next, they'd probably urinate on the wall. Donley opened his desk drawer and set Lou's revolver on the desk. He kept it close when he worked late. He noticed Max Seager's business card, picked it up, and thought again about calling to make an appointment. Now was not the time. He set it aside and read a treatise Ruth-Bell had opened to criminal arraignments. He'd grasped the procedural aspects, which were not complicated, but he would go through the treatise and his notes again for the nuances. Lou had taught him the courtroom was a stage, with lawyers and judges the actors. It didn't just matter what you said; it mattered how you looked saying it. He suspected Ramsey and St. Claire would attempt to make him look inexperienced in front of Milton Trimble, and Trimble had a reputation of devouring young, unprepared lawyers.

Ruth-Bell had also been accurate in her assessment of the arraignment. The key was to not enter a plea but to waive time to allow the defense attorney the chance to review the evidence and prepare a defense. That would eventually be either Lou, who right now needed as much time as Donley could get him, or if Lou didn't make it back, someone with more experience, like Larry Carr.

The strain of the prior two days made Donley's head heavy. He contemplated the empty coffeemaker, but remembered Ruth-Bell's admonition that caffeine would make him edgy and decided against it. Instead, he lowered his head. He'd take a five-minute nap to rejuvenate. Then he would go over his notes again.

September 1978

Donley flicked the tubular-shaped fuse and watched it tumble over the stair edge, clattering down the staircase and rolling across the hardwood floor to a darkened corner near the front door. Beads of perspiration trickled down his face and ringed the collar of his white T-shirt—an Indian summer had brought soaring temperatures and the kind of dry, windless days San Franciscans quietly called earthquake weather.

He sat halfway up the staircase, waiting, listening to the clock in the living room tick off the seconds. His eyes had long since adjusted to the dark, and he peered between the bannister slats at the golden football trophies his mother kept prominently displayed on the entry table for the recruiters. Part of the facade. His high school football coaches told the recruiters that determination and hard work had made Peter Donley one of the best high school football players in the country.

They were wrong.

Football didn't drive Donley to lift weights to near exhaustion. It was rage. The anger built inside him like compressed air, which Donley vented in the weight room, at practice, and during games. It was the only thing that kept him from exploding.

Just above the trophies, black-and-white photographs hung on the wall. In one, a young man in a tuxedo looked as if he were about to fall face-first but for an arm draped around his bride's shoulders. Donley didn't recognize the man or the woman in that picture. In the ensuing eighteen years, his father's lean and angular face had become pale and fleshy, and his six-pack stomach now hung well over his belt. The James Dean curl in the picture no longer sat atop his head like a rooster's crown but drooped like a beaten dog's tail.

Donley's mother had once been beautiful, lustrous dark hair, blue-green eyes, and soft features. At thirty-six, her hair had streaked prematurely gray, and her smile was missing two teeth. Her figure had grown thin and frail.

The familiar sound of the Impala's engine drew Donley's attention back to the front door. It still caused a Pavlovian chill to trickle down his spine. As a child, that chill caused him to slide beneath his bed. But he was no longer a child. And he was no longer scared.

The car's headlights pierced the shuttered windows, casting slatted shadows on the wall.

The clock chimed twice.

The man was nothing if not predictable.

The car jerked to a stop at the curb, the engine sputtering and finally dying with a last gasp from the carburetor. The driver's side door creaked open—a dent had creased the panel—then slammed shut with the same forced snap.

Donley stood.

The familiar sound of heavy boots trudged up the concrete walk in an uneven shuffle. God, how he hated that sound. He'd prayed nightly not to hear that sound, prayed it would be the night his father did not come home, left for good. But each night, the boots returned.

Keys rattled in the lock.

Donley stepped down one stair and parted his legs shoulder-width, balanced.

The deadbolt flicked upright.

The hairs on the back of Donley's neck twitched—an angel's breath, his mother called it. Donley pressed down on the balls of his feet and felt his jeans tighten around the muscles of his thighs as the front door swung open.

He was home.

◆ ◆ ◆

The bang startled Donley from sleep. He sat up quickly, saw a dark figure hovering over him, stood, spun, and drew his arms across his body. In the same motion, he'd shifted his weight to his back leg, his front leg coiled and ready to strike. The figure never moved. It remained a headless image on the wall. He looked to the window, to where Ruth-Bell had hung his suit above the radiator, now backlit by the street lamp leaking through the blinds.

Just a shadow.

He released a held breath and ran a hand through his hair. His sweatshirt was damp to the touch. The radiator banged again, then went back to its usual ticking and hissing. What time was it?

He picked up his watch from his desk. Midnight. Damn. He'd fallen asleep for nearly an hour.

A chill brought goose bumps along his arms. He felt the room shrinking, as it had when he'd visited Father Martin's cell. The same feeling of claustrophobia enveloped him, suffocating. He couldn't catch his breath. His skin prickled, and his joints ached. He felt light-headed, dizzy. He needed to get out. He needed to get home. He stuffed books and papers into his briefcase, shoved his wallet and keys into his gym bag, and hurried from his office into the reception area, feeling as though he were being chased. He exited the building peering over his shoulder, certain someone or something was about to step up behind him. Even when he slid inside his car, the feeling of being pursued persisted, enough that he repeatedly checked the rearview mirror on the drive home.

Not until he'd merged onto the freeway did his body begin to relax, and his thoughts shifted from his father to Kim. He imagined her sitting at the kitchen table sipping a mug of tepid tea, a medical book open, Bo asleep at her feet. They'd spoken on the phone at eight, when Donley called to say good night to Benny. He'd told her not to wait up, that he would be late preparing for the priest's arraignment. She said she needed to study, but he knew that was only an excuse. Kim didn't like going to bed knowing he remained at the office. She worried about his safety. She'd be really worried now. Donley wished he'd called her before leaving the office.

When he reached home, Donley did not raise the electric garage door for fear the vibration would wake Benny. He parked in the sloped driveway and walked along the side of the house, where he'd fenced in a dog run, to reach the door at the side of the house. Entering the garage, he heard Bo's paws clicking on the hardwood overhead as he made his way to his spot at the top of the back stairs, ready to greet his master. Donley couldn't go upstairs, not yet. He still felt the rush of anxiety pulsing through his body.

He heard the door at the top of the stairs open.

"Peter?"

"Yeah," he said.

"You coming up?"

"Need a few minutes."

He pressed "Play" on the boom box. Bruce Springsteen shouted out "Born in the USA," the part about a dog being beat too much, spending half its life just covering up. The heavy bass beat of the E Street Band played as Peter's hands and feet pounded the canvas heavy bag and rattled the metal chain that suspended it from an overhead joist.

Barefoot and bare chested, he attacked the bag from all angles, feinting and rising, left fist after right, combination kicks. He was fast but felt off-balance and imprecise, nothing like Kim had taught him. Without protection, his feet and knuckles soon became a raspberry red and began to ache, but he kept at it, feeling the release. His breathing became strained, and his arms and legs felt leaden. Springsteen gave way to Bono and the Irish band U2. Bono sang about streets with no names. The guitars pulsed; the drums pounded. Bono shouted about wanting to run and hide and tear down walls.

Peter ducked and dipped, weaving from side to side, continuing the onslaught, rising to land another punch or kick. The heavy bag spun until his arms and legs weakened to the point that his punches slowed and lost force, becoming long, looping swings. His chest heaved, and he exhaled raspy gasps of air until finally, unable to continue, he draped his hands around the bag, clutching it for support. Beads of sweat trailed down his neck and chest.

Kim turned off the cassette player. "Peter?"

Until then, he hadn't heard her come down the stairs. Didn't know she was there. He let go of the bag and stumbled backward against the unfinished concrete wall.

"Peter, what's wrong? What's the matter?"

"He's back."

He never referred to his father by name. He didn't have to. Kim knew the history of abuse, and she knew his father had died in an accident in their home. She didn't know the circumstances. He'd never told her. He'd never told anyone, except Mike Harris.

Kim cupped his face in her hands and gently turned it, forcing him to look her in the eyes. "Your father can't hurt you anymore, Peter. He's gone."

"No," he said. "He's not gone, just buried."

Chapter 10

December 24, 1987

Dimmed lights cast a pallid glow down the sterile hall. Nurses sitting behind counters adorned with Christmas lights reviewed charts, starting their morning shifts. One ate cereal from a plastic bowl. Christmas Eve, but not here. Here, it was just another morning, a place that did not know weekends or stop for holidays. Donley walked down the sparkling linoleum, past gurneys, linen bags, and carts with teetering stacks of empty dinner trays. He stepped into Lou's private room in the cardiac-care ward. Most of the tubing that had pierced Lou's body in the intensive-care unit had been removed, along with the tube down his throat. The room had much less the feel of impending death.

The same doctor who had confronted Donley in the intensive-care ward walked through the door and startled at the sight of him. "This is getting to be a bad habit," she said. At 5:00 a.m., visiting hours didn't begin for another three hours.

"I just needed a few minutes. I won't disturb him."

They moved to the doorway.

"They took the tube out of his throat," he said.

"He's breathing on his own. He's made remarkable progress," the doctor said, but cautioned that she could not quantify the damage or determine whether any of Lou's paralysis would be permanent until he was strong enough to undergo a series of tests, probably within a few days. They had, however, established that the stroke had not impaired Lou's vocal chords.

"When we removed the tube from his throat, he said, 'Goddamn thing was choking me to death.'"

Donley laughed. "That sounds like Lou."

In a very short time, Lou had charmed them all. "He's becoming a favorite here among the nurses. I get the impression your uncle is excitable?"

"That's an understatement."

"I think he pretty much willed himself through this one. Then again, it's likely he caused it by his diet and the work hours his wife says he keeps."

Donley nodded. "It comes with the job."

The doctor lowered the clipboard, looking at Lou. "Probably not anymore, I'm afraid."

"What do you mean?"

"He'll have to consider retirement."

"That's not going to happen."

She fixed her gaze on Donley. "Even if he could go back to work, I wouldn't recommend it," she said, looking grim. "This might have been a blessing. If he changes his eating habits and lifestyle, your uncle could live a long time."

The reality of the doctor's statement that Lou needed to retire hit Donley like a slap across the face. "Don't tell him," he said. "He loves his work. He really does."

"He'll have to learn to love something else." The doctor started from the room. "Just a few minutes."

Donley returned to Lou's bedside and put a hand on his uncle's shoulder. Lou opened his eyes. "You're awake?" Donley said. Half of Lou's face smiled. The other half twitched, the muscles struggling. "How do you feel?"

"I hurt like hell from all the needles they've been sticking in me." Lou sounded as if he had just returned from the dentist's office and the Novocain had not yet worn off.

Donley leaned forward to make it easier for Lou to see him.

"Don't you start hovering over me like your aunt; this isn't a goddamn funeral. I'm not dead yet."

Donley smiled. "I doubt there would be this many people at your funeral. I'm just hanging around for my inheritance."

"You'll be bitterly disappointed." He grimaced.

Donley looked up at the pulsing monitors, though he had no idea what any meant. "Are you all right?"

"Relax. I just have a pain in my side from lying here so damn long. How are things at the office?" Like most lawyers, Lou needed to know what was happening at work.

"Everything is fine. Ruth-Bell took charge like Alexander Haig."

"*Took* charge? She's run that office since the day I hired her, or hadn't you noticed?" He turned his head on the pillow. "You look worse than I feel."

"I'm fine. Just a little tired."

"The priest?"

"You know about that?"

"You ought to know me better. I've read the newspaper every morning for the past fifty years. I wasn't about to let a little heart attack keep me from my morning routine. I had your aunt read it to me."

"You should have skipped the article."

"I saw the photograph. When you see a priest in the paper, it's usually a bad sign. They don't write about the good things."

"That's what the archbishop said."

"He's always stolen my best lines. He came by to see me. He said you convinced him to let you represent Father Martin."

"Just until you get better," Donley said. He reached into his briefcase and pulled out a copy of the morning edition, holding it up for Lou to see. "Here's today's headline."

Priest of Polk Street
Arraignment Today
District Attorney Promises to Act Swiftly

"Today?"

"Bright and early before Maximum Milt."

His uncle let out a sigh. "Ramsey is such a jackass."

"I met him yesterday."

"What'd he want?"

"I'm not certain. I think he wants to make a deal, but everyone says I'm crazy."

"What kind of deal?"

"A plea if Father Martin confesses. At least that's what he hinted at."

"Life without parole?"

"We didn't get that far. The minute I brought it up, he backed off like I was out of my mind."

Lou furrowed his brow.

"The thing is, I can't figure out why he'd even hint at it. According to Ramsey, they have all the evidence they need to convict the priest. About the only thing I can figure is that he doesn't want to get his hands dirty before his final campaign push . . . actually, that was Ruth-Bell's theory. I just adopted it. Ramsey supported Father Martin and the shelter."

Lou didn't look or sound convinced. "Do they have aggravated circumstances?"

Donley put down the paper. "They say the kid was beaten and tortured before he was killed."

Lou momentarily closed his eyes and shook his head. "You don't have to do this, Peter. This is not something you have to do for me. Just find him another lawyer. Don says he had Larry Carr on board. Let him handle it."

"You know I can't do that, Lou."

"Have you called Max Seager yet?"

The question caught Donley off guard. "How do you know about that?"

"Never mind how I know. I know. Call him. He can pay you a hell of a lot more money and offer you things I can't. You don't owe me a thing. Your responsibility is to your wife and son."

"We don't need to have this discussion now."

Lou said, "Listen to me. When you were a boy, you were always sad. Your mother was always sad. I suspected something, but she was too proud to say anything. It just wasn't our way back then. You married who you married and you stayed married, in good times and in bad, for better or for worse. And I was always too goddamn busy . . . there was always a case, or a client, or a friend who needed me." Lou shut his eyes, but a tear leaked out and rolled down his face. He quickly wiped it away. "You were my family. You were my nephew. I should have done something."

"Lou, you don't have to—"

He put up a hand. "Don't tell me what I can and can't do. I suspect your aunt is going to be doing enough of that from now on." He swallowed with some difficulty. Donley found a cup on the tray by the bed and guided the straw to Lou's lips. He sipped the water before continuing. "I was wrong, Peter. I should have stepped in and stopped it. I'm sorry. I wanted you to know that."

Donley tried to make a joke. "Is this a deathbed confession? Because I spoke to your doctor, and she says you're not dying."

"You can bet your ass I'm not dying. Your aunt would kill me if I died." He took a deep breath, again with a grimace. "All I'm saying is, if you don't want to take this case, you just tell Judge Trimble that you're in the process of securing defense counsel for Father Martin. If he gives you any crap, tell him I'll climb out of this bed and personally kick his ass."

Donley smiled. "Will you bail me out of jail?"

Lou touched Donley's hand. He couldn't remember Lou ever touching him. "You don't need me to bail you out of anything. In case you missed it, that was the point of that beautiful speech I just gave. You're an excellent lawyer, Peter, better than I ever was at your age. You have perfect instincts, and you're quick on your feet. More importantly, you have a good heart." Lou took another deep breath and squeezed his hand. "I went out on my own about your age because I wanted control over the clients I chose to represent and what I charged them, even if it meant charging them nothing. I made less money, but I was a hell of a lot more satisfied at the end of the day. I was scared at first. You take a lot of bumps and bruises. Next thing you know, it's been forty years, and doctors are telling you that you can't do it anymore."

"You heard that?"

Lou nodded. "But that was my life. It doesn't have to be yours. Talk to Seager. If he offers you a job, take it and don't look back."

"We'll discuss that later. I have an arraignment this morning."

"Did you talk to the priest?"

"I tried, but he just sat there in his cell with his eyes closed."

Lou seemed to give that some thought. "Let me tell you one more thing. When they brought me in here, I was strapped to a gurney, lights blurring past. I couldn't move. For the first time in my life, I had absolutely no control over the situation. I suspected it was bad. The thought crossed my mind that I was dying, that I might never see my wife again. People were asking me questions, sticking me with needles. I had piss in my underwear and tubes coming from places I didn't even know existed. I wanted to grab somebody by the hand and tell them my name, tell them that I had a wife. I wanted to see a familiar face. Then I felt someone grab my hand, and I heard your voice, and I knew you would take care of things."

Donley felt a moment of pride. His father had never praised him, not even for his football exploits. They seemed only to make him angrier, probably because they made him realize the depth of his own failures. "You think the priest is scared."

"Wouldn't you be?"

Donley nodded. "I'll handle things, Lou. You just get better."

"You've climbed higher mountains than I ever had to climb, but you have one more mountain to climb, and you know it. The past is always the highest peak, and the hardest to scale. But when you finally pull yourself to the top and peer over the edge, there's nothing before you but the rest of your life."

The nurse walked in the door and nodded to Donley.

It was time to go.

Donley parked his Saab on Bryant Street, a block from the Hall of Justice. At precisely nine in the morning, or in little less than thirty minutes, deputies would escort Father Martin from his cell in solitary confinement to a holding tank, where a tape recording would advise him of his right to a jury trial, the right to confront and cross-examine witnesses, the right to remain silent, and other constitutional guarantees. Then they would lead him into the courtroom of the Honorable Milton Trimble.

"Maximum Milt" had earned his nickname as a deputy district attorney who always sought the maximum penalty for convicted offenders. Based on what Donley had been able to learn, Trimble's years on the bench had not softened him.

Donley turned off the car engine and tried to rub the fatigue from his face. The four Advil he'd chased with a glass of water had helped to alleviate the throbbing headache but had done nothing to remove the cobwebs. He picked up the morning newspaper from the passenger seat and reconsidered the article he had not shown Lou. Andrew Bennet's relatives in the Midwest, the same relatives who hadn't spoken with him in years, were said to be sorting through the résumés of plaintiffs' lawyers, some of whom had flown across country to pitch their services and try to convince the family that death could be an economically prosperous event.

Nauseated by the thought, Donley put down the paper and reached for the door handle just as someone knocked on the passenger-side window, startling him. Mike Harris stood in his police uniform holding two cups of coffee, his breath small, white wisps.

Donley inserted the key and lowered the window. "What are you doing here?"

"Freezing my ass off. Open the door."

Donley disengaged the locks, and Harris pulled open the passenger door and handed Donley a cup.

"Thanks."

"That's not for you." He slid his long legs into the passenger seat and took back the cup, setting it in the cup holder that popped from the dash. "That's for Rochelle. I'm going to be late getting home, and this is my peace offering."

"How'd you know I'd be here?"

"You called me, remember?"

"Yeah, like yesterday."

"Sorry, but I had the shift from hell. I called your house after I got off. Kim said you had the hearing at nine. I figured you'd be too cheap to pay to park in one of the lots and looked for the car." Harris frowned. "You look like shit."

"I feel like shit. What else did Kim tell you?"

"She said you were a terrible lay, but then we already knew that."
Donley laughed.

Harris sipped his coffee. "She's worried about you; she said you've been having a rough couple of days. She said you mentioned your father."

Donley and Harris had met at the Potrero Hill Boys' Club. Harris came from a broken home but had become an all-city basketball player and escaped by playing in college and briefly in Europe. He'd wanted to be an FBI agent, but the background check revealed three juvenile arrests, one with Donley. He'd joined the San Francisco Police Department instead.

"I'm all right."

"So, why'd you call?" Harris spoke over the collar of his jacket, which was pulled up to cover his neck. "Turn the heat on in here."

"It's not that cold."

"I can see my breath. It's like a refrigerator. This time next week, I'll be sunning my black ass in Hawaii and sipping tropical drinks in the sand."

"I didn't think black people tanned."

"Please, white boy, do not make me hurt you. Turn on the damn heater."

Donley turned on the engine and flipped a few switches. "There's something strange going on, Mike. I met with Ramsey yesterday, and he hinted at a plea—"

"Not for murder one." Harris shook his head. "DA doesn't plea murder one."

"How come everyone knows that except me?"

"'Cause you're a dumb shit."

"Maybe so, but I'm telling you Ramsey did everything except say the word."

Harris seemed to contemplate this. "You didn't hear this from me, OK? It could be my job."

"OK."

"Word is, they have some major problems with the evidence against your guy."

"What kind of problems?"

"Problems with the way they got it, which means problems with using it."

The light went on. "No warrant. Illegal search and seizure," Donley said.

"One of the detectives apparently went to the scene and turned everything upside down, including breaking down some locked doors and opening locked cabinets."

"They're worried," Donley said. "It's a business, but it also could be considered the priest's personal residence—maybe even the boys'. Different rules apply." He wished he'd have known earlier, so he could have done some research.

Harris sipped at his coffee. "I don't know about the legal crap, but I can tell you the detective was suspended."

"You think they might be hiding him?"

"I don't know, but this guy is liable to say or do almost anything," Harris said. "He's a GI Joe–type, medals in Vietnam, hero cop. He's also a racist, homophobic asshole, though he does a pretty good job of hiding it. I don't know what happened at the shelter that night, but I suspect there is more to it. Connor is an asshole, but he's not dumb when it comes to police procedure and evidence."

"Connor? That's the detective's name?"

"Dixon Connor. He's been in homicide more than twenty years, and his old man was a cop before they kicked him out, too."

"So, he had to know that breaking down doors would cause problems," Donley said.

"One would think, my friend. One would think." Harris reached for the door handle. "I need to get home so Rochelle can get to work. Remember, you did not hear any of this from me. I'll see you tonight."

"Tonight?"

"At your party. Christmas Eve? Goodwill to men? Ho, ho, ho?" Harris took his hand out of his pocket long enough to give Donley a halfhearted handshake. "I love you, brother. Give that asshole Ramsey hell."

Donley waited for Harris to leave before stepping from the car. The traffic on Bryant Street had become more congested. Black-and-white police cars lined the curb, along with television trucks. Men taped cables to the sidewalk with duct tape while well-dressed men and women holding microphones mapped out positions with camera crews so the news shot would include the large seal of the State of California affixed to the building. Apparently, everyone was expecting a show. Donley wasn't about to provide one. Get in and get out, as Ruth-Bell and Lou had both said. He went over his three main notes. Do not enter a plea, waive time, and otherwise say as little as possible.

The second floor of the Hall of Justice was a marbled tunnel, devoid of windows and dimly lit by fluorescent lights. The mood seemed subdued for a morning calendar. A few anxious-looking men sat huddled on worn benches talking to their lawyers as security guards and court personnel strolled past in no apparent hurry. One wore a red-and-white Christmas hat, but that was it for the Christmas spirit.

As Ruth-Bell advised, Judge Milton Trimble would temporarily preside over Courtroom 13, the ceremonial courtroom usually reserved for public functions. Ramsey expected a crowd and was likely to get it. Donley checked the criminal calendar posted on a bulletin board just outside the fifteen-foot doors. The clerk had placed the arraignment of case number C87–0545, *State of California v. Thomas Wilson Martin*, first on the calendar, likely to get it over with and get back to routine.

Donley turned when he heard a commotion in the hall behind him. Gil Ramsey and Linda St. Claire had stepped from the elevator followed by five or six reporters, including a camera crew. Both had dressed in navy blue and were smiling so bright they could have been doing a chewing-gum commercial. Donley wanted no part of it. He reached for the handle to the large wooden doors. Locked. Nowhere to run. Nowhere to hide.

"This is Peter Donley," Ramsey said as the horde arrived. "He has been retained to represent Father Martin."

The questions came rapid-fire, some too idiotic to generate a response.

"Will Father Martin enter a plea this morning?"

"Do you have any comment on reports the evidence in this case is overwhelming?"

"The police say pornographic material was found in Father Martin's office. Can you confirm that?"

"Was there an accomplice?"

"Will the archdiocese be involved in his defense?"

Donley knew he should say, "No comment," but his competitive juices kicked in when he saw St. Claire and Ramsey enjoying the attack. He cleared his throat. "I am aware of no such evidence. If the district attorney has overwhelming evidence of Father Martin's guilt, they've certainly done a good job of hiding it from all of you folks. Your articles and news stories have been a bit bland."

The reporters smiled. "What have you been told?" a woman in front asked.

Donley gave an exaggerated shrug. "I'm afraid the DA has kept the defense in the dark also."

Ramsey stepped forward. "As you know, this matter is moving quickly. The evidence and authorized statements were withheld pending notice of the deceased's next of kin. They will be presented to the court this morning."

"I'm just surprised all of you were able to find the next of kin so quickly when the DA apparently couldn't," Donley said, holding up the *Chronicle*. The group chuckled. Ramsey did not. Donley continued. "As for the evidence, let me say this." He looked to Ramsey. "The police department engaged in an unauthorized search, without a warrant, of Father Martin's shelter in violation of his Fourth Amendment right against unreasonable searches."

Ramsey and Linda St. Claire exchanged a glance. The reporters moved the tape recorders closer to Donley's chin. Others wrote furiously, firing off additional questions. Donley talked over them.

"We are considering bringing a motion to suppress all evidence illegally obtained as a direct result of that unlawful search. I would also seek to question the detective who conducted that search, but I understand he has been suspended for his acts of indiscretion." Donley paused. "But as the district attorney said, I'm getting ahead of myself. I'll leave that to him and Ms. St. Claire to present to the court this morning."

The crowd shifted to Ramsey and St. Claire. Timing being everything, as Lou liked to say, someone had unlocked the wooden doors. Donley pulled one open and ducked inside as the reporters began again with their series of questions.

Inside, Donley realized he'd failed at the first of his three notes—say as little as possible. His temper and competitiveness had gotten the better of him again. Lou would have called it an amateur's move: you push me, and I'll push you back. Donley thought of Mike Harris and hoped no one would put two and two together. Then he thought again of Lou and smiled.

It had been a hell of a lot of fun.

He pushed through the swinging gate in the wooden railing that separated the gallery from the temporary altar of His Holiness, Milton Trimble. He set his briefcase on the table closest to the jury box and removed his notepad, file, and his notes and then set them on the table, along with the silver Waterman pen Kim had given him upon his graduating law school.

The volume of voices from the hallway increased, indicating the doors had opened behind him. Spectators filed in, and within minutes the courtroom, usually as reserved as a funeral parlor, bristled with energy and hushed voices. A reporter seated behind the railing tried to get Donley's attention, but Donley ignored him. He crossed his legs and stared straight ahead, calm and poised, his courtroom demeanor well rehearsed. It had been that way since his first trial. His nerves usually raged until he entered the courtroom and spoke his first words. Then he relaxed. The singular focus of a hearing or a trial inside a courtroom brought Donley a certain sense of peace, though this courtroom was bigger than any in which he had previously appeared. The centerpiece was an ornate, elevated bench flanked by flags and bathed in a dull light from candelabra-style light fixtures along the walls and chandeliers hanging from the ceiling. A massive gold seal of the State of California hung on the dark-wood walls behind the bench.

The decibel level in the room continued to increase, voices echoing off the marble floor to the twenty-foot ceiling. Donley did not need to turn around to know that St. Claire and Ramsey had entered, likely striding down the aisle like a wedding couple. He heard the gate swing open. St. Claire nodded as if the confrontation in the hallway had not happened and moved to the other table. As she did, the bailiff entered from a door to the left of the bench and called out, "All rise and come to order. The Honorable Milton Trimble, judge, presiding."

The words had barely escaped the bailiff's mouth when Trimble burst through the door and vaulted the four steps behind the bench like a man chasing a windblown $100 bill. Despite the acrobatics and for all his reputation, Trimble's entrance was a letdown. Short and thin with a receding hairline, he looked more like a besieged accountant during tax season than a judge. The regal courtroom dwarfed him. When he sat in the black-leather chair, he momentarily disappeared from view. Sitting forward, he looked like a child at his father's desk. Perhaps sensing this, he leaned on his forearms as if to prop himself higher, and he busied himself moving stacks of files while looking out at the packed gallery over bifocal glasses. He ran his fingers over strands of hair, which he parted low on the side and combed over to unsuccessfully cover a bald spot. He did not look happy to be there.

"Call the first case."

The clerk spoke in a monotone. "Case number C87–0545. The people of the State of California versus Thomas Wilson Martin."

The door to Donley's right opened, and two burly deputies escorted Father Martin into the courtroom. The priest wore an orange top and pants, white socks, and rubber sandals. Despite the cast on his left wrist, Father Martin held his hands at stomach level to provide enough slack in the chain that extended between his legs to shackles around his ankles. It seemed to take him forever to shuffle his way across the marble floor. Nearing the table, he stumbled. The two guards caught him under the arms.

Trimble looked up from the file he'd been reading. "Remove those shackles immediately."

St. Claire spoke instantly. "If it pleases the court—"

"It doesn't." Trimble shot St. Claire a look that knocked her back onto her heels. "Remove the shackles. This is a courtroom, not a zoo." The murmur in the gallery was instantaneous, as was Trimble's solid, single wrap of the gavel. "I will not tolerate any outbursts in my courtroom this morning," he growled. "If there is a single shenanigan, I'll close it."

Maximum Milt was taking charge, setting the ground rules on the first day of school.

The deputies removed the shackles and led Father Martin to the chair beside Donley. The priest looked worse than the day before, his jaw now covered by pronounced stubble. Recalling Lou's advice that the priest was likely scared, and recognizing he had an audience behind him that had read his client was a monster, Donley made a point of reaching out his hand. Father Martin hesitated before taking it.

"State your appearances, counsel," Trimble instructed.

"Linda St. Claire on behalf of the people of the State of California, Your Honor."

"Peter Donley specially appearing on behalf of the defendant, Father Thomas Martin."

"Specially appearing? What does that mean?" Judge Trimble sounded annoyed.

"I'm appearing today on Father Martin's behalf. I have not, however, been retained by Father Martin."

"What are you, decor?"

The retort brought muffled laughter from the gallery. Trimble was wasting no time taking Donley apart. "My partner, Lou Giantelli, would normally be here, but he's suffered a heart attack and stroke and is in the hospital," Donley said. "Father Martin and I have not spoken, and therefore, I do not know whether he seeks my counsel or not."

Trimble fidgeted in his seat. "Mr. Donley, my comment was misplaced. I apologize. I heard about Mr. Giantelli and didn't know the connection. How is he doing?"

"He's fighting."

"I'd expect nothing less. Please give him my personal wishes for a speedy recovery."

"I will do that, Your Honor." He'd played a hunch based on Ruth-Bell's statement that Lou and Trimble had sparred. He figured it meant Trimble had been a good lawyer, and Donley suspected that had led to mutual respect.

"Under the circumstances, I will proceed on the assumption that Father Martin has not yet retained counsel," Trimble said.

St. Claire interrupted. "Your Honor, Father Martin did meet with—"

Trimble cut her off. "Ms. St. Claire, let's get something straight. When I talk, you listen. When I want your input, I'll ask for it. It's simple. Stick to it, and we'll have no problems. Fail, and it will be a long morning. Understood?"

"Understood, Your Honor," St. Claire said.

Trimble turned to Father Martin and read from a prepared statement. "Thomas Wilson Martin, you're here in San Francisco Superior Court. You are in the custody of the San Francisco County Sheriff, and you are here for the purpose of arraignment." He looked up at the priest. "Did you hear the tape recording of your rights played in the holding cell?"

"Yes," Father Martin said.

Trimble looked to Donley. "Have you discussed the charges with Father Martin?"

"My office received a faxed copy of the complaint late last night. So, no, I haven't discussed it with Father Martin."

Trimble ran a hand over his chin as if considering his shave. "All right, for the record, I'm going to read the criminal complaint filed by the district attorney. Then I assume we are going to have some discussion. Father Martin, a copy of a complaint has been provided to Mr. Donley. It charges you with a violation of the law on December 21, 1987, in the San Francisco Judicial District, in the county of San Francisco, state of California. In count one, you are charged with felony violation of Penal Code Section 187, to wit murder, that you did then and there cause the death of a minor, Andrew Bennet. In count two of the complaint, you are charged with violation of Penal Code Section 190.2 (a) (17), the commission of a felony while the defendant was engaged in the commission, or attempted commission of a felony." Trimble stopped and looked over at St. Claire. "What is the felony, Ms. St. Claire?"

"The State intends to prove there exist sufficient facts to warrant special circumstances."

"I can read, Ms. St. Claire. What are those facts? What is the felony?" Trimble repeated, impatient.

She postured slightly toward the gallery. "On the basis that the murder of Andrew Bennet was committed with such heinous disregard for human life that it constitutes infliction of torture, warranting special circumstances."

The courtroom buzzed. Whether the district attorney would seek the death penalty and why had apparently been questions on everyone's mind. *So much for any plea deal,* Donley thought.

Trimble shook his head. "Ms. St. Claire, in case you didn't notice, this mammoth piece of wood I'm being forced to sit behind this morning is up here. That means I'm up here. You can address your arguments to the bench. I assume all of that evidence is set forth in the documents?"

"It is, Your Honor. If I may present the report of Alfred Shirk, county medical examiner?"

"You may do so."

She handed a copy of the report to Donley and one to the court clerk, who stood on her toes and reached to hand it up to Trimble. Donley placed the report on counsel table, trying to show no emotion.

Trimble turned to him. "I take it you have read this report, Mr. Donley?"

"No, Your Honor, this is the first I've seen it."

Judge Trimble turned his copy over. "Then we're not going to read it now."

St. Claire looked exasperated.

Trimble looked to Donley. "I assume you have some things to discuss with the court?"

"Your Honor, given that we received the complaint late last night, after work hours, and we are receiving the medical examiner's report and Riverside documents now, the defense asks for a continuance to enter a plea."

"Your Honor, the People object to any attempt to delay these proceedings," St. Claire said.

Trimble raised his reading glasses onto the tip of his nose. "I disagree, Ms. St. Claire. The accused cannot reasonably be expected to enter a plea if he is unaware of the charges against him. Seems fundamental to me. I'm going to continue these proceedings—the Christmas holiday being noted. Mr. Donley, how much time do you need?"

"I'd suggest after the new year, Your Honor?"

"Very well. The court clerk will send out notice." Judge Trimble raised his gavel.

Donley let out a sigh. A reprieve would give him a chance to catch his breath, enjoy the Christmas holiday, and allow him time to find Father Martin competent counsel.

"But I'm not guilty."

Donley turned to the priest and felt the back of his knees go weak.

Trimble lowered his gavel and leaned forward. "Father Martin?"

Donley leaned closer to his client, whispering, "You don't need to enter a plea."

"You're not obligated to enter a plea, Father Martin," Trimble said. "Your counsel has sought and been granted a continuance."

"I understand that, Your Honor. But I'm not guilty. I did not kill Andrew Bennet." The coal-black eyes were gone, replaced by a soft hazel. "I don't need more time to enter a plea."

The courtroom buzzed. This time it took several bangs of Trimble's gavel to silence it. Trimble shot Donley a glance before turning his attention back to Father Martin. "Does the defendant wish to enter a plea at this time?"

Donley looked from the priest to the bench. "Your Honor, I request a moment to confer with my client?"

"Your Honor, Mr. Donley said he was not here representing Father Martin," St. Claire shot back.

Trimble raised a hand. "He is if Father Martin enters a plea."

Father Martin leaned toward Donley, who raised a legal pad to block the gallery's view of their conversation. "I'm not guilty. I didn't do it," he said.

"You don't need to enter a plea even if you're not guilty," Donley said. "This buys us time to get the evidence."

"I understand, and I appreciate your counsel, but I wish to enter the plea of not guilty."

Donley studied the priest's face and saw that he was resolute in his conviction. "You're sure it's what you want to do?"

"I am."

"Mr. Donley?" Judge Trimble said.

The courtroom slowed to a crawl. In his mind, Donley saw and heard a collage of people. Mike Harris sipped at the rim of his coffee, telling him there were problems with the evidence, that a veteran cop had made a rookie mistake. Ruth-Bell stood in his office, telling him that the district attorney did not plea murder-one charges, and Lou lay looking up at him from his hospital bed, telling him to trust his instincts.

"Mr. Donley?" Trimble said, growing impatient.

Donley exited the tunnel. Father Martin smiled at him. "I'm not guilty."

Donley faced the bench. The gallery seemed to lean forward, as if the courtroom had slipped off its foundation and listed toward the front of the room.

"My client pleads not guilty, Your Honor."

The gallery rumbled.

Milton Trimble nodded, though his brow furrowed. "The court will accept the defendant's plea of not guilty. I'm making an independent Riverside determination of probable cause. Does your client waive time, Mr. Donley?"

Now on the offensive, Donley decided not to back off. He was not about to give Ramsey and St. Claire more time to clean up their evidence. "Your Honor, the defense requests an immediate preliminary examination of the evidence. We intend to challenge the police seizure of the alleged physical evidence in this case as being the product of an unlawful search, without a warrant. The evidence obtained, and all evidence generated from it, is tainted and therefore inadmissible."

The courtroom buzzed like the din of a large engine.

St. Claire rushed to respond. "Your Honor, all of the evidence obtained would have otherwise necessarily been obtained. It was found on the premises, across a hallway from a murder scene. It clearly falls within the exception enumerated in *Nix v. Williams*."

"Maybe so, Your Honor," Donley countered. "But now is not the time for the prosecution to make such a circular argument. Ms. St. Claire justifies the police department's illegal search by already convicting Father Martin. She concludes a warrant would have been granted to search locked offices where Father Martin also kept a private residence, but she provides no rationale as to the probable cause that brought the police to the shelter in the first place. What the detectives came upon was a dead body at a shelter where Father Martin works and lives. They cannot try and convict him of a crime in order to justify their illegal search. We also intend to prove the illegally obtained evidence is flawed. To argue Father Martin's fingerprints or footprints were found in the room is ludicrous given that Father Martin works—"

Trimble banged his gavel, cutting him off. "I want to see counsel in chambers. Now."

Trimble's judicial chambers contained the same rich oak paneling but a more modest desk. Antique law books, framed photographs, and elaborate miniature trains of all shapes and sizes, an impressive collection, filled the shelves. In the far corner sat a baby's crib, complete with bumpers, a quilt, and a Mickey Mouse mobile. Donley picked out a photograph of Judge Trimble's multiple grandchildren on a shelf behind his desk, though he doubted they would be swapping baby stories this morning.

By the time St. Claire and Ramsey entered his office, Trimble had already removed his robe, revealing a light-blue, short-sleeved shirt and a tie decorated with ornate Christmas trees. His scowl let everyone know he was not happy.

"Be seated." They complied. "What happened today will not happen again in my courtroom. The justice system is about dispensing justice. It is about the rights of the victims and the accused. It is not about you."

"Judge," Ramsey said in a conversational tone.

"I'm not finished, Mr. Ramsey. The best attorneys I've had in my courtroom are the ones I can't recall. They're the ones who did their jobs efficiently and without fanfare. The ones I recall are the showboats and grandstanders. That is not what the legal system is about. From this moment forward, I am absolutely forbidding any of you, or your witnesses, from speaking to the press."

"Your Honor—" St. Claire started.

"You are either a television commentator, or you're an attorney, Ms. St. Claire. Decide."

"Your Honor, I resent—"

"And I resent being a part of the display that went on this morning," Trimble growled. "I resent lawyers who demean the courtroom and legal system like used-car salesmen. I cannot control the press, but I can control you. While you are in my courtroom, you will be lawyers. All of you. Outside the courtroom, I expect you to conduct yourselves as professionals. You will not discuss this matter with the press. I want a free exchange of the evidence. From this point forward, Mr. Donley is to be given unlimited access to the evidence in your possession."

He turned to Donley. "Mr. Donley, I will not tolerate courtroom theatrics. If I find out that your client's demeanor or your request for an expedited preliminary hearing was to serve that purpose, I will come down on you very hard. Understood?"

"Understood," Donley said.

Trimble sat. "Your motion will be heard next Thursday."

Donley nodded. It was a very short time, particularly with the Christmas holiday, but he was in no position to negotiate. Judges were not sympathetic when they were also working over the holidays. He also suspected Trimble was giving him a lesson in "be careful what you wish for." Put up or shut up.

For the next ten minutes, they discussed courtroom procedure for motions, witnesses, and other matters. Trimble set ground rules to prevent the case from overwhelming his staff and calendar. Judges, like schoolteachers, were overworked and underpaid given the importance of their position in society. Lou had advised Donley on more than one occasion to avoid making more work for a judge than was absolutely necessary. They wouldn't thank you for it, but the alternative was far worse.

Donley nodded when appropriate, but most of the time, he heeded Ruth-Bell's third piece of advice and kept his mouth shut.

"Your Honor," Ramsey said, "given the tight timetable the court has set for the preliminary examination, we would request that Father Martin submit to a blood test."

Judge Trimble looked at Donley. "How about it, Mr. Donley? It's a fair request."

Donley knew Trimble was inclined to grant such a motion and saw no need to appear unreasonable. He would gain points if he was cooperative. "I'll consult with Father Martin. I don't anticipate a problem. I'll advise Ms. St. Claire."

Before anyone could utter another word, Judge Trimble dismissed them. "I've missed enough family holidays during my career. I don't intend to miss Christmas Eve. I'm Santa Claus this year."

They all smiled and quickly departed.

In the hallway, Ramsey called to Donley and handed him his umbrella. "I believe you left this in my office yesterday."

Donley took the umbrella, but Ramsey did not immediately release his grip. He smiled. Then, without a word, he turned and walked toward a rear door, apparently no longer interested in facing a media to which he couldn't pander.

Chapter 11

Donley placed his briefcase on the table as the metal door shut. Father Martin stood across the county jail's attorney-client room, staring out a rectangular, double-paned window. Through it, at a certain angle, Donley knew the priest could see the San Francisco skyline. Though it was only a short distance, it must have felt like a great divide.

"Father Martin?"

Father Martin turned and walked toward the table. "Please, call me Tom, Mr. Donley. Nobody calls me Father Martin."

"Peter. Nobody calls me Mr. Donley."

They shook hands, then pulled out chairs and sat on opposite sides of the table.

"I'm not a murderer, and I'm not a pedophile," Father Martin said.

"I'm not a criminal lawyer," Donley replied. "Well, I mean I've never defended anyone accused of murder. If we go down this path, I'll need to bring in someone with more experience. The court will mandate it."

"I understand."

"I wanted to apologize for running out of the room the other day—" Donley started.

Father Martin raised a hand. "I don't blame you; you must have thought I was a lunatic."

"Why wouldn't you speak to me?"

Father Martin lowered his head. When he looked up, his eyes were moist. "I don't know. Shock, perhaps. A lot of things, I suppose. The painkillers on an empty stomach; the feeling that I had somehow killed Andrew. I had gone back into that place I left behind many years ago when it was me against the world. You were an unfamiliar face. I thought you were from the public defender's office."

"I understand the feeling," Donley said. "But what do you mean that you felt you had somehow killed Andrew?"

Father Martin took a breath before starting. "The boys called him Alphabet. I called him Andrew. Nicknames demean because they come from the streets. I use the names God gave each boy."

"So, you did know him," Donley said, reaching into his briefcase for his notepad and pen.

Father Martin shook his head. "I knew more *of* him. I don't know anyone who actually *knew* Andrew. It's not unusual. A lot of these kids live multiple lives. The person they display on the street is not who they are. They put up walls to survive."

Donley understood all too well about putting up walls.

"Andrew survived the streets because he was smart and resourceful, but like most heroin addicts, he was always looking for a way to make or steal a buck. No one on the street had a good handle on him. He wasn't interested in anybody's sympathy or help, which is why I was so surprised when he came to the shelter that afternoon."

"What time did he get there?"

"Early, about five o'clock. If he wasn't the last person I expected to see, he was close to it."

"Did he say why he came?"

"No. And I didn't press the issue. He was agitated. I thought it was the drugs, but I decided to let him stay. I don't normally do that. I won't allow the shelter to be used as a crash house. I guess I held out hope his coming was his way of reaching out for help. I didn't want to turn my back on him, or spook him. The hardest part is getting the kids to the shelter. My chances of helping them improve dramatically once they are there. Do you follow?"

Donley did.

"I left Andrew alone. When I went back to the dormitory later that night to check on him, he was gone."

"What time was that?"

"When he left? I can't say for certain, but I noticed he was gone around seven, right before I sat down to pay the bills. I figured he couldn't take it, that he needed a fix. But I also couldn't shake the feeling that I should have spent time with him, talked with him, that if I had, maybe he would have stayed. I let the stress of the shelter get to me; financially, it's been tough."

"I'm going to need details," Donley said. "And I'm going to force you to be painfully specific."

"I understand," Father Martin said.

Aileen O'Malley sat behind her desk thinking, *Déjà vu all over again,* or whatever the hell the saying was. Gil Ramsey and Linda St. Claire continued to grill both her and Detective John Begley.

"I don't know how he found out." Begley held out his hands like he was presenting a sacrificial lamb to the gods. "These things tend to take on a life of their own; I can't control what everyone says. Hell, it could be the friend of a wife of an officer who happened to run into someone in a grocery store who happened to know Donley."

Ramsey paced the office. O'Malley had never seen him so agitated. He extended a finger in her direction. "This will reflect poorly on your department and you. If they fight this, I can't guarantee the evidence will get in."

She brushed aside the threat. "What's done is done. He would have learned of the problems with the evidence eventually. It wasn't going to stay hidden forever. The question now is, how to deal with it."

Ramsey turned to St. Claire. "Do you think he orchestrated Father Martin's entering a plea so he could seek an expedited motion on the evidence?"

"You're giving him too much credit. He's bluffing," St. Claire said.

"Really? Because it felt like he was calling our bluff."

"Then let's play our hands. I like my cards a hell of a lot better than his. I told you forensic—"

Ramsey cut her off. "The blood? The fingerprints? You heard him in court today. He'll argue that away in a heartbeat. If the evidence gets thrown out, we have no murder weapon and no motivation. We have a priest who lives at a shelter who rushed to the aid of a dead boy. Donley will paint Father Martin as the damned Good Samaritan."

O'Malley stepped into the fray, hoping to move the conversation toward conclusion. She looked to Begley. "What do we have, John?"

"Forensics picked up blood samples from the office, fingerprints, possible murder weapon. But Mr. Ramsey's right; that might not matter. Father Martin lived at the shelter."

O'Malley asked, "What do you mean 'possible' murder weapon? I thought we had a positive?"

Begley shook his head. "The ME will say only that the stab wounds are consistent with the puncture wounds he would *expect* the letter opener to make, not that it is the weapon."

"So, undetermined," she said.

"It had the kid's blood all over it," St. Claire scoffed, as if everyone in the room was stupid. "How else did it get there?"

Begley shook his head. "Why would the priest kill the kid at the shelter and leave the murder weapon in plain sight? Why would he sit there with blood all over himself?"

"Where was he going to go?" St. Claire said. "I've tried murderers who killed their entire families, then sat down to make a sandwich with the same knife. You guys have found them at the table dipping it in the mayonnaise jar. Who knows why these people do what they do?"

"It doesn't make a lot of sense," Begley said, sounding tired of the debate.

"I'll make it make sense," St. Claire said.

Ramsey shook his head. "You better hope Trimble is in a better mood." He turned to O'Malley. "Where are we on the declarations for the warrant to search the shelter?"

"Just about done."

"Good. I want to get in there as soon as possible after the holiday." To St. Claire, he said, "I want the warrant to include any private residence the priest maintains, including the shelter. And put a guard at the entrance of the building until we can get in."

"A guard has been posted at the shelter since John froze the building," Begley said.

Ramsey turned to Begley. "What about other witnesses?"

"Scattered like rabbits. The only one we know for sure was there that night is the one Connor put in the hospital, and he's so drugged up on painkillers right now, he can't give his name."

"There have to be records," St. Claire said. "The shelter receives state funding."

"Did you find anything like that?" Ramsey asked Begley.

Begley shook his head. "Didn't look."

"Put it on the subpoena," Ramsey said to St. Claire.

"I'll pull the victim's juvenile file and see if there's anything of interest," Begley offered.

"No," Ramsey said. "It's irrelevant unless we make it relevant. Leave it alone." He turned to St. Claire. "Call Donley. See if his client has agreed to give a blood sample; if the priest's blood is found at the crime scene, the landscape changes."

"There is something else," O'Malley said. "After I suspended Connor, I had John pull his files so I could distribute his active cases. Not exactly the Christmas bonus my detectives expected." She looked to Begley.

"Connor had two files that caught my attention," Begley said. "Two other street kids recently murdered."

"Is there any evidence of a correlation?" Ramsey asked.

"I don't know. One kid was shot. His body was found at Fort Funston. The other died by strangulation and was found in a dumpster south of Market."

"Do either of them have any connection to Father Martin's shelter?" Ramsey asked.

"Uncertain. The investigations haven't gone anywhere," Begley said. "They could have just been drug related; both victims were known to use heavy drugs."

Ramsey stood in the doorway, his jacket draped over his arm. "I don't want to go off half-cocked on a wild goose chase. Unless there is some connection, let's concentrate on this case. We need to keep our focus." He looked at his watch. "It's getting late. We all have places we need to be tonight."

◆　◆　◆

Donley had loosened his tie, unbuttoned the collar of his shirt, and rolled his sleeves halfway up his forearms. Father Martin finished a Styrofoam cup half-filled with what was supposed to be coffee and tossed it into the wastebasket.

"The sadness just overwhelmed me," Father Martin said. "The loss of a life so young is such a waste, but for someone to kill Andrew and place him in a manger . . . what kind of sick individual would do something like that?" Father Martin shook his head, took a breath, and blew out a burst of air. "From there, everything just spun out of control. It was like I was in the middle of a bad dream and couldn't wake up. Do you know what that's like?"

Too well, Donley thought.

"When you came to my cell, you were just an extension of that nightmare. It wasn't until the archbishop came to see me that reality hit."

"There was no need to enter a plea today," Donley said. "It's extremely rare at a first hearing."

"So is a packed courtroom full of media."

Donley smiled. "You did it on purpose."

"As you shook my hand on purpose. I learned while promoting the shelter that you can use the media or be used by it. I saw the courtroom today as a forum to let Andrew's killer know this is not over."

"Let's talk about your defense. The first thing you need to understand is that the legal profession is not the real world," Donley said, mimicking a phrase Lou used with clients. "What may be black and white is often gray in the courtroom."

Father Martin stood and paced. "You're telling me what's true and what you can prove are two different things."

"Exactly."

"I understand, and I'm somewhat familiar with the judicial system. I got in my share of trouble as a kid."

"What will they find?"

"A couple of convictions for petty theft, a joyride in a stolen car, malicious mischief, one or two others that don't come immediately to mind. My mother raised seven children by herself. She had a lot of irons in the fire and couldn't always be there."

"None of those are relevant; no way Judge Trimble lets those in."

"Maybe not, but the press will print them."

Donley sat back, stretching his legs. The stress of the past two days had started to subside, and his body slumped as though it was slowly deflating. He thought about his conversation with Lou that morning, about how scared Father Martin must be, especially if he were innocent.

Donley pointed with the tip of his pen. "I couldn't help but notice the tattoo."

"I grew up on the streets," Father Martin said, sounding defensive. "I ran with kids who grew up on the streets, and I got in trouble for it. I tried drugs and alcohol, lost more fights than I won, and lost my virginity when I was thirteen."

"Thirteen? Wow."

"Where I grew up, the only thing you had was how you carried yourself. I keep the tattoo and the earring to remind me of how far I've come. It gives me hope with my ministry."

"I was just going to say I like it," Donley offered. "I have a panther on my calf."

Father Martin stopped pacing. "Sorry, I guess I can get a little sensitive about it. Why a panther?"

"High school mascot."

"You were an athlete?"

"A football player. Why a hawk?"

"A nickname." Father Martin turned his head so it was in profile and pointed to his nose, which looked to have been broken at least once.

Donley nodded. "So, how did you become a priest?"

"I wish I had a better answer to that question."

"I don't doubt you get it a lot."

"All the time. It would certainly make for a better story if I could tell the kids that I had some epiphany, you know, like the gates of heaven opening and a large hand pointing a bent finger at me through the clouds."

"If you did, I might be able to get you off on insanity."

Father Martin smiled. "Growing up, the church was always a part of my life. In fact, I might not have become a priest if I hadn't grown up where I did. My mother used to drag all of us there every Sunday. I complained to keep in good graces with my brothers, but for me, when I reached those steps and opened those big wooden doors, the whole world changed. I smelled the incense and saw the flickering light off the gold and silver, and I just felt at peace. I felt at home."

When Father Martin stared at the floor, Donley knew the priest was wondering if he would ever feel that peace again. Father Martin lifted his gaze. "Is it true what the prosecutor said? Was Andrew tortured?"

"She was reading between the lines," Donley said. "The autopsy report raises more questions than it answers in my mind. It would be pretty tough for St. Claire to conclude that a street prostitute was raped and tortured. I think she was playing to the press."

"But there was some indication?" Father Martin persisted.

"There's some indication, yes. Let's talk about that night," Donley said. "Start with the power outage. Was it the fuse?"

Father Martin shook his head. "I don't know. I never got the chance to find out."

Donley made a note to find out if there had been a power outage that night in the electrical grid on which the shelter was located.

"Any idea where the photographs came from?"

"All I've come up with is one of the boys could have brought them in when they checked in that night and stashed them in their locker."

"And the letter opener?"

"Mine. How Andrew's blood got on it, I don't know."

"When's the last time you saw it?"

"Earlier that night. I used it to open bills."

"So, it was on your desk." Donley made a note to ask for the names of every boy who'd checked into the shelter. "OK, how does someone get a body—alive or dead—into the shelter without anyone noticing?"

"May I?" Father Martin held out his hands for Donley's notepad and pen. He diagramed a crude layout of the shelter's floor plan as he spoke.

"I've thought about this. From my desk, I can see anyone who comes up the stairs. Across the hall is the recreation room. In other words, nothing gets past me. I set it up for that reason."

"Any other entrances?"

Father Martin nodded. "In the back of the recreation room, there's a staircase that leads down to the furnace room. A door leads outside to a park, which is just a slab of asphalt surrounded by a chain-link fence. The homeless sleep there. The stairwell is not far from the street. I keep the door in the recreation room and the door to the park locked. Neither door has a handle on the outside, just a metal plate. You can't get in unless someone opens that door for you from the inside."

"Who knows that beside you?"

"A few of the boys who've stayed before; I've found the door propped open for friends to get in after curfew. I try to check it regularly, but . . . it should have been locked."

Donley sat back, thinking. "It would be a hell of a gamble for someone carrying a body—dead or still alive—to take a chance the door might or might not be open."

Father Martin nodded. "I agree."

"So, someone had to have propped both doors open."

"Andrew would have been my first choice, but of course, that makes no sense, unless maybe the killer double-crossed him."

"You didn't check the door that night?"

"No."

"Anyone else ever check it for you?"

"Danny will on occasion."

"Who's Danny?"

"Danny Simeon. He helps out nights at the shelter." Father Martin shook his head. "Danny wouldn't do it, but he might have better insight into who could have."

"Where can I find him?"

"He keeps a room in the back of a bar. It's called the Grub Steak or Grub House, something like that. At least, that's what it used to be called."

"What about the other boys at the shelter that night? How would I find them?"

Father Martin shook his head. "I'm not sure you will. They disappear, and they don't speak to anyone they don't know or trust."

Again, Donley understood. After so many years of waiting for someone to help him and his mother, he had eventually given up hope.

"Let me worry about that. How would I determine who was at the shelter that night?"

"I keep a log. It's required by the state."

"Where?"

"In the upper right-hand drawer of my desk. I keep the log inside my Bible."

Donley stopped writing and looked up from the pad.

"The success of the shelter depends upon trust. Except for state funding, I keep the names in that book, and what each boy brings to the shelter, strictly confidential."

Donley reviewed his notes. "I should be getting the police and witness statements this afternoon. The show I put on in court was pretty much from the hip. Right now their case is blood and fingerprints. They'll use a lot of scientific data and statistics to impress the jury, but I can argue that away. The rest might not come into evidence because they didn't have a warrant to search your office. There are ways around that, but we have a chance because you also used it as your personal residence. We'll have to argue that whoever left the photographs also bloodied the letter opener, but without something more solid, we'll look like we're grasping at straws." Donley put the cap back on his pen and stood. "This will get me started." He picked up his briefcase and put on his jacket.

"Do you pray, Peter?"

Donley fixed his cuffs. "I'm afraid not too much, Father."

"I believe that God is nearest in our darkest moments."

Donley disagreed but wasn't about to debate it. "I'll have to take your word on that one."

They shook hands. Then Donley walked to the metal door and knocked twice.

"Merry Christmas, Peter."

The door opened. Donley had forgotten again. Christmas Eve. "Merry Christmas," he said. He stepped into the hallway, and the heavy door swung shut behind him.

Chapter 12

Father Martin knelt at the side of the metal-frame bed attached to the wall, an empty dinner tray on the thin mattress. It was the first meal he'd eaten in more than forty-eight hours, but it still hadn't been satisfying. The fried chicken and mashed potatoes had a chalky, high-carbohydrate taste. The green beans were overcooked. Still, he ate every bite.

Peter Donley had given him renewed hope.

He refocused his attention on his daily prayers, and he dedicated those prayers to Donley. He didn't know what was in Donley's past that had darkened his perception of the world, but he had worked long enough with troubled young men to recognize one. Donley had carefully crafted an appearance to hide whatever it was that had made him so guarded and jaded, but Father Martin knew that never lasted long. He suspected an alcoholic household and parental abuse, likely by Donley's father.

As he prayed, Father Martin's concentration wandered and he thought he detected the faint sound of Christmas music. He was uncertain whether he was actually hearing the music, or if his mind was filling in the notes he'd come to know so well. Either way, he deduced the song to be "The First Noel."

The jail had extended visiting hours for family, and he had overheard one of the guards say there would be some semblance of a Christmas party, though not for Father Martin. He would not be let loose in the general population. On the ladder of crimes, pedophiles and child killers were at the bottom rung. The other inmates wouldn't hesitate to kill him.

The sound of the lock on his cell door disengaging interrupted the music and refocused Father Martin's attention. He looked up from the side of the bed as a deputy sheriff with a meaty face and thick, wedge-shaped mustache walked into his cell, holding the handcuffs and chains. He'd never seen the man before.

"Let's go."

"Go? Go where?"

"Blood work."

"Tonight?"

"That's what they tell me."

"It's Christmas Eve."

"No fooling. And I get off as soon as I deliver you. So let's go."

Father Martin stood and forced his stocking feet into the rubber slippers. He hesitated and picked up Peter Donley's business card from the bed. "I'd like to call my lawyer," he said.

"You can make that call after your blood work. Transporting you is the last thing I have to do tonight."

Gil Ramsey was pleased, though not surprised, at the large turnout for his Christmas Eve party at his spacious home in Pacific Heights. Limousines and expensive automobiles pulled up the circular driveway to the valet, and men and women in expensive suits and dresses emerged beneath a temporary awning. Inside, a five-piece orchestra played in the foyer beneath a crystal chandelier, and the caterer's staff walked through the crowd in white coats carrying silver trays with hors d'oeuvres and crystal flutes of chilled champagne and expensive wine.

The crowd, a who's who of the state's politicians, had been ensured by Augustus Ramsey and included a former US senator, a current US senator, a Congresswoman, a former White House chief of staff, an ambassador to France, a California Supreme Court justice, a Superior Court judge, a handful of actors and actresses who called the city home, and enough blue blood San Francisco families to make the New York Stock Exchange take notice.

Gil Ramsey greeted each guest beneath a large oil canvas—a portrait of his father painted when he served as governor. He took particular notice when Linda St. Claire walked in the front door in a white-silk gown with a plunging neckline, her arm entwined around the arm of a prominent San Francisco plaintiff's lawyer. Ramsey would have liked more time to admire her figure, but this was not a social affair. Not for him. This was business. After greeting his guests, he flowed from one group to the next, holding conversations on a variety of subjects. Well versed and well read, Ramsey took pride in his ability to discuss the 49ers as readily as the Asian-tapestry exhibit currently on display at the de Young Museum. When prompted, he'd even discuss politics, though his standard line for the evening was, "No politics tonight. Eat, drink, and be merry."

But, of course, the night was all about politics. With the upcoming election, Ramsey did not have time to eat, drink, and be merry. He barely had time to take a piss. While his father had not been able to parlay the governorship of one of the richest electoral-vote states in the union to the White House, Ronald Reagan had, and Augustus Ramsey believed the same fate could await his son. Neither was about to let Christmas get in the way of the first step toward that goal.

As Ramsey charmed the curator of the Asian Art Museum, a hand touched the back of his elbow. Without losing eye contact with his guest, Ramsey leaned back far enough for the assistant to whisper in his ear. Ramsey nodded once, giving no other outward indication that his attention had been diverted. Then, at an appropriate break in the conversation, he excused himself and glided past his guests, promising to return. The aide waited for him in the corner of the kitchen.

"Did he give you a name?" Ramsey asked, annoyed.

The young woman shook her head. "But he was very persistent. He's in your study."

"And he said this was about the campaign?"

She nodded.

Ramsey groaned. "Talk to the caterer. Tell them the punch is flat, and the caviar tastes like shit."

He walked through the kitchen, which tonight served as the caterer's battleground, and dodged trays on his way to his study at the back of the house. Stepping in, he smelled the aroma of one of his Cuban cigars. A trail of smoke wafted above the back of his green-leather chair, which faced away from him, toward the view out the French doors leading to the back deck.

"Can I help you?" Ramsey asked.

The chair swiveled.

Ramsey dropped his glass, shattering it.

Donley mingled among the crowd in his living room wearing a red-wool sweater and a Santa Claus hat trimmed with white fur. The ball at the tip of the hat flopped to the side, weighted with Christmas bells. Kim was in the kitchen, dressed similarly, the kind of "couple's outfit" Donley had sworn he'd never wear. At least the bells thrilled Benny, who continued going strong an hour past his bedtime. At the moment, he was wearing out his grandfather's knee getting horsey rides on the living-room couch. Donley suspected the sugar pulsing through his son's system from the chocolate fudge, cream puffs, and candy canes could have powered an entire grade school.

Most of the guests were Kim's relatives, close friends without local family, and a few clients. Four years earlier, Kim had had the idea of a party for a few friends whose families lived out of state. The party had evolved from there. In years past, Lou and Sarah had come. Donley missed having them.

He did his best to deliver refills on drinks and collect empty bottles and glasses as he worked his way toward the kitchen, where the aroma of Kim's crab hors d'oeuvres enticed. Making his way through the crowd was proving difficult; everyone wanted to talk to him, and most conversations started with the person having seen Donley on the evening news. The stations were particularly fond of playing the part outside the courtroom where Donley had confronted Ramsey and St. Claire about the problems with the evidence.

Judge Trimble would not be happy.

Still, Donley was doing his best to not think of Milton Trimble, Linda St. Claire, or Gil Ramsey. Several beers had helped, though they had not quieted his thoughts about Father Thomas Martin.

God comes in our darkest moments.

Donley wondered how a man who dealt with so much despair, who witnessed children abandoned on the streets like discarded furniture and abused by sick and twisted adults, could have such faith.

Where was their God?

Where had God been those nights Donley hid beneath his bed, praying? God had not answered his prayers. God had not helped him or his mother in their darkest hours.

The smell of crab intensified, and Donley bumped and grinded through the crowd to the sound of Christmas carols sung by Elvis Presley—the tape a gift from Mr. Anitolli's three sons. The judge had ruled in their favor.

Kim held the tray of crab hors d'oeuvres in gloved hands and was issuing a warning to the group of bodies between her and the wooden cutting board.

"Coming through. Coming through."

Donley walked past her, did a spin move to avoid the tray, and pinched her butt. She ignored him until she'd put the tray down, then turned and smiled. He picked out two of the wedges and popped one into his mouth.

"Hot," she said. Too late.

He fanned his tongue, the crab burning, grabbed a bottle of beer from an outstretched hand, and took a long drink.

"Damn," he said, running his tongue along the roof of his mouth and feeling it already starting to peel.

Kim laughed. "I tried to warn you."

He spotted a tray of custard-filled, chocolate-topped cream puffs, popped a whole one in his mouth, and planted a messy cream-and-chocolate kiss over Kim's lips. The crowd in the kitchen hooted.

"Doorbell," Kim said, wiping the chocolate from the corner of her mouth.

"What?"

She pointed at the buzzer located over the entrance to the kitchen. "Get the door."

Donley kissed her again and made his way through the dining room, dropping off two beers and a glass of white wine on his way. He pulled open the front door. Mike and Rochelle Harris and their two children stood on his porch dressed in the same matching red sweaters and hats, bells dangling to the side. Harris's son and daughter raced past Donley in search of Benny. Rochelle stepped in holding a tray of stuffed mushrooms. Donley tried to steal one.

She swatted his hand. "They're not cooked yet. Where's Kim?"

"Kitchen duty. I'm on drink patrol."

Rochelle turned to her husband, who held a bottle of wine and wrapped presents. "I'll be in the kitchen giving Kim a hand. Be good. You still have a bike to put together tonight." She left the two men standing under the mistletoe.

"You can stand there, but I'm not going to kiss you," Donley said.

Harris looked past him. "You have any other brothers at this party, or am I the Christmas token, again?"

"If I wanted a token, I'd have found someone a hell of a lot cooler than you."

"You're in a good mood." Harris stepped in and Donley closed the door. "How many have you had?"

"Enough to forget."

Harris handed Donley the bottle of wine. "You were front and center on the six o'clock news, pal."

Donley put a hand to his face. "I'm sorry, Mike."

"I should have known you'd take on Ramsey and The Chair. You just can't help yourself." He handed Donley the presents. "Merry Christmas. It's another sweater."

"Thanks for the surprise." Donley laughed. "Come on in. I'll get you a beer."

Donley found a beer in the fridge, twisted off the top, and handed it to Harris. "I assume you don't want a glass?"

"Bottle is fine."

Donley watched Kim answer the phone in the small nook off the kitchen. She put a finger in her ear as she walked out the back door onto the deck. After a moment, she returned, made eye contact with Donley, and mimed that the phone was for him.

Thinking it could be his aunt Sarah, he walked out onto the deck. The temperature was brisk. "Who is it?"

"The county jail," she said.

Donley took the phone, expecting to hear Father Martin's voice. "Hello?"

"Peter Donley?"

Donley stuck a finger in his ear. "Yes. Who's this?"

With one sentence, Donley's Christmas Eve came to an end.

Dixon Connor removed his black wingtips from the corner of Gil Ramsey's desk and stood. Behind him, French doors to the English garden framed the Golden Gate Bridge, a silhouette outlined by sparkling white lights that reflected off the darkened waters of the San Francisco Bay and stretched to the Marin Headlands.

"What the hell are you doing here?" Ramsey asked.

"Long time no see, Gil."

"I'm calling the police." Ramsey walked to the edge of the desk and picked up the phone.

"Wouldn't," Connor said.

"Breaking and entering is a crime, Connor."

Connor picked up the remote control from the desk and pointed it at a television on a built-in shelf across the room. The television blinked. Ramsey turned his head. The image was grainy and dark, but he could make out two people.

"Not the best quality," Connor said. "But good enough, don't you think?"

Ramsey lowered the phone back to its cradle and walked closer to the television screen. Whoever had been filming zoomed in, and Ramsey froze. Stunned. Unable to speak.

"The eyes don't lie, do they, Gil?" Connor waited a moment before clicking off the remote, leaving Ramsey staring at his reflection in the darkened glass.

"Shocking, isn't it? Who would have thunk it? I mean, a video camera, of all things. Never would have thought the little shits were that enterprising, would you?" Connor walked around the room, picking up and putting down things from the desk and shelving. "Almost as surprising as you and me ending up at the same shindig. What are the chances of that, huh?" He sniffed the air. "Something smells good. What's in the oven?"

Ramsey pulled his gaze from the television. "What do you want?" he asked, voice barely a whisper.

"I'm sorry. Did you say something, Gil?"

Ramsey swallowed with difficulty. His voice croaked. "What do you want? Why are you here?"

Connor shrugged. "I can't say I've honestly made up my mind. You see, Gil, in the vernacular, now I got *you* by the balls, just like you once had a grip on my old man's nut sack. What do they call this . . . poetic justice?"

"I—"

"I only wish he were still alive to see it. God, he would have loved this. Opportunities like this don't come around but once in a lifetime. So, a man has to be judicious with how he uses something like this. He can't rush his decision. He has to be patient and prudent." Connor pointed the cigar. "You look a little pale, Gil." He motioned to the chair behind the desk. "You want to take a seat?"

Ramsey did not respond.

"Cat got your tongue? Why don't I try for you? Holy shit!" Connor yelled.

Ramsey flinched and turned quickly to the door.

"What's the matter? You afraid one of your other guests might hear me? Hell, I don't have to yell." Connor started for the door. "I'll just go mingle through the crowd and whisper in their ears. Or maybe I'll pop the video in the family television."

"No," Ramsey said.

Connor turned. "I must be losing my hearing. Did you say something?"

"What do you want?" Ramsey asked again.

"I told you, I'm really not sure, but I'm thinking half a million. Cash. Can't accept a check or credit card, I'm afraid."

Ramsey's jaw dropped. "I don't have that kind of money."

"Of course you do. You and your father could probably scrounge that up tonight if you stood at the door and held out a hat. Hell, you should consider it cheap, because it is. And we both know it. The alternative is murder one—"

"Murder? What the hell are you talking about?"

"Let me fill you in on this bit of police procedure I picked up humping my ass for the past twenty-five years. It's something my dad taught me before . . . well, we don't really have to get into old history tonight, do we? After all, it's Christmas Eve. Anyway, as I was saying, police procedure, detective stuff. If you want to solve a crime, you always look for the guy with the motive. Who has the motive, Gil?"

Ramsey shut his eyes.

"You need a drink or something, Gil? You really do look like you're going to be sick." Connor pulled a slip of paper from his pocket. "I figured it out. If you take my old man's salary, what he would have earned until he *voluntarily* resigned, which I think was the way you put it, plus the full pension he lost, along with the equity in the house and the stocks he had to cash in to pay his attorneys' fees, it comes to just about $223,000. Hell, he was just a civil servant. Wiped him out." Connor again pointed the cigar. "Now that's just the hard costs. I'm adding a fee for pain and suffering. What do they call that, punitive damages? You understand. But, hey, I'm not totally unreasonable. I didn't add even a penny of interest." Connor winked. "That's just the kind of guy I am."

Ramsey pulled loose his bow tie and undid the top button of his shirt. "I'll need some time to think this over," he said.

Connor blew smoke in the air. "Sure." He held up his watch. "You have sixty seconds to accept my proposal. Otherwise . . . it's showtime!"

"You're joking?" Ramsey said.

Connor stepped forward. "Do I look like I'm joking, Gil?"

"I can't get the money in sixty seconds."

Connor held the cigar close to the tip of Ramsey's nose. "I know that, you dumb shit. I just want your word, Gil. I am a man of utmost honor, and when I say I'm going to do something, you can trust that I will do it. I ask nothing more of you." He smiled. "Otherwise, this time it will be your old man who goes down. And you? You can kiss Sacramento bye-bye, along with this beautiful house and all the beautiful people out there you call friends, though we both know that really isn't true. They're just sucking up to you because they think you're going places. People like that are parasites, Gil. They're just along for the ride. You'd be better off without them. You have one week to get the money."

"I could go to the police," Ramsey said.

Connor picked up the telephone from the desk and handed it to Ramsey. "There you go, Gil. All you have to do is press nine-one-one. While we're both waiting for the police to arrive, let's talk about how a dedicated homicide detective dotted his *i*'s and crossed his *t*'s to get enough evidence—"

Ramsey hung up the phone.

"What's the matter, Gil, not the Christmas story you want to hear?"

"Why should I trust you? What assurances do I have that you will keep your end of the bargain?"

Connor blew more smoke. "None. Like I said, this time I'm the guy holding your nut sack." Connor shook his head, looking disgusted. "You know, it would be just like you not to trust a man at his word. That's the difference between me and you. You throw your word around like cheap confetti. It ain't worth shit. But I'm willing to trust you, anyway, Gil. And you sure as hell better trust me." Connor waved the cigar and turned again for the door. "Or I could just meander through your guests—"

"No."

Connor turned around. "I didn't hear you, Gil?"

Ramsey stood rigid. "I'll get you a job. I'll put you on the payroll. You won't have to do a thing."

Connor laughed. "You mean, like, maybe your bodyguard? That would be cool. You and me hanging out in Sacto? We'd be a pair, wouldn't we?" Connor's eyes narrowed. His jaw tightened. "And my old man? Are you going to get him a job, too? Are you going to dig him up and prop his corpse in a chair somewhere?" Connor's face turned dark. His voice hardened. "I don't want a job, Gil. I want justice. I want what my old man was entitled to. Five hundred thousand. You have one week."

Connor started for the French doors.

"The kid you put in the hospital provides the defense a key witness," Ramsey said.

Connor turned.

"And there's a log of the boys who stay at the shelter each night. Apparently, everything they bring in is catalogued."

"Not my problem, Gil," Connor said.

Ramsey stepped forward, teeth clenched. "I'd say it's both of our problem. If someone figures this out, you no longer hold anyone's nut sack. I'll be holding yours. And I'll squeeze until you turn blue. You want five hundred thousand dollars, earn it."

Connor smiled. "Don't get tough with me, Gil. It's not your style."

Ramsey pointed. "If this comes apart, Connor, you won't want to see my style."

Connor grabbed Ramsey's finger and bent it violently backward. The pain dropped Ramsey to his knees. Connor pressed the tip of the cigar into the palm of Ramsey's hand. "Don't scream, Gil. You don't want anyone coming through that door. How would it look, you on your knees and all?"

Ramsey gritted his teeth, groaning. His forehead dripped perspiration.

"Do not threaten me," Connor said. "One week. After that, the price goes up a hundred grand a day." Connor patted Ramsey's cheek and released his finger. As he passed the desk, he opened the humidor and helped himself to a handful of cigars. "You don't mind, do you, Gil? It being Christmas and all. Don't get up. I know my way out." He stepped through the French doors onto the deck, stopped, and turned back. Ramsey remained on his knees. "And Gil . . ."

Gil Ramsey lifted his head.

"I know my way back in, too."

Donley bounced the Saab into the parking lot and jerked to a stop near the emergency entrance, beneath a black-and-white sign mounted on the wall. He didn't bother to read it. He really didn't care.

Mike Harris struggled out of his seat belt. "This is a doctor's stall, Peter."

"They can tow it."

Donley jogged to the emergency entrance, Harris following. He had a pit in his stomach the size of a softball. The emergency-room doors slid open. "Father Thomas Martin," he said, approaching a nurse seated behind the counter.

She ignored him. He wasn't in the mood to be ignored.

"Father Thomas Martin," he said more forcefully. "The sheriff's deputies brought him in about thirty minutes ago."

The nurse put a defiant hand on her hip. "Are you a relative?"

"I'm his lawyer."

Donley noticed two deputies at the end of the hall and started for them. Harris grabbed him by the arm and wheeled him in the opposite direction. "Take it easy, Peter. This isn't her fault."

Donley pulled his arm free, directing his comments to the deputies. "Whose fault is it? Who's going to take the blame?"

Harris flashed his badge and pulled Donley farther down a short hall to a room with vending machines. He held him by the shoulders. "Take a seat."

Donley resisted. The adrenaline pumped through his system, the way it felt back in high school on the football field, when he was about to unload on a ball carrier.

"Take a seat, Peter. You aren't going to be of any help to him or anyone else if your ass is in jail."

Donley walked away, pacing while Harris walked down the hall to talk to the deputies. The telephone call to Donley's home had been from a sheriff's deputy at the jail who said he found Donley's business card on the ground near the priest's body but could provide no further information on Father Tom's condition.

Harris returned after several minutes. "Sit."

Donley kept pacing. "He's dead, isn't he?"

"No, he's not dead. Sit down."

Donley realized he was taking out his anger on the wrong people. He sat on a bench. Harris fished change from his pockets and purchased a soft drink from a vending machine, holding it out to Donley.

Donley waved it away. "Just tell me what happened?"

"They're not certain."

Donley rolled his eyes. "Come on, Mike."

"An order came down for Father Martin to have his blood drawn."

Donley looked at him wide-eyed. "Tonight? They did it tonight?"

"Keep your voice down, Peter." He looked down the hall at the deputies. "They didn't have to tell me anything. The order said *immediately*. When an order comes in, it's carried out. The time of day or night is not relevant. These guys are on the clock twenty-four-seven." Harris cracked his neck. "But to answer your question, no, it didn't have to be carried out tonight. The deputy who transported Father Martin completed a shift and went home. Nobody has been able to reach him. When Father Martin was finished, there was a whole new shift on duty."

Donley took another deep breath. "So, what happened?"

"Apparently the deputy who came on duty to transport Father Martin back to his cell had been off duty the past seventy-two hours. He had no idea who Father Martin was."

"And?"

"And he put him in general population."

Donley felt the softball in his stomach drop. "Oh, shit."

"It happens," Harris said, though he didn't sound convincing.

"Bullshit. We both know that's not the case. This is my fault."

"How is it your fault?"

It had all been fun and games, toying with St. Claire and Ramsey, but now it could have cost Father Tom his life. "You told me to keep it quiet. You said to keep my mouth shut. All that stuff I said today in court about the evidence and the motion—they don't think they can win."

"Who?"

"Ramsey, the DA's office, whoever is behind this."

"That's a huge jump, Peter."

"Is it? You said this guy Connor is not the kind of cop to screw up a crime scene, but he did. Father Martin didn't have to have his blood drawn tonight, but he did. Then he somehow ends up back in general circulation. Something is not right about any of this, Mike."

"What are you saying? That there's some conspiracy to get Father Martin?"

"All I know is, Father Martin didn't kill Andrew Bennet."

Harris looked him in the eye. "You sure about that?"

"Don't go all cop on me now, Mike."

"That's not fair, Peter."

The vending machines hummed from down the hall. "I'm sorry." Donley wasn't sure he wanted to know the answer but asked the question, anyway. "What did they do to him?"

"They found him unconscious on a cell floor. Of course, nobody saw or heard anything, but one of the gorillas down the hall said your boy gave as good as he got. He just got overpowered."

Donley leaned his head against the wall to wait.

After forty minutes, a man in surgical scrubs approached the nurses' station and spoke to the nurse, who pointed to Donley and Harris. They stood as the doctor approached.

"I'm Dr. Araj," the man said, removing a blue surgical cap.

"How is he?" Donley asked.

"Not good. We've relieved the pressure from the swelling in his brain and stopped the internal bleeding, but he sustained a serious head injury. He'll be in the recovery room for another forty-five minutes or so. I wouldn't plan on speaking to him tonight. It will be a while."

After the doctor had departed, Donley held out the keys to the Saab. "Go on back to the party. There's no sense both of us waiting. Your kids shouldn't be punished for this; Benny's too young to know the difference."

Harris shook his head. "My kids will be in bed soon. We'll handle this together, just like we used to."

"I hope not. We didn't always handle things too well."

Harris studied the linoleum floor. "We've done all right, considering where we came from." He finished the soft drink and played with the can, flexing the aluminum, making crinkling noises. "Maybe it's time you told Kim what happened that night."

Donley shook his head. "And what exactly would I tell her?"

"The truth. Just tell her the truth. She loves you, Peter. That won't change."

Donley wasn't so sure.

◆ ◆ ◆

Danny Simeon lay in the dark, small bursts of red, orange, and green lights pulsing on the consoles all around him. He continued to float in and out of consciousness and suspected it was the drugs being administered through an IV drip in his right arm, making everything fuzzy. His tongue felt as though it was coated with hair. When he turned his head or shifted his eyes, the room followed a split second behind, like a time-lapsed photograph. At least the excruciating pain in his side and jaw was better now, just a dull ache.

The doctor said he was lucky. He said X-rays revealed the nightstick had not ruptured his spleen or kidneys, though they were bruised and he continued to pass blood. Simeon had also suffered bruised ribs that would keep him in pain for the better part of the next few weeks. When he coughed, he felt like someone was stabbing him with a knife. Connor had also cracked two of Simeon's teeth, but his jaw was not broken. He would not be eating pureed food through a straw.

Simeon concentrated on a small orange light blinking across the room. He felt an urgency to stay awake, to leave, but he was having difficulty remembering why. In fact, it was difficult to remember much about the past three days. His body wanted to let the soothing warmth of the drugs help him drift to sleep, but his mind fought against that desire. Each time he closed his eyes, drifting on the gentle waves, images jarred him awake: Father Tom being led from the shelter in handcuffs, covered in blood.

Then he would drift again, wake, drift and wake, drift . . .

Slipping toward sleep, he was vaguely aware when the door to his room had opened, a wedge of light spilling into the darkness. He heard the voice a split second before the hand gripped his throat, cutting off the flow of air.

"Hello, Dingo. Did you miss me?"

Simeon opened his eyes, the room remained fuzzy, but the voice was unmistakable. Dixon Connor. He'd used what had been Simeon's street nickname.

Connor drew closer, his wide face and flat head a spinning blur in the dark. Simeon gasped for air. Connor squeezed tighter.

"Are they taking good care of you? This must be heaven for a junkie lowlife like you. Free drugs, a clean bed, and a pretty little nurse."

Connor's breath smelled of alcohol and cigarettes.

"We have some unfinished business, you and me," Connor said.

Simeon grabbed Connor's wrist, but it was thick as a tree limb, and his own arms felt weak from the drugs.

"The side effects of prescribed narcotics can be a bitch, especially for someone who has abused drugs and alcohol. A hospital can't be held responsible. Organs can shut down. A patient can suffocate or drown in his own spit." Connor leaned closer, whispering, "And nobody would even look into it."

Simeon felt himself losing consciousness. He struggled to breathe, inhaling short, thin breaths.

Connor maintained pressure. "See how easy that would be? Just like squishing a bug. Now, I'm going to ask you a question, and you're going to give me an answer. You give me the right answer, and I leave you alone with your plastic bottle here. You don't, and I ask the question again. And Dingo, I don't like to ask questions more than once. Got it? First question: Does Father Martin keep a record of the little pricks who stay at the shelter each night?"

Simeon tried to speak, but it came out a gurgle, like water flowing through an obstructed drainpipe.

Connor loosened his grip and turned his head. "I couldn't quite understand you. Let's try that again."

Simeon hissed in air through clenched teeth. He tried to speak, but his lips would not respond to what his brain wanted. He stuttered. "F-F-F-F . . ."

Connor lowered his ear near Simeon's mouth.

"F-F-F-F-F . . . fuck y-y-y-you."

Connor straightened. "You know, I'm trying to be nice here, because I can see by the chart that you are in considerable pain from those ribs. And I know how that can be." He slid his hand down Simeon's side and let it rest on the bandage. "Awful painful," he said, applying pressure.

The pain shot through Simeon like an electric jolt. He moaned, but Connor's left hand covered his mouth as the right hand continued to apply pressure. Simeon gripped the metal handrail, causing it to rattle and bang. His legs kicked at the thin white sheet.

Connor released the pressure. "I assume from your prior response there are records. Next question. Where does he keep them?"

Simeon spit through the gaps in his teeth. His chest heaved from the pain pulsing through his body, but the pain had also helped him to focus through the drugs. Connor no longer floated about the room.

Connor patted the bandage wrap. "Where are the records, Dingo?"

Simeon slowly and cautiously moved his right hand, feeling beneath the thin sheet.

Connor put pressure on the wrap. "Don't be stubborn, Dingo."

Finding the nurse-call button, Simeon pressed it. "F-F-Fuck you."

Connor pushed hard on the bandaged ribs. Simeon's back arched into a bridge. He screamed through Connor's hand, a horrific moan.

The door to the hospital room swung open, the nurse rushing in. "My God, what happened?" She stepped between Connor and the bed, trying to keep Simeon from thrashing.

"He's in horrible pain." Connor stepped back. "I was talking to him, and he just screamed and started flailing his arms and legs. I was trying to hold him down. I was afraid he would hurt himself."

The nurse checked an array of machines behind Simeon. "His pulse is racing." She pressed the call button, seeking assistance.

"Maybe it's the drugs. You know, he's had a problem before," Connor said.

"I'm sorry. I know you traveled a long way to see your nephew on Christmas Eve, but we're going to need some room. We have to get his pain under control."

"I understand," Connor said. "I only want what's best for Danny."

"You'll have to wait outside." Others hurried into the room as the nurse undid the IV needle from the plastic implant taped to Simeon's arm. Connor reached out and put a hand on Simeon's cheek. "You do just what the nurse says, Danny. And remember, I'm not far away."

Donley looked across the emergency room to where a woman sat hunched over, clutching her knees to her stomach. Donley overheard her tell the nurse she fell into the corner of a table, but the woman also had a black eye. Next to her sat a bald, overweight man with a graying goatee.

"They'll separate them," Harris said, his head tilted back against the wall. "They'll ask her questions when he isn't around. It doesn't matter, though. They have to go home sometime."

Donley knew that to be the truth. He used to sit for hours in the park at the top of his street watching the San Francisco skyline late at night, thinking of reasons not to go home. He'd watch the red taillights of cars driving east on the Bay Bridge and think of the people in those cars, wishing he could be one of them, going anywhere but back to that house. But leaving was not an option; he couldn't leave his mother alone with his father.

Donley shifted his attention to two men huddled in another corner of the room. One appeared to be in considerable pain. Pale and gaunt, he looked fifty years older than his partner. Donley tried not to eavesdrop, but it was clear they were afraid this could be their final trip to the hospital.

"M&M?" Harris held out a pack of candy he'd bought from the vending machine.

Donley took the pack and poured several colored candies into his palm. The taste of chocolate made him remember the buffet he was missing at home, which made him remember the party he was missing at home. Maybe it was the sugar, but something sparked the thought that followed.

"Where do they take people who can't pay?"

"What's that?" Harris asked.

"People who don't have medical insurance. Where do they take them?"

"Here."

"You're sure?"

"I've done it enough times myself. We'll pick people up off the street and bring them here to general. The private hospitals won't keep them."

Donley stood.

"Where're you going?" Harris asked.

"Be right back."

Donley approached the nurse at the station. She edged her seat away from the counter. "I wanted to apologize for my behavior earlier. I was upset."

She nodded but offered no forgiveness.

"I was wondering, where would I find admissions? Where would I go to see if a patient has been admitted?"

"Was he admitted to the hospital, or did he come in through the emergency room?"

Donley thought for a moment. "Emergency room. December twenty-first."

She turned to a computer screen. "Admission will be closed or short-staffed tonight. What's the patient's name?"

Donley tried to remember the name Father Martin had provided. "Danny."

She gave him an inquisitive look.

"Simon," he said. "Danny Simon."

The nurse typed. A moment later she ran her finger down the front of the screen.

"Simeon?"

"That's it," Donley said.

"Daniel Simeon." She ran a finger across the computer in a straight line. "He was moved this morning to a room on the third floor, west wing. Three twenty-seven. But you won't be able to see him," the nurse said. "Visiting hours are over."

Donley called down the hallway to Harris. "Let's make some phone calls home."

◆　◆　◆

When they exited the elevator onto the third floor, a stocky nurse stepped out from the nurses' station. "Do you have a patient named Danny Simeon?" Donley asked.

"Mr. Simeon is resting." She looked frazzled. "You'll have to come back in the morning. I just sent his uncle home."

"His uncle?" Donley looked to Harris, thinking it unlikely Simeon, who'd grown up on the streets, had an uncle who cared enough to pay him a visit on Christmas Eve.

"What did he look like?" Harris asked.

"Excuse me?"

"His uncle. What did he look like?"

Donley started quickly down the hallway, scanning the numbers of the rooms on the wall.

"I don't remember." The nurse turned to Donley. "Sir—"

Harris badged the nurse. "What did the man look like?"

"He was white. Six foot two or three, I think. Husky, over two hundred pounds. He had a crew cut." She called out to Donley. "Sir, you can't go in there."

Donley pushed open the door to Room 327 and slapped at the wall switch.

The thin, white sheet lay crumpled in a ball, the tube from an IV bag dripping clear fluid onto the floor.

Chapter 13

December 26, 1987

Frank Ross wedged a knee beneath the steering wheel, balanced a cup of coffee in one hand, and dunked a cinnamon-twist doughnut with the other, maneuvering the dripping pastry to his mouth. Nothing better on a cold Saturday morning. If the best things in life were free, the next best things could be bought for less than two bucks at the local 7-Eleven.

Unfortunately, the cinnamon twists would be a casualty of his New Year's resolution, a begrudging concession to his inner conscience, bathroom scale, and wife. The day after Christmas, he'd weighed in at 270 pounds, too heavy even for his six-foot-five-inch frame, and the slide to three hundred was a slippery slope getting more slippery by the doughnut.

This morning, however, not even the thought of his last doughnut could depress him. He felt rejuvenated and excited to get to his office for the first time in a long time. After a few days in Tahoe for the Christmas holidays, he was going to work with a sense of purpose. When was the last time he could say he was working on something real and substantial, not the dime-store cases that had become a vivid reminder of how far he'd fallen?

He clenched the doughnut between his teeth, steered the black 1965 Fleetwood past the OK Barber Shop and Elk Motel, and turned onto Eddy Street. A blinding glare greeted him, the sun reflecting off the rain-soaked pavement and building windows. Ross lowered the visor and quickly corrected the steering wheel as the Cadillac drifted precariously close to a parked car.

The hard rains might have washed other areas of the city glistening clean, but it had done little to improve the brick and stucco buildings of the Tenderloin. The ten square blocks of graffiti-splattered buildings, wedged tighter together than impacted teeth, still looked in need of a massive paint job. Ross honked the horn at an orderly line of homeless waiting for a hot meal at the St. Vincent de Paul Society's shelter. No one reacted. Even the homeless had become accustomed to Ross, another of San Francisco's misfits. Ross could have taken a more scenic route to the office, but he'd turned on Eddy to see the homeless, a reminder that no matter how bad things got, he still had a roof over his head, and he sure as hell wasn't starving.

Halfway up the block, he spotted a parking spot, thanked the Lord for small miracles, and nudged the curb. Coffee spilled over the rim of the cup, missing his leg and splattering on the floorboard to be soaked up by discarded napkins and old sports pages. He finished the last bite of the cinnamon twist, licked his fingers, and stepped from the car to a high sky of billowing clouds that offered some hope of relief from the persistent rain.

Ross pushed aside a shopping cart filled with other people's discards and placed the brown bag containing a second cup of coffee and cinnamon twist near a blue sleeping bag on the tile entryway.

"Rise and shine, Annie. Breakfast."

The mound stirred. Two arms stretched out the top of the bag followed by dark hair and dark skin. Annie squinted and raised her hand to cut the glare.

"Lordy. You must be an angel. Couldn't be no Frank Ross because he gone and deserted old Annie."

"Now, you know I wouldn't do that, Annie. I told you I was going to Lake Tahoe for a couple of days. How do you like sleeping in that bag?" It had been a Christmas present. Ross couldn't afford it, but Annie couldn't afford to freeze, either. Her old bag and plastic tarp had been stolen.

"Like a caterpillar in a cocoon," she said in her raspy voice. "Warm. Too warm. Can't shake the sleep now; it's got a grip on old Annie for sure." She brightened at the sight of the brown bag and removed the plastic top on her cup of coffee to dip the twist the way Ross had taught her. "Mmmm. Mmmm," she said.

Ross handed her a paper napkin. "Is it going to rain again today, Annie?"

Annie set the coffee down and balanced the cinnamon twist on the rim. Then she took a deep breath of the chilled morning air. "Smells like rain. Yep. It does smell like rain."

Ross considered the sky. "I'm tired of the rain, Annie."

"Not the rain that makes a man tired. It's his soul. You have a tired soul, Frank Ross."

Ross looked up and down the block. "Yeah, Annie, I guess I do." He reached into his pocket and handed her spare change. "But not today. You keep an eye out for those meter maids. No sleeping on the job."

"They ain't pulled one by on Annie yet, has they? Annie knows when they're coming."

Ross stepped past her and pulled open the glass door, gathering the newspapers and mail delivered while he'd been away. He hadn't wanted a vacation, not with Lou Giantelli hiring him to work the case involving the priest of Polk Street, but he also knew he couldn't disappoint his wife. It had been their first vacation since they'd lost Frank Jr., and neither wanted to be in the house during the holiday, not with the memories still so fresh. Lou had told Ross to go. He said nothing much would happen over the holiday, anyway.

Ross thumbed through his mail as he walked up the tiled steps to the second floor. The windowless hallway smelled like damp carpet. He hoped it was damp carpet and not the lingering odor of the accountant's rotting corpse. Paramedics had found the man sitting upright in his chair, a heroin needle stuck in his arm. He'd gone unnoticed for nearly a week, until he failed to pay his rent and the landlord brought a locksmith. *Surprise.* They'd carried his body out in a sitting position.

Ross had chosen the office closest to the exit, in case of a fire. He'd had to pay six months' rent in advance before the landlord would stencil the black letters on the smoked glass window of his office door.

2c

FRANK ROSS
PRIVATE DICTECTIVE

Mr. Chang proved to be more adept at collecting rent than spelling. He'd promised to correct the mistake, but Ross wasn't holding his breath, except when he walked down the hallway and "dictected" the lingering smell of the accountant.

Ross pushed open the door and stepped into an office bathed in a light blue from the arched, stained-glass window behind his desk. On sunny days, the room shaded a color of a particular windowpane depending on the time of day and time of year. Ross had rented the office on a cloudy day, not realizing he was destined to sit inside a kaleidoscope until the first sunny day.

He dropped the newspapers on his desk and hit the button on the answering machine, listening to his messages as he sorted through the stack of mail, depositing most pieces into the garbage can at the side of his desk. He stopped when he heard Nathaniel Collins's nasal whine. The wealthy lawyer from Pacific Heights was convinced his young wife was cheating on him with her tennis instructor. He wanted photographs to prove the affair. Under the terms of the couple's prenuptial agreement, Abigail Collins stood to make a tidy $1.5 million if the couple divorced, but she received nothing if Mr. Collins could prove she'd been unfaithful. What a way to start a marriage. Collins's terse message indicated his displeasure with Ross's efforts to catch his young wife and lover. Apparently his mistress, the next Mrs. Collins-in-waiting, was growing impatient.

The second message was from the owner of Fotomat kiosks whose cash registers weren't adding up at night. On other days, the messages would have depressed him. Today, Ross just smiled. Before settling at his desk, he pulled the cap off a black marker and put an x thru the days he'd been away. Three additional days. Sober.

One day at a time.

He sat and unfolded the newspaper for Tuesday, December 23. His eyes stopped on the black block headline indicating the priest was to be arraigned the following day, Christmas Eve.

"What the hell?" he said, quickly opening the paper to where the article jumped to an inside page. Ross noticed a second headline and quickly sat forward, knocking over his cup of coffee.

◆ ◆ ◆

The Sunset District, forty city blocks bordered to the north by Golden Gate Park and to the west by the Pacific Ocean, was one of those odd San Francisco neighborhoods where the weather in the winter and fall was actually better than in summer and spring. In the summer, pea-soup fog driven by heavy winds off the ocean often prevailed, but the winters could be crisp and clear. The day after Christmas was one of those days. Donley sat huddled in the Saab, the collar of his leather jacket pulled up around his neck to ward off the cold. As with most streets in the Sunset, foliage was sparse, sporadic trees planted in dirt squares in cement sidewalks. The one-story, detached houses had been cut from the same developer mold: two-bedroom-and-one-bath buildings with flat roofs. The front door, centered between two windows, faced the street. The houses varied only in the color of the stucco and amenities to the gardens. It was Anywhere, USA, and according to real-estate records, it included the house once owned by Max and Irene Connor, where their son, Dixon, currently lived.

The exterior of Connor's home seemed to confirm everything Harris had said about the man: cold, dark, and uninviting. Swatches of moss that thrived in the damp climate spotted the beige-stucco exterior. The small patch of lawn had died and sprouted dandelions, and the planter boxes beneath the windows were empty.

Donley needed to subpoena Connor to appear at the evidentiary hearing on Thursday. He'd done it before. When you were a small practice, you became a jack of all trades. Harris said Connor was a mean son of a bitch who did not like lawyers, which meant he definitely wouldn't appreciate being subpoenaed to answer questions in court, but Donley had a job to do. He was hoping that Connor might have an ax to grind against the department for suspending him, which might make him willing to talk.

Even if Connor refused to talk to him or to attend the hearing, Donley might be able to use his refusal to seek a continuance, or to argue against the court admitting the evidence since an inability to cross-examine the detective who found it would greatly prejudice Father Martin's defense.

Donley might never know. He'd thought the day after Christmas would be the best time to find Connor, but no one had answered the front door, and no car was parked in the driveway down the side of the house. He was beginning to wonder if Connor had gone away for the holidays.

Donley started the ignition and pulled away from the curb. Harris had told him that Connor frequented a local bar in the Sunset called The 19th Hole, which was near Golden Gate Park Golf Course, just a few blocks from Connor's home. The bar was next to a small grocery store, both likely built when neighborhoods were still where people lived, shopped, and socialized, before cars became individual neighborhoods.

Like Connor's house, the stucco of The 19th Hole needed painting and repair. Gangs had tagged the building, and a fender-high hole revealed mesh where a car had jumped the curb and come to an unplanned stop. The neon sign overhead displayed a green flagpole with a white flag, and the bar's name in pink, though part of the tubes no longer lit, so the sign actually read, THE 1 HO.

Donley stepped from the car and zipped his leather jacket against a chill wind as he crossed the street. He pushed through weathered, swinging doors. The interior was a narrow, windowless corridor, the bar set along the west wall. The only light came from the portholes in the doors and a light beneath the bar that illuminated the bartender in strange shadows that brought to mind a set in a black-and-white horror film.

Sitting on a bar stool, his thick shoulders and a broad back hunched over a cocktail glass, was a man who fit Harris's description of Dixon Connor. His arms looked to be putting the seams of a tweed sports coat to the test. A crew cut shaped his head square. Two other men sat several stools away, keeping to themselves, watching a college football game on a television mounted in the corner of the room.

Feeling like he was plunging into shark-infested waters, Donley sat down on an empty stool one removed from Connor. When the bartender approached, Donley took out a ten-dollar bill.

"Corona."

"They don't serve that Mexican shit in here," Connor said, without looking at him. "Why don't you order an American beer?"

The detective's gaze remained on the television. Donley looked up at the bartender. "Budweiser."

The bartender pulled a Budweiser from under the bar and put the bottle on a paper coaster adorned with the 19th Hole neon sign and made change at an old-fashioned cash register.

Donley took a pull on his beer. "What's the score?"

Connor gave no indication he'd heard the question. He sipped from a highball glass, probably Scotch or whiskey over ice, and returned to cleaning his teeth with a toothpick.

"I got fifty bucks on the Forty-Niners tomorrow," Donley said, "but I'm worried about the spread. It was eight and a half this morning. That's a lot of points, no matter who they're playing."

Connor took another drink and spit an ice cube back into the glass.

"Can I buy you a drink?" Donley flagged the bartender. "Whatever he's drinking."

The bartender gave Donley an inquisitive look before pulling a glass from under the counter and pouring Jameson Irish Whiskey over ice. He put the glass on the bar. Connor ignored it.

Donley let a few plays pass. "You're Dixon Connor?"

Connor continued to work the toothpick between his teeth.

"I'm Peter Donley. I represent—"

Connor raised his left hand and placed a .44 Magnum handgun on the bar. The bartender stopped washing glasses. The two men sitting nearby froze with their beer bottles at their lips.

Donley took a swig from his bottle, fighting to remain outwardly calm, though his insides were churning. He was already evaluating potential options should Connor raise the gun.

"I know who you are." Connor spoke without looking at him. "And I know who you represent."

"I want to talk—"

"Want?"

Connor glanced at Donley. His face was fat and fleshy, his eyes as dark as checker pieces. He smelled like the bar—a mixture of cheap cologne, perspiration, alcohol, and cigarettes. God, how Donley hated that smell.

Donley's pulse quickened. "All right, I need to ask you a few questions about what happened at the shelter the night you arrested Father Martin."

No response.

"I understand you've been suspended."

Connor slid the second drink in front of Donley. "Don't *want* your drink. Don't *want* to answer your questions. Don't like lawyers who represent murderers. Don't give a shit what you want or need."

A voice in Donley's head cautioned him to get up and walk out. But there was that stubborn streak again, and Donley hated bullies. "I'm just trying to do my job, Detective."

"So was I," Connor said.

"I don't doubt that."

"Don't kiss my ass."

"Fine. Why did they suspend you if you were only doing your job?"

Connor didn't answer.

"I could subpoena you, Detective."

"You could."

"I will."

Donley reached into his pocket for the subpoena at the same time Connor lifted the Magnum off the counter and pointed the barrel directly at Donley's head. The bartender stepped away from the bar. Donley heard the doors behind him creak open and closed, presumably the other two men leaving, but Donley didn't see anything except the barrel of the gun. Mike Harris had once told Donley that looking down the barrel of a gun was like looking down a sewer pipe. You saw nothing but the black hole. It had been an appropriate analogy.

"You don't want to do that, counselor."

Donley froze, hand still in his jacket.

He won't shoot. There's a witness. He's just trying to intimidate you.

But the more Donley tried to convince himself, the more he saw the reality in Dixon Connor's black, lifeless eyes. He would shoot. And as if to emphasize that point, Connor pulled back the hammer.

Frank Ross struggled to read the coffee-dampened newsprint. Lou Giantelli had been taken from a courtroom on a stretcher, but nothing indicated what kind of shape he was in. He searched through the other articles but did not find a name identifying the attorney representing the priest.

Ross opened the second paper. The priest not only had been arraigned but had entered a plea of not guilty, and the court had scheduled a preliminary evidentiary hearing that week. The article mentioned an attorney named Peter Donley. Things were moving fast, and Ross was well behind, assuming he was even still working on the case. Ross picked up the telephone and pressed the buttons for a number committed to memory. "Detective Frank Ross for Sam Goldman," he said out of habit.

After a moment, an animated voice boomed through the receiver. "How are you, hero?"

Sam Goldman called everyone hero, great hero, friend, and chief.

"Curious," Ross said, holding the phone from his ear. "When are you guys going to print some stories with some meat on the bones?"

Goldman laughed. "You've been complaining since the day you walked into my journalism class twenty-five years ago and haven't stopped since."

"Hey, at least I'm consistent."

"How were the holidays?"

"Good. Spent a couple of days in Tahoe to recharge. Now I'm back reading about the priest. What's going on, Sam?"

"Is that something or what? The circus is in town, friend."

"I thought I'd call the premier newspaperman on the West Coast and try to find some of the facts your reporters left out of their stories."

"You can flatter me all you like, hero, but I can't give you what I don't have."

"If you don't have it, Sam, no one does."

"The DA's office has been tight-lipped. We're prying, but the jaws are clenched. The party line is, they were waiting to notify the next of kin. Then Judge Trimble issued a gag order. I'll tell you this, though. A lot of people are going to get dirty on this one. All those people who openly supported that guy and his shelter will be trampling one another to get out from under the avalanche. Step back, and watch the dominos fall."

"Do you know who the detectives were? Who arrested the priest?"

"I don't know, but I can find out."

"What about the victim? Anything more on how he died?"

"Stabbed, according to the ME. I can tell you The Chair is handling it. What's your interest in this, hero?"

"Lou Giantelli hired me to take a look."

"Lou Giantelli's in the hospital. Collapsed in court."

"Read that, too. So, why the warp speed on the court proceedings?"

"I guess Ramsey wants one more high-profile conviction on his résumé."

"Paper mentioned an attorney named Donley."

"Works for Lou Giantelli. Barely wet behind the ears, though. Likely won't be the priest's lawyer for long." Goldman changed subjects. "Have you heard anything?"

"On my reinstatement? No, nothing. Last time I spoke to my attorney, he said the police commission is stonewalling him. I think he's stonewalling me. I'd fire him if he wasn't my brother-in-law."

"OK, chief, I got to run. You keep your chin up. Something will break through. How's private enterprise treating you?"

"Better before I learned my client was in the hospital," Ross said.

"So, when do I get to see the great Sherlock Holmes in action?"

Ross looked at his surroundings, just the hint of red now shading the room. The rising sun had reached the glass pane over his right shoulder. "Boring stuff, Sam. Let's meet for lunch. I'm out an awful lot. Probably easier if we picked a spot."

"All right. All good things must come to an end, hero. I have sources to call, deadlines to meet, and teaching plans due after the new year. I still think I could have made a damn good reporter out of you."

"You're an optimist, Sam. I can't even type a grocery list."

Ross hung up. He'd once been like Sam Goldman, a guy who saw the world as a glass half-full. Now he saw the glass empty. He'd finally gotten a real case to work, and his client has a heart attack and ends up in the hospital. As for the appeal of his dismissal from the police force, he'd filed it only because it offered a glimmer of hope he wouldn't be sitting inside the kaleidoscope the rest of his career. Still, he wasn't naïve or ungrateful. Things could have been a lot worse. It had taken one hell of a lawyer just to keep him out of jail. Ross had been drunk when he'd hit the small sedan carrying a mother and her two children. He could have killed them.

Lou Giantelli had been that lawyer.

Ross retrieved his raincoat from the hook behind the door and locked the office behind him. He needed to find Peter Donley and find out who would be representing the priest. In the interim, he needed to pay this month's rent, and that meant catching employees dipping into the cash register and getting pictures of a debutante screwing around on her husband.

◆　◆　◆

Donley forced a smile, though inside, his rage burned. "You going to shoot me, Detective?"

Connor didn't answer.

"You have a witness. Is this wise?"

"Maybe I'll shoot him, too," Connor said.

"Take it easy, Connor." The bartender turned to Donley. "Mister, I don't know who you are, but you got more balls than brains. Why don't you just get up slowly and leave? Right, Connor? No problems. He just gets up and leaves."

Donley slowly pulled his hand from his jacket without the subpoena. The rage inched its way through his body, overtaking him. When he'd been younger, he hadn't been able to control it. His coaches had taught him how to focus it on opposing teams. Kim had taught him to release it, but he was finding it more difficult. For now, he was focusing it on Dixon Connor. He picked up the beer bottle, never taking his eyes from Connor's face. He finished the beer, a long pull, put the bottle on the bar, and slid backward off the stool.

"I'll leave now."

Connor's lip curled into a grin. He lowered the hammer on the gun and turned to put it back on the counter.

Donley grabbed the hand and bent it back violently at the wrist. The gun clattered to the floor. Donley kicked it away and bent the arm at the elbow, yanking it halfway up Connor's back. He thrust his left hand forward and pressed Connor's head against the bar, upending a bowl of bar mix, the wooden bowl flipping off the counter.

"I don't like bullies, Detective. And I don't like people sticking a gun in my face."

Connor was strong, stronger than Donley had anticipated. Even with an arm twisted violently behind the man's back, Donley could feel his power.

"Hey!"

Donley looked up. The bartender held an ax handle above Donley's head. "Let him go."

Unbelievable.

Donley maintained pressure on Connor's arm. The detective continued to strain, his skin red, veins bulging. Donley stepped back quickly, kicked the legs of the bar stool out from under Connor, and hit him in the sternum with his right fist. The force of the blow knocked the detective over the stool, both crashing to the floor.

Donley ripped the subpoena from his jacket and tossed it on Connor's chest. "Consider yourself served," he said, backing quickly to the swinging doors. Outside, he turned and ran for the Saab.

◆ ◆ ◆

Late that afternoon, a uniformed guard sat posted outside Father Thomas Martin's hospital room. Donley found the priest asleep, bandages wrapped around his head. The confrontation in the bar remained vivid, but the adrenaline rush had subsided, and now Donley felt an oncoming headache and fatigue. He sat in a chair beside the bed and leaned his head against the wall. He'd known trying to serve Connor was a risk, but Donley had spent his whole life taking risks and courting confrontations. Still, he'd never for the life of him thought the detective would point a loaded gun at him. It had unnerved him, and the episode lingered. Though he'd washed his hands and face in a bathroom sink, he couldn't get rid of the smell of Dixon Connor—cigarettes, sweat, and cheap cologne. It clung to his skin and clothes and permeated his nostrils. Each time he closed his eyes, the image of Connor's face and those dark, hollow eyes returned—eyes that looked capable of just about anything.

It was that familiar smell and those eyes that kept pulling Donley back to a place he didn't want to go, back to a night he had fought so hard to bury, determined not to let it, or his father, ruin his life. But now that night seemed just as determined to push through the walls Donley had so carefully built around it.

◆ ◆ ◆

Head down, his father struggled to remove the key from the front door lock, unaware Donley stood on the staircase, watching.

When Donley had been younger, his teachers at Assumption Middle School had assured him there were no such things as monsters, and that the boogeyman was make-believe. But his teachers had never smelled that smell, something not quite human, stale and putrid, like a wet basement. They'd never seen those dark, lifeless eyes.

Monsters were real. The boogeyman existed.

Night was something to fear.

His father freed the key from the lock, closed the door, and started for the stairs.

"What the?" The keys clattered when they hit the floor, and his father rocked back on his heels, eyes straining to see. He pawed at the wall and flicked the light switch, but the house remained dark.

"What are you doing, boy?"

Donley did not answer.

His father continued to flick the switch. "What's wrong with the lights? What're you, deaf, boy? Where's your mother?"

"Gone."

"Gone? Gone where?"

Donley didn't answer.

"She'll be back." He started up the stairs.

Donley stretched an arm across his father's path, gripping the bannister. His father turned his head. They stood face-to-face, no longer a boy and man. Same height. Same weight. Same size.

"Get out of my way." His father pushed against Donley's arm.

Donley tightened his grip.

His father's eyes narrowed. "You bucking me, boy?" His breath was tart and acidic. "I asked if you're bucking me. Move your arm . . . before I break it."

Donley didn't move. He would not be bullied. Not any longer.

They stared at each other for a long moment. Both of them had known for some time this confrontation had been inevitable. As Donley had grown, so, too, had the tension in the house. They had avoided each other as much as possible, but it was like putting a lid on a boiling pot. Eventually, it would explode.

Tonight.

His father stepped down one stair and turned as if to descend. "I want a beer, anyway."

Donley relaxed. Mistake.

The back of the hand struck him hard across his face, knocking him backward. His head struck the plaster wall with such force, the wall fissured. Donley lost his balance and slipped off the stair, landing hard on his back, dazed and in pain. He saw stars.

His father stepped past him. "I warned you to get out of my way, boy."

Donley shook the pain and stars and scrambled to his feet. He lunged, grabbing his father by the back of the collar. He yanked, and his father fell back into him. They rolled down the steps, the wood railing snapping and giving way. They hit the floor hard, shaking the house and rattling the windows. Donley got up first. For a moment, his father did not move. Then, slowly, he got to his knees—wheezing, guttural sounds escaping his throat.

"Who do you think you are? This is my house."

Rather than turn and run, as he had as a boy, only to be cornered and beaten, Donley stepped forward. "Not anymore. You don't own it, and you don't pay the rent."

His father stood. The first swing was wild. Donley easily ducked beneath it. The second fist struck him in the shoulder, but his legs absorbed the force. He raised his arm and grabbed the third punch, stopping it.

Donley countered with a right hand, and his father crashed into the front door. Stunned by the blow, he wiped a hand across his mouth and looked disbelieving at his own blood. Then he charged forward, yelling.

Donley shifted to the side like a bullfighter, grabbed his father by the waist, and hurled him into what remained of the bannister. More wooden poles cracked and splintered. The hallway table spilled the trophies and framed pictures, glass shattering.

His father rose, clenching a piece of the railing, swinging it wildly. Donley avoided the blows, retreating into the living room. He blocked the wooden stick with a forearm and countered with a punch to his father's stomach that buckled the man's knees. Donley lowered his shoulder and barreled into him, slamming him hard against the brick fireplace. The years of pain and anger exploded. Donley rained blow upon blow, knuckles striking bone again and again and again. His father slumped under the assault. Donley grabbed him by the collar, lifted him to his feet, and drove a knee into his stomach, hearing the air escape his lungs. Then he gripped him about the throat, blind with rage, squeezing. His father gasped and gagged and grabbed at Donley's arms, but Donley was determined not to let go.

He looked up and found himself staring at an unfamiliar, grotesque face, eyes bulging and bloodshot, nostrils flared, teeth bared.

A reflection in the mirror above the mantel.

His face.

Horrified, he released his grip, stepped back, and hurled a lamp from an end table at the mirror. The glass exploded, cascading to the floor.

He grabbed his father and lifted him to his feet. "It's time for you to leave," Donley said, breathing heavily, barely able to get the words out. "We don't want you here. We don't need you. I won't leave her here with you. So it's time for you to leave. Tonight. Now. And if you ever come back, if you make any attempt to contact her, I'll find you. And next time, I will kill you."

He released his grip and stepped away. His father fell like a weighted sack, slumped against the hearth.

Glass crushed beneath Donley's shoes as he made his way to the front door to leave. He reached the entryway when he heard the noise behind him. A low hum, it sounded at first like a distant motorcycle that grew in intensity and volume. When Donley turned back to the living room, his father charged, the scream becoming a deafening roar.

Chapter 14

Frank Ross adjusted the notched knob between the eyepieces and focused the oversize binoculars on the front entrance of the brick apartment building. Bronze-plated numbers illuminated beneath a small light confirmed the address.

He lowered the binoculars and looked up and down the block of manicured trees and three-story apartment buildings, but did not see Michael Whitney's blue BMW sports coupe. Ross wondered how a tennis instructor afforded such a luxury item or rent in a high-end apartment building.

Earlier that afternoon, Ross had driven by Lou Giantelli's office, but it was closed. A sign on the door indicated the office would be open sporadically throughout the end of the year. Until Ross found out whether he was still on the case, he was resigned to chasing down an unfaithful wife.

He picked up the handheld tape recorder and pressed the "Record" button while considering his watch. "Ten forty-two p.m. I have confirmed the address to be 1281 Clay Street. According to retrieved information, apartment 6B is occupied by a tenant of the last name, Whitney. DMV and credit-card records confirm the address. Mr. Whitney currently leases a navy-blue, two-door BMW sports coupe. He was seen leaving the Geary Theater with a woman fitting the description of the subject, Abigail Collins."

Ross turned off the recorder. "The guy must be a hell of a lay." He depressed the "Record" button. "Attempts to confirm relationship with Abigail Collins earlier in the evening unsuccessful."

Ross had been unable to snap any clear pictures of Collins and Whitney as they left the 8:00 p.m. performance of *The Phantom of the Opera*. The crowd of attendees on Geary Street, dressed in bulky raincoats and carrying large umbrellas, made it impossible for Ross to raise his camera and snap off a couple of quick shots. Thinking like a guy, Ross suspected Whitney would bring Abigail Collins back to his apartment. Whitney was paying a pricey chunk of change for his Pacific Heights address and would see no reason to spend money on a hotel. The fact that they went to a public show confirmed Mrs. Collins and her lover were unconcerned about Mr. Collins, who had deliberately left town to tempt his young wife.

Ross opened a thermos as old and conspicuous as the football-size binoculars and poured hot coffee into the cap. His car phone rang, an extravagant item for an underpaid private "dictective," but Ross had put the $2,100 cost on his credit card to pacify his wife. She worried about him, and unlike his time on the police force, the department could not reach him on the radio. "Hi, honey."

"That's the nicest thing I've been called all week, hero. How are the bad guys?"

"Sam? How did you get this number?"

"I charmed a pretty lady with a sweet voice."

"Did she at least hold out for a bribe?"

"Not a penny."

"I tell you, she's forgotten everything I taught her."

Sam Goldman roared. Even after a full day, he still sounded wired. "Business must be good if you can afford one of those fancy portable phones."

"Portable, my ass. The damn thing feels like I'm holding a brick and sounds like you're in a tunnel."

"Where I am talking to you?"

"I'm in my car."

"Imagine that. Beam me up, Scotty."

"To what do I owe the pleasure, Sam?"

"I got some news on the priest."

"I hope you're a better reporter than the gal who wrote the afternoon piece for the *Examiner*. That was worthless."

"I told you, everyone is keeping quiet. It's like the Kremlin."

Ross sipped at the coffee. "What's the big secret?"

"Don't know yet, but I'll find out. They can run, but they can't hide. You asked me about the detective who found the victim?"

"You have a name?"

"Dixon Connor. From what I'm told, Connor caught the priest red-handed. No pun intended. I checked with the people here who monitor police and fire frequencies. A call came in around nine twelve that night. Connor beat everybody there—materialized at the shelter like Hamlet's father."

"How did Connor get there so fast?"

"Don't know. But the real fireworks apparently started when Connor got back to the station. I'm told Mr. United States War Hero threw a fit in Lieutenant O'Malley's office, and she suspended him. Internal Affairs is involved," Goldman said.

"Any idea why she suspended him?"

"The priest's attorney is contending the search was illegal, that Connor kicked in doors and busted locked cabinets without a warrant."

"What's Connor's response?"

"Silence. Like I said, he cleaned out his desk and left. He's not answering his phone. So, are you going to tell me your angle on this investigation?" Goldman asked.

Ross had known Sam Goldman a long time. He considered him both a friend and a mentor. But Goldman was a reporter first, and Ross knew he could be sitting on potentially explosive information, a story that any good journalist would like to investigate, but it was too early. He knew it would be unfair to tell Goldman the angle, then have him promise not to look into it. Giving a good journalist a tip you didn't want in the paper was like lending money to friends. You just didn't do it. Besides, if he was still working on the case, he had a duty to not disclose anything.

Ross threw him a bone. "I'm working on something, Sam. When I feel like I have enough to make it worth your interest, we'll sit down, just me and you."

Goldman dismissed it. "You know me, I'm always on the go. The missus said you were working. Top secret? James Bond stuff?"

Ross looked at the mess in the Cadillac and picked up the mammoth binoculars. "Yeah, Sam. I'm a real secret agent. Thanks for the information."

"No problem. Enjoy that phone while it lasts, hero. Those things will never catch on. Who wants to be bothered morning, noon, and night?"

Ross set down the phone. He thought of Dixon Connor. He thought of Father Thomas Martin. And he thought of the victim, Andrew Bennet. He wondered how they all might have interacted with one another. He had enough material to have somebody take a close and serious look at three different files: three teenage prostitutes, all murdered, all unsolved . . . and Dixon Connor's name now appeared as the detective on all three.

When he looked back to the front entrance of the apartment building, the BMW was parked at the curb. Michael Whitney had opened the passenger-side door, and his date was stepping out. Ross reached quickly into the backseat for his camera, opened the case, and removed the Nikon, fumbling with the telephoto lens. He started shooting as

Whitney and Abigail Collins entered the front door and disappeared into the lobby. He knew he had a blurry photograph of the backs of a well-dressed man and woman.

Nathaniel Collins would not be happy, and an unhappy client was unlikely to pay. Ross picked up the tape recorder.

"Ten fifty-two p.m. Ross screws up. Subjects evade tail. No photographs. Wife makes one-point-five million. Frank Ross, private 'dictective,' makes nothing."

◆ ◆ ◆

"You OK?"

Donley had opened his eyes. Momentarily confused, he realized he'd fallen asleep in the chair beside Father Martin's bed and the priest was talking to him. He sat up and shook away the cobwebs. Father Martin had his head turned on the pillow, watching him.

"I was going to ask you the same thing," Donley said. He was sweating and breathing heavily. He unclenched his hands, which had been balled into fists, stood, and walked to the side of the bed.

"Vicious headache," Father Martin said.

"The turban becomes you."

"Never thought being bald would be a virtue; at least they didn't have to shave my head."

Donley smiled. "One of the officers who brought you in said you put up a hell of a fight. He said you might not be alive if you hadn't."

"I always did have a problem with that 'turn the other cheek' thing. What day is it?"

"Saturday."

Father Martin turned his head to look out the window. "It's late. You should be home with your wife and son."

"I'm doing hospital rounds. I went to visit my uncle earlier and thought I'd come check on you."

"How is he?"

"Ornery as ever, which means he's getting better. They have him walking the halls. He keeps threatening to walk right out the door. He would, too, if my aunt wasn't there. Walk right to the office, probably. You feel up to a few questions?"

"Sure."

"I tried to see your friend Danny a couple nights ago."

Father Martin's eyes widened. "Is he all right?"

"I don't know. He left the hospital in the middle of the night. Apparently, Detective Connor paid him a visit just before he did."

The priest's gaze shifted to the ceiling. "He's scared."

"With good reason. I paid Connor a visit myself earlier today to see if he would talk to me and to hand him a subpoena."

"How'd that go?"

"Let's just say I wouldn't count on him as a character witness."

"Connor hates the shelter."

"Why?"

"People like Connor hate just to hate. They don't need a reason. It's part of their DNA." Father Martin's eyes fluttered. He yawned.

"I'll let you rest."

"What about you?" the priest asked.

"No rest for me," Donley said. "I have an evidentiary hearing to prepare for, though I intend to ask for a continuance with you lying here looking like a Saudi oil sheik and Connor refusing my subpoena. No guarantees Maximum Milt will grant it, since you really don't need to be present, and I'm sure the district attorney will argue I'm only stalling."

Father Martin said, "It looked like you were having a nightmare."

Donley dismissed it. "Nothing like the one you must be having."

Father Martin paused. Then, apparently not wanting to push the subject, he asked, "How old is your son?"

"Benny? He's two, almost three. Why do you ask?"

"He's with your wife?"

"Actually, he's with his grandmother. My wife's on call tonight."

"She's a doctor."

"A resident."

"So, he stays with your mother."

Donley shook his head. "My wife's mother. My mother is dead."

"I'm sorry."

"It's been a few years," he said.

"How'd she die?"

"Cancer. I was in law school. They found it too late. She died sixty days from diagnosis. The really amazing thing is, she waited a month to tell me because she didn't want it to interfere with my semester exams. She went through hell by herself. That still bothers me."

"What about your father?"

Donley shook his head, and for a moment remembered his nightmare, which was all too real. "He died in an accident a few years before that."

"I'm sorry."

"Don't be. He was a lot like Dixon Connor, angry at everyone and everything. Blamed everyone else for his problems. Hated just to hate . . ." Donley checked his watch. "I better get going."

"It's all right to be angry, Peter."

Donley nodded, but no words came.

"It's all right to be angry at God. He and I battle all the time. When my mother died, I was angry because she gave her life to him, and I thought she deserved better. But we don't know why God does what he does until sometimes much later. My mother's death forced my older brothers to grow up and realize they had a responsibility to step up and take care of the rest of us. If they hadn't, social services would have split us up, and they likely would be dead, given the direction they'd been heading. Maybe me as well. They protected me, and when I got to the seminary, they made sure I stayed there."

"My mother used to say something similar," Donley said. "But I never did find much comfort in the 'everything happens for a reason' answer, Father."

"Do you know the story of Saint Paul?" Father Tom asked.

Donley smiled. "Not very well, I'm afraid. From what I recall, he persecuted the Jews until God knocked him from his horse and struck him blind."

"Paul didn't just persecute the Jews," Father Martin said. "He murdered them. And yet, he was the disciple God chose to spread Christ's message. God made us sinners, Peter. But he also forgives those sins. That's his divine mercy. But first, we have to forgive ourselves."

Donley wasn't in the mood to go to confession. The memories of his father had returned from wherever Donley had buried him. With those memories, Donley's resentment and anger had also returned. If he was being honest, Donley was scared he wouldn't be able to control it, and what he might do as a result.

"I'll keep you posted on what happens," he said, and left the room.

Inside the building, Ross walked down chandelier-lit hallways with high ceilings. He wore coveralls he kept in the trunk of his car and a nylon-mesh baseball cap. Apartment 6B was the last door on the right. Ross pulled the bill of his hat low over his eyes and knocked. He held a clipboard in one hand and a toolbox from the trunk of his car in the other. Fastened around his waist was a tool belt. In the front pouch, a hidden camera lay inside what appeared to be a twenty-five-foot measuring tape.

"Who is it?" A man's voice. He sounded aggravated.

"Roto-Rooter."

"I didn't call Roto-Rooter. You have the wrong apartment."

Ross lifted the clipboard and pretended to read from it. "Apartment 6B, 1281 Clay Street?"

"Yes, but—"

"Got a call from the superintendent."

Michael Whitney opened the door dressed in slacks and a V-neck T-shirt that showed off a thick gold-chain necklace. Thin as a rock star, Whitney pulled his long blond hair back in a ponytail.

"Do you know what time it is?" Whitney asked.

Ross checked his wristwatch. "Eleven twenty-four."

"I meant—"

"And I'm hoping this is my last call of the night because, boy, my dogs are barking. Ms. Jamison in 4C appears to have developed a problem with her waste line, and I don't mean her figure, you know." He laughed out loud.

Whitney didn't find it amusing.

Dolt.

"Anyway, superintendent has asked that we check each of the units on the same line."

"Who is it?"

The question came from inside the apartment, the voice of an impatient-sounding woman.

Whitney leaned forward. "This is not a good time right now."

Ross winked. "I understand, partner. Tell you what, if you have any raw sewage come floating up into your bathroom from the toilet, give us a call. We'll have somebody out here within seventy-two hours. Stuff towels under the door to keep it contained. It can be a health hazard."

Ross turned to walk away.

"Raw sewage?" Whitney asked with alarm.

"Ruined Ms. Jamison's party," Ross said. "Every time someone in the building flushes the toilet, she ends up with turds on her bathroom floor. We think it's probably a tree root. Tree roots can grow right on up the pipe. You can snake the lines from here to China, but until you get the tree root out of the pipe, you're just wasting everybody's time. No pun intended."

Whitney gave no response. This guy had the IQ of tree bark.

"How long do you think this will take?"

Ross winked. "I'll have you back in the saddle in no time."

Whitney opened the door, and Ross stepped into the apartment and turned left in the direction of the woman's voice. Abigail Collins reclined on pillows by a fireplace sipping from a wineglass. Articles of clothing littered the room. Mrs. Collins pulled a blanket tight around her, but not before an enhanced breast tumbled out.

Click.

"Evening, ma'am. Sorry to disturb you so late."

Click.

Collins looked to be in her mid-thirties, fifteen to twenty years younger than Mr. Collins.

"Who the hell are you?" she hissed.

"I'm Marty. I'm here to check your toilet."

Click.

"It isn't my toilet."

Click.

Whitney grabbed Ross under the elbow. "The bathroom is the other direction, first door on the right."

Abigail Collins reached up playfully and grabbed Whitney's hand.

Click. Click.

Whitney stumbled and fell onto the pillows. Abigail Collins leaned across him, her breast again popping free.

Click. Click. Click. Click.

"Could be hair in the drains," Ross said, snapping pictures as quick as the camera allowed. "Hair in the drain will be the end of the entire sewage system in all of the largest cities."

Whitney pointed as he struggled to get up from the pillows. "Down the hall. Down the hall."

"Got it," Ross said. Mr. Collins had enough photographs to do a photo shoot, and Ross had just paid the mortgage for the next four months.

He shut the door to a green-marble bathroom with gold fixtures, removed a socket wrench from the toolbox, and knelt down to rap on the pipes. On a glass shelf above the bathroom sink, he spied a framed picture of Michael Whitney with Abigail Collins in front of the bicycle shop on Angel Island. Ross had once taken Frank Jr. there. What caught his attention, though, were the two little girls on miniature bikes with colorful streamers protruding from the handles. The girls were dark-skinned with rugged chins and bore a striking and unmistakable resemblance to their father. He put the picture back and sat on the toilet feeling sick to his stomach. Then he dropped the wrench into the toolbox and walked back into the living room.

Whitney and Collins sipped wine on the pillows. "You're done?" Whitney asked.

Ross looked past him to Abigail Collins. "The picture, those are your daughters?"

"Yes," she said, looking and sounding uncertain.

Ross tipped his cap. "They're beautiful," he said. "And precious. You folks have a nice night. I'll see myself out."

Ross closed the door behind him. Andrew Collins had said he and his estranged wife had no children. The son of a bitch was going to use the pictures not just to keep his wife from getting the money. He wanted to keep her from battling him about child-support payments—using Ross to get out of taking care of his kids while he drove down the coast to screw a young girl who worked in the golf shop at Pebble Beach.

Ross removed the tape measure from his belt buckle, located the clasp on the side, and opened it, exposing the film. He'd find another way to pay the mortgage.

Chapter 15

December 28, 1987

Gil Ramsey looked up from his desk as Linda St. Claire walked into his office on Monday, holding a sheet of paper. "Nice party the other night. How's the hand?" she asked.

Ramsey squeezed his bandaged right hand, which still stung from the cigar burn. He'd told the guests that he'd burned his hand on the oven. "Did you get laid?"

She smiled. "He owns the biggest private defense practice in the city, Gil, and a ranch in Portola Valley. Just doing my part for the campaign."

Ramsey turned toward the window. "Is that why you're still smiling?"

St. Claire laughed and sat in one of the leather chairs, crossing her legs. "Actually, the news I have will put a smile on both our faces, and neither of us will have to remove an article of clothing."

"Too bad," Ramsey said.

She held up the paper. "The lab tests on Andrew Bennet's clothing came back. They detected two types of blood. The kid is B positive. They also found O. Guess whose blood type is O."

"Father Martin."

St. Claire lowered the piece of paper. "What's wrong with you? I thought you'd be jumping up and down."

"I don't jump up and down. What did Donley say about a plea?"

She shook her head, exasperated. "He didn't take the bait. Who cares? Did you hear what I just said?"

"I heard. Call Donley, and make the bait a little more intriguing. Give him this latest bit of information."

St. Claire was incredulous. "Why? We have a positive match."

"Which means shit, if it isn't admissible," Ramsey said.

"This wasn't found in the locked office, Gil. It was found on Bennet's clothing. It's over."

"If the other evidence doesn't come in, we have no murder weapon and no motive. We have O-positive blood. I'm O positive. It is the most common type out there."

"This is the hammer, Gil. If he survives the beating he took, Father Martin's facing a death sentence," St. Claire said.

"Exactly. And Mr. Donley knows there is no guarantee he will win his motion and keep the evidence out, and we can't guarantee the judge will let it in," Ramsey said. "The difference is, if we gamble and lose, we have options. We may find more evidence when we go into the shelter, and even if we don't, we go forward with our case and get to a jury. If he gambles and loses, he has no options. This evidence will convict his client, and after his appeals are exhausted, Father Martin will die by lethal injection."

St. Claire sat back. "He can't take that chance."

"No, he can't, no matter how big a set of balls he has. So go to your office, get on the telephone, and tell him the news. Then tell him Father Martin has until Thursday morning, *before* the hearing, to plead guilty. If he does, we will strongly consider a sentence of twenty-five years to life and recommend twenty-five years. If he does not, the offer is off the table, we will seek the death penalty, and Mr. Donley will be playing Russian roulette with Father Martin's life."

The door to the office opened without a knock. Augustus Ramsey paused in the doorway, considering St. Claire.

"Hello, Governor," St. Claire said, standing.

"Hello, Ms. St. Claire. Did you enjoy yourself the other night?"

"I did. Thank you for having me." St. Claire turned to Gil Ramsey. "I'll go make that call." She excused herself and walked out.

Augustus Ramsey followed her with his eyes. When the door closed, he turned to his son. "Are you getting a piece of that?"

Ramsey returned to his desk. "Why are you here, Dad?"

"Your mother and I missed you Christmas Day. We missed seeing our grandchildren."

"Change of plans," Gil Ramsey said. "Linda wanted to see her parents."

Augustus Ramsey didn't pursue it. He sat in the chair St. Claire had vacated.

"I'm very busy, Dad."

"Just thought I'd check in and see how the priest case is coming along. I understand you have a positive match on the blood."

Gil Ramsey felt his stomach grip. "How would you know that, Dad?"

"A man has his sources."

"Not all men, Dad. Just you." Ramsey walked to the window behind his desk but closed his eyes to the view, feeling nauseated. "Why are you so interested in this case, Dad?"

"I told you why. I'm just looking out for your best interests. It's unfortunate what happened to the priest. I heard he nearly died. Mistakes happen, I guess."

Nothing had been printed about the screwup at the county jail that resulted in the priest's jacket file being changed from red to yellow. Yellow-coded jacket files indicated general-population prisoners. Red was for isolated prisoners. The deputy who had come on duty swore that Father Martin's jacket had been yellow. Other than the sheriff's office, which was investigating the matter, and Gil Ramsey, no one knew that information. Ramsey hadn't even told St. Claire.

Ramsey turned and looked at the man sitting in the chair across his desk. "How do you know that?" Augustus Ramsey did not answer. "What the hell did you do?"

Augustus Ramsey lifted his hands like a priest greeting his congregation. Irony had always been one of his strengths. "I did what a father does for his son. I took care of things for you."

The nauseated feeling intensified. "For me? Or for you?"

"I wouldn't have had to do anything if you had done your job and convinced that attorney to take the plea," Augustus Ramsey said. "Instead, he made you look incompetent on national television. I hope this time you'll be more persuasive."

Ramsey looked at the man sitting across from him and felt nothing but disgust. "I'm washing my hands of this."

"Don't be a fool."

"I'm no fool, Dad."

His father did not reply.

"And I want no more of this. I want no more of you. I want you out of here. I want you away from me and my children. If you interfere again, I'll . . ."

Augustus Ramsey smiled. "You'll what? Go to the police? How is that going to look, the district attorney offering a murder-one suspect a plea agreement?"

"What are you talking about?"

"Why would you do that when everyone knows the DA doesn't plea murder-one suspects? Why would you do it in this case unless you had some personal interest?"

For a moment, Ramsey couldn't speak. His throat had gone dry. He licked his lips. "You set me up?"

"My career is over," his father said. "Who has the most at stake, the most to lose? Who had the greater motivation to make this go away, to make that kid go away? It's a crime to use your office to obstruct justice."

A cold sweat overcame him. He felt chilled to the bone. His legs weak, he sunk into his chair. "You knew. You knew about the tapes," he said, his voice barely a whisper.

"I've had reason to suspect they existed, yes."

"And Connor? You're aware of Connor?"

"Not initially, no. We'll raise the money and put this behind us."

"And you used me," Ramsey said. He looked up at the ceiling and laughed, disbelieving.

August Ramsey picked a piece of lint from his coat sleeve and rubbed it from his fingers, watching it float to the ground. "Grow up, Gil. Here's a news flash: Everybody uses everybody. It's how you get to the top. It's how you stay on top. And I intend to stay on top. The only question is, do you?"

Late Monday afternoon, Donley sat in a chair in Linda St. Claire's office in the Hall of Justice building. Donley had spent most of the weekend and all day Monday researching the law for his motion to exclude the evidence. So far, the results had not been encouraging. The last thing he'd needed or wanted was a call from St. Claire. She had greeted him without the same confrontational demeanor she'd displayed in their first two encounters, surprisingly cordial, even friendly. In fact, her whole appearance had softened, with her hair pulled back in a loose clip. She wore khaki slacks and a red-knit sweater.

She handed him a single sheet of paper. "They've confirmed Father Martin's blood type on Andrew Bennet's clothing."

Donley remained determined not to allow St. Claire to do another tap dance on his face, but her words struck hard, like an anvil to the chest. "The evidence is not going to come in, Ms. St. Claire. It was obtained illegally."

She shook her head. "The clothing was not in the locked office. There's no argument to keep it out." Before he had a chance to respond, she stood and raised a hand, though again it seemed conciliatory. "Look, I know you're confident in your legal position, but I believe the law is more favorable to admitting the evidence. It would have been found eventually under *Nix v. Williams*. Be that as it may, I'm not here to debate the law with you. You'll argue your case, and I'll argue mine. But you have to agree, at the very least, neither of us can predict what Judge Trimble will ultimately do."

She was back to the plea. Donley remained silent.

"I guess the real issue is consequences," she continued. "If you lose your motion, how do you explain this evidence to a jury?" St. Claire again raised a hand as if to cut him off, though Donley had no intention of answering her question. "You have to acknowledge it is a problem." She sat back in her chair. "If I lose this motion, I still have a dead boy at Father Martin's shelter with Father Martin covered in his blood and his blood type on the victim's clothing. I know you'll argue Father Martin lived there and went to the boy's aid, but how do you explain Father Martin's blood? I also think I still have a better than fifty-fifty chance of getting the letter opener into evidence. It was in plain sight on his desk and not locked in a cabinet. It's circumstantial, certainly, but if I'm right, I have the murder weapon, the body, the circumstances, and now, the blood. Murder one. Father Martin goes away for life—I think that's the worst I do. If you lose, it all comes in, and I have aggravated murder. Father Martin gets the death penalty."

"And you have something for Father Martin to consider in light of that risk?" Donley asked, tired of the hints.

She sat forward. "We're prepared to recommend a sentence of between twenty-five years to life and let Trimble decide the number."

Donley tried to show no emotion. "A chance with Maximum Milt? Not much of an offer."

She put up a hand. "We would strongly recommend Father Martin receive twenty-five years, with the possibility of parole after twenty. When he gets out, he's still a relatively young man, mid-fifties."

Donley sat back. "You know, I've been told numerous times now that the DA doesn't plea murder ones."

St. Claire diverted her eyes. "Sometimes doing justice requires that we consider reasonable plea agreements."

It sounded like a rehearsed speech. "But this isn't what *you* want, is it? No offense, but your record speaks for itself, and I can see it in your demeanor. You'd prefer to try Father Martin. I'm not casting aspersions. It's just a deduction."

St. Claire wasn't about to say, but her lack of fire and brimstone betrayed her. "It's simple percentages, Mr. Donley. I'm weighing the percentages and calculating where this is likely to shake out. It's a gamble. We all realize that. But you're the only one who'll be gambling with Father Martin's life."

Father Martin sat up in his hospital bed. "Peter. I didn't expect to see you tonight."

Donley dropped his briefcase at the foot of the bed and undid the knot of his tie. "They found your blood type on Andrew Bennet's clothing."

Father Martin closed his eyes.

Donley paced, one hand rubbing his forehead. "I can't keep that out. It wasn't in the office. How do we explain it?"

Father Martin sighed. "I'm sorry, Peter."

Donley stopped and turned. "Stop being sorry, OK? That's not getting us anywhere. How do we explain it, Tom? I need to know, because I am running out of time and options."

"Do you see any reason why a man in custody, going nowhere, has to have his blood drawn at eleven p.m. on Christmas Eve when the officer is going off duty?"

"No, I don't, but now we're going from someone planting evidence to a vast conspiracy to frame you, and the farther we go out on that limb, the weaker it becomes. When we first met, I told you the courtroom was not the real world. It's the world I create. How do I sell that to a jury? How do I sell a conspiracy theory to a jury when we don't have a clue who the conspirators might be, or what their beef is with you?"

"You indicated the other evidence was illegally seized, that it might not come into evidence."

Donley put up a hand to cut him off. "I said that I would bring a motion to exclude it. I can't guarantee anything. I've been doing research for three days, and I'd say our chances are less than fifty percent of keeping it out."

"What do you want me to do, confess to a crime I did not commit? I didn't kill Andrew Bennet."

Donley stopped pacing. "The DA is offering twenty-five years with the possibility of parole after twenty."

Father Martin shut his eyes. "If I plead guilty."

"Yes. I can't guarantee you I can do better than that, Tom, and I'm obligated to bring you the offer. If we lose, best-case scenario, you get life, no parole. Worst-case, the State of California puts you to death."

Father Martin opened his eyes. "You've never guaranteed me anything."

"What?"

"From the very beginning, you have told me the evidence against me was very bad. You told me the chances of keeping it out are, at best, even. I listened to your counsel because it is your job, but what I truly care about is that you believe me when I tell you that I did not kill Andrew Bennet."

"Whether I believe you or not is not important—"

"It is to me."

Donley looked away and blew out a breath.

"If I have to spend the rest of my life in prison, then so be it. I'll accept it as God's way of calling me to minister to those who need it most."

Donley spoke without turning. "Do you know what they do to child molesters in prison?"

Martin scoffed and spread his arms. "Uh, yeah!"

Donley faced him. "They'll kill you this time."

"Another reason for me not to plea to any deal. This is my decision, Peter. Do not put this burden on your shoulders. If this is my cross to carry, then I will carry it. I make it willingly and knowingly. I am prepared to die, if that is my fate, and nothing you do or not do will have contributed to it. Do you understand that?"

Donley didn't answer. How could he not feel like it would be his fault? "That's very noble," he said. "But just the same, I'd prefer you didn't die on my watch."

"I ask only two things of you."

"What?" Donley said.

"Believe me when I say I did not kill Andrew Bennet."

"I believe you," Donley said.

Father Martin nodded. "Thank you."

"What's the second thing?"

"Andrew's killer remains free. Find him. Find him for all the boys I was trying to help. Do it for them, not for me."

Donley thought about it, and the more he did, the more he realized Father Tom had just hit on maybe the only thing that would save his life—finding the killer.

Chapter 16

December 29, 1987

Donley pulled out the business card and double-checked the address. The inordinate number of cheap motels and corner liquor stores with gated entrances and barred windows confirmed the building remained in the heart of the Tenderloin, just blocks from his own office, though the deterioration was significant. How like Lou to choose a private investigator who couldn't afford a business address better than the Tenderloin. He hoped Frank Ross was a better investigator than his choice of neighborhoods would otherwise indicate. After a fitful night of sleep, Donley was more convinced that Father Martin was correct—the only way Donley was going to win was if he found Andrew Bennet's killer. Arguing some vast conspiracy without the evidence to support it was not going to get them anywhere. In fact, it would make them look desperate.

Donley's breath formed white wisps as he dodged a couple of cars crossing the street. The stucco of the three-story building had been tagged with graffiti, and the wood trim had flaked so badly, he couldn't be sure what color it had once been painted. A homeless woman sat on the top step pulling a dark-blue ski cap low on her head and dipping a doughnut into a steaming cup of coffee.

The building lobby smelled like mold, though the floor was a cracked orange tile. A glass-enclosed, black-felt board identified the building tenants, though so many of the white letters had fallen and become wedged at the bottom of the case, the board looked like an unsolved crossword puzzle. Donley ran his index finger down the list of remaining vowels and consonants.

F ANK RO s P IVA   DIC ECT V

Frank Ross's office was on the second floor at the end of a drab, dimly lit hallway. Donley noted the misspelled word *Dictective* on the smoked glass. When he knocked, the door swung open, the office empty.

He called out. "Mr. Ross? Hello?"

The bright December sun streamed through a stained-glass window, coloring everything purple. Enough time in here, and Donley would have a major headache.

Uncertain what to do, Donley stepped inside. The furnishings were spartan, an industrial-size metal desk and chair, multiple cardboard boxes, and a tattered couch. Built-in shelves held framed photographs, a few books, and miscellaneous stacks of paper.

Donley picked up one of the frames and considered the picture. A young man with a crew cut sat in a police officer's dress-blue uniform. The officer's brown eyes sparkled like he wanted to smile but had been given an order to look serious. Donley put the picture back on the shelf. The other photographs were of the same officer, older, shaking hands with a former mayor, Muhammad Ali, and 49ers quarterback Joe Montana. The Ali and Montana photographs were both autographed *To Frank*. A medal draped over a framed certificate from the city and county indicated Frank Ross had received the police department's Gold Medal of Valor for bravery.

On the second shelf a framed wedding picture sat between two photographs of a boy in a football uniform. The boy was big for his age, a smaller version of Frank Ross.

"You better have a good reason for being in here."

Donley startled at the sound of the voice. Turning, he said, "Sorry, the door wasn't shut all the way. It opened when I knocked."

Ross checked the latch and shook his head. "I was in the head."

"You don't lock your door?"

"Somebody wants to steal the stuff in here, I'll help them carry it out."

Donley gestured to the door. "*Detective* is misspelled."

"Don't remind me. What can I do for you?"

"I'm Peter Donley. I work with Lou Giantelli. I tried to call." Donley glanced at the answering machine. A red light blinked. "Your answering machine must be full."

"I have a client who isn't too happy with me at the moment." He stuck out his hand. "Frank Ross."

"Lou said he hired you to work on the Father Martin case."

"He did, but I wasn't sure about my status with Lou in the hospital. How's he doing?"

"Getting better, but not fast enough to handle this."

"So, you're representing the priest?"

"At the moment, and I have an evidentiary hearing Thursday—"

"Read about it in the paper." Ross looked about. "I'd offer you a chair."

"Couch is fine."

"Wouldn't. Guy in here before me made movies. I haven't had the manpower to get it out of here."

Donley stepped away from the couch into a stream of purple light and raised a hand to deflect the glare. "Isn't that window a bit distracting?"

"I rented the space on a foggy day. Had I known . . ." Ross shrugged huge shoulders. He was a big man, but there was a gentleness to him that belied his size—a soft voice, his eyes friendly. As big as he was, Ross seemed to slump, as if carrying an enormous weight on his shoulders. Given whom he had apparently once been based on the pictorial history on his shelves, and where he now conducted business, Donley reasoned it a safe assumption the man had taken a serious and painful fall. He knew Lou had represented a lot of cops and wondered if that was the connection. "You were a cop?"

"I was. Tell me about your client."

Donley rubbed at his chin. "Well, to start, he says he did not kill Andrew Bennet."

"I know."

"How would you know?" Donley asked.

"I read it in the paper." Ross put up his hands to depict a banner. "Big headline. Priest says, 'I didn't do it.' Sounds like it was a hell of an arraignment. Most are boring."

Donley smiled. "Right. So, what exactly did Lou ask you to do?"

Ross spoke as he moved to the chair behind the desk. "Ask around and find out what I could about what went down that night at the shelter and anything else I thought might be important."

"Did you find anything?"

"First, tell me about the priest. Do you believe him?"

"Yeah, I believe him."

"Why?"

Donley took a moment to gather his thoughts. "The night of Andrew Bennet's murder, Father Martin said he was on his way to lock the front door when the power cut out."

"I believe there was a storm that night," Ross said.

"There was, but I've checked with PG&E. There was no power outage for the grid that included the shelter, and they did not shut off power to the building. That means either the power failed, which would have been a hell of a coincidence, or someone pulled the fuse. The fuses are located in a closet in the back of the room where Andrew Bennet's body was found."

Ross seemed to consider this for a moment. Then he asked, "How would someone get in the building unnoticed?"

"According to Father Tom, there's a door in that room that leads to a staircase that goes down to a basement. Another door leads to the back of the building. He keeps both locked at all times. Someone had to have let the killer in, or at least propped the door open."

"So, two people?" Ross asked.

"Seems that way."

"What else?"

"The day I visited Father Martin in jail, he was under lock and key, a high-profile defendant on suicide watch being kept in isolation."

"Given what he's accused of doing, that would be the protocol," Ross said.

"So, tell me why, on Christmas Eve, he gets transported to give a blood sample at the end of a shift, and somehow when he's brought back, he's placed in general population and nearly killed."

"The paper said it was an administrative error."

"Yeah, and occasionally the power goes out, but that's two coincidences. Then there's the fact the DA keeps hinting at a plea."

"DA doesn't plea murder ones."

"They do now. Gil Ramsey hinted at it in his office once. Yesterday afternoon, after hitting me with the news that they'd found my client's blood type on the victim's clothing, Linda St. Claire offered twenty-five years to life with parole at twenty for a guilty plea."

"She made the offer after telling you the blood type matched?"

"Strange, huh? You'd think it would have made them pull the offer off the table."

"What did your client say?"

Donley shook his head. "He won't plea. He didn't do it."

"Gutsy."

Donley nodded, but inside he couldn't shake that feeling he was leading Father Martin to the gallows.

"You have a motion to exclude evidence pending," Ross said. "Maybe they're worried the blood type won't come in."

"My motion won't keep out blood on the victim's clothing, and as Ms. St. Claire was so kind to remind me, even if I win, I still have to defend against a murder charge. If she wins I've given Father Martin a one-way ticket to Colma," Donley said, referring to the city famous for having more graves than citizens.

"How does your client explain the blood?"

"Someone had to doctor the clothing."

"So, a third person involved?"

Donley heard Ross's skepticism. "My client was taken to the hospital the night of the murder for a broken wrist, Mr. Ross."

"Frank," he said. "How did he break his wrist?"

"He slipped and fell on Andrew Bennet's blood. I have the hospital records. There is no mention that my client was bleeding. Look, I know where your questions are heading, Frank, and I don't disagree that, at the moment, I don't have a lot to back up a conspiracy theory. So, I'm screwed royally unless I can figure out who did kill Andrew Bennet."

"Solve the case?"

"That might be the only way."

"Did your priest know the victim?"

"Knew *of* him. He was surprised when Bennet showed up at the shelter that night."

"Why?"

"Bennet was a tough kid who did heavy drugs, heroin apparently. Father Tom said when Bennet came in, he was agitated. He thought Bennet was coming down off a high or was in need of a fix, but before Father Tom had the chance to talk to him, Bennet took off."

"He left the shelter?"

"At some point. Then his body turns up back at the shelter. That got me thinking. What if it wasn't drugs that made Andrew Bennet agitated? What if he was agitated because he was afraid someone was going to kill him? Maybe Bennet went to the shelter because he was scared."

"Then why would he leave?"

"I don't know." Donley shook his head. "The problem is, I have until Thursday morning, bright and early, to figure this out. I can't afford to lose that motion, but at the moment, I don't believe I can win."

"Ask for a continuance. Your guy is in the hospital."

"I did. The court denied my motion. The judge doesn't need Father Martin present to hear it. Can you help me?"

Ross sat back, pausing before he answered. "Maybe. I spent the weekend and all day yesterday running some things down." Ross opened a drawer and pulled out a file. He placed it on the desk and opened it. On top was a newspaper article. Someone, likely Ross, had written the date in ink at the top above a simple, nondescript headline.

Body Found in Dumpster

"Sixteen-year-old runaway from Illinois named Jerry Burke," Ross said. "He was strangled. The killer stuffed his body in a green garbage bag and dumped it in a bin behind a bar in the Castro. Burke had a long history of solicitation and drug-related charges." Ross turned the article over and handed Donley a copy of a police report, two sheets of paper stapled at the top. "The driver for the garbage company that serviced the area found the body when he went to dump the contents. Actually, he saw a foot sticking through the bag. But for that, the driver said he would have buried Jerry Burke under a mound of garbage, perhaps forever. There were no other statements. There were no witnesses."

Ross took back the report, put it in the file, and set the file aside. He opened a second file. It appeared to be organized in the same manner, a newspaper article clipped to a police report. "Two weeks later, the body of Manuel Rivera, seventeen, was found at Fort Funston."

Donley and Kim sometimes ran Bo at that park, which was situated on a bluff above the coast.

"A woman walking her dog found the body. More accurately, her dog found it in a thick bramble of bushes."

"How'd he die?"

Rivera was shot once through the head. He was also described as a street prostitute with a long criminal record, including drugs and solicitation. The police report was similar to the first, scant. The only witness statement was from the woman who stumbled on to the body."

"You think these cases are related to Andrew Bennet's killing."

"I can't say that, but the autopsy report on Jerry Burke revealed his lungs were filled with water, and the garbage bin in which they found him was a long way from any body of water. He also had fresh burn marks on his body, like someone had used him as an ashtray. Rivera didn't have any water in his lungs, but he also had the burn marks. Torture is done either because the killer is a sick, sadistic son of a bitch, or he's trying to get information."

"Bennet had burn marks on his body. It's in the ME's report."

"So, we have three street kids all about the same age, all tortured, all murdered within weeks of one another. All three investigations remain open, and here's what I learned more recently. Dixon Connor is the lead detective in all three investigations. At least, he was until he got himself suspended."

That got Donley's attention. "Connor is the detective who broke down the door to Father Tom's office. He claims that's where he found the letter opener and photographs." But just as Donley started to get excited, he deflated. He shook his head. "The State will object this is all irrelevant, and I don't see Judge Trimble letting in any evidence related to Rivera or Burke without something more to tie them to Andrew Bennet."

"I agree. But you were talking about coincidences. How much do you know about San Francisco Homicide?" Ross said.

"Not much."

"Fourteen detectives, one lieutenant, and one secretary. They work in seven teams. Since murderers don't conform to regular business hours, the detectives are on call twenty-four hours a day, seven days a week. To ease that burden, they rotate, like doctors on call. They call it standby. Connor was on standby the nights of each of the three murders. From twenty years of police work, I can tell you that's rare. Even less likely is Connor being stupid enough to break in a locked door at a crime scene and jeopardizing the evidence."

"What can you tell me about him?"

"Dixon Connor is a third-generation San Francisco police officer. His grandfather walked the beat, his father followed him, and it's the only job Connor ever wanted to do. Only it isn't a job for him. It's a way of life. His father, Max, was a legend in the Sunset District. *Infamous* is probably a better word to describe him. Max Connor ran the Police Athletic League. His teams were white boys, and they were tough. Max Connor was a good cop, but not so good a person."

Ross told the story like he was building up to something.

"What do you mean *was*?" Donley asked.

Ross picked up a pen and ran it between his fingers like a tiny baton. "Max Connor didn't exactly take to having women and minorities on the police force. He made life miserable for the few female officers we had back then. Most of them didn't want to make waves, didn't want to buck the system and come off as too sensitive for the job—it was still pretty much an old boys' network back then. So most tolerated his crap."

"But not all?" Donley said, picking up the thread of the story.

"Maria Gonzalez grew up in a tough neighborhood. The facts are a bit sketchy, but if you believe her, Max Connor forced himself on her after a night of drinking. She said that when she resisted, punches were thrown. Max Connor claimed she set him up, came on to him, then started screaming. He said she had an ax to grind and wanted to get him dismissed from the force. It was classic 'he said, she said.' The review board sided with Gonzalez and dismissed Max Connor. That was enough to kill him, but it turned out that was the least of his problems. The district attorney was the political type, and the dismissal, which got a lot of press, was an opportunity to stand up for women and minorities, and maybe get a few votes in the process. Augustus Ramsey decided to make an example of Max Connor. And he assigned a young DA to the case named Gil Ramsey. His son."

"So, what happened?"

"They couldn't make a rape case, so they went after Connor for assault and battery. The old boys' network couldn't save Connor the humiliation of a criminal trial."

"No wonder Connor hates lawyers. Was his father convicted?"

Donley shook his head. "Like I said: He said, she said. The jury hung. But Gonzalez wasn't about to let it drop. She sued Connor for civil damages and won. I heard she took him for just about everything he had but his house. After that, Max Connor disappeared. I didn't hear anything about him for about a year. Then I picked up the paper one morning, and there he was. He'd shot himself with his service revolver. Dixon Connor found him lying on his bed wearing his dress blues, medals pinned to his chest. A memory like that eats at a man."

Donley knew.

"Then there's the cumulative effect of the painkillers Connor chases with alcohol to deaden the pain from the bullet in his back that they can't remove without permanently damaging his spine. Suffice it to say, I wouldn't put anything past the man."

Donley recalled the sight of the barrel of Connor's gun, as big as a sewer pipe. He started to pace, feeling both energized but anxious. "So, if he kicked in the door, there had to be a reason. Right?"

Ross crossed his arms. "You got a theory?"

Donley ran a hand through his hair. "Maybe he killed Bennet and planted the evidence to frame Father Martin."

"If that were true, why screw up the evidence? Why not just plant it and let someone find it?"

Donley shook his head. "I don't know."

"Theories without motivation aren't much good. Ninety-nine percent of all murderers have a motive: money, jealousy, revenge. Maybe one percent kill for pleasure. Those are your psychopaths. Connor is not that one percent. Did he have anything against your guy?"

Donley continued to pace. "Father Martin said they sparred a few times over the shelter, but nothing that would warrant something like this. Maybe Connor is a closet homosexual, you know? Maybe he likes boys—"

Ross shook his head. "Second rule: know your suspect. Connor is not a closet homosexual. He detests them as much as he detests women and minorities on the force."

"OK, what theory would you start with?"

Ross rocked back in his chair. "A guy like Connor? I'd guess revenge above anything else."

Donley stopped pacing, a thought coming to him. "Connor showed up at San Francisco General on Christmas Eve to talk with a young man from the shelter he put in the hospital the night they arrested Father Tom. Why would he do that unless maybe he was looking for something?"

"What are you getting at?"

"Maybe I'm coming at this from the wrong angle. Maybe Connor didn't kick the door in because he wanted to plant evidence. Maybe he thought there was something inside the office he wanted. Maybe that's why he broke open the desk and the file cabinets."

"What'd the young man say?"

"I don't know. After Connor's visit, he took off. I haven't been able to find him."

"So how do you know this happened?"

"Because I was at the hospital and tried to talk to him."

"Christmas Eve?"

"That's the night I got the call about Father Martin being beaten. I missed Connor by minutes."

Ross folded his hands in his lap. "Christmas Eve. That's admirable."

"I owe it to Lou. The archdiocese is his biggest client."

"Bullshit," Ross said. "I know a lot of attorneys who wouldn't have done what you did, no matter how big the client."

Donley looked to the framed photographs and certificates on Ross's shelves. He suspected Frank Ross, once a decorated police officer, wasn't sitting in a Tenderloin office that smelled of mold by choice. Something had happened in his past that had relegated him to this life.

"All right. I'll tell you straight up. No bullshit. I need to exorcise some demons from my past to get on with my life, and I think defending Father Tom might help me do that."

Ross stared at him, but for a brief moment, his eyes flicked to the photographs on the shelves.

"So, will you help me?" Donley asked.

Ross ran a hand across his chin and looked down at the flashing light on his answering machine. "I have a client who is not going to be too happy with me. He'd like his deposit back, and I'm not inclined to give it to him. He lied to me. Common sense says he should go away quietly, but he's a lawyer, and no offense to you, they don't usually have much common sense."

Donley smiled and picked up the phone. "What's his number?"

Father Martin had told Donley he'd chosen the location for his shelter, six blocks west of the Polk Gulch, because it was an easy walk straight up O'Farrell and Ellis streets. The four square blocks that ran north and south between Geary and Ellis and east to west from Van Ness to Polk represented the mouth of The Gulch. Ellis was a main tributary, a one-way street that emptied onto the main artery, Polk Street. At night, Polk Street was alive with local bars, trendy restaurants, and not-so-trendy liquor stores, corner markets, adult-video stores, and an occasional fast-food eatery.

Ross drove the Cadillac past the shelter. Yellow police ribbons criss-crossed the front entrance, and an unhappy-looking police officer stood on the top step with his hands shoved deep in his pockets. He kept his shoulders turned to avoid the cold winds blowing small tornadoes of dirt and litter up the street.

"Overkill," Ross said. He turned the corner and drove down an alley so narrow, Donley thought the sides of the Cadillac would scrape the buildings' concrete walls, but the big car emerged unscathed.

"You always want to start with the crime scene," Ross said.

"I told you, I don't have time to get a motion filed for an expedited view," Donley said.

"No, you don't." Ross turned right on Ellis and parked next to a ten-foot-high, chain-link fence enclosing a square slab of concrete.

The back side of the building formed one of the walls in the park. Amid graffiti and gang symbols, someone had spray-painted a square approximating a baseball strike zone. Round marks indicated where a ball had been repeatedly thrown. The park was twenty feet lower than the front entrance to the building on Eddy Street, a configuration not uncommon in San Francisco because of its steep hills. Buildings were pitched on slopes. A jungle gym sat atop a rubber mat that looked like a puzzle missing several of the interlocking pieces.

"Show me that map again. Where was the priest before he found the kid?"

Donley took out the sheet of paper with the crude sketch Father Martin had drawn during their visit. "At seven that evening, he went here, to his office, to pay bills and do paperwork. At about ten minutes after nine, he put the log of residents in his Bible and locked both in his desk. Then he got up to lock the front door to the building." Donley used his finger to demonstrate Father Martin leaving the office and walking toward the front entrance. "He said he stalled and went to the dormitory. That's the room here, at the opposite end of the hall. He stayed there for a few minutes, talking with a new kid who had checked in that night, then he left to lock the front door."

"I assume the kid is long gone."

"I would assume so, but if we can find Danny Simeon, he can vouch for Father Tom's presence in the dormitory."

"Simeon's the guy Dixon Connor visited in the hospital?"

"That's right."

"What does your guy say happened after he left the dorm?"

Donley finished explaining what Father Martin said happened up until the moment he found Andrew Bennet.

"What's the estimated time of death?"

"Medical examiner's preliminary assessment has it between six and nine thirty p.m. Can't be any more specific."

"What's the report say about whether the body was moved or not?"

"Inconclusive. The report indicates a blow to the back of the head but concludes the body was stabbed at the shelter."

"Somebody could have knocked Bennet out and carried him in."

"That'll be my argument—if I get to make it."

"What about the drops of blood?"

"Could have come from blood spatter or dripped from the murder weapon."

"The letter opener."

"Again, the ME can't say with certainty."

"Who wrote up the report?" Ross asked, sounding frustrated.

Donley had to dig the report out of his briefcase and flip to the last page. "A Dr. Wendle Tong."

"Dr. Undetermined," Ross said.

"What's that?"

"Tong has a well-deserved reputation of never wanting to go out on a limb and provide a definitive cause of death. They refer to him as Dr. Undetermined. That could help you." Ross looked up at the building. "Make me a list of what you want."

"You're going in?"

"Can't think of a better way."

Donley considered the building. He'd broken into more than a few during his teenage years, but now, he would be putting his career at risk. Then he thought of Father Martin turning down a plea of twenty-five years.

"If you're going in, I'm going with you." Donley folded the diagram and put it back in his pocket.

Ross shook his head. "There's not much anyone can do to me if I get caught. You have a career."

"Maybe not after Thursday," Donley said, and pushed out of the car.

Ross met him on the passenger side of the car and offered Donley a stick of gum. "Chew it good."

Donley chewed the gum as he followed Ross between a gap in the chain-link fence to the back of the building. Ross paused to study a ground-floor window protected by iron bars, then continued to an overgrown hedge. He pushed it aside, revealing a sunken stairwell. The door at the bottom had no handle, just a metal plate.

"That's got to be the door that leads to the boiler room," Donley said.

Ross looked about the playground. "At night, it would have been completely hidden." Ross walked down the steps, surveying the concrete. Donley knew he was looking for drops of blood. They found none.

They moved to a fire escape hanging from the second story, a San Francisco building-code requirement. Ross considered the lowest rung, which was out of reach, then stood with his back to the building and cupped his hands. "Give me your foot."

Donley stuck the sole of his shoe in the cup, and on the count of three, Ross lifted him up and he grabbed the lowest rung. The fire escape unfolded in a rush, like an accordion, the clang of metal echoing in the quiet canyon of the concrete park. They froze, but the sentry wasn't interested enough to leave the comfort of the front steps.

Ross followed Donley up the fire escape stairs, which swayed and shook, to a landing outside a locked door. Ross searched the door frame for an alarm before kneeling and removing a black-leather case from his blazer.

Donley took the piece of gum from his mouth. "Do you want my gum?"

Ross looked at it with disgust. "Why would I want your gum?"

"I assumed you needed it to cut off the alarm or something."

Ross shook his head. "You've been watching way too much television. You looked nervous. Chewing gum helps relieve anxiety."

Donley must have looked unconvinced.

"Seriously, it's a medical fact," Ross said, sliding on a pair of surgical gloves. He handed Donley a second pair, then unzipped the case, revealing a set of stainless-steel tools.

"Tools of the trade?" Donley asked, putting on his gloves.

"I confiscated it from a burglar when I was a beat cop. The deputy DA used it to convict the guy, and I expressed admiration for the stuff. I like things like this. Don't ask me why. Bet he never thought I'd use it to break into a building."

"Can you?"

Ross smiled. "Oh ye of little faith. Time me." He removed a miniature can of graphite spray and looked at Donley. "I'm serious. Time me. I like to challenge myself."

Donley played with the buttons on the side of his watch. "OK, MacGyver. Go."

Ross sprayed the lock, explaining the graphite freed the tumblers of dirt and grime. He then explained that he was using an Allen wrench and a tool known as a "rake" to apply force to the lock and worked to free the tumblers. After several attempts, the lock clicked. He turned the handle and pushed open the door. "Time?"

Donley looked at his watch. "Two minutes twenty-three seconds."

Ross smiled and put away the tools.

Inside, they walked down the hall past a small kitchen and a larger room with a worn-looking pool table. At the end of the hallway, they came to a closed door. Ross turned the knob and pushed it open, revealing metal-framed beds.

"Dormitory," Donley whispered.

"Reminds me of the army," Ross said.

Six of the beds had covers thrown to the side. "How many were here that night?" Ross asked.

"Father Martin said eight checked in, including Bennet."

Ross nodded to two beds still made. "Maybe someone else besides Bennet wasn't planning on staying."

They left the dormitory. Donley's shoes squeaked as they made their way down the linoleum to the other end of the hall, stopping at a door near the stairwell.

"Should be the office," Donley said, referring to the diagram.

The lock had been busted. Ross pushed open the door and stepped in. Donley followed. The space was cramped, with a metal desk and a three-drawer, green file cabinet. Athletic lockers lined a wall. The padlocks had been broken. Donley opened each locker. Inside, he found cash, rings, gold chains, cigarettes, and a Walkman tape player.

"Good instincts," Ross said, keeping his voice low. "Someone *was* looking for something, but it wasn't money or something they could pawn."

As Ross stepped to the window and looked down at the front entrance to ensure the police officer had remained there, Donley turned his attention to the desk. The locks on the drawers had also been punched in. He pulled open the upper right-hand drawer. The Bible with the log of occupants was not there. He checked the other drawers but did not find it.

"It's not here," he said.

Ross looked in the drawers. "You sure he said the desk?"

"I thought so. Maybe he meant the file cabinet." Donley turned his attention to the top drawer. "This is where Connor claims to have found the photographs."

The manila files inside the cabinet were neatly arranged and individually tabbed.

"Somebody this anal isn't likely to leave the murder weapon lying on the desk," Ross said.

Donley did not find the Bible.

He pulled open a door at the back of the office, revealing a room no bigger than a walk-in closet with a metal-framed bed. Hooks screwed into the wooden sill beneath a small window served as a place to hang clothes. A lamp had been mounted to the wall over the head of the bed near a shelf holding half a dozen novels. Father Martin liked thrillers. On the wall above the bed hung a small crucifix. Splinter cracks radiated from the nail in the plaster. If Father Martin was to spend the rest of his life in a cramped jail cell, he was well prepared to do so.

But there was no sign of the Bible or logbook.

Donley walked back into the office. "It's not here."

"And it wasn't on the list of evidence they took that night?"

"No."

"Then somebody had to have taken it," Ross said. "Come on. We've got to keep moving." He started for the door. "Let's check out the recreation room."

Across the hall, yellow police tape crisscrossed two tall doors. Ross reached under the tape, pushed open the door, and ducked into the room. It reminded Donley of the many gymnasiums found in the upper stories of city buildings in which he'd played as a kid. There was only so much space for concrete parks. Basketball hoops hung on the walls at each end of the room. A knotted climbing rope dangled motionless near a pegboard. At the front of the room, a white cloth covered a folding table set up beneath a wooden crucifix. The image of Christ, head bowed, eyes closed, hung limply from the wood. The Nativity scene was to its left.

Dried blood, nearly black in color, saturated a small wooden manger stuffed with straw. Donley looked away, moving to the metal door behind the altar. Painted the same color as the wall, the door was almost imperceptible. He pushed it open. Heavy and spring-loaded, it shut automatically. Had he not braced it, it would have shut with a thud. He opened it again and examined the other side. Like the door at the bottom of the stairs in the park, it had no handle, only a metal plate.

As Donley started into the stairwell, Ross grabbed him by the collar. When he turned, Ross had a finger to his lips. He pointed with the other hand to the waffled sole of a shoe sticking out from under the cloth-draped altar.

"Let's get out of here," he said. "We'll go through the boiler room."

Ross let the metal door slam closed and released the snap of his shoulder holster.

The cloth covering the altar fluttered, and a boy crawled out backward, feet first. He stood, took one look at Ross and Donley, and started running. Donley caught him halfway across the room, subdued him with an armlock, and walked him back.

"Just take it easy, and tell us what you're doing here," Ross said.

The kid looked to be in his late teens, his red hair shaved on one side and long and straight on the other. He wore a silver ring in his right nostril, faded blue jeans, and heavy black work boots. A black T-shirt with a skull and crossbones and an unbuttoned, long-sleeve flannel shirt completed the ensemble. He didn't respond.

Donley tried a softer approach. "What's your name?"

The kid continued to study the linoleum.

"Look," Ross said, "if you won't talk to us here, I have to take you downtown. You know the routine. So, tell me what you're doing here."

The boy lifted his head. "Nothing."

"Strange place to be doing nothing," Ross said. "How long have you been staying here doing nothing?"

"Just last night."

"Never before last night?"

"No."

"Then why did you stay last night?"

The kid shrugged. Ross looked to Donley and arched his eyebrows to indicate he wasn't buying it.

"Were you here last Wednesday?" Donley asked.

"No."

"You wouldn't lie to us, would you?" Ross asked, making the question sound rhetorical.

"No."

"Liar."

"Do you know what happened that night?" Donley asked.

The kid shook his head.

"Really? Didn't hear a thing?" Ross said.

"No." The kid shifted his gaze between Donley and Ross. He said, "Fine, I heard the priest killed that kid. We all heard it."

"Did you know Andrew Bennet?" Donley asked.

"Not really."

"Not really, or not at all?" Ross asked.

"Not really."

"Wasn't well liked, was he?" Ross said. "Did heavy drugs, didn't he?"

"I don't know. I didn't know him."

"Heroin, crack, crystal meth. He was a junkie, wasn't he?"

Another shrug.

Donley couldn't help but feel sorry for the kid. "How old are you?"

"I don't know."

"You don't know how old you are?" Ross said.

"My mom wasn't big on birthdays," the kid said, voice dripping sarcasm.

"Where's your mom?" Donley asked.

The kid smirked. "Guess." He continued to shift from foot to foot.

"You need to go to the bathroom?" Ross asked. "You look like you got ants in your pants. You know that's a tell when a person is lying."

The kid stopped shifting.

Donley said, "You know a guy named Danny Simeon? Worked here at the shelter."

He shook his head. "I told you, I've never been here before."

"How did you get in here?" Ross asked.

"Window in the kitchen," he said. "There's a dumpster to stand on."

Ross looked to Donley and shrugged. "Would have been easier." He reached into his pocket and handed the kid a business card. "Put this in your pocket. I want you to ask around, talk to all your buddies. I want the names of anyone who stayed here the night Bennet was killed. You call me at that number tomorrow at noon, and tell me what you've found out. You don't call, and I'll come looking for you."

The kid reached for the card, but Ross did not release it. "I'll find you. You know that, right?"

◆ ◆ ◆

Dixon Connor watched Frank Ross come out the back door from the boiler room, followed by the red-haired kid and the lawyer, Peter Donley. "Frank Ross," Connor said to himself.

He raised the newspaper as Ross and the lawyer drove past in the Cadillac. Less than a minute later, the red-haired kid was at the passenger's-side window.

Connor pushed the door open. "Get in." Red slid into the passenger seat. "Did you find it?" Connor asked.

Red shook his head. "I didn't see any book with names in it."

"What did they want?"

"I don't know."

Connor whipped the back of his hand across Red's mouth, splitting his lip. Blood dripped onto the kid's shirt. "You get blood in my new car, and you are really going to be in a lot of pain. Now, tell me what they wanted."

Red held his shirt to his mouth. "They wanted to know if I knew someone named Simeon," he mumbled. "They wanted to know if I was there that night."

"What did you tell them?"

"I said no."

Connor grabbed Red's hand, forced open the boy's index finger, and put the first knuckle between the blades of pruning shears. "If I find out you're lying to me, I'll start with the first knuckle and take them off one at a time. You understand me?"

Red's eyes went wide. "I didn't say anything. I swear."

Connor let go of the hand. "Get the hell out of my car. You're stinking it up."

Chapter 17

Donley and Ross went in search of Danny Simeon. Ross said he recalled the Grub Steak, which was where Father Tom said Simeon kept a room, but that restaurant had gone out of business, explaining why Donley had trouble finding it.

Ross rubbed the cold from his hands and turned on the heater. It brought the distinct smell of hamburgers, which Donley assumed was from the fast-food bags discarded on the floor.

"I'm hungry," Ross said. "You hungry?"

Donley had been staring out the window, recalling his first memory of his father beating him, and how close he'd come to running away and possibly living on the streets, maybe like the kids Father Tom was trying to help. He couldn't remember the reason for the beating; there didn't need to be one. His father beat him for any number of digressions, from spilling his cereal over the rim of his bowl to talking back. Mostly, he beat him because he was alive.

"Hey? You with me?" Ross asked.

Donley turned from the window. "What do you think makes a kid like that run away from home?"

Ross shrugged. "First thing you got to understand is that with these kids, you never know what's the truth and what's fiction. They'll bullshit the hell out of you, and they're adept at it. It's like some Vietnam vets; they all have a story. They all experienced combat and watched women and children being shot and mutilated. They all had their lives ruined. Listen, I was there, and I know that some did, no doubt about it, but for others, it's just a sob story to separate you from some of your money. With these kids, sometimes it's drugs; sometimes it's broken and abusive homes. Sometimes it's just the kid. Did you believe him?"

Donley shook his head. "Something didn't seem right."

"Like why he was there?"

"Not the first cold night we've had," Donley agreed.

"And if he's never stayed at the shelter, it means he has other places to go. These kids usually stick to what they know."

"You really think he'll call?"

Ross chuckled. "Stranger things have happened. I just wanted to give him the option and let him think I wasn't done with him."

"What if he runs?"

"Where?" Ross looked over at him. "Where's that kid going to run?" Ross shook his head. "People say the same thing about the homeless. 'Why don't they go someplace warm like Florida?' Like they could just pack up the family station wagon and drive three thousand miles across country. They stay where it's familiar, where they know the services and the angles, where they have a network. Those kids have no place to go. They don't trust anyone. That's the sad part."

Donley knew.

They parked at the corner of Polk and Larkin. The Gulch in the morning was everything it was not at night—quiet, deserted, mostly subdued. The lunch crowd wouldn't arrive for an hour. Donley looked up at a neon sign of a green cactus wearing black sunglasses. The cactus held an umbrella to shade it from a bright tropical sun. Tequila Dan's.

"You sure this is the place?" Donley asked, considering the knotted-wood facade and bamboo-pole railings that made the restaurant look like a tropical shack dropped in the middle of the city.

"This used to be the Grub Steak," Ross said. "Before that, it was a hamburger-and-fries joint. Believe it or not, it used to look like a cable car. I'll bet you ten bucks you can't get a hamburger or steak in here now."

"No wonder I couldn't find it," Donley said.

Donley fed the parking meter and followed Ross up the wooden ramp.

Inside the restaurant, seashells and other beach finds filled a fishing net draped over the entrance. To Donley's right, colorful fish swam in a large tropical fish tank. Reggae music and chirping birds played at a moderate level from speakers attached to beams made to look like beach logs and palm trees. Weathered tables and chairs sat beneath thatched roofs.

"Can't believe what an active imagination and a good bank loan can do," Ross said. They took stools at a horseshoe-shaped bar decorated to look like a Club Med bar at a resort in the Caribbean. A bartender in a flowered shirt and khaki shorts put paper coasters in front of them. Then he picked up a stack of playing cards, separating and burying the top card using just one hand, like a magician. They ordered coffee.

The bartender set down two mugs and filled them from a coffeepot. Ross stirred in three packets of sweetener. "Looking for a kid named Danny Simeon. Sometimes goes by the name Dingo."

The bartender set the coffeepot back on a burner and returned to flipping the cards, showing them the ace of spades, burying it, and flipping it up again. "Who are you?" He asked the question without stopping the card trick. His thick mustache draped over his mouth, preventing them from seeing his lips move, like a ventriloquist act.

Ross and Donley had discussed the scenario in the car. If Simeon lived in back of the restaurant, he did so illegally. The owner and employees wouldn't be eager to talk about it, but they might to someone perceived to be a friend of Father Martin.

Donley set a business card on the counter. "I represent Father Thomas Martin. Danny Simeon may be able to help."

The bartender did not pick up the card or give any indication he read it from behind rose-tinted glasses, but the moment Donley mentioned Father Martin, the man stopped flipping the deck of cards.

"Thought you looked familiar. Saw you on the TV. How's he doing?"

"Not too good."

The bartender shook his head. "The whole thing is a tragedy."

"Father Martin said Danny kept a room in the back. I think he could be in some danger. I'm trying to find him before there's another tragedy."

The bartender paused for a second, picked up Donley's business card, twirled it between each of his fingers, and made it disappear. "Wait here."

He came back a few minutes later. "It's in the back off the bathroom." They started from their stools. "I could get in trouble for letting someone live here; just trying to help him out."

"You've got no problem with us." Donley pushed a twenty-dollar bill across the counter.

The bartender pushed it back. "Give it to the shelter."

They walked past two men studying a chessboard of odd-shaped tiki pieces. Ross stopped and studied the board, then reached down and moved a black piece. "Checkmate."

The player returned the piece to its original position, looking irritated. "Nice try. That's a rook."

Ross shrugged at Donley. "Damn thing looked like a knight."

They continued down a short hallway past a unisex bathroom to a room stocked with restaurant supplies. At the back of that room they encountered two doors. One led to an alley. On the other door someone had stenciled **PRIVATE**. Donley knocked once, turned the handle, and opened the door. He got one foot inside when he heard a sharp click.

A muscular young man sat on the edge of a bed holding a six-inch switchblade in his right hand.

Ross walked into the room without pausing. "Down, boy."

Danny Simeon had a gray blanket wrapped around his shoulders. Pale and sweating profusely, he looked sick and spoke in a halting voice. "Which one of you represents Father Tom?"

"I do," Donley said.

Simeon looked about to say something more; then his eyes rolled back in his head and he dropped the knife and slumped off the edge of the bed and onto the floor.

Ross and Donley paced Donley's living room like two expectant fathers waiting for their spouses to give birth. When Kim walked in, they asked the same question. "How is he?"

"He's better," Kim said. "But he's dehydrated and in a lot of pain. His body is fighting off the effects of the drugs they were giving him for the pain, and I doubt he's eaten or drunk much. Mostly he's weak and tired and needs to regain his strength."

"Can he talk?" Donley asked.

"Not for a while. He crashed. From how you described it, when he sat up, the blood likely rushed from his head, and he passed out. I've given him some Tylenol with codeine for the pain, which should knock him out for a while. That will give me a chance to get an IV in his arm and pump him full of fluids. But I have to go to the hospital to get that. I'd say late this afternoon, maybe tonight." She became quiet and gave Donley a look he recognized.

"What is it? What's the matter?" Donley asked.

Her eyes shifted to Ross.

Quick to pick up on the signal, Ross excused himself. "I'll wait in the car."

After Ross had left, Kim said, "I'd feel more comfortable if he was in a hospital."

"He's not safe there, Kim, and I doubt he would go."

"Is it safe having him here? I'm worried about Benny."

At the moment, Benny was at day care.

Donley rubbed his forehead. He'd asked himself the same questions. "I didn't know where else to take him. I knew I couldn't take him to the hospital. I thought of you. I'm sorry. Listen, Father Martin says he's a good kid. And nobody knows he's here. But if it makes you feel better, why don't you and Benny stay at your mother and father's for a few days? At least until I figure out what's going on."

"I don't want to split us up. I'm worried about you."

"I'm fine. And I'll feel better if I know you and Benny are safe."

Frank Ross opened the front door and stuck his head in.

"I'm sorry to interrupt," he said. "We need to go."

"What is it?" Donley asked.

"Someone who might be able to help."

◆ ◆ ◆

Back inside the Cadillac, Donley fastened his seat belt and looked back up at the front window of his house. Kim was not there. "Everything all right?" Ross asked.

"She's worried about me."

"My wife's been worrying about me for twenty years. She worried every night I was on duty. Worrying is a part of loving."

"Yeah, I guess. I'm worried about her and my son."

"You got a boy?"

"Benny. He's almost three."

"How long have you been working for Lou Giantelli?" Ross asked.

"Little over three years; Lou's my uncle."

"Small world. He was my attorney."

"Really," Donley said, though he'd suspected it.

"There was a time when you couldn't find anyone in law enforcement who *didn't* know Lou Giantelli. He's represented a lot of cops. Word of mouth spread quickly he was a good guy to know."

"Does Lou representing you have to do with why you're no longer a cop?"

"It has more to do with why I'm still alive."

"I didn't mean to pry."

"No worries."

After a beat, Donley changed subjects. "How old is your son?"

Ross didn't answer.

"I saw a picture in your office."

Ross adjusted in his seat. "He would have been nine last month."

Donley felt his stomach drop. "Frank, I'm sorry."

Ross nodded. "My son disappeared two years ago. He walked out the front door and never came home, disappeared without a trace."

Donley sat stunned, uncertain what to say, a hollow pit in his stomach.

"We searched for a long time, and that kept me going, that hope that we would find him. But every day you lose a little more hope. I couldn't sleep. When I did, the nightmares usually woke me. When I was awake, the nightmare was real." He shook his head, fighting off his emotions. "I developed a little problem with the bottle." He looked at Donley and smiled wanly. "My name is Frank, and I am an alcoholic. I have been sober seven months, twenty-two days."

"Congratulations."

Ross looked out the windshield. "Yeah. The end of the day used to hit me like a ton of bricks. That was when I was forced to spend time with my thoughts. When I didn't feel like thinking, I climbed into a chair with a bottle of Jack Daniel's. It helped for a while, but you can do that only so long before your world crashes. One night I drank until two in the morning, passed out, woke up at five or six, and started in again. My wife had left me by then. She was grieving in her own way. There was no one to stop me. No one to tell me I was in no condition to drive. I ran a red light and hit a van with a mother and two kids on their way to school."

"Were they hurt?" Donley asked.

"Not seriously, thank God. But that was right about the time California was coming down hard on drunk drivers. The family got a lawyer, and it got ugly. Your uncle handled it for me."

As Ross told the story, something familiar about it caused a spark of recognition. "I remember that case. I think the last thing was the insurance company settling. I might have even written a coverage opinion."

"Like I said," Ross continued, "your uncle was a name around the station. He persuaded the insurance company to pick up my defense, so I could keep my home and what little savings I had. Then he got the department to put me on leave, so I wouldn't lose my pension and keep open the chance that I might someday be reinstated—as remote a possibility as that is. He kept me out of jail by getting the court to agree to a diversionary program for alcoholics. Then he went and found my wife to go through it all with me. I'm most grateful for that. He didn't have to do that."

"That was you?" Donley asked.

"That was me," Ross said.

Twenty minutes later, they were seated at a table in the back of a narrow and crowded Bon Appetit sandwich shop on Market Street. Donley seasoned a roast-beef sandwich with salt and pepper. Frank Ross lifted a spoon of clam chowder from a sourdough-bread bowl, blowing on it before tasting it.

"Nothing better on a cold day," Ross said, shaking what seemed like an entire pepper shaker into the bowl.

"I thought you said we were going to meet a friend?" Donley asked.

"Are you complaining?"

"No. I'm actually starving." Donley bit into his sandwich.

Ross nodded to the door while raising the spoon to his lips. "Here he comes."

Donley looked back over his shoulder as a short, curly-haired man with large-framed glasses walked in the door and surveyed the tables. When he saw Ross, the man's eyes widened, and his smile broadened. He walked toward them, leaning forward like a man traveling downhill, his feet trying to catch up to his body.

"Hello, hero." He pushed the glasses onto the bridge of his nose and slid into a chair next to Donley.

"Sam Goldman, metro editor at the *Chronicle*," Ross said to Donley. "Can I buy you lunch, Sam?"

Goldman adjusted the knot of his tie. "You know me. I never stop long enough to eat. It's my own diet. I call it work."

Ross turned to Donley. "Sam was my journalism instructor during a very brief career choice in college. He's also the best journalist in the city."

Goldman beamed. "Don't you believe a word he says, friend. He's buttering me up for something."

Ross sipped chowder off his spoon. "Sam, this is Peter Donley."

Goldman looked like he'd just walked in on his own surprise party. "You're kidding."

Donley smiled. "Guilty as charged."

Goldman leaned across the table. "You? Or the priest?" He laughed and glanced at Ross. "So, this is why you called the other day with all the questions. You're working for the priest?"

"Not all the questions." Ross put down his spoon, ripped off a piece of bread, and dipped it into his bowl. "But yeah, I'm working for the priest."

"Best detective I know," Goldman said to Donley. "Frank Ross is like Allstate Insurance. You're in good hands. Lou Giantelli taught you well."

"Lou's his uncle, Sam."

Goldman redirected his attention to Donley. "You're full of surprises, hero." He seemed to be studying Donley's face. "Do I know you from someplace else?"

Donley's last bite of his sandwich lodged in his throat. He washed it down with a sip of Coke. "I don't think so," he said.

Goldman looked at him like he was trying to figure out a puzzle. "You sure? I'm good with faces and like Webster's with names."

"Donley's pretty common," he said. "And I've been in the news a bit lately."

Goldman kept his eyes locked on Donley's face. "It'll come to me." He smiled and broke eye contact.

"Sam has met just about every important person in the world who's come through this city," Ross said, "but he's not easily impressed. He likes a good story better."

"Those people put their pants on one leg at a time, just like you and me." Goldman turned back to Ross. "Did I tell you I met the Pope last year? How do you like that? I had my photographer take a picture of the Jewish kid kissing the Pope's ring. They blew it up and put a poster on the door to my office. We howled for weeks." He turned to Donley. "So, what's the story? Did the priest kill that kid?"

"Off the record?"

"Careful," Ross said between another spoonful of clam chowder.

Goldman raised his hands as if surrendering. "OK, hero, off the record."

Donley said, "We're all going to find out."

"So, what do you got for me, Sam?" Ross asked.

"Aside from never getting to see you anymore, I got some information for you on the victim. Seems he wasn't exactly a choirboy."

"I figured that."

Goldman smiled like a kid with a secret. "It gets better, friend." He opened a black satchel and pulled out sheets of paper. "The kid was a street prostitute, but according to my reporter who wrote that sidebar the other day, he was older, seventeen."

Ross looked dismayed. "Seventeen is older? What am I, a dinosaur?"

"If you are, then I'm a fossil." He turned to Donley. "She tells me they're on the street at ten and eleven, sometimes younger. By the time most kids are learning how to drive and thinking about the junior prom, these kids have already passed middle age. It's a tragedy."

"Just go down Haight Street on a Friday night," Ross said. "They're still romanticizing the hippies and flower children. They end up hooked on heroin, one step from death's door."

Goldman nodded. "She's trying to do a feature on the kid, but nobody down there is saying much, not even to her, and she looks like she could belong—purple hair and more body piercings than a bulletin board. She says they're all scared. They say kids are dying."

Ross gave Donley a look but didn't say anything. "So, what do we know about the victim?" he asked Goldman.

"The kid landed in Hollywood by bus, going to be a star. After two years living on the streets of Santa Monica, Venice Beach, and West Hollywood, he ended up in the Gulch a junkie. He was also apparently a con man and petty thief. His juvenile records were sealed, but we got a copy of them after he died. He's got a rap sheet as long as *War and Peace*. Possession. Intent to distribute. Breaking and entering. Car theft. But it's the one not on there I think you might find most interesting."

"Yeah?" Ross said. "What is it?"

"Extortion."

Ross stopped the spoon halfway to his mouth and lowered it back to the bread bowl.

Goldman smiled. "I thought that might interest you." He turned to Donley and pointed to his temple. "I still don't use a computer. I type off a portable, and I store the information up here. When I went through the rap sheet, something clicked, and it all came back to me."

"What was it?" Ross asked.

"A little story a while back about a kid blackmailing men, threatening to expose them for having sex with a minor. Most were scared enough to pay the money."

Frank Ross nodded. "I remember that story. That was *this* kid?"

"That was this kid."

"What happened?" Donley asked.

"The exact specifics might forever remain a mystery, hero. There was no court proceeding."

"How did that happen?" Donley asked.

"Don't know, but the kid got off easy. Not even a note on his record."

"Who was he blackmailing?" Ross asked.

"A mover and shaker in the restaurant business who owned a trendy nightclub south of Market Street. Ring any bells?"

"Yeah, it does," Ross said, looking like he actually heard bells ringing.

"Jack Devine," Goldman said.

Ross snapped his fingers. "That's it. That's the name." Ross turned to Donley. "From what I remember, Devine said the kid made his acquaintance after a big spread in the newspaper hyping Devine and his latest restaurant."

"The kid wanted money," Goldman said, "and kept after him."

"And Devine was married to a wealthy girl with deep San Francisco roots."

"Ruth Catchings," Goldman interjected.

"Ruth Catchings," Ross said.

"Devine paid at first, close to a couple thousand bucks," Goldman said. "But then the kid got nasty and really started putting the screws to him. Devine didn't have much choice but to go to the police."

"They did a little undercover sting operation of their own, and from what I was told, the police tape is not pleasant," Ross finished.

"Where's Devine now?" Donley asked.

"Great minds think alike, hero." His eyes grew wide. "Maybe a revenge killing; wouldn't that be something? They'd make a movie and star Jack Nicholson. Here's Johnny!" Goldman's roar caught the attention of the adjacent table. "Apparently, after the little sting operation, Devine sold the restaurants, left San Francisco, and took his family to the wine country. He owns a house and grows grapes near Saint Helena. According to our reporter, Devine is edgy. Says about fifty witnesses will confirm he was at the winery that night, no further comment, and he'll sue the pants off us if we print another story."

"Extortion," Ross mused while ripping a chunk of bread from the top of his bowl and wiping at the remnants of his clam chowder as he glanced at Donley. "How about that?"

"Story is going to run front page in the paper tomorrow morning. Care to make a statement, friend?" Goldman asked Donley.

Donley shook his head. "I don't think so."

Goldman stood. "OK, I got to move. Too long in one place, and I grow roots." He took another look at Donley. "You sure I don't know you?" he asked.

"I'd remember you," Donley said, causing Ross to laugh.

◆ ◆ ◆

Ross and Donley drove across the Bay Bridge in the direction of Saint Helena, Napa Valley wine country.

"He's quite a character," Donley said of Goldman. "Is he always that animated?"

"That was subdued," Ross said as if surprised. "And he's not a character. He's the genuine article. With Sam Goldman, what you see is what you get. He loves life, and he loves being a newspaperman."

"I couldn't tell what he liked better, having the information or giving it to us," Donley agreed.

"Make no mistake about that," Ross cautioned. "Sam's a reporter. Getting information is what makes a man like Sam click. Once he's got it, it's old news. He's already looking for the next story." He looked over at Donley. "He'll be hot on your trail. He won't stop thinking about how he knows you until he figures it out."

Donley tried to dismiss it. "Probably high school football. I had a lot of stories written about me back then."

"You were a star, huh?"

"Something like that."

Ross nodded to the white lunch bag on the cherry-red seat that contained half of the roast-beef sandwich. "You appeared to have lost your appetite awful quick."

Donley changed the subject. "You think this guy Devine could have killed Bennet?"

"Don't know, but I doubt it."

"You said motivation was number one. Devine had the motivation."

"*Had* being the operative word," Ross said. "Devine apparently got away with it. Why would he look a gift horse in the mouth and come back for more?"

"Because he can't help himself; I mean, if we go with the assumption that he's a pedophile."

"Maybe, but I'm betting old Jack Devine never wanted to see or hear about Andrew Bennet again."

"Maybe Bennet found him."

"Again, not likely. I don't see Bennet getting on a bus for the wine country. But let's not get ahead of ourselves. Let's see what kind of guy Jack is and what he has to say."

"What if this guy Devine wasn't the only person Bennet blackmailed?"

"I like that assumption better."

"He could have made the wrong enemy."

"Plausible," Ross agreed.

The lightbulb turned on for Donley. "The lockers. Someone broke into the lockers looking for something. What if what they were looking for was something Andrew Bennet brought to the shelter with him? Goldman said that Bennet was blackmailing people. He had to have some evidence, something to make them concerned." The idea came to him quickly. "Photographs. Photographs like the ones Connor claims he found in the office. Maybe Bennet tried to blackmail the wrong guy. Connor?"

"Like I said, not likely," Ross said. "But it could have been the priest."

"I believe my guy," Donley said. "What about someone Connor was working for?"

"Again, I don't see Connor working for a pedophile, no matter how much the guy was willing to pay."

Donley gave it further consideration. "You said revenge was likely what motivates someone like Connor. Maybe he wanted the photographs to blackmail someone himself."

"I like that theory a lot better," Ross said.

An hour and a half later, they drove through Saint Helena, a quaint town of trendy antique shops, expensive restaurants, and bed-and-breakfasts nestled in the heart of Napa Valley. The businesses appeared to be keeping winter hours; many of the storefront windows were already dark. Saint Helena was one of a string of wine-country towns serving as weekend escapes for the residents of San Francisco and its crowded Bay Area suburbs. The valley had become a getaway retreat for those with a lot of money seeking warm weather and wine tasting amid lush valley brush and two-hundred-year-old oak trees. They built multimillion-dollar homes with tennis courts, swimming pools, vineyards, and guesthouses. It was here that Frank Ross and Peter Donley would find Jack Devine.

Donley spotted the two rock pillars, a landmark that a woman at a restaurant had provided. No other markers identified the Devine estate from the road. As the Cadillac bounced up a narrow dirt road cut through tree limbs and brush, Donley was convinced Ross was right, that Jack Devine wanted it that way. He wanted to be lost. He wanted the shrubs and grass and oak trees to grow over the road and his shady past. Then Ross steered the Cadillac around a corner, and they came upon a mammoth wood-and-river-rock structure that was anything but subtle. Towering above the tree line, the building was surrounded by well-manicured grounds with picnic tables, gravel footpaths lined by flower beds, and antique horse carriages.

What Donley initially mistook to be Devine's home turned out to be the facade to a winery. They had apparently driven in the back entrance. The main road, paved asphalt, circled through gnarled grapevines stretched across sloped hills at the top of which sat an equally impressive mansion that looked like it belonged in the hills of Tuscany. Jack Devine had apparently landed on his feet following his exposure as a pedophile. He had survived the pain and humiliation quite nicely, thank you.

Ross parked in one of several spaces open along the side of the winery. "Not bad," he said, speaking for them both. "Not bad at all." They pushed out of the car.

"Let's get the lay of the land," Ross said.

They circled the building and found several parked cars at the back, including an emerald-green Mercedes parked in a spot reserved for J. Devine. The sign was unnecessary. The Mercedes came with a personalized license plate: DEVINE.

"So much for Jack seeking anonymity and a little humility," Ross said.

At the front entrance, Donley pulled open a mammoth redwood door and stepped into a peaked-roof structure. Vines and plants hung from the beams of a cathedral ceiling, and a small pond and waterfall trickled into a lazy stream along a gravel path that led to a tasting bar. A young woman stood beside a muscled, silver-haired man aglow with orange skin that beamed tanning salon. They both wore white-knit shirts with an image of the winery embroidered just above the left breast.

"We'll be closing in fifteen minutes," the man said pleasantly. "We don't have much of a selection left, but I can pour you a glass of our chardonnay. We're going to be putting two out to market this year, and both are particularly nice."

"No, thanks," Ross said, getting to the point without pleasantries. "We're here to see Jack Devine."

"Jack?"

"He's expecting us. We have an appointment."

The man tapped the counter, uncertain what to do or say. Ross's no-nonsense stare apparently convinced him. "OK, I'll let him know. Can I tell him who it is?"

"Tom and Jerry," Ross said, breaking into a wide grin. "I'm Tom." The man turned and left the counter.

Donley walked around the winery, considering wood and metal wine racks, corks, books, T-shirts, and other novelty items. Air-conditioning chilled the room. It took longer than it should have for the man to return. When he did, he was still smiling, but now it looked forced.

"I'm sorry. Jack left early today."

After an hour-and-a-half drive, Donley was not ready to go home without speaking to Devine, but before he could call bullshit and tell the orange man that Devine's car was sitting in the parking lot, Ross chimed in.

"We're sorry to have troubled you; I guess we got the day wrong. Can I borrow your pen?"

The man unsnapped a pen clipped to the front of his shirt and handed it to Ross. Ross took a napkin from the counter, wrote on it, folded it in half, and handed the note and pen back to the man. "Could you do me a favor and give this to Jack when you see him? It's important. He'll want to read it *right away*."

Outside, they walked around the back of the building and waited near the Mercedes. "What are we doing?" Donley asked.

"Waiting."

"For what?"

Ross looked at his watch, then at the back door. "That."

The man storming out of the building was dressed in a tennis outfit and looked the part with a trim build, sandy-blond hair pulled into a ponytail, and a red face that was definitely not from the sun or regular visits to a tanning salon. Jack Devine marched forward like a disgruntled five-year-old sent off to bed. He spoke before his feet stopped moving, a shrill whine.

"You have no right to be here. You have no right to be here." The only thing missing from his tantrum was stomping feet.

"Take it easy, Jack." Ross made the name sound less like Devine's first name, and more like an insult. He sat on the hood of Devine's Mercedes, and the car sagged beneath his weight. "Your winery is open to the public, and last time I checked, we're part of the public." He looked at Donley. "Aren't we part of the public?"

"We're as public as they get," Donley said. "Nothing private about us."

"I called my lawyer. He's on his way. You can talk to him. I have nothing to say to either of you." It was a bluff and not a very good one. For one, Devine was standing there when he could have stayed in his office. Whatever Ross wrote on the napkin, it had worked.

Ross let out an exaggerated sigh. "You didn't call your lawyer, Jack, because you don't want to drag your past into your cozy life here in the Napa Valley. The way I figure it, you'd like to forget all about the past."

"I did. I called my lawyer," Devine said, becoming less and less convincing, if that were possible. "My next call will be to the police."

Ross stood. His enormous size dwarfed Devine. "Tell you what, Jack. I'll make that call for you. You see, on the drive up here, I had a friend of mine go on the computer and look up whether you were a registered sex offender. Imagine my surprise when she told me no." Ross made a face like he was shocked. "I assume that was part of the deal your lawyer cut with the DA. Am I right?"

Devine did not answer. His coloring had gone from red to a chalky white.

"You managed to avoid just about everything except the papers, didn't you, Jack? Well, that will change with just one call to the *Napa Valley Register*. Big story for a small town like this—big man on campus a possible murder suspect in the death of a teenage prostitute he once used to frequent. You feel like moving again? I hear Idaho is nice in the summers, but the winters can be a bitch."

Devine's chest sunk. He pinched his nostrils and cleared his throat.

Ross turned to Donley. "Allergies. I hate those. I hear stress can trigger them. You stressed, Jack?"

Devine removed an inhaler from his pants pocket and took a puff. Donley thought the man might have a heart attack right on the spot.

"We're not with the press," Ross said, "and we're not the police. So pull your panties out of your ass, and don't start hyperventilating on me." Ross pointed a thumb at Donley. "He represents the priest. I know you know the story, so don't bullshit us and say you don't."

"I can get you ten names that will all say I was here that night." Devine sounded like a man trying to hold his breath while talking.

"You told the reporter fifty. You lost forty alibis already?" Ross said. "That's not good."

"I haven't been back to San Francisco in over a year," Devine rushed.

"You're not missing much," Ross said. "A lot of construction. And traffic is still the shits."

"What is it you want?"

Donley said, "We want to know more about the victim, about what happened between the two of you."

"Victim?" Devine scoffed and rubbed a hand over his head as if feeling for a stray hair. Finally, he said, "Why would you want to know anything about that?"

"Because I think it might help my client. Because I think somebody is trying to frame him for a crime he didn't commit."

Devine closed his eyes. "God help him if they are."

"Why is that?" Donley asked.

Gravel crushed beneath shoes. The young woman who had been at the counter walked toward them. "Have a good night, Jack." She forced an uncertain smile before getting into a blue Toyota.

Devine gave Ross and Donley a nod to follow him. They walked through the door at the back of the building and passed several stainless-steel vats with pipes extending in various directions. At the top of a metal staircase, they followed Devine into a spacious office. Large picture windows faced the vineyards, offering a view of a fading winter sun that left traces of red and purple along the horizon. At the bottom of the valley, surrounded by a plush green lawn and oak trees, was what Donley presumed to be Devine's house and, next to it, a children's playground, complete with slides, swings, and forts, all being doused in the arc of water from a sprinkler.

"Have a seat," Devine said.

Ross and Donley sat in two of three chairs on the opposite side of an oak drafting table Devine used as a desk. His chair faced the windows. The wall behind him included framed awards for his winery and the wines it produced.

"What is it you want to know?" Devine did not hide his impatience.

Donley gathered his thoughts. The trick was to ask questions without sounding like it, and to take paths not expected. "We already have much of the police report," he said to make Devine believe he couldn't hide anything and shouldn't try.

Devine's cheeks flushed. "That file was supposed to be sealed."

"It is," Donley assured him, though he didn't know. "But people aren't as anal about those kinds of things after the person is dead. Given the nature of this crime, I argued it was relevant to my client's defense. Your name was expunged from the record."

"Then how did you find me?"

"I found the reporter who wrote the story," Ross said. "Your name was not expunged from the newspapers."

"Don't remind me. It nearly ruined me. It nearly ruined my marriage. I was humiliated. We had to leave everything behind and start over."

Devine was whining again, and Donley couldn't muster sympathy for an acknowledged pedophile living the lifestyle of the rich and famous while his former victim lay on a slab in the morgue. But now was not the time to tell Jack Devine the newspaper was about to do a rerun.

"It must have been terrible for you and your family," he said, the words leaving a bitter taste in his mouth. "I can only imagine there was a tremendous amount of pain for all of you."

Devine nodded. "It was my kids I worried about. I have two boys."

Donley pointed to a picture on the shelf behind Devine. "They look like you. How old are they?"

Devine retrieved the picture. "Kevin is nine. Mark is seven."

"They're good-looking boys." Donley smiled.

Devine put the picture down. The red had faded from his cheeks. "Obviously, they know nothing about any of this. And I plan to keep it that way."

"I understand," Donley said. "No reason not to."

Devine continued. "I'm in counseling now. It was mandatory at first, but I continue to attend on my own." Donley nodded. Devine kept talking. "My wife's family wanted her to divorce me, but we got through it."

Which explained the winery, restaurant, and otherwise cushy life-style—his wife's family might hate Jack Devine, but they loved their daughter and grandchildren, and were likely footing the bill to keep their daughter and grandchildren in the style to which they had become accustomed. Donley wondered how voluntary Devine's attendance at the counseling sessions really was. He guessed Jack was kept on a short leash.

"I'm trying to rebuild my business . . . and my family," Divine said, making the latter sound almost like an afterthought.

"That's admirable of you," Donley said.

Ross interrupted. "What can you tell us about Andrew Bennet?"

Devine made a face. "He was a despicable character. Don't get me wrong—"

"Wouldn't want to do that," Ross mumbled.

"I'm not happy that he's dead, but I'm not going to shed any tears, either. He ruined my life."

I'm sure you didn't do a lot for his life, either, Donley thought but did not say. "How did you meet him?"

Devine stared at his desk. "I was partying a lot back then; it was part of the nightclub scene." He reached into his pocket and took out a tube of ChapStick, applying it as he spoke. "When I was at the club, four or five people a night would buy me a vodka or want me to do a bump in the bathroom. My wife partied as much as I did, though her family doesn't know that." Divine looked out the window and rubbed a finger over his lips, spreading the lip balm. "It was a business, and I did what needed to be done to make the business succeed. The nightclub did well from the start because of me, but the restaurant took more time. You have to develop an identity and get some publicity. My wife's family had some connections. Her father made a couple of telephone calls, and we were featured in the *Chronicle*. I used to keep the article framed on the wall in the restaurant."

"How often did you see Bennet?" Donley asked.

"Who?"

"The victim."

"Not often. He lied. He told me he was eighteen."

"How did you find him when you wanted to see him?"

Devine shrugged. "I asked for Alphabet. That was the name I knew. I'd send my wife home and tell her I was going to close. There were places to go."

"How did he blackmail you?" Ross asked, clearly wanting Devine to get on with it.

"How?"

"Yes, how? Did he send a letter, stop by the house—"

Devine closed his eyes and shook his head. "I wish. The little fucker had a video."

Ross and Donley exchanged a glance.

"How did he get a video?" Donley asked.

Devine gave them a grim look. "I was so stupid," he said. "At first, we stayed in my car. I stuck with him, you know, in case the police were doing an undercover thing."

Donley wanted to vomit. Frank Ross looked like he'd bit into a lemon.

"One night he told me about a place he wanted to take me, a room below a video store on O'Farrell. A party room. I was pretty wasted and wasn't thinking clearly. We went there, and he turned on this strobe light and loud music. I couldn't see or hear anything." Devine cleared his throat and looked out the window. "They filmed us."

"They?" Donley asked.

"Well, I assume he had someone else filming. He had to, didn't he? Anyway, he must have seen the article in the *Chronicle* about the restaurant with my picture and name because he showed up at work one night and had a waiter hand me a copy of the videotape. I met him in the alley in back. He asked for five hundred dollars."

"And you paid it," Ross said.

"What was I supposed to do?"

"But he didn't go away," Donley said.

"No," Devine said. "He said he had copies. When I told him I wouldn't pay any more, he threatened to mail the tape to my wife. He threatened to go to my boys' school and put it in the VCR. I was up against the wall. The restaurant wasn't doing well. Two of my chefs had quit. I couldn't handle it anymore. So I went to the police. Then I had to tell my wife."

Donley had no doubt that was the order of Devine's confessions. "Did the investigation reveal the names of the other boys who did the filming?"

"I don't know."

"I'm curious," Ross asked. "How did you get the DA not to prosecute you, to let you go without even having to register as a sex offender?"

Divine shrugged. "I don't know. I left that to my father-in-law and his lawyer. He knew the governor."

"Augustus Ramsey?" Ross asked.

Devine nodded. "They knew each other through the Bohemian Club. They golfed together on Saturdays."

"Outside you said, 'God help him' when I said I thought some-one was trying to frame my client," Donley said. "Why did you say that?"

Devine looked to the window before reengaging Donley. "Because of something he said to me once when I told him I wouldn't pay."

"Bennet?"

Divine nodded. "He said he had a lot of tapes of people like me. And he said he was going to make them all pay."

"And you believe that to be true?" Donley asked.

Devine looked off again, like he was seeing all the way back to those years. "I called his bluff once and paid for it with my life," he said. "I wasn't about to call his bluff again."

◆ ◆ ◆

They drove along the same dirt path, away from the winery. With the sun having set, Ross turned on the Cadillac's headlights. The beams cast two funnel cones on the road and shimmered in the brush and tree branches. In town, the remaining storefronts in Saint Helena had darkened, the old-fashioned street lamps lighting the streets. It wasn't for half an hour, until they reached the freeway and started south, that Ross spoke, his voice subdued.

"I have to commend you. I wanted to reach across the desk and tear his face off. Tell me where in life it says that guys like Jack Devine *always* end up on their feet? Why is that?"

"It's just the way it is," Donley said. "You know that. We all know that. People say the justice system is color-blind, but it isn't. It sees color, and it sees green. It will always see green. We like to think our courts are the great equalizer between the powerful and the powerless, but more times than not, money and power still prevail. To the Jack Devines of this world, Bennet wasn't the victim because in Jack Devine's way of thinking, everything was OK because he paid for it."

"Bennet was just trying to survive," Ross said. "He wouldn't have been doing it if it wasn't for the Jack Devines of the world."

"You're preaching to the choir," Donley replied.

"He's not even sorry. That's what pisses me off most. I could tell watching him sitting there that the son of a bitch wasn't even sorry for what he did."

"I once heard a judge tell a defendant there was a difference between being sorry for his actions and being sorry he got caught," Donley said. "I agree with you. Jack Devine is only sorry he got caught."

"He's not on the road to recovery; he's on the road dictated to him by his wife and his father-in-law," Ross said.

"You're probably right." Donley watched the yellow line at the side of the road blur past the window. "That's why I kept thinking about his kids."

Ross remained agitated. "Don't worry about them. I'll bet old Jack doesn't spend much quality time alone with the boys."

"They're suffering just the same," Donley said. "They're growing up with a bad father, which is worse than growing up without a father. When I was a kid, all I wanted was for my father to leave." He continued to focus on the hypnotic yellow line. "It wasn't until Benny was born and I sat in that hospital room holding him and thinking of all the things we would do together, all the things I would teach him, that I realized the beatings weren't the worst part about having a bad father. The worst part was all those things my father could have offered me and didn't, all the things he could have been for me and wasn't."

Frank Ross adjusted in his seat. "I'm sorry."

Donley didn't respond.

"So, that's the demon you're trying to exorcise."

Donley looked at him, half his face in the shadows. "You said you hated nights—that you couldn't sleep because that was when you were alone with *your* demons? You couldn't have hated nights more than I hated them. My demon was flesh and blood, and usually drunk."

They sat somber, like two penitents. In the distance, one of the spires of the Golden Gate Bridge peaked over the ridge, red lights flashing a warning to planes. Beyond the spire, the lights from the San Francisco skyline were a soft glow in the darkening sky.

Donley spoke without taking his eyes off the horizon. "You wonder how I listened to a guy like Jack Devine without going across the desk? You didn't see me gripping the chair. I've been gripping the chair with both hands all my life."

Chapter 18

The video store was across the street from the O'Farrell Theatre, an infamous flesh house where patrons paid a high price to watch naked women engage in live sex acts with one another. San Francisco's streets were starting to buzz with energy, the storefronts lit with flashing lights, people milling about or cruising in cars to loud music. Donley watched a group of Japanese businessmen enter the O'Farrell, then turned his attention to the video store. He could guess its primary customers; it wasn't competing with the new-releases section at the local Blockbuster.

"You're sure this is the place?" Donley asked.

"Let's go find out," Ross said.

When Donley and Ross walked in the front door, several young men dressed in tight blue jeans and T-shirts, despite the brisk weather, eased their way to the exit, leaving the lingering, sweet smell of marijuana. A quick inventory revealed the merchandise was not limited to videos but included magazines and sex gadgets not for the faint of heart. *No soft porn here,* Donley thought. *Hard core all the way.*

The man behind the counter was bald and dark-skinned with a silver loop earring and a manicured goatee. Donley guessed him to be of Middle Eastern descent. He seemed unbothered by Ross and Donley, ignoring them while continuing a conversation with a tall black woman with flowing hair and dressed in high heels and a tight, red-sequined dress.

Ross gave the woman the thumb as he approached the counter. "Take a hike, sweetheart."

The woman blew them a kiss. "You too old for me, sugar." She turned to Donley. "But you look yummy."

"Lucky you," Ross said to Donley.

On closer inspection, the woman had a more prominent Adam's apple than Ross.

She gave them a flirtatious flick of her hair with two-inch, bright-red fingernails before sauntering out.

Ross turned to the man behind the counter. "Sorry to burst your bubble. You the owner?"

The man straightened but kept both palms flat on the counter. "Yeah. So what?"

"So, what's your name?"

The man smirked. "Joe."

"OK, Joe," Ross said, apparently willing to play along. "Do you know an Andrew Bennet, goes by the street name Alphabet?"

"Never heard of it; lots of other movies on the shelf, though."

"Cute." Ross laughed. "Here's a better clue. He was stabbed to death last week. Prior to dying, he ran quite a little business for himself making videotaped movies. Something tells me a kid like that can't afford a studio. How do you think he got access to one, Joe?"

Joe shrugged. "Wouldn't know. Name doesn't ring a bell, and I don't read the paper. It's too depressing."

"Still no bells, huh?" Ross snatched Joe's wrist, pinning his hand to the counter. His other hand flicked out just as quick and gripped the earlobe with the earring, pulling Joe closer. The remaining customers scattered. "Maybe you didn't hear me standing all the way over there," Ross said, bending down to talk into Joe's ear. "I said Andrew Bennet. Stabbed. Video equipment. The party room below your store. Illegal.

Violations of building and fire codes. Jail. Heavy fines. Loss of business license. Am I making myself heard now?"

Joe grimaced. His free hand inched under the counter.

Ross twisted the earring. "Don't be stupid, Joe. If you move your hand another inch, I'll rip this earring right out of your ear."

Joe put his free hand back on top of the counter.

"You have a piece under there, Joe?"

Joe shook his head.

"Then what is worth losing your earlobe over?"

"Alarm," Joe said through clenched teeth.

"Alarm? Don't bother."

"You guys been hassling me for two weeks. I'm tired of being hassled."

"Who's been hassling you, Joe?"

Joe gave him a curious look. "SFPD."

"Same guy or different guys?"

"Same guy."

"Big guy, crew cut, square head?"

"Yeah," Joe said.

Ross looked to Donley. Then he let go of the earring.

"You need a lawyer? It's your lucky day. I brought one." Ross turned to Donley. "You're a lawyer. What is your assessment of Joe's operation here?"

Donley grimaced as if weighing the consequences. "I have to be honest, Joe. A quick review indicates illegal drugs and probably illegal reading and viewing material. Plus, if we find the party room, you're looking at perhaps accessory to extortion and a host of other crimes. Hell, they'd probably even want to question you regarding Andrew Bennet's death. I could make a pretty good case, couldn't you, Detective? Greedy store owner got worried about his liability, decided to kill his partner. I wouldn't want to stand up in court and argue in your defense, though I would, after you paid me a hell of a lot of money. My advice to you would be to listen to the detective and answer his questions. It will be cheaper in the long run."

Joe stepped back, massaging his earlobe.

"We already know about the room downstairs. We just need you to show it to us," Donley said. "I'm not here to hassle you."

"Yeah, right, lucky me. And I'm nobody's partner. I'm not worried about that crap."

"So, you do know Andrew Bennet?" Ross said.

Joe paused. "I recognized his picture from the paper, OK?"

"Is that the paper you don't read because it depresses you?" Ross asked.

"I thought you weren't here to hassle me."

Ross pointed to Donley. "He said he wasn't here to hassle you. I am."

"I didn't have anything to do with anything like that."

"Good," Ross said. "So, show us the room."

Joe stretched his neck, a simple gesture of a beaten man trying to maintain a sense of dignity. "Meet me in the alley in five minutes," he said.

"One minute," Ross said. "Don't even stop to take a pee. If you are one second late, I'll come back here every night and sit right in the front of your store. You got the rules, Joe?"

Joe nodded.

"Good." Ross looked at his watch. "Time's running."

Joe called into the back room in a foreign language Donley thought to be Farsi. The way he looked at Ross as he spoke, Donley surmised that Joe was calling Ross every swear word he knew. A moment later, a glassy-eyed man who looked to be a younger version of Joe, a brother, came out from behind the curtain.

"Watch the counter," Joe said. "I need to go for a walk."

228

The alley smelled of rotting garbage emanating from a beat-up dumpster. Though the facades of the buildings facing the street had been refurbished with stucco, the walls that formed the alley remained original brick and mortar, orange in color from the dull ambient lighting. The pavement under Donley's feet was uneven and looked wet. He tried not to think about what he was stepping in.

Ross said, "You're pretty good at this. You picked up the good-cop-bad-cop routine better than some partners I've had."

"I watch a lot of television."

"Am I that predictable?"

Donley shook his head. "You would never be on television."

A soft yellow light flicked on over their heads, a bulb in a metal cage. A moment later, Joe appeared in the alley with a set of keys. He waved them to the garbage bin, and they helped him push it to the side, revealing a reddish-brown door painted the color of the brick. At night, it was nearly undetectable. Joe opened the door, and Ross and Donley followed him down a dimly lit stairwell to another door. Joe unlocked it, pushed it in, and flipped on the light.

The room was concrete, the walls painted dark purple with a black ceiling. Worn couches lined the perimeter along with a few sporadic tables and chairs.

"What does that do?" Ross asked, pointing to a machine hanging from the ceiling in the center of the room.

With a look of pride, Joe flipped a switch. Pulsing strobes of lights colored the walls and made their movements look slow and jerky. Joe flipped a second switch, and music burst from speakers hanging in the four corners, causing the air in the room to vibrate. Donley had been in a few similar clubs in the Haight-Ashbury District before Benny was born, before wake-up came at 6:00 a.m., rain or shine.

Joe stood smiling at Ross, who had his fingers in his ears. "Turn it off," Ross yelled.

Joe flipped the switches, and the room stopped spinning and vibrating. "What, you don't like to party, Detective?"

"I'm a wine-and-cheese guy, can't you tell?" Ross looked at Donley. "I thought my office gave me a headache."

"It was built during Prohibition," Joe said. "They used to gamble and drink down here."

"We'll erect a historical plaque on the wall," Ross said.

"Now it's a place for people with what you call alternative lifestyles. It's popular with the vampire crowd. Tonight the punks have it. They bring their own music. I just rent the room. Helps pay my monthly rent the city keeps jacking me for."

"Where are they tonight?" Ross asked.

Joe shrugged. "It's early, Detective. They don't even go out until ten o'clock, sometimes midnight."

"And you don't pay any more attention to it than that?" Ross asked with skepticism.

Joe's goatee sagged. He shook his head. "I don't care what they do here. I just take the money. You want to bust me, go ahead. There are about two dozen other places like this around the city. The way I figure it, I'm doing the city a favor. At least they're not on the street."

"Remind me to nominate you for a citizenship award," Ross said.

"What do you know about Andrew Bennet?" Donley asked.

"I don't." Joe put up a hand to protect his ear. "Like I said, I recognized the kid's picture in the paper. He and his buddies used the room. They had a video camera. I figured they were making movies. Porn stuff, you know. They usually came on an off night during the week. Thursday through Sunday, the place is booked."

"He had buddies?" Ross asked.

Joe nodded. "I haven't seen them in a while, though. I heard one overdosed. I don't know. Not my business."

"Would you recognize them?" Donley asked.

Joe shook his head. "I doubt it. I'm like the three monkeys. You know, hear no evil, see no evil, speak no evil."

"Car unlocked?" Donley asked Ross.

"In this neighborhood?" Ross tossed him the keys, and Donley hurried around the corner to the front of the building.

Joe looked uncomfortable alone with Ross. After a beat he said, "I'm not into any of this stuff. I don't even watch the videos. I got three kids of my own at home. I'm just a businessman."

Ross rolled his eyes. "Right, Joe, and I'm a vampire."

Joe became defiant. "This wasn't my career choice, Detective, but we had to leave Iran, and you do what you do to survive. My son wants to be a doctor. My daughter is an honor student in engineering at Berkeley. I'm giving them a better life." He waved toward the room. "You think this is all weirdos and freaks, but you'd be surprised who comes here at night when it's dark and no one can see them. You would be damned surprised. In the morning, they put on their suits and ties and go off to their downtown offices with their secretaries and pots of coffee. But at night, they come here."

Donley returned with his briefcase and pulled out the files Ross had given him documenting the deaths of Jerry Burke and Manuel Rivera. He opened both and showed Joe the photographs. Joe held them up, considering the faces. "Yeah. Yeah, I think that's them." He handed the photos back to Donley.

"Is this the only room?" Ross asked.

"You want to rent it, Detective? I'll make you a good deal."

"Nah, I like a room with a view."

"Do you know what vampires and lawyers have in common?" Joe asked Donley.

Donley sighed—another lawyer joke.

"They both bleed you dry but never leave you satisfied."

Donley smiled. "It's not even ten o'clock yet, Joe. I don't start drinking blood until midnight, but I might make an exception for you."

Donley and Ross leaned against his Cadillac, eating Philly cheesesteaks and juggling Cokes while watching the night world pass. After experiencing the nightclub in the alley that smelled like urine, and watching young men and women parade past with hair more shades of color than a carpet factory, and bodies glistening with enough piercings to open a hardware store, Donley felt like he was a hundred years old.

Ross spoke through a bite of his sandwich. "So, Burke and Rivera were making videos with Bennet. We have ourselves a connection and a motive."

"Blackmail," Donley said. "Somebody got caught and didn't like it."

"It also gives us a connecting thread to Connor. He had all three files open, and he screwed up the evidence. We're making good progress. I've had worse days." When Donley didn't respond, Ross asked, "Something else eating at you?"

"Something that Devine said. He said his father-in-law played golf with the governor, Augustus Ramsey. Why would the governor go to bat for a pedophile? Seems he'd run fast and far."

"Because money talks in politics, and August Ramsey is so crooked, he couldn't put on a straight-leg pair of jeans. I'm not surprised he'd bend the rules for a potentially wealthy contributor to the Ramsey political campaign, especially for his son."

"Maybe, but when I met with St. Claire about the plea, she wasn't the same fire and brimstone she'd been up to this point, either."

"I'm not following."

Donley shook his head. "The plea wasn't her idea. I'm sure of that. She wasn't happy being the messenger."

"You think it came from Gil Ramsey?"

"Had to. She couldn't do it without his blessing. But I can't figure out why, and I'm not buying the argument that Ramsey just wants to get out of Dodge unscathed. Twenty-five years to life with a recommendation of twenty-five and parole after twenty is a hell of a concession, especially with a match of Father Tom's blood type."

"I agree. Your guy's got courage, I'll give him that," Ross said.

"I can't win, Ross."

"What?"

"The motion. I've done the research. I can't win. The evidence will come in under the case law. It might have been illegally seized, but they would have found it eventually. Trimble is going to have to let it in."

"Then he lets it in. They still have to prove it to a jury, and they still won't have a motive. All you need to do is show a reasonable doubt."

"It's a hell of a gamble."

"It always is when they're talking murder one. Look, this thing is a marathon, not a sprint. You lose that motion, we press on."

"And an innocent man is put to death."

"Not because of anything you did, Peter. You won't have Father Martin's blood on your hands; the State will. You're defending him, not sentencing him."

It didn't feel that way.

Ross walked around the hood and removed a parking ticket stuck beneath the windshield wiper. He opened the driver's-side door and threw the ticket into the backseat. "Tomorrow, maybe we pay old Augustus Ramsey a visit and ask him about Jack Devine. He won't talk, but we can rattle some chains, let him know we know he's pardoning pedophiles. That won't go over well for his son's political future. And it might also be time to give Aileen O'Malley a call and have a heart-to-heart with her."

"Who's she?"

"Connor's lieutenant. We worked homicide together, back in the day. She might want to bring Connor in for a chat. I'll pick you up. You like cinnamon rolls?"

Donley pulled open the passenger door. "If I keep eating with you, *I'm* going to need to go on a diet."

"Humor a condemned man. I only have a few more days left before the new year, and then I'm eating carrots and broccoli."

Chapter 19

Kim greeted Donley at the door with a hug and warm kiss. Dressed in a T-shirt and blue jeans, she never looked more beautiful. He followed her into the living room and detected the smell of something spicy coming from the kitchen.

"I hope you're hungry," she said. "I made lasagna."

Donley smiled, hoping his breath didn't smell like Philly cheesesteak. "Starved. Is Benny asleep?"

"God, no. They've been playing for the past two hours."

"Simeon's awake?"

She nodded. "They're in the bedroom. He's really good with Benny, and he's a nice young man. Why don't you go in and get Benny ready for bed?"

Donley walked into the bedroom. Before Benny was born, they'd painted the walls a bright yellow and trimmed it with a border of Noah's ark animals. Danny Simeon was reading Benny a children's book. Benny looked up from the bed and smiled when Donley entered the room.

"Hi, Daddy."

"Hi, Ben."

"Daddy done working?" he asked.

"Daddy's done working." He picked up his son and hugged and kissed him.

Benny squirmed. "Put me down."

It was a game they played. "Put you down?" Donley held him upside-down by his ankles. Benny squealed. "Who loves you, Benny? Who loves you?"

"Daddy! Daddy!"

Donley turned him right side up and lowered him back onto the bed. He shook hands with Simeon and reintroduced himself. "I hear you're a pretty good babysitter."

Simeon smiled. He looked better than he had in his room at the back of the restaurant, though he still appeared worn out and pale, with dark circles under his eyes. "This kid's smart. I'd get him into computers if I were you. They're going to be the wave of the future."

"You think so? Pretty expensive."

"Trust me. Every home in America is going to have one. They'll be turning on your lights and televisions automatically. You let me school him, and he'll be teaching the other kids in his day care how to program."

"I might take you up on that." Donley changed subjects. "I'd like to talk to you about a few things."

Simeon sat up, grimaced, and took a second to let the pain pass. Then he said, "Shoot. Anything you want."

"Let me take care of Dad duty first. Then we'll talk." He picked up Benny. "Let's go, Ben. Bedtime."

Benny resisted, but the struggle was short-lived. Donley took Benny to his and Kim's bedroom, where Kim had set up the portable crib. After reading Benny *Go, Dog. Go!*, Donley put him in the crib and got him settled. Then he went to talk to Simeon. He pulled the plastic crate they used to store toys close to the bed and sat.

"How's Father Tom doing?" Simeon asked.

It felt like weeks had passed, but Donley realized Simeon did not know Father Martin had been beaten and was in the hospital. Donley leaned his elbows on his knees and picked at his fingernails. "Father Tom's in the hospital. It's a long story, but basically, some guys in jail did a pretty good number on him."

"Is he going to make it?"

"Yeah, he'll be OK, but he'll be there a couple more days."

Simeon's face contorted. "This is all screwed up."

Donley nodded. "You feel up to talking? How're the ribs?"

"Sore."

"I need to establish Father Tom's whereabouts that night."

"You need an alibi? I'm your man."

"Father Tom told me he was in his office between seven and nine that night, paying bills. Can you verify that?"

"Absolutely."

"What I mean is, did you see him? Talk with him? Can you place him in that office during those two hours?"

Simeon nodded. "I brought Father T a burger and fries right around seven forty-five, eight o'clock."

"You remember that for certain?"

"I walk down the street to Burger King around seven thirty, after I check in with him for the night. I get him a number six: Whopper, fries, and a chocolate shake. That's all the man ever eats. I get back to the office, like I said, near eight, and we eat together. Then I go to the dorm, I'd say eight thirty, to keep an eye on the residents and work on the computer."

"That's the computer in the back of the dormitory?"

"It will be if I ever get to finish it—a kick-ass computer, too."

Donley smiled. "Father Tom said he checked on the dormitory before going to lock up. He says he spent about ten minutes there."

"Father T came down to the dormitory at nine ten exactly."

"How can you be so specific?"

"Because he stalls ten minutes every night before closing the front doors; you can set your watch by him. Like I said, the man is a creature of habit."

"I take it he wasn't covered in blood when you saw him?"

"What? No."

"When's the next time you saw him?"

"I heard the sirens and went into the hall. The police were already coming up the stairs. Father T was in the recreation room with his back to the door. He was on his knees, hunched over, holding Bennet. Next thing I know, I'm up against the wall."

"What time was that?" Donley asked.

"Maybe nine twenty, nine twenty-five."

"Can you be more certain?"

Simeon shook his head and grimaced, holding his side for a moment. "I don't think so. Things got crazy after that."

Donley had just narrowed Father Tom's time alone from over two hours to about twenty minutes, maybe less. Still, it might not be enough.

"OK, so Father Tom came to the dormitory at nine ten. How long did he stay?"

Simeon thought for a moment. "Just a few minutes. We pulled the fire gag on a new kid."

"Fire gag?"

"You can't smoke in the shelter. Sometimes the new ones hide a cigarette or two. They think I'm one of them. Like I said, I was preoccupied with the computer and probably wasn't paying attention. This red-haired kid was sitting by the window smoking—"

Donley sat up. "Red-haired kid?"

"Yeah."

"Shaved on one side, earring in his nose, black T-shirt, plaid shirt?"

"You know him?" Simeon asked.

Donley stood. His heart raced. "He was there that night? You're certain of it?"

"I checked him in."

"And you've never seen him there before? He's never been to the shelter before that night?"

"First time that I know of. We don't get the punks too much."

"Punks?"

"Punk rockers."

The kid Ross and Donley had found at the shelter had lied. He'd been there that night. Donley was certain he'd just figured out how the killer got in the recreation-room door. He tried not to rush his questions, to proceed deliberately. He needed evidence. He needed to prove the red-haired kid had been at the shelter that night. "Father Martin says there's a log-in sheet where he keeps track of everyone who comes to the shelter."

Simeon nodded. "We log in everyone and everything they have. It's all locked in a locker. I logged them in that night."

"He'd be in it?" Donley asked. "The sheet would show the red-haired kid's name?"

"He wouldn't give his name. Just Red. Father T ordinarily insists on their names, but he told me to let it slide because it was the kid's first night."

"What about Bennet? Did you log him in, too?"

"Earlier, yeah. But he left."

"What did he bring to the shelter? Do you remember?"

Simeon shrugged. "Not really. I'd say cigs and stuff."

"You don't remember a videotape?"

Simeon grimaced. "I don't. I'm sorry."

"Could he have put one in the locker without you knowing?"

Simeon gave this some thought. "Yeah. I mean, it's possible. I'm not watching them the whole time. I ask what they have and write it down. He could have just slipped it in the locker without declaring it."

Donley fought to remain calm. "I went back to the shelter to try and find Father Martin's logbook. It wasn't there."

"That's because I took it."

Donley stopped pacing. "You have it?"

"When I saw the police lights, I went down the hall. I saw the flashlights coming up the stairs and I hid in Father Tom's office, and I remembered the book, the Bible. Father Tom puts the sign-in log in there. I took it and shoved it in my pants pocket and locked the door when I stepped out. I had it at the hospital when Connor showed up. It's in my room back at the restaurant. I put it under the mattress."

Donley smiled. He thought of calling Frank Ross. "Why'd you take it?"

"Father T once said he didn't want the police getting it. It's confidential. Some of the kids bring in some shit with them, drugs, you know. We don't ask questions. Rule is they can't use at the shelter and they can't be high when they check in. We just lock it in the lockers. Connor wants the book. I can tell you that."

Donley stood. "That's why he came to your hospital room Christmas Eve. He told you he wanted the book?"

"Wanted it bad," Simeon said.

And that was why Red went back to the shelter that morning. Connor wanted the book because Red's name would be in it, and maybe a note of a videotape attached to Andrew Bennet's name. What better place for Bennet to store it, someplace he didn't think Connor could reach?

"When Bennet left, did he take what he'd put in his locker?"

Simeon shook his head. "He didn't ask me, and I know he didn't ask Father T because he was surprised Bennet had left."

"How would I find Red? How would I find a kid like that?"

Simeon started to get out of bed, then stopped, grimacing. "I can show you some spots he might hang," he said, sounding out of breath.

Donley put out a hand and glanced at the door. "No can do, Danny. You're not well enough yet, and my wife is tougher than I am. I can't tell her where I'm going."

Simeon thought for a moment. "Punks hang together. They don't usually come to the shelter . . . what's the matter?"

Donley looked at his watch. The vampires would start venturing out in a couple of hours, but Joe said the punks had the club tonight.

◆　◆　◆

The night doorman at the *Chronicle* sat behind a counter with three television monitors. Frank Ross handed him a business card and told him he had an appointment to see Sam Goldman. The man used the phone to seek clearance before releasing the elevator in the lobby.

Frank Ross had been on his way home when Goldman called on the portable phone. He advised Ross that he was working on a late-breaking story and asked Ross to come by the newspaper office.

Goldman met Ross on the third floor in a secure lobby. With rich, dark paneling and stained glass, it looked more like a church vestibule.

"So, tell me what couldn't wait until tomorrow," Ross said.

"Today's news is old tomorrow. You know that," Goldman said, leading Ross down a red-tile hallway lined with plaques commemorating awards won by the newspaper. Cubicles and filing cabinets cluttered every available inch of the newsroom. Despite the late hour, reporters faced terminals, keyboards clattering, while they talked into headsets. Ross followed Goldman into a conference room with framed photographs of *Chronicle* reporters who had won the Pulitzer Prize. At the front of the room, a cluttered bulletin board displayed the front pages of local and national newspapers. Someone had marked up the pages with red ink.

"Things move fast around here," Ross said.

"This? This is nothing," Goldman said. "You ought to be around at four in the afternoon when everyone is filing stories. Right now, we're trying to verify a report on a sniper taking shots at cars on the 101."

"Really? Anyone hit?"

"Thankfully not, but we have an eyewitness who says there are at least two cars with bullet holes, and the police are descending on the place like reporters to a banquet table." Goldman closed the door. "I want to show you page one for tomorrow." He handed Frank Ross a mock-up of the morning paper. It still had blanks, but Ross caught the headline in the middle of the page.

Priest's Attorney Once a Murder Suspect
Peter Donley Accused of Killing Father

"I told you I knew him." Goldman pointed to his temple. "I racked my brains for the better part of the afternoon before it came to me. It was a hell of a story."

Ross read the article as Goldman spoke. "Donley was a high school All-American linebacker and running back from Potrero Hill. He had a full ride to just about every school in the nation, but he chose Berkeley. It was a real 'local boy does good' story. Couple weeks before school is set to start, the police get a nine-one-one call from a neighbor. She says it sounds like they're beating the hell out of each other next door. When the police get there, they find the old man covered in glass and lying on his back in the driveway. He fell ten feet through a plate-glass window. Your boy, Donley, is sitting on the steps, bleeding, and the inside of the house is a shambles."

"What about the mother? Was she there?"

Goldman's eyebrows arched above his black-framed glasses. "Not home. Went to visit her sister."

Ross pulled out a chair and sat, feeling sick to his stomach. His mind went over his conversation with Donley on the drive back from Saint Helena.

"The police arrest the kid on suspicion of murder and take him to the hospital," Goldman said. "They stitch him up, but he isn't saying anything. Not a word. He goes to county jail and stays there for two days until his uncle, Lou Giantelli, convinces a judge he's bailable. Three weeks later, the district attorney drops the charges."

Ross looked up. "Why?"

"Lack of evidence. Only two people knew what happened in that house that night, and one was dead and the other wasn't talking. Rumor had it Giantelli convinced the DA the kid was worth saving and the father wasn't. Whatever happened, the official word was the father's death was an accident. Donley went off to college, and the rest is history."

Ross ran a hand over his face. Donley had said his father beat him and his mother. At eighteen, Donley would have grown big enough to do something about it, and time was running out. He had a scholarship to a premier school and a bright future, but what would he do about his mother?

Ross rubbed the tip of his ear and let out a sigh. "I don't suppose there's any way I could talk you out of running that story, is there, Sam?"

Goldman pulled out a chair and sat.

"Maybe you could hold it for a few days. I mean, with the priest in the hospital, the story isn't breaking news."

Goldman leaned in. "What is it, Ross? We've known each other a long time. It would take a hell of a lot for you to ask me something like that."

"I know, and I would never take advantage of our friendship, Sam, but Donley has a family now. He has a wife and a son, a little boy. They don't need this. This is going to drag up a lot of bad, bad memories."

"It's news, Ross."

Ross nodded. "Yeah, it is. And I know you have a job to do. I just don't know that twenty-five thousand people need to know about it at this very moment. He was cleared. They didn't charge him."

"So was Jack Devine."

Ross sighed.

Sam Goldman took off his glasses and sat back. Without his glasses, his eyes looked smaller, and he looked tired. "According to police sources, there was blood on the main circuit breaker to the house. Speculation is the kid pulled it, that he was lying in wait for the old man to get home, then put the fuse back after the fight."

"Maybe. Or maybe the old man was waiting for him."

They sat staring at each other. Point made: nobody knew what had really happened except the two men in the room, and one was dead.

"And the DA dropped the charges," Ross said.

Goldman made a face. "We both know that was because of Lou Giantelli."

Ross knocked on the table. "I'll make you a deal, Sam. What if I told you that Donley and I have been doing some digging, and we know enough that I can tell you the priest did not kill that kid, that there are at least two other related murders. And there are rumors of more Jack Devine–like videotapes, and a cop could be involved."

Goldman leaned forward, his voice a shocked whisper. "Connor?"

"You'll have to take me at my word. We're very close, and if we get there, it will make this look like a fluff piece," he said, tapping the table again. "But we don't have it all yet. We need some time."

There was a knock on the door. A young man in a wrinkled shirt stuck his head in the room. "Sam? Sorry to interrupt, but I got confirmation on the sniper. He's now taken out three cars and put two people in the hospital. I've spoken with two of the families and have the husband of the third calling me back in fifteen minutes. The police will have a statement for me at the end of the hour. That's after the eleven o'clock news signs off. We'll be first in the morning. I'll have a minimum of forty-eight inches. Can we fit it?"

Sam Goldman sat swinging his glasses, considering Ross. After a beat, he looked back to the reporter. "Yeah, we can fit it. Page one, center."

Donley pushed through the door of Tequila Dan's and maneuvered through a crowd to the horseshoe bar. He had not been able to reach Frank Ross. Ross had left Donley his home number, but his wife said Ross had gone to a meeting, which sounded odd for that hour of the night. Donley hoped Ross wasn't out drinking.

At the counter, Donley made eye contact with the bartender. The man no longer wore his rose-tinted glasses, and the scowl he gave Donley indicated he was not happy to see him.

"I thought we had a deal?"

"What are you talking about?" Donley asked.

He motioned Donley to an area just to the right of the bar, away from the noise. "You said I didn't have a problem."

"You don't," Donley said.

"Then why the hell did the police show up here busting my balls?"

Donley had a sinking feeling. "The police came here?"

"Yeah, a major asshole, said he was going to shut the whole bar down because I was letting Danny live in the back."

Donley felt the bow of the ship sinking. "Was his name Connor?"

"Who?"

"The cop. Was his name Dixon Connor?"

"I don't know. He didn't say, and I didn't ask."

"Big man? My size. Square head with a crew cut."

"Yeah, that was him. A real prince."

"Did you show him Danny's room?"

"No, but he went back there, anyway. Tore the fucking place apart. You want to tell me what the hell happened?"

Donley ran a hand through his hair. He'd just lost a critical piece of evidence.

◆　◆　◆

Donley sat in his car on the side street perpendicular to the corner video store on O'Farrell, watching a group of young people congregating in the alley. Though it was cold out, most wore nothing more than short sleeves and tank tops, displaying exotic tattoos and a lot of piercings. Some wore dog collars; others military-style pants and black boots. All seemed to have thick chains dangling from their pockets and innovative hair colors and styles: Mohawks, spikes, shaved heads, and elaborate carvings. Donley did not see Red, and he doubted he'd find anyone who'd tell him where he could.

He got out of the car.

"Ragtop. Nice car."

A man wearing an army fatigue jacket, black ski hat, and worn shoes sat atop a four-foot-high concrete wall. He wasn't one of the punks. He had bags in a shopping cart positioned below him. One of San Francisco's many homeless.

"Watch that car for you for a couple of bucks. Make sure no harm comes to it. Ragtops are easy to break in. Rip the top, open the door, do all kinds of damage."

Part of Donley wanted to knock the man off the wall and tell him that if any harm came to the car, Donley would find him, but that was just the anger he could feel building inside him. And it was stupid. The man held all the leverage. He had no place to go. Donley did.

Donley walked closer and smelled the cheap wine and mildew. He reached up and handed the man two dollars. "Do I get a wash and wax with that?"

The man studied him, uncertain. Then he broke into a gap-toothed grin. "That'll be extra."

"I thought so." Donley handed him another dollar.

The man took the money. "Thank you, brother."

Donley turned to cross the street.

"Hey, you going to the O'Farrell?"

Donley shook his head. "I'm working tonight."

The man cocked his head. "Working? What do you do?"

"I'm an undercover cop," Donley said.

Donley crossed the street and continued around the block to the end of the alley farthest from the door to the party room. He stood behind the wall, occasionally peering around the corner to watch the entrance to the underground club. The lightbulb over the door cast an orange glow that colored the alley a blood red. A bouncer stood just outside the door in a sleeveless T-shirt with hair that looked like the plume of a peacock's tail.

Donley waited forty minutes, fighting the cold. As he peered around the corner, he sensed someone approaching. He turned and recognized the transvestite from the video store sauntering up the street wearing the same red-sequined dress. Donley started to turn away, then got an idea.

"Cold tonight," he said, engaging her.

"Very cold." She leaned against the wall and flipped her shoulder-length hair, which Donley concluded to be a wig. "Hey, I know you." She grinned. "You were in the store. Are you a cop for real?" She squealed the last part of the sentence.

"Not me," Donley said. "What's your name again?"

"Crystal. Delicate and expensive. Who you waiting for?"

"He's in the club down this alley."

Crystal pursed her lips, a pout. "I'll make you forget him."

Donley pulled a fold of money from his pocket. It looked substantial, but was actually two twenty-dollar bills, a five, and a lot of ones.

He held the money at his side. "Would you take a look and see if he's in there for me?"

Crystal considered the money but shook her head. "Uh-uh. Punks have the club tonight."

Donley looked down the alley. The punks continued to file past the bouncer or stood in the alley smoking. No sign of Red. "It's very important to me." He peeled off the twenty. "I can describe him."

Crystal looked again at the money. "What do I have to do?"

"Just tell him I'll meet him at the corner by the video store. Tell him Connor is waiting for him."

Crystal squealed again. "Connor. That's a cute name."

"Do it for me, and I'll have another twenty for you when you come back. Easy money."

Crystal let out a sigh and looked back down the alley. Donley could tell she was waffling. "What do I have to do?"

"Just what I said." Donley described Red. "Just tell him Connor is waiting for him, and if he doesn't come out, I'm going to come in."

Crystal looked skeptical. "Are you sure you're not a cop?"

"Would a cop be making this transaction, Crystal?"

"Some would." She contemplated the alley. "They're mean. Punks are mean."

"In and out. That's all you have to do. Deliver the message and get out."

"What if he's not there?"

"If he's not there, you still get the money. Easiest forty dollars you ever made."

"Make it a hundred."

Donley shook his head. "Fifty. That's the best I can do."

She looked back down the alley for what seemed the hundredth time. "There's a five-dollar cover at the door."

Donley flipped through the stack, pulled out the five, and handed it and the twenty to her. "Just deliver the message. You'll get the rest when you return."

Crystal took a deep breath and started down the alley, walking comfortably in a pair of spiked heels despite the uneven pavement. Donley knew the door was the only entry and exit, and there were only two ends to the alley. If Red was inside, he'd think Connor was at the other end.

Crystal reached the club entrance. Donley watched as she stopped to speak to the bouncer with the multicolored spikes. Just when Donley thought Crystal would be turned away, the man nodded toward the entrance, and Crystal disappeared into the doorway.

Five minutes later, Crystal hurried back down the alley. When she reached Donley, he saw she was wiping blood from her nose.

"What happened?" Donley asked.

"I got slammed into a wall," she said, no longer sounding so feminine.

"Are you all right?"

"That's how they dance."

"Did you find him?"

"I gave him the message."

"He was there? You told him what I told you to say?"

"I said I did."

"You wouldn't lie to me, would you, Crystal?"

"You said I'd get the money either way. Why would I lie? Red hair, shaved on one side, earring through his nose. But I don't think he's going to come. He looked freaked when he heard *your* name."

Donley handed Crystal the rest of the money. "Thanks, Crystal. That's all I need."

Crystal put the money down the front of her dress. "If you change your mind, you know the name. Crystal. Delicate and expensive," she said, and walked off down the block.

Donley watched the door to the club. People continued to file in. No one was coming out. Then Red stepped out, followed by another boy. Donley's pulse quickened. The two boys looked down the alley in the direction of the video store, where they expected to find Dixon Connor. Then they turned and started running to where Donley waited. Donley pressed his back against the wall, listening for the sound of heavy-soled boots on pavement. He tensed his legs, timed their arrival, and burst from the wall as they reached the edge of the alley.

He hit Red square with his shoulders, knocking him backward into his friend, and took both to the ground. He pulled Red from the pavement by his shirt collar and dragged him quickly up the block, shoving him into the entryway of an apartment building. The second boy came up the stairway with a knife. Donley spun and kicked the blade from the kid's hand. Red made a move to flee, but Donley grabbed him and threw him up against the wall. Then he dragged the second kid up the steps and also pushed him to the ground.

Red glanced at the knife.

"Don't," Donley said. He leaned closer. "Why did you lie to me?"

"I didn't lie."

Donley grabbed him by the collar and pulled him to his feet. "You're lying to me now. You were at the shelter that night. You checked in. I got a book with your name on it and witnesses who say you were there."

Red's friend started to get up.

"Tell him to stay down."

"Stay down," Red said. His friend slumped back against the marble wall.

"Don't lie to me. I know you were there. You were smoking in the dorm room. The priest came in and told you to quit. I know it, so don't you lie to me."

"OK, I was there."

"Why? Who sent you in?"

"No one."

Donley shook him. "Who sent you in?"

"No one."

"It was Connor, wasn't it? He had you prop open the two doors, the one at the bottom of the stairs off the park and the door into the recreation room."

Red shook his head. "No." But his eyes betrayed him. He clearly knew the name Connor because it had just scared him enough to flee the club.

Donley forced him against the wall. "Here's a news flash. Connor has killed three young men already. You think he won't make it four? You think you can survive out here, avoid him forever? You're a witness. You know what he did. That means he'll come for you. He'll come because he knows I'm onto him. So if you want to live, right now I'm the only one who can help you."

Red's voice broke. "Why? Why would you help me?"

The emotion startled Donley. He noticed Red's lip was swollen, and dried blood had scabbed over a cut. The kid's eyes were wide with fear. Donley let go of Red's collar and stepped back. He took a breath to calm himself. "Because I know what it's like to be afraid, to have someone like Connor chasing you. And I know you can't run forever. Eventually, he'll get you. You know that."

Red did not speak.

"Let me tell you how this works." Donley spoke softly, deliberately. "The police will consider you an accessory to Bennet's murder. I'll tell them you refused to cooperate. You're what, sixteen, seventeen? They'll consider you an adult because you likely have a police record. That means you go to state prison. The other alternative is, I leave you on the street for Connor." He let the choices sink in. "If you want my help, you have to be honest with me. You have to tell me the truth. People are forgiving, but you have to be accountable. You have to tell me what happened. You do that, and I'll take you someplace where Connor can't touch you."

Red shifted his gaze to his friend.

"We didn't know," his friend said.

"Didn't know what?"

"Didn't know Connor was going to kill anyone," Red said. "He's crazy."

"Tell me what you do know," Donley said.

"Connor said he'll kill me."

"Tell me what you know, and I'll keep you safe from Connor. You have my word." Donley stepped back, leaving the stairway clear for the boys to run. Neither did. "Tell me what happened."

Red ran a hand through his hair and pulled the long strands to the side. "Connor busted us for coke. He said it was enough that he'd make sure we did time."

"What did he tell you to do?"

"He told me to check into the shelter and unlock the two doors."

"Was that it?"

"Mostly."

"What else?"

"He wanted us to get something."

"What?"

Red was breathing heavily. "I didn't know he was going to kill anybody. I just didn't want to go to jail."

"Was it a book?"

Red shook his head. "A videotape. He said Bennet had it. He said he put it in a locker in the office."

"Did you get it?"

"I couldn't. The lockers were locked, and the priest was in there."

"What did you do when the police showed up?"

"Just ran."

Jack Devine's whiny voice resonated inside Donley's head.

The little fucker had a videotape.

Bennet had told Devine he had a lot of videotapes, and that he was going to make a lot of people pay. He'd been blackmailing someone with a videotape, but he was also running for his life from Connor. His two accomplices were dead. Where could he go? Ross said kids like Bennet had no place to go, nowhere to turn, nowhere except perhaps to a priest who had started a shelter for kids just like him. His two friends were dead. He was afraid. So he stashed a videotape at the shelter and took off. That's why Connor broke down doors and busted locks. He was looking for the videotape Bennet had stashed. In the process, Connor planted enough evidence to blame the murder on Father Martin. He'd kill two birds with one stone.

But why was Connor so interested in a tape? What was on it? Ross said no way Connor was on the tape, but Donley was no longer so sure. It was like Joe from the video store said. You'd be surprised what skeletons people kept in their closets.

Donley knew.

He listened to the distant sound of a siren screaming toward an impending tragedy, echoing as they had ten years earlier when the police cars had sped up the hill, one after the other, lights flashing, and pulled to a stop in front of Donley's home. He considered the two boys, backs against the wall, knees to their chests, frightened, distrustful.

He knew what he had to do to have any hope of saving Father Martin's life. He had to get that tape before Connor used it for whatever purpose he intended, and Donley's instincts were telling him he didn't have a lot of time. Things were coming to a head. Connor knew it, too.

Whatever Donley was going to do, he had to do it now.

Chapter 20

December 30, 1987

The windshield wipers slapped a steady beat. Donley slowed the car to a crawl, the headlights blunted by the thick fog. With the temperature warming after a two-day cold spell, gray mist and fog had rolled over the Sunset District, nearly obscuring the pink-and-green neon sign of the 19th Hole.

Donley parked across the street, stepped out, and walked toward the doors. He'd driven by Connor's house, but it had been dark, with no car in the driveway. Now he was playing a hunch.

He stepped to the swinging wooden doors of the 19th Hole and peered through the porthole. He recognized the hulking figure slumped on the same bar stool. Dixon Connor.

Turning, he noticed a brand-new Range Rover, the only vehicle parked in front of the building. He put a hand on the hood. It was warm. He pressed his face to the glass and shone a small penlight through the windows. He didn't see a videotape or a Bible on the seats or the floor.

He hurried back to his car and pulled from the curb, driving past Connor's house. Then he turned, and parked three houses to the west on the opposite side of the street. He killed the engine and took a moment to consider the neighborhood. Christmas lights and televisions glowed muted colors in the gray mist, but Donley detected no activity. No late-night dog walkers patrolled the sidewalks. No busybody neighbors stuck their heads out from behind curtained windows. The fog blunted all noise but for the low howl of the wind off the Pacific.

Donley pushed aside the words of caution repeatedly streaming through his head. He couldn't wait for Ross, whose wife said he was not home. Connor would not stay out much later. The bars closed at 2:00 a.m. Besides, Ross would talk Donley out of what he knew he had to do. He'd tell Donley that he had a career and a family to think about. He'd tell Donley that Connor was not someone to mess with. He'd tell him to call the police, to get a search warrant. But that would be too late. Connor would ditch the book and the videotape. And Father Martin would fry. If Donley had any hope of finding either, he needed to act now, before Connor realized the extent to which Donley and Ross were on to him.

Besides, Donley had heard the same admonitions before, and he'd learned the hard way that if you wanted something done, you had to take care of it yourself. No one was going to help you.

Donley's only chance, Father Tom's only chance, was Connor's arrogance. He wouldn't think anyone knew about the videotape. He wouldn't think anyone would dare to come looking for it. He wouldn't think anyone would be so brazen as to break into a cop's home.

Donley's hand drifted to the passenger seat, feeling the walnut-wood grip of Lou's police service revolver. In the thirty years Lou had kept it in his desk, it had never been fired. It had probably never been cleaned, but it was always loaded. Donley had no idea if it would fire or explode in his hand. He hoped he wouldn't have to find out tonight.

He took a deep breath, steeled himself, and stepped from the car. He shoved the barrel of the revolver into his pants at the small of his back and covered the handle with his leather jacket. He shut the car door with care. A neighborhood dog, as if sensing his presence, barked.

The fog blew moist pellets in his face as he crossed the street and walked up the sidewalk. He passed the walkway leading to Connor's front door, took a final look over his shoulder, and ducked down the driveway beneath the sill of a window. At the end of the driveway, he came to a wooden gate. He looked over the top into the backyard before pulling on the knotted string. The gate unlatched with a click and swung open. He crept into a bleak backyard of crabgrass and dandelions. Weeds stood four feet high in planter beds along a dilapidated redwood fence. In the corner of the yard, a rusted clothesline resembling an oversize television antenna rotated in the breeze, whining like the strings on a violin.

Donley moved to a small wooden porch off the back of the house and started up three steps to a back door. The steps sagged beneath his weight, and the railing shook, likely rotted. The persistently moist salt air was hard on the homes.

Closer, he noticed a large hole had been cut in the bottom of the door and covered with a plastic flap. Dog door.

Damn.

He hadn't thought of a dog. Connor didn't seem like the pet-loving type. Dogs unnerved Donley. He'd never had a pet growing up, and the dogs in his neighborhood had served one purpose: security. Even after Kim talked him into getting Bo for those nights Donley worked late, his innate fear of man's best friend persisted.

He surveyed the yard but did not see where an animal had trampled the tall grass, nor did he see a doghouse or a bowl or smell dog poop. He looked through the windowpane. The interior was dark. He knelt and cautiously lifted the flap of plastic covering the opening. No large animal lunged out and took a hunk of flesh from his face.

With no dog, the dog door became a blessing. Donley stuck his head inside the opening and saw a washer and dryer—a laundry room off the back of a kitchen. He recognized the familiar floor plan. His shoulders were too wide to squeeze through the hole and his arm just inches too short to reach the latched deadbolt above the doorknob.

He slid back out and retreated down the steps, rummaging in the tall grass until finding a dilapidated flower trellis along the fence. He snapped off one of the redwood sticks and considered its length. It might do.

He slid into the dog door again and used the stick to reach the latch on the deadbolt. After several failed attempts, he managed to push the latch straight up. Standing, he threw the stick into the grass, braced the glass pane with the palm of his hand so it would not rattle, and turned the door handle. The door stuck in the jamb, and he momentarily feared it remained locked. Then it popped free.

He was in.

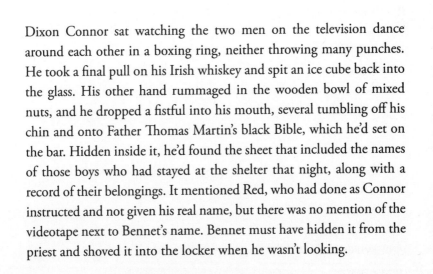

Dixon Connor sat watching the two men on the television dance around each other in a boxing ring, neither throwing many punches. He took a final pull on his Irish whiskey and spit an ice cube back into the glass. His other hand rummaged in the wooden bowl of mixed nuts, and he dropped a fistful into his mouth, several tumbling off his chin and onto Father Thomas Martin's black Bible, which he'd set on the bar. Hidden inside it, he'd found the sheet that included the names of those boys who had stayed at the shelter that night, along with a record of their belongings. It mentioned Red, who had done as Connor instructed and not given his real name, but there was no mention of the videotape next to Bennet's name. Bennet must have hidden it from the priest and shoved it into the locker when he wasn't looking.

Didn't matter. Connor now had the videotape and the sheet. Case closed. Now, the fun could really begin. In just a little more than twenty-four hours he would have exacted the type of justice his old man deserved.

"Two Mexicans dancing around up there and getting paid to do it," he said to the television. "Is it any wonder this country is going to hell?" He shook the ice in the glass and sucked at the remaining drops of whiskey. The bartender turned from a conversation at the other end of the bar and glanced with disinterest at the television.

"Not like the old days with real fighters. Guys stood in the center of the ring and went toe-to-toe. Jake LaMotta. Rocky Marciano. Jack Dempsey. Those guys were fighters. The Rock beat the shit out of that nigger, Joe Louis. My dad sat right here, and I stood next to him listening to the radio." Connor pointed. "Eddie Buchanan and Charlie Lawlor recreated every punch right in that corner over there. Then, *boom*, the Rock knocks that big black son of a bitch into the ropes, and the place erupts like fireworks on the Fourth of July."

Connor put the glass on the bar and motioned for the bartender to pour him another Jameson. The bartender took his time walking to Connor's end of the bar. He retrieved the glass and leaned across the wood, inching into Connor's personal space.

Connor leaned back. "What are you, a fag?"

The man straightened and stepped back. "Take it easy, Connor."

Connor looked around the bar. "What? Somebody got a problem with me?"

No one said anything.

"Nobody's got a problem with you, Connor. It's just a little loud," the bartender said.

"You mean *I'm* a little loud."

"Yeah, OK, you're a little loud. Just take it down a notch. Let me pour you a cup of coffee, heat you up a couple of hot dogs."

"Shit, I wouldn't eat that crap. You don't know what they're putting in those things. You never should have closed the kitchen if you wanted people to eat." He swiveled his stool. "There used to be a kitchen on the other side of that wall, before the Chinaman bought this place and made it look like a boxcar."

"I know," the bartender said, his voice weary. He dunked the glass in a sink of soapy water behind the bar. "And I've told you, I didn't close the kitchen, and I didn't construct the wall. I just pour the drinks."

"Then pour me another drink, and shut up. I've been drinking here for twenty-five years, sitting on this same damn stool . . . my father's stool. I've been here long before the Chinaman, or you."

The bartender reached under the bar with a look of contempt, pulled out the bottle of Jameson, scooped ice into a glass, and poured the drink. He slid it to Connor on a fresh napkin. Connor sipped his whiskey and considered what the 19th Hole had once been. The Chinaman took more than square footage. He took the bar's soul. He'd put a big partition right down the center of the room and squeezed in a grocery store on the other side, though all he sold were cigarettes and dirty magazines. He'd covered the walls with cheap wooden paneling that was now bowing in spots and made the bar long, narrow, and dark. Then he'd walled in the large, tinted window that looked out onto the sidewalk. He said the window was a hazard. He feared vandals, but vandals and gangs had steered clear of the 19th Hole because at any moment, there could be half a dozen off-duty police officers inside, Max Connor usually one of them.

Not anymore. The bar was just like the police force. The regulars were gone, kicked out and replaced. The life had been squeezed from it. The Chinaman had killed it. Minorities were killing the city, just like they'd killed his old man.

Connor took another drink. "My dad would have beat the shit out of those Mexicans. Look at them, dancing around up there. Looks like they got jumping beans in their shorts. Stand and fight!" he shouted at the television. "They should give them dresses and put on a record." He finished his drink in one long pull and put the glass on the counter.

"Give me another one."

The bartender ignored him, washing and stacking glasses.

"Hey, you deaf?"

"Go home and sleep it off."

"I said, give me another one."

The bartender picked up the telephone. "I'll call you a cab."

Connor swore and slammed a hand on the counter, spraying the bowl of peanuts. "What is this world coming to? I got a bartender who won't pour a drink in a bar?" He picked up his glass and hurled it at the rows of bottles, as if throwing a baseball at milk bottles stacked in a carnival booth. Glass exploded, cascading to the floor.

"Goddamn it, Connor." The bartender dropped the phone and pulled the ax handle from two clips under the bar. "That's it. I've had—" He froze, looking like the rusted tin man cutting wood in *The Wizard of Oz*.

"Go ahead." Connor pulled back the hammer on the .44. "But this isn't baseball. You only get one swing. So I suggest you make it a good one."

Donley stood in the laundry room, listening to the sounds of the house while allowing his eyes to adjust to the darkness. His mouth was dry, and he was fumbling with the rubber gloves Frank Ross had given him when they went inside the shelter.

Gloves on, he walked across the linoleum hearing every squeak of the floor. The kitchen looked unused, the tiled counter clear, the Wedgewood stove's metal polished, the liner of the garbage can pristine. Donley walked from the kitchen into a dining room with a table and chairs, sideboard, and a china cabinet filled with plates and ceramic figurines. Time looked to have stopped somewhere in the 1960s.

The living room was off the dining room, its windows and the front door facing the street. Two floral couches covered in plastic were arranged perpendicular to each other, with a glass coffee table in the middle and end tables with lamps. A recliner faced a television. No plants or flowers to indicate anyone lived in the house on a daily basis. The air smelled like an old person's clothes left in a closet with mothballs.

Built-in bookshelves included a framed photograph of a man and woman, presumably Max Connor and his wife. Next to it was a photograph of Connor in his dress blues. He was the spitting image of his father, the same square head and death-cold stare. The shelves were packed with videotapes, movies like *Roman Holiday*, *Run Silent Run Deep*, *Trapeze*, *On the Waterfront*.

As Donley stepped from the room, the television suddenly burst to life. He jumped and reached for the gun, feeling his heart skip a beat, then realized the television must be on a timer. He took a moment to regain his composure and catch his breath, wiped perspiration trickling from his temples, and walked through the dining room into a hallway. The bathroom was directly ahead. He turned left, toward the back of the house and a closed door. He turned the knob and pushed the door open. Light from a street lamp cast shadows on a queen-size bed that took up most of the space in the room. In the center of the bedspread was a large, dark-brown stain. Blood. A chill ran up Donley's back as he remembered Frank Ross telling him that Dixon Connor had found his father's body. He realized not only that this was the room in which Max Connor had taken his life but that Dixon Connor had kept it preserved. Not wanting to linger, Donley quickly opened a closet door. The closet was empty, not even a hanger on the bar.

He shut the door to the room behind him and walked to the closed door at the other end of the hall. He put an ear to the door, hearing only the sound of his own breathing. Gathering himself, he opened the door. The room was dark, the window covered by a shade. He removed the small pen flashlight from his pocket and began his search.

◆　◆　◆

Connor fumbled to insert the key in the Range Rover lock, pulled open the door, and slid in to the smell of new leather. He slammed the door closed with a thud that seemed to shake the whole neighborhood and sat for a moment watching fog billow up the street. As thick as it was, it couldn't mask the 19th Hole's now-tattered appearance. The Chinaman hadn't put a nickel into the place since he'd bought it. Word was, he wanted to tear it down and build an apartment building. There had been a time when such talk would have caused punches to be thrown. The 19th Hole had reflected the neighborhood. The 19th Hole was the community. Tearing it down would be like tearing out the neighborhood's soul.

As a boy, Connor used to ride his bike down the street at sundown and push through the swinging doors feeling like Matt Dillon in *Gunsmoke*. Everyone greeted Max Connor's kid. His father would have Connor make fists and punch in combinations while Mike O'Shea lowered his voice to sound like a ring announcer echoing over a microphone.

Ladies and gentlemen, the next heavyweight cham-peen of the world, Dixon Connor.

He hadn't made it that far, but he had won a city Golden Gloves championship.

Everything had revolved around the stool at the corner of the bar. Not anymore.

They'd killed the bar, just like they'd killed his father.

Connor had just had his final drink at the 19th Hole. Thursday morning, he'd pick up his money. Then he'd vanish, to hunt and fish the rest of his life. For the fun of it, he'd screw that prick Gil Ramsey and his father. He'd send a copy of the tape to the local media. What had gone around was coming back around. Payback was going to be a royal bitch.

He turned the key and started the engine.

◆ ◆ ◆

The tiny penlight revealed an unmade bed. On it was a large canvas bag stuffed with clothes and toiletries. Donley's instincts were correct. Dixon Connor was leaving town, in a hurry from the looks of it. Unopened mail and debris littered the floor and obscured a desk. Donley stepped closer to what, at first, appeared to be a strange wallpaper pattern. Instead, his penlight revealed dozens of articles pinned and taped to the wall—a seemingly unorganized collage.

He moved the light from article to article. The collage covered the arrest and criminal trial of Max Connor, and the civil trial that had followed. Equally prevalent were articles on then–District Attorney Augustus Ramsey and the young assistant DA he had assigned to handle the case, Gil Ramsey.

Frank Ross had been accurate in his assessment that the Ramseys had been unable or unwilling to let the matter go. There were articles about the Hispanic community and women's groups pressuring the DA to ensure Max Connor would be held accountable to the fullest extent of the law. The police association had predictably stood by one of its brethren. It had accused Augustus Ramsey of conducting a witch hunt and pandering to special-interest groups, especially when an internal investigation questioned the veracity of the female officer's allegations that Max Connor had raped her. But it had not been enough to save Max Connor.

Ross had been right about Dixon Connor having slipped off the ledge of rational thinking; he'd just underestimated how far Connor had fallen. The bloodstained bedspread and the bizarre collage represented the work of a man obsessed with revenge and seething with anger.

Donley realized he'd underestimated the danger he'd put himself in. He needed to get out of that house as quickly as possible. He stuck the penlight between his teeth, and quickly went through the canvas bag but did not see or feel any videocassettes or books.

He picked through the mess on the desk and floor, checked under the bed, and went through the closet. He pulled open drawers of a dresser, pushing aside clothes. Nothing.

He hadn't figured Connor to be the kind of guy who would get a safe-deposit box or hide the tape someplace else, but maybe he'd also misjudged Connor's paranoia. He left the room, stepped back into the dining room, and suddenly thought of the videotapes on the shelves in the living room.

He moved quickly into the room and ran a gloved finger over the titles, pulling tapes from the shelves and sliding out the cassettes to check whether the title matched the case. There had to be close to fifty tapes. It would take too long to go through them all. As if to prove that point, two cones of light pierced the curtain. A second later, Donley heard the hum of an engine turning in to the driveway.

◆ ◆ ◆

Dixon Connor stopped the car at the end of his driveway and reached out the window, but with the new vehicle being higher, he could not reach the lock on his mailbox. He put the car in park and stepped out, opening the lock. Inside, he found nothing but junk mail and a bill from PG&E. He'd requested the postal service to cease delivery the day after tomorrow, providing no forwarding address. He didn't care if he ever got another scrap. He'd listed the house with an agent to sell after he'd left, and set up a bank account for the real-estate agent to deposit the funds upon closing. Once the check cleared, he'd transfer those funds into a different account. He'd load his duffel into the back of the Range Rover, pick up his money from Gil Ramsey, retire to the little cottage he'd bought in the Northern Idaho wilderness, and live out his life the way he was entitled, the way his father had talked about but never got the chance.

As he slid back onto his leather seat, a light in the front window caught his attention. The television. The timer was off its cycle again. Probably a power shortage.

He tossed the mail onto the passenger seat, about to continue down the driveway when another flicker of light caught his eye—a sharp, more directed light. Not the television. Connor swiveled his head and looked up and down the block. The wind continued to blow the fog thick and thin. He saw a car parked on the south side of the street, the only one. A red Saab convertible. It faded and reappeared in the fog like an apparition. After forty years, Connor knew what belonged and what was out of place in his neighborhood. The street cleaners cleaned the south side of the street every Wednesday morning at 6:00 a.m. The fines for not moving your car were steep. Anyone who lived in the neighborhood knew the schedule.

The car did not belong.

Neither did the light that flickered again inside his home.

Connor took his foot off the brake and drove forward.

Outside, the headlights crept down the side of the house and disappeared. The engine died.

Donley started out of the room, took one last look at the shelf of videotapes, and stopped. A videocassette rested atop the video player below the television. Donley quickly picked it up. *Dirty Harry*. The cassette was the only one not in a case. Given how organized the rest of the house was, it seemed particularly out of place. He looked but didn't see the empty case.

Outside the window, a car door opened and closed. Donley's heart raced. He wiped perspiration from his eyes and quickly ran the penlight over the titles again.

Get out, his inner voice shouted. *Get out!*

Heavy footsteps approached the front door.

Dirty Harry.

He pulled the case from the shelf. It contained a tape. He slid it out. Unlabeled. Footsteps sounded on the front porch. He quickly switched the *Dirty Harry* cassette for the unlabeled tape inside the case and slid it back onto the shelf.

Keys rattled in the lock. Donley crossed to the kitchen as the front door opened behind him. As he crossed to the laundry room, he heard the sound of keys dropping on a wood surface.

Donley pulled open the back door and stepped onto the porch. A light inside the house came on. Donley shut the door and grabbed the porch railing, intending to vault it to get out of the line of sight, but when he jumped, the railing snapped, and he sprawled into the grass. He felt the gun dislodge from the small of his back. On his hands and knees, he frantically searched the tall grass, but it was like a thicket. He couldn't find the revolver. He didn't have time to look.

Move!

He scrambled to his feet, unlatched the gate, and slid between the car and the side of the house, ducking low to stay below the windows. At the corner of the house, he paused and leaned out. Seeing no one, he bolted for the street, the videocassette bouncing inside his coat pocket. The fog now became his ally, helping to obscure him.

Fear caused him to burst into a dead run. At his car, he fumbled with his keys and looked back over his shoulder, but the fog had grown so thick, he could barely see the outline of the house.

The key rattled in the lock. Donley's hand shook, unable to find the teeth. Gusts of wind shook the car. Donley inserted the key. He had visions of it snapping off in the lock, but it turned, and the door latch popped up.

He pulled the door open, slid behind the wheel, and shut and locked the door. Only then did he allow himself to let out the breath he'd been holding, to feel a sense of relief. Yes, it had been a risk, but it had paid off. He had the tape, and he was certain whatever was on it would be the final piece to the puzzle he needed to exonerate Father Tom. He inserted the key in the ignition lock between the two seats. A further sense of relief washed over him when the engine kicked over. He felt like shouting. He felt like laughing out loud. He felt as if a huge weight had been lifted from his shoulders.

Something fluttered in a gust of wind.

He looked up at the convertible top. A wedge-shaped piece of the canvas roof flapped like a bird's wings.

Ragtops are easy, the homeless man had said. *Rip the top, open the door, do all kinds of damage.*

And in that moment he smelled the feral, inhuman smell, just before he felt the muzzle of the gun press against the back of his head.

"Hello, Counselor."

Chapter 21

Frank Ross walked into his house through the back door, opened the refrigerator, and pulled out a bottle of mineral water. Old habits died hard. The mineral water used to be beer. He drank the water to settle his stomach.

His wife, Julia, walked into the kitchen wearing a bathrobe and slippers, drying her hair with a towel.

"You waited up this late," he said, surprised to see her.

"I couldn't sleep. Thought a hot shower would help." She leaned against a counter. "Everything OK?"

"Sam just needed to talk. I didn't think I'd be this long, or I would have called. I was afraid I'd wake you."

"What did Sam want this time of night?"

"He wanted to show me a story the *Chronicle* was going to run tomorrow about that attorney I told you about, the one representing Father Martin."

"That doesn't sound good," she said. "He called, by the way."

"Peter Donley called here? When?"

"Earlier. He called twice."

"Did he say what he wanted?"

She shook her head. "No. Didn't leave a number, either."

Ross wondered if it had to do with Ross picking up Donley in the morning, if Donley had a change of plans. It was too late to call now.

On the drive home, Ross had thought about what Donley had told him in the car, about being abused by his father, and the deadly confrontation that eventually resulted.

"So many people really get cheated in life, don't they?" he said. "Kids, I mean. They don't do anything except get born, and then they pay the price for someone else's mistakes and disappointments." He felt his emotions bubbling to the surface and wiped away tears. "We gave Frankie a good home, two loving parents. Why him?"

This time, the tears felt different. Instead of stinging like a thousand needles piercing his skin, they felt like they were somehow washing him clean, absolving him. "Why would God take him when there are so many others out there living in such crappy conditions?"

She put her arms around him and pressed her cheek to his chest. "I don't know, Frank. I don't know."

"He's dead," Ross said, sobbing. "Frankie's dead, isn't he?"

Now she was crying, too, holding him tight. "I think so, Frank. I think he is."

"I hope he is," Ross said. "Does that sound terrible . . ."

"No."

"To hope that your own child is dead? I just don't want him suffering. I don't want him hurting. I want him to be in a better place, someplace where no one can hurt him. Someplace where he can feel our love, where he knows we still love him, and that we tried. We really tried to get him back."

"He's there, Frank. He's there, and that's where we'll think of him from now on. We'll think of him in that better place, with your parents and mine watching over him."

"My pop loved Frankie."

"Yes, he did. So that's what we'll think. We'll think they're up there fishing together on a big lake with a bright-morning sun and doughnuts and coffee—"

"Hot chocolate and cinnamon twists," he said.

"Hot chocolate and cinnamon twists."

He clutched her to him, holding her in a fierce embrace.

"He's in a better place," he said. "So much better than this world has to offer."

◆　◆　◆

The nauseating odor of alcohol and cigarettes filled the car as they drove east on Sloat Boulevard, making their way across town—to where, Donley did not know. His mind raced, and he fought to slow his thinking and remain calm, but there was a howling in his ears like the wind blowing off the Pacific Ocean. Beads of sweat trickled down his brow, the salt stinging his eyes.

He thought of hitting the brakes and trying to wrestle the gun away from Connor. If he crashed and died, it didn't matter. Connor was going to kill him, anyway. At least he'd take the son of a bitch with him. The light fixtures along the sides of the road were metal poles but made to break away if hit. He looked for something solid to impact.

Dixon Connor spoke from the back of the car, like the devil on Donley's shoulder.

"Keep your eyes forward. If you make any sudden movements, or do something stupid, I'll blow your brains out."

"It's over, Connor. People know I came here. People know I came to your house."

"No, they don't. You know how I know that? Because I saw you and Frank Ross together, which means you're working with him, and if Ross knew you were thinking of breaking into my house, he never would have let you do it. I actually admire your courage, Counselor. You got balls."

"You're wrong. I called Frank. I left a message. I told him where I was going."

"Well, then, he's too late, isn't he?" Connor chuckled. "Good old Frank. Is he still crackers? He was a good man until someone stole his kid."

Donley searched the deserted streets. "We found the red-haired kid. He told us everything. He's giving the police a statement right now. We also know about the other two boys you killed, Jerry Burke and Manuel Rivera."

"Without the video and the priest's little black book, you don't have shit. Do you think I picked that kid at random? He's a druggie and a liar. Did he tell you he had hippie parents or give you the story about his father dying in Vietnam? He comes from Orinda, Counselor. His father's a doctor. He's just a punk loser whose parents threw him out of the house. He's also a compulsive liar. But that's all irrelevant because nobody is going to prosecute me." Connor leaned forward, speaking into Donley's ear. "You can count on that."

Connor picked up the videocassette and held it between the bucket seats. "They had no idea what they had. I thought it was all bullshit, the rumors about three punks blackmailing people with videotapes. Then I paid a visit to that restaurant prick, Devine, and he cried like a baby. So I started thinking if they had clients like Jack Devine, who knew what else they had? When I got ahold of Burke and he told me he'd seen one of the guys on a local billboard, I nearly shit my drawers."

"Bennet took the tape to the shelter, didn't he?" Donley said. "He tried to hide it in one of the lockers."

"Not bad, Counselor. Keep going."

"You sent Red in to get it, but the lockers were locked. So you had to get it yourself. But you had another problem: two open files, Burke and Rivera. Three would set off alarms. So you framed Father Tom for Bennet's murder."

"Actually, the locks on the office door and lockers turned out to be a stroke of luck."

"Because screwing up the evidence makes people more nervous the priest might walk, or this matter could go to trial," Donley said.

"People tend to listen better when they're nervous."

"That's why Ramsey is pushing a plea."

Connor gave him instructions to turn on to back streets, avoiding the freeway and major arteries across town. They turned onto Third Street, an industrial area of cement plants, abandoned steel mills, and warehouses. The condition of the area declined as they drove south.

"Slow here," Connor said, looking out the windshield. "Turn."

Donley made a right turn onto a gravel road. The Saab lurched and pitched up an incline toward a ten-foot-tall chain-link fence with a single roll of barbed wire strung along the top.

"Pull up to the fence."

"Where are we?"

"A long time ago, I was investigating a missing person's report. The family became convinced a boyfriend killed their teenage daughter. The problem was, we couldn't find the body. The boyfriend's old man owned this wrecking yard. Eventually, the poor dumb bastard broke down and led me here. He and the son dumped the girlfriend's body in the trunk of a car, flattened it, and sent the car inside the building, where it was melted down at about ten billion degrees. No car. No girlfriend. No body. Ingenious. I didn't think the guy was that smart. Apparently, there's a soil-contamination problem, so the yard has sat unused since father and son went off to San Quentin together."

"Why not just take the tapes? Why kill those three kids?"

"Don't go getting all sentimental on me, Counselor. They were going to die, anyway, with all the drugs and crap they were putting in their veins. I just helped along the natural order."

"Ross is right. You really went off the deep end. What happened to the decorated police officer and war hero? Your father must be looking down at you awful proud tonight."

Connor grabbed a handful of Donley's hair, pulled his head back, and bit down on the tip of his ear. A searing pain shot through his body, his back arching as if Connor had embedded a knife in his spine. Connor kept a grip on Donley's hair and spit the tip of the ear onto the passenger seat. Donley felt warm blood dripping down the side of his neck.

"Did you know the ear is all cartilage?" Connor said, still spitting. "That's the reason it atrophies so bad. You see those wrestlers with the big cauliflower ears? They can't fix 'em. Plastic surgery doesn't work. You hurt someone's ear and they're scarred for life. You want to talk about my father? My father taught me that when I wrestled. He said go for their ears."

Donley grimaced at the sudden, searing pain. Spit projected through the gaps in his teeth. He had trouble focusing, thinking clearly. The pain caused his hands to clench into fists and bile to inch up his throat.

Connor sat back, laughing. "You want to know what happened?"

Donley tried to swallow, but his saliva stuck in his throat. Connor slapped the ear with the cup of his hand. "Hey, you with me? I asked, do you want to know what happened?"

Donley buckled over as far as the seat belt allowed, his ear on fire. Mentally, he tried to absorb the anger and the pain, to redirect it, to use it to help him focus. "Yeah, Connor, what happened? I'm dying to know."

Connor leaned between the seats and whispered in Donley's ear. "What happened is this whole world fell apart, and you're part of the problem. Lawyers have screwed it up for everybody with your bullshit lawsuits. Civil-rights crap. Affirmative action. Equal opportunity. Sexual harassment. It cost my old man the only job he loved. It wasn't just that bitch that killed him; it was guys like you. You sucked the life out of him. Twenty-five years he put his ass on the line every day, and they killed him because of one lying bitch."

"I didn't do anything, Connor. I didn't even know your father."

Connor sat back. "Lawyers and politicians love to talk about the public welfare, but they don't give a shit about public welfare. It's about money. Everything is about how much cash everyone can stuff in his pockets. You don't give a shit about the consequences so long as you get your money."

Connor leaned forward again. His breath brushed against Donley's ear, the same bitter, acidic odor Donley had smelled so many times when his father came into his room, belt in hand.

"It used to be survival of the fittest. Nature's way, just like the animals. You fought for what you got, and whoever fought the hardest got the most. You got a job and a promotion because you earned it. What went wrong is this country lost sight of the natural order. We're no longer Americans. We're Mexicans and Latinos, blacks and Chinese, and a thousand other things. Men want to be women, and women want to be men. And everybody wants to be treated special. Everybody is entitled to something. You don't earn anything anymore. You just whine about something long enough, and the politicians hand it to you. If you don't like what you get, you hire a lawyer, and he sues to get you more. Well, I'm getting what my old man should've got, what he was entitled to, and what I'm entitled to. And I'm getting justice in the process."

He pulled the key from the ignition between the seats and grabbed the tape and the Bible, putting them in his jacket. "Get out."

Donley took a breath, the pain making him disoriented. This would be his one chance. He needed to pull it together. He pushed open the door, swung his legs out, and stood, though he felt off-balance.

Connor motioned to him with the gun. "Step away from the car, and turn around. Don't even think about running. I'll shoot you in the back."

Donley took two steps, fighting to focus. He felt dizzy. When he heard Connor push the seat forward and get out of the car, Donley leaped. His left leg swept in an arc head high, but he was too far away. Connor leaned back, and Donley's foot shot past him. He landed on his left leg, raised his right leg, and kicked out, his foot uncoiling, but Connor had stepped to the side, and Donley had lost the moment of surprise. Connor grabbed the leg and yanked it toward him, pulling Donley off-balance. He fell backward, landing hard, his head slamming against the ground.

Connor held Donley's leg in the air, one foot pressed against Donley's cheek, grinding his face into the dirt.

"Fool me once, shame on you. Fool me twice, shame on me. Still, I would have been disappointed if you hadn't at least tried." Connor removed his foot and dropped Donley's leg. "Get up."

Donley got to his knees, panting from the exertion and the searing pain in his ear. He stumbled trying to get to his feet. His eyes searched the ground, but he did not see anything he could use as a weapon. Connor kicked him hard in the face, knocking him onto his back. Blood streamed from his lip and nose, filling his mouth with a metallic taste.

"I said get up."

Donley stumbled to his hands and knees and slowly stood.

"Turn around."

He complied. Connor pushed him toward the chain-link fence. Donley bent under a locked chain and squeezed between the gates. Connor followed. He directed Donley to walk down an aisle of flattened cars stacked two stories high. Rusted car parts littered the ground. The air smelled like petroleum.

"Stop," Connor said. "Well, what do you know?" Connor motioned to a stripped-down Chevy Impala. "Looks just like the one I used to drive. Must be fate. You can't say I didn't pick a proper final resting place. Open the trunk, and try it on for size, Counselor."

Donley faced Connor. "No. I'm not making this that easy for you, Connor. If you're going to kill me, do it here while I'm looking at you. I'm not some young kid you can bully."

Connor smiled. "Why is it at the moment when it matters least, everyone becomes so brave?" He shrugged. "Have it your way," he said, and aimed the gun.

Frank Ross lay on his back, staring up at the ceiling. Julia rested her head on his shoulder, rubbing her hand through the hairs on his chest.

"Frank," she said in that soft voice.

Ross closed his eyes. She wanted another child. He knew it. She wasn't getting any younger. Neither was he, but her biological clock was ticking. He also knew it wasn't fair to her. She'd stuck by him through his drinking, the car accident, and the year it took to get back some semblance of a life. She had ignored her own pain and suffering to help him, and he had been too self-absorbed to see that she was hurting, too. But now, he felt different, accepting that Frankie was in a better place. It was time to care for her again.

"I was thinking," she said, "you know, about what you said in the kitchen, about there being so many kids out there who need a good home, good parents."

His chest rose, shuddered, and fell.

"I know it's hard for you to think about, and I'm not trying to replace Frankie. I just want us to have a family, to be a family again. You're a good dad. You're a good father. So many kids out there need a good father like you."

He shifted so he could see her face. "What are you saying?"

"We could adopt, Frank. We could help some of those kids out there who are lost. We could give them a better life, a chance."

He didn't know what to say. He thought of his conversation with Peter Donley about children with bad fathers; not necessarily fathers that abused them, but fathers who ignored them, didn't spend time with them, didn't offer them all of the things that a good father could offer and teach. Ross had been a good father. He had so much to offer.

He kissed the top of her head. The moisture from her cheek dampened his chest. "What did I do to deserve someone as good as you?" he asked.

"Will you at least think about it, Frank?"

He already had.

The telephone rang.

"Saved by the bell," his wife said with a trace of humor.

Ross reached over his head and blindly lifted the receiver, thinking it might be Sam Goldman, or Donley. "Hello?"

"Frank? It's Lieutenant Aileen O'Malley."

Ross sat up.

His wife rolled to the side. "Who is it?"

Ross mouthed, "O'Malley."

"Aileen?" Julia said.

"Frank, I'm sorry to call so late. I'm sure I'm not a voice you expected to hear."

She might have been the last voice he expected to hear. "Can't say I did."

"I don't doubt it. But I got a kid down here telling one hell of a story, and I think you'll want to hear it."

"Come again?"

"He has your card in his pocket, and he says you gave it to him."

Ross swung his legs over the side of the bed. "Red-haired kid?"

"He says Peter Donley dropped him off here and told the officers the kid had a story to tell me."

"Dropped him off?"

"That's right."

Ross got a bad feeling. "Donley isn't with him?"

"No. The kid said Donley told him not to be afraid anymore, to just tell the officers the truth and we'd keep him safe."

"Did he say where Donley went?"

"That's what concerns me. The kid said this had to do with Dixon Connor and that Peter Donley said he was going to take care of the problem. Do you know what the hell he's talking about Frank? Frank?"

"I'm here, Aileen."

"Do you know what he meant?"

Ross did. "Aileen, I'm going to need your help. I'm going to need some black-and-whites to meet me at Dixon Connor's house in the Sunset and do what I tell them. Can you do that, for old time's sake? There might be a life at stake."

◆　◆　◆

Donley heard the growl before the thick, dark shape materialized, darting from the shadows between the canyon of gutted car frames.

Connor, too, turned at the sound, but the Rottweiler had already closed the distance. Its paws impacted Connor's chest with the full force of its weight and momentum, knocking him off his feet. The big gun exploded, off target, echoing like a cannon blast. Connor rolled, but the Rottweiler had seized the arm holding the gun, locking its teeth into flesh, shaking its head.

Connor howled, a horrific cry of pain.

Donley backed away, uncertain what he had just witnessed, what he was continuing to witness. Then the inner voice of instinct shouted.

Run!

The videotape and Bible lay on the ground, having fallen from Connor's pocket. Donley grabbed both, turned, and ran. He ducked his way through the maze of gutted car frames, searching for a way out. The holes where the car headlights had once been followed him like hollow eye sockets, the front grills menacing grins. He ran blindly, uncertain of his direction or his path.

Behind him, the dog growled, and he heard Connor yell again in anguish.

Donley chose another row. Circles. He was running in circles. He turned yet again and skidded to a stop at the base of the cyclone fence.

Dead end.

He started back in the direction he had come but stopped when he heard the same guttural growl from somewhere in the dark. It came out of the darkness and shadows.

A second dog.

The impact knocked Connor backward, as if he'd been hit by a train. His legs came out from under him, and when he hit the ground, a sharp pain exploded at the small of his back, followed by an intense heat and electric jolt. It felt like the time he'd been shot.

Something had embedded deep in his flesh, but Connor was in no position to try and dislodge whatever had impaled him. The dog had bit down with such force, Connor thought the bones in his arm would snap. Blood saturated the sleeve of his sport coat. He feared the taste would send the dog into a primal frenzy.

Connor had spent eight years with the canine unit, and through his pain and shock, he still could recognize that the dog was well trained, attacking and immobilizing the arm holding the weapon. The junkyard was clearly no longer abandoned. The dog would not let go. There was no one to call it off. Still, as long as the dog had its jaws clamped around Connor's arm, it could not go for his throat, and that gave Connor a chance. The problem was, with the dog's jaws immobilizing Connor's arm, he could not use the gun to kill it.

He felt the strength in his grip waning and rotated his body to kick at the animal, but the dog dragged him in a circle, causing the sharp object to embed deeper into Connor's flesh, the pain now searing.

Connor squeezed the trigger, hoping the sound might scare the animal, but it had no effect. The dog maintained its grip. Connor rolled onto his right side and reached behind him with his left hand, feeling something cylindrical protruding from his back. It was his only chance. He gripped it, took a deep breath, clenched his teeth, and yanked the shiv free, swallowing the pain. He flipped his legs around the dog's thick body, momentarily straddling it like a bull, raised the jagged metal, and struck.

The second Rottweiler stepped from the shadows. As big as the one chewing on Connor's arm, the dog thrust out its front paws, lowered its head, and bared its teeth, daring Donley to get past it.

Donley heard an anguished cry of pain. So did the dog. Its ears perked and it turned its head, but only momentarily. It returned its attention to Donley, inching closer.

Donley looked over his shoulder at the fence. He could climb it, but not as fast as the dog would attack. He thought of Kim and what she had taught him for so many years about finding an inner peace even during moments of chaos. He just didn't know if he had the courage to do it, but he also knew he had no choice.

With no other option, he slowly dropped to a knee. The dog lurched forward, digging its front paws into the dirt, barking and growling. Donley paused, then, slowly, he lowered to his other knee. He kept his eyes down, each movement slow and deliberate.

"Easy, boy. Easy now," he whispered.

The dog made another false charge.

Donley fought not to panic. He fought his instinct to get up and run. Instead, he willed himself to lower his body onto the ground.

The dog bared its teeth and made another charge, but this time Donley sensed it did so because it was confused. Donley slowly brought his knees to his chest and cradled his face in his arms, assuming a fetal position, trying to slip into that place of tranquility. He could hear the chain around the dog's neck rattling and the low growl as it circled. Dog breath warmed the side of Donley's face. He did not dare move. The dog gripped his forearm with its jaws and pulled, but it did not bite down. The leather jacket offered some protection, but Donley could still feel the power in the dog's jaws. Strong as a bull, the animal dragged Donley's body inches along the ground.

When Donley did not resist, the dog dropped his arm. Then it sniffed at Donley's face, moving closer to his bloodied ear.

Frank Ross slowed at an intersection to allow a car to pass, then gunned the Cadillac through the red light. Dixon Connor lived in the Sunset District near the ocean. It was Connor's parents' house, less than five miles from Frank Ross's home. Ross remembered thinking it was too close. Now, he wished it were closer.

Red was in a conference room in homicide talking about Connor and videotapes, and generally confusing the hell out of Lieutenant Aileen O'Malley and Detective John Begley.

Before leaving the house, Ross had called Kim Donley, but she said Peter wasn't home, that he'd eaten dinner and said he had to go back to the office to work on his motion to exclude the evidence. He gave her his car-phone number and asked her to call him back when she'd heard from her husband. Kim Donley called Ross back five minutes later and said she'd called the office but no one had answered. Now stricken with worry, she said she'd asked Danny Simeon if he knew where Peter had gone. Simeon had told her Peter had said he was going to find a red-haired kid who'd stayed at the shelter, but he had no idea where else Donley would have gone. Frank Ross did.

Peter Donley was going after the evidence. Donley had told him as much. He'd said, to win, he had to find Andrew Bennet's killer. Now he had.

Headlights appeared to his right. Ross slammed on the brakes, sending the Cadillac into a skid on the fog-slickened pavement. He turned the wheel hard against the spin, correcting. A horn blared. He punched the accelerator. The back end fishtailed, but he avoided the oncoming vehicle. His heart raced, and for a brief moment he'd flashed back to that morning when he'd hit the minivan, but he dismissed it. He needed to focus. Connor was a trained cop, a good one, and one mean, strong son of a bitch. He would think nothing of blowing a hole in Peter Donley if he found him in his house.

Ross skidded the Cadillac to a stop at the curb. Within seconds, the patrol cars Aileen O'Malley had sent pulled up behind him. Ross jumped from the car, slapping a clip into his SIG. He quickly apprised the uniformed officers of the situation and said Connor would be armed and should be considered extremely dangerous. Beyond that, he had no idea what they would find inside.

He approached Dixon Connor's house in a thick blanket of fog, using arm and hand signals to tell the officers to fan out. Two went down the side of the house. Two went to the front door. Ross touched the hood of the SUV in the driveway. It was cold. He pressed his back against the stucco exterior and looked inside the windows. A television glowed. He went down the side of the house to a gate and peered over the top into an overgrown back yard. He unlatched the gate and went in, the officers following. As Ross approached the back door, he noticed that the staircase handrail was broken, the railing lying in the tall grass. He stepped on something hard, bent down, and picked up a police service revolver. He knew Connor's preferred weapon was a .44 Magnum. This was not it.

He stuffed the revolver in his pants, held the SIG in front of him, and stepped onto the porch, feeling the wood sag. He tried the door handle and found the back door unlocked, which seemed unlike Dixon Connor.

He nodded to the two officers. One used a radio to alert the two officers at the front door that they were going in. They entered the house combat-style, low to the ground, aiming left and right. The kitchen was clear. So was the dining room and the living room. Ross turned to the hallway and two closed doors.

Connor sat with his back pressed against a car frame, the sleeve of his jacket bloodied and torn. He couldn't be sure of the extent of the damage in the dim moonlight, but he suspected it was bad. He took off his jacket and used the metal shiv to cut strips of cloth, tying two strips tight around his forearm. He could do nothing about the wound in his back, which he sensed was also bad. The dog lay nearby on its side.

Connor holstered the .44 with his good hand and stumbled to his feet. A searing pain burned down both legs. His shirt stuck to his back. He didn't have time to dwell on it. Peter Donley was here somewhere, and he had the tape and Bible with the log-in record. Without them, Connor was screwed.

In pain, he stumbled forward, through the rows of cars.

The dog circled, sniffing at Donley's cheek and ear, nudging him with its bony head, growling. Then it stepped back and barked. Donley didn't move, thinking of those red taillights he used to watch on the Bay

Bridge, thinking of himself in one of those cars, leaving. Across the junkyard, a dog yelped, followed by a gunshot. The first dog was dead.

Connor was coming.

The chain around the animal's neck rattled and shook. Donley opened one eye and watched the dog step back, maybe four feet, and turn its head in the direction of the sound. It took two steps down the path, sniffing the air before turning back to Donley and growling, as if to warn him not to move. Then, just as quickly as it had appeared, the dog darted between the rows of cars. This time, Connor would not be surprised. He would kill the second dog immediately.

Donley jumped up quickly, stumbled to the fence, and started to climb. Poorly anchored, the fence swayed like unsecured netting, making it difficult for Donley to pull himself up, to find the next toehold. It forced him to climb cautiously, fearful of losing his grip, of falling and having to start over. He put his toe in another link, climbing higher, chain link by chain link. The fence looked a hundred feet tall.

The second dog barked, followed by the echo of another gunshot.

Connor was coming.

Donley fought against the urge to rush, maintaining a methodical pace. At the top of the fence, he grabbed the metal tube with his hands, but he lost his toehold in the chain link and, momentarily dangling, kicked at the fence. The rattle echoed in the empty yard, giving away his position. He regained his toehold, pushed up with his legs, and wrapped one arm around the top of the fence. He had to figure out quickly how to get over the barbed wire.

He slid one leg over the top so he was straddling the metal pole. Carefully, he removed his leather jacket and flung it over the wire.

He looked down into the yard. A shadow step from behind the rows of cars and started down the dirt path. With a full moon, Connor would see Donley atop the fence like a target in a carnival booth. Donley didn't have time to climb over and down the other side. He gripped the metal pole with his hands and lifted himself up so that both feet were on the bar, like a swimmer bent over on the starting block. The fence swayed. He hesitated a split second when he realized he could see nothing below him but darkness.

Then the big gun thundered, and Donley jumped.

He had no idea how far he would fall.

His heels jarred upon impact with the ground, splinters of pain shooting up both legs. Donley fell forward, like a board pitching end over end, his hands unable to break his fall, unable to stop his momentum. He tumbled repeatedly, the ground slamming hard against his chest, his legs whipping over the top.

When he had finally stopped rolling, he slid headfirst. Sharp brush whipped against his bare arms and face. He grabbed a branch, but it ripped from his grasp. He reached again, failed, reached, gripped, and held on. His lower body slid past in a half circle, like someone clinging to a rope after falling over the side of a building.

When his momentum stopped, Donley lowered his head to let the avalanche of dirt and debris pass. Stunned and dazed, he lifted his head to assess his situation. He lay on an incline pocked with scrub brush. The fence at the top of the hill looked like a toy model, but he could just barely make out his jacket still hanging from the barbed wire.

Inside the pocket was the video and Bible.

His only hope was that Connor didn't see it or was too injured to climb up and get it.

Donley rolled onto his back. He was in so much pain, he couldn't be certain whether Connor's final shot had hit him or not. He sat up and took a brief moment to catch his wind and assess his condition. When he tried to stand, the pain in his right shin felt like someone had stabbed it. He fell back to the ground. He didn't have to be a doctor to know his leg was broken.

That didn't matter.

Connor was still out there, and he would come. He needed to be sure Donley was dead. He needed the tape. He would come.

Donley turned and faced up the slope, then slid downhill using his good leg to push through the thick brush. The process was laborious and slow. He tried not to think about how much time was passing or the pain radiating throughout his body. At the base of the hill, he got to his feet, balancing on his good leg. A cluster of corrugated-metal warehouses was visible in the near distance. It looked like miles across open desert. He picked up a discarded board and leaned on it like a crutch, making his way toward the warehouses, trying not to rush, afraid he would stumble and fall. He groaned with each hop forward, putting his weight on his good leg, propping the board in front of him, lunging.

When he reached the warehouses, he was drenched in a chilled sweat, though his forehead burned. The pain in his leg caused tremors throughout his body. Suddenly nauseated, he lurched forward and vomited, then wretched again, dry heaves.

When the nausea passed, he braced himself on the two-by-four and hobbled toward the back of one of the buildings. He tried a metal door, not surprised to find it locked. Near it were two smoked-glass windows reinforced with chicken wire. He leaned against the wall and wiped the sweat dripping from his forehead, feeling light-headed and weak. He picked up the board and used it to batter one of the windows. The glass cracked but did not shatter. He continued to beat at the glass until the chicken wire gave way. He punched through. When he'd busted out most of the glass, he put the board across the sill and struggled to lift himself onto it. He leaned forward, like on a teeter-totter, and slid. His right leg crashed against the top edge of the window, and this time, he could not swallow the pain. His screams and moans echoed throughout the warehouse.

He didn't know how long he lay on the cold concrete floor. At one point, he was sure he'd passed out. When the forty-foot ceiling above him quit spinning, Donley managed to sit up. Rows of metal shelving filled with paint cans and paint supplies pulsed in and out of focus. He used one of the racks to pull himself to his feet and shuffled through the maze of cans of paint thinner and acetone, searching for an office and a phone. At the end of the row, he came to a long white counter in front of a glass-enclosed room. It looked like an oasis.

The door was unlocked. Inside, he found a counter with a computer terminal, stools, desks with swivel chairs, filing cabinets, and a telephone.

◆ ◆ ◆

Ross went room to room, officers fanning out, yelling "Clear!" as they entered and exited.

He flipped on light switches and entered what was presumably Dixon Connor's bedroom. It looked like a storm had swept through it.

"Holy crap," one of the officers said, noticing the montage of newspaper articles tacked and taped to the wall, most yellowed with age. Ross felt sick to his stomach. Dixon Connor had indeed gone off the deep end.

Chapter 22

Donley could not move his arms. His shirt, saturated with sweat, stuck to his skin. His fingers and hands felt numb, and he was shivering uncontrollably. He didn't know how long he'd passed out, whether a minute or an hour, but judging from the darkness inside the warehouse, he had not yet made it through the night. He remembered picking up the phone but couldn't be certain he'd called anyone.

When he sat, a sharp pain shot up his leg. He gathered his strength, gripped the counter, and pulled himself to his feet. A muted light streamed through skylights, casting shadows off the metal shelves and drums of paint, making it difficult to determine what was real and what was reflected in the office windows. Overhead, an automatic air-conditioning system hummed, pouring cool air through a grill, a strip of red fabric flapping in the breeze.

Donley started for the phone on the counter but froze when a beam of light swept across the warehouse. Someone was coming. He slid open drawers, looking for a weapon. In one of the drawers he found a long pair of scissors. He grabbed it and pressed his back against the wall near the door.

It was all he could do.

The figure passed the counter and disappeared from view. Donley looked down and watched the doorknob turn. The door pushed in, but no one immediately entered. The beam of light swept across the room. Donley clenched his teeth and raised the scissors, not about to go quietly.

The overhead lights in the office clicked on. Donley spun from the wall, scissors raised.

"Whoa." Frank Ross reached up, stopping Donley's arm.

"Ross," Donley said, collapsing against the big man, feeling a sense of relief.

Ross directed him to a stool and lowered him down. "How bad are you hurt?"

"I think my leg is broken."

"Connor?"

"I don't know. Still out there somewhere."

"Let's get you out of here."

Ross draped Donley's arm around his shoulders. One of two officers who stepped forward came to Donley's other side.

"How did you find me?" Donley asked.

Ross gave him a concerned look. "You called your wife. She called nine-one-one. You don't remember?"

The retort of a big gun echoed, and the glass window of the office exploded not far from their heads.

Ross acted instinctively, pushing Donley to the floor and slapping at the light switch, plunging them back into darkness.

Connor.

From the trajectory of the bullet, Ross figured Connor had to be somewhere above them, on the catwalk.

A second shot shattered another window.

Ross crawled from the office on his hands and knees to the two officers who had taken cover below the counter.

"Connor carries a forty-four Magnum," he said to them. "It sounds like a cannon, but at that distance, it's not very accurate." He raised his head, looking for shadows and movement. "He's somewhere on the catwalk. Give me some cover."

Another shot rang out, skipping off the Formica, causing Ross to duck again. The son of a bitch always was a good shot, but the shot had also given away Connor's location.

"He's at two o'clock," Ross said to the officers. "Take a broad range and provide me with cover."

On the count of three, the officers rose and fired, their guns echoing as if in a drum.

Ross ran, firing the SIG over his head. When he reached the cover of the metal shelving, he slid down the aisle, staying close to the cans. A bullet skipped off the concrete floor a foot behind him. He returned fire at the catwalk, backpedaling down the aisle and around the corner. The front entrance was to his left. The broken window he and the officers had found walking the perimeter was about ten yards to his right, at the back of the building. The metal rack and paint drums, his cover, ended five yards short. As he slapped in a fresh clip, he noticed the labels on the cans.

Flammable.

Not good.

Ross decided to go for the window. He took half a step from behind a row of cans, but had to draw back when another shot skipped off the cement.

He pressed his back to the cans, wishing he'd given up the cinnamon twists a year earlier. He made the sign of the cross and bolted for the window, firing blindly at the catwalk. Nearing the window, he lowered his head and dove through the opening, hitting the ground outside and rolling onto his back.

He scrambled to his feet and staggered down the side of the building, hearing additional shots being fired from inside. At the Cadillac, Ross climbed inside, about to start the engine when a loud explosion and flash of flames blew out windows near the roof, raining glass onto the hood of the car. Ross turned the key and threw the car into reverse. He drove away from the warehouse, made a sudden U-turn, and punched the accelerator. The Cadillac's back tires spun in the dirt and gravel, gripped, and propelled the car forward across the dirt lot toward the building's corrugated-metal doors. His instinct was to hit the brakes, but Ross suppressed it and pressed down on the accelerator. He pulled his seat belt tight, and braced his hands on the steering wheel.

God forgive him, he was about to retire the Cadillac.

The car hit a bump, bounced, and became airborne. The force caused Ross to lurch forward, straining against the belt, but he had the presence of mind to hit the brakes when the Cadillac impacted the doors. The car burst through with a metallic thud, landed, and skidded across the slick cement, toppling metal shelving and sending cans and drums flying. Paint splattered across the hood of the car as it shot forward. Another drum shattered the windshield.

The car slid to a stop near the office.

Ross reached for the SIG and fell out the door, gripping the gun in both hands, aiming at the catwalk, not seeing anyone. Flames leaped high over the metal racks. A second explosion launched a drum of paint like a depth charge off the back of a destroyer. It hit the counter, bounced, and crashed through the office windows.

"Move!" Ross yelled to the two police officers taking cover.

He put his shoulder under Donley's arm, assisting him into the back of the car as a third explosion rocked the warehouse and a plume of flames and smoke shot toward the ceiling. One of the officers crawled into the back seat with Donley. The second jumped in the front seat. Ross threw the car into reverse as another explosion rippled toward them and the metal shelving overhead teetered.

The Cadillac's engine revved, but the car did not move, the tires spinning on the paint-slickened concrete, spewing a plume of white smoke. Another explosion sent a rolling ball of flames directly at them. Ross punched the accelerator, and the tires gripped and finally lurched backward as the shelving above them collapsed in a pile of twisted metal.

For an instant, he saw nothing but the flames and smoke. Then it cleared, and the Cadillac shot outside, across the lot.

Chapter 23

December 30, 1987

Frank Ross stood outside what remained of the paint warehouse. An ambulance had taken Peter Donley to the emergency room, but Ross had stayed to coordinate with the detectives and discuss the situation with Aileen O'Malley, who was en route. Though the fog layer had burned off, a stubborn morning haze and lingering smoke and ash particulates choked the air. The explosion and three-alarm blaze had burned out of control for hours, providing the news stations spectacular film footage and making for a busy night for San Francisco firefighters. The warehouse had been reduced to blackened rubble. Even the cement foundation had melted, leaving pieces of rebar sticking up like the charred remains of trees after a forest fire.

One of the fire units continued to pour water on the smoldering debris. Others shoveled through it. The flames had been so intense, the firefighters initially could not get near the building and hadn't been eager to do so. Ross still did not fully understand exactly what had happened. Donley had been in no shape to talk. His pain and shock had made him delirious. The one thing he'd kept repeating was that he needed his jacket, even after paramedics had covered him with multiple blankets.

Then he'd passed out.

Ross looked up at the sound of footsteps. Aileen O'Malley approached.

"He is one crazy son of a bitch," she said, surveying the damage.

Ross nodded. "That he is."

"You OK?"

Ross shrugged. "I could use a cinnamon twist and cup of coffee, but yeah, I'm OK."

She smiled. "How's Peter Donley?"

"Don't know. They're working on him. He's pretty banged up— broken leg and a lot of bumps and bruises. They're monitoring him for a concussion. Slipped into shock, but physically, I think he should be fine." Ross paused. "Mentally, I think it's going to take longer to heal."

Ross watched a fireman turn off the final stream of water. Others had begun to stretch their hoses, preparing to roll them up. "Any word on Connor?"

O'Malley shook her head. "No, but he won't get far. Where's a guy like Connor going to run? Can't imagine he has any friends left."

"Don't count on him making it easy on you," Ross said. "He won't do it himself like his old man."

"I know," O'Malley said. She took a deep breath. "There's something bothering me about this one, Frank. My stomach's been bothering me from the start."

"Never knew you to have a queasy stomach, Aileen."

"I made some telephone calls to try to find out what happened with Father Martin on Christmas Eve."

"The blood test?"

"I haven't been able to get anything concrete, but from what I can tell, the sheriff didn't act on an order from the district attorney's office."

Ross gave her a look. "So, who gave the order to have it done that night?"

She shook her head. "Don't know, but it had to be someone with some pretty good credentials."

Ross contemplated the information. "What does Ramsey have to say?"

"Haven't spoken to him yet. He's been stumping down south for votes. Last I heard, he was in Orange County. I was hoping you might have some insight."

"Into that specifically?" Ross shook his head. "No."

O'Malley leaned against the police cruiser, the two of them side by side. "At least it looks like this nightmare is over for Father Martin."

"The kid came clean?"

"About everything."

Ross shook his head. "I'm not sure it will ever be over for Father Martin. Something like this . . ."

"How about you, Frank? How're you doing?"

Frank Ross tilted his head and looked up at the sky. For the first time in nearly two years, he thought he just might be OK. Never the same. But OK. He really couldn't ask for more than that, not with his son gone.

"Sober for more than seven months now and plan on staying that way. I miss my son and know I'll always be a little crazy as a result, but I'm OK with that. Maybe I can make some good come from it."

"Maybe I can help."

Ross looked at her.

"I've put in a request for state and federal funding to form a child-exploitation detail. San Jose's had a pilot program that's showing success. They work with local FBI, Customs agents, US attorneys. I need somebody committed."

Ross shoved his hands in his pockets, giving it some thought. After several seconds he said, "I'll think about it. I have to discuss it with my wife. We're talking about starting a family again."

"Yeah?"

"Adopting."

"Good for you, Frank."

Ross looked down the street at the police barricade and saw Sam Goldman waving to him. "Thanks. I'll get back to you, but yeah, I think I'd like that. Right now, I have to keep a promise to a friend."

◆ ◆ ◆

Donley awoke to the glare of bright fluorescent lights that hurt his eyes and made him squint. When he stirred, his leg felt weighted. He looked down at a robin's-egg-blue cast that extended to just below his right knee, elevated in a stirrup. As more of the room came into focus, he saw Father Martin sitting in a chair by the bed, a bandage still around his head, but he was dressed in civilian clothes. Father Martin stood and approached.

"Well, this is a switch," Donley said, his voice rough and his throat so dry.

Father Martin reached onto a tray near the side of the bed and handed him a plastic cup with a straw. Donley sipped tepid water. A small amount dribbled down his chin.

"Welcome back," Father Martin said.

"Have I been out long?"

"Through the night and most of today."

"What?"

"They kept you sedated to deal with the pain."

"How did you get out?" Donley asked.

"Lou."

"He's out of the hospital?"

Father Martin nodded. "He is. He made some calls from home."

"Sounds like Lou." Donley considered the cast. "Light blue?"

"Your friend Mike wanted pink. You're lucky they were out."

"Mike is here?"

"No, but he called from Hawaii. You had a lot of people worried about you."

Donley looked about the room with a little trepidation. "Is Kim here?"

Father Martin nodded to the hallway. "She just stepped out to talk to your doctors. I'll get her." He took a half step.

"Wait. What about Frank?"

"Frank's fine. He stopped by earlier, said he talked to a lieutenant about what happened."

"They have Connor?"

"No. They haven't caught him yet." Father Martin stepped closer to the bed. "But they will. I'm in your debt, Peter."

"I knew you didn't kill Bennet. I want you to know that."

Kim appeared at the door, and Peter winced, though not from the pain. He now fully realized the stupidity of his actions, and he wasn't eager to face her. Father Martin gave him a wink and walked out, touching Kim's arm as he left. Kim walked to the window and pulled back the drapes. Streams of sunlight shot into the room.

"What time is it?" he asked.

"After three."

He struggled with the cobwebs. "Is Benny with your parents?"

She crossed her arms. "My parents are at the cabin. I can't reach them. Probably better I don't."

"Who's watching Benny?"

"Anne's at the house. And Danny is still there."

Donley struggled with what to say.

"Are you going to stay awake this time?" Kim walked closer and held his hand. With the other, she gently touched his forehead.

"I understand I've been in and out a few times?"

"Once or twice," she said.

"I feel like somebody beat me all over my body with a two-by-four."

"You look like somebody beat you all over your body with a two-by-four."

He smiled wanly. "Some bedside manner you have, Doctor." Donley stretched the muscles in his neck and grimaced. The soreness was sharp and tight.

"Whiplash," she said. "You'll be sore for a while."

"What's the rest of the diagnosis?"

"You broke your femur, but it was a clean break and should mend nicely. You'll be on crutches for several weeks, maybe longer, and in a cast for six weeks. Then they'll reevaluate. You have scrapes and bruises on your arms, one deep enough to require six stitches. The rest were cleaned and disinfected and bandaged. You could have some scars. Judging from your face, I'd say you'd better learn how to fall."

"That bad, huh?"

"It's not pretty. They're monitoring you for a concussion. You'll have some headaches and dizziness, but it shouldn't be prolonged."

Pieces of the night continued to come back to him. He reached up and touched a bandage on his ear, wincing at the recollection of Dixon Connor biting down on the tip.

"I left that one out," Kim said.

"How bad is it?"

"You're lucky you were passed out for that. The ear is cartilage. They can't give you a local anesthetic. They used a razor to cut it straight."

He grimaced at the thought.

"They say it was a human bite." He could see now Kim was fighting back tears, and he felt horrible knowing how much worry and pain he had caused her. "You lost a piece at the top, but it's toward the back. From the front, you really can't tell. Just face forward when you talk to the jury. Or you can grow your hair long again like in the seventies." She wiped tears rolling down her cheeks.

"Hey, come here."

She crossed her arms and didn't move. Her voice hardened. "What happened? What the hell were you doing?"

"I don't know," he said.

Her tone changed. "I'm your wife, Peter. I have a right to know. I was awake all night worrying."

"I'm sorry, Kim. I—"

"When Ross called and said you were in the hospital, I didn't know what I'd find down here. I didn't know if I was going to be retrieving a body or just bits and pieces."

"I'm all right. It's going to be OK now."

She stepped back. "Don't pacify me. You can shut me out, but I won't allow you to pacify me. Not anymore. That's not good enough. Why did you do it? Why did you go out there by yourself? Do you have a death wish? Why don't you let people help you, Peter?"

"Because I don't know how," he said. He looked away to wipe the tear forming in the corner of his eye. "No one ever helped, Kim. No one ever helped me or my mother. I waited eighteen years for someone to help us. No one did."

"And are you going to hold the whole world responsible, Peter? What did it prove? What did going after Dixon Connor prove?"

He turned and faced her. "That I cared. It proved that I cared about Father Martin and those boys he killed—that I wasn't going to turn my back on them and look away."

"You nearly got yourself killed in the process," she said. "You nearly left me a widow with two babies." The last words came in a sob.

Donley searched her face and felt himself go numb.

"I'm about six weeks." She put a trembling hand over her mouth. "Oh, God. Oh, God. I didn't want to tell you like this."

Donley reached out to her and pulled her close. He shut his eyes, but it did not stop the flow of tears down his face. He felt a mixture of joy and sorrow and guilt, recognizing the selfishness of his act. Kim was pregnant. My God, what had he been thinking?

After a minute, she grabbed a tissue from a box on his tray and sat on the edge of the bed blowing her nose. "I wanted to wait to tell you until a quiet moment when we were alone. I was hoping to surprise you Christmas Eve, but that sort of fell apart." She sobbed again. "I want you back, Peter. I want my husband back."

Donley pulled her to him and leaned his head against hers, but it caused a sharp pain in his neck. He grunted, and when she lifted her head, she hit the bandage on his forehead. He groaned and winced. His eyes watered. Their clumsiness made her laugh through her tears.

"Peter, if you don't want to talk to me about your past, I know some people here at the hospital."

He looked out the window. She reached out and gripped his hand.

He faced her. "I think that would be good," he said. "But there's something I also have to tell you."

"What is it?"

He felt the emotions again, unable to speak.

"Just tell me, Peter."

"It's about my father. It's about the night he died."

Kim sat holding his hand. Donley took a deep breath and started slowly, explaining how his father had never wanted to marry his mother and had never wanted a child. He worked his way through the years, telling her everything he had never told her about the physical and verbal abuse. He told her about how he blamed himself for it all, how his father told him it was his fault. He told her everything—the times he wanted to run away, the times he wanted to die, the times he wanted to kill his father.

"It got really bad when I was about nine. The rest of those years are a blur. I tried to block them out. When I got the scholarship to

Berkeley, it was the happiest and saddest day of my life. I was leaving. I was finally leaving, but I knew I couldn't leave my mother alone in that house with him. I knew as soon as I left, the beatings would start again, and he would have eventually killed her."

He looked down at the cast on his foot. "I called Lou and Sara and told them that I thought Mom was depressed and could use a weekend away. I asked them to take her. Her birthday was that week. It was a good excuse." He raised his gaze and engaged her. "When it got dark, I walked out back and removed the main fuse."

He saw in her face that she was figuring out on her own what had happened, and he saw that it scared her. He told her how he had sat on the steps waiting for the sound of the car engine chugging up the hill.

"The strange thing was, for the first time that I could remember, I wasn't afraid. For the first time in my life, I felt a sense of peace and relief. I had struggled with the decision for so long that, I think, to finally see the end of the tunnel actually made me feel free."

Kim sat silent.

"He hit me first. He always did. But this time, I didn't just take it. I was stronger than him by then. I was bigger, and the years of abusing his body had taken its toll on him physically. I had his throat in my hands, Kim. I had his throat in my hands." He bit down on his lip.

"What happened, Peter?"

He shook his head at the recollection of his contorted and grotesque face in the mirror above the mantel. "I realized I couldn't do it. I couldn't kill him. I knew that if I did, I would be just like him, and it would always haunt me. I think he knew it, too. I think he wanted me to kill him. I think he wanted it to be over."

He looked up at her. "But I let him go. I let him go, Kim, and I turned to leave. I intended to leave. And that's when I heard it."

The sound grew to a deafening roar.

His father rushed across the room, swinging a shard of glass like the blade of a knife. Surprised, Donley raised his arms, and the glass split his forearm, opening a deep wound.

Donley stumbled backward, falling over the debris of the bannister, landing hard on his back. His father attacked again, slashing, but his foot slipped on the blood flowing from Donley's arm, and he stumbled, giving Donley a momentary chance to roll and avoid the blade. As he rolled, Donley swept his right leg, hitting his father in the calves, knocking him off-balance.

It gave him time to scramble to his feet and grab a seat cushion off the couch, which he used as his father recovered and advanced. The shard of glass shredded the cushion. Donley tossed it aside. His father slashed again. Donley leaned back, but the tip of the blade grazed his cheek.

Donley shoved the hallway table into his father's path. The man kicked it aside like a toy. Donley backed into the living room, dodging and ducking, looking for an opening. It came when his father swung wildly, leaving his side exposed. Donley drove a fist into his father's kidney and a left hook that hit him square in the jaw and knocked him back against the wall.

His father just stood there, breathing heavily and perspiring profusely, wiping blood from his nose. For a moment, Donley thought he'd have the sense to just leave, to let them be, but they were beyond that now. They were too far along.

His father charged, his advance lazy and the swing of his arm looping and slow. Donley ducked beneath it and came up fast and hard, driving his shoulder into his father's gut, lifting with all the strength he could summon from the muscles in his legs, stomach, and back, and hurled his father up and over his shoulder.

The plate-glass window behind him exploded on impact, the sound reverberating like a thunderclap. Shards of glass cascaded like falling rain.

Donley stood in the living room, a breeze blowing in through the gaping hole where the window had been. He looked down at his father's contorted body. He lay sprawled on the concrete driveway, his neck and head twisted at an awkward angle, his body outlined in glass crystals reflecting the light from the street lamp, glistening like thousands of tiny diamonds.

And just like that, it was over.

◆ ◆ ◆

Kim guided Donley's face back to hers, lifting his chin, forcing him to look her in the eyes. "We'll get through this," she said. "Together. We'll get through it."

"I was taken to the hospital and stitched back together," he said. "For three days, I sat in that room not saying a word, not to my mother, not to Lou, not to anyone. I didn't eat. I didn't sleep. I really didn't want to live, Kim."

"It wasn't your fault, Peter."

"Lou and my mother gave the district attorney a full account of the abuse, and Lou was able to convince him that my father had attacked me and I had acted in self-defense. Since I was the only one who knew what happened, they declined to prosecute me. Three weeks later, I checked into the dorms at Berkeley, anonymous. Both my mother and I had a chance to start over. Things went well for a while; Lou got Mom a job at the courthouse and moved her into an apartment, and they brought her to every one of my games. It was the first time I ever recalled her looking and sounding happy. Then, in law school, the doctors diagnosed her cancer."

He shook his head. "After all she had been through, after all the crap she had endured. People say there is a God, but at that moment, I didn't believe it. I couldn't believe it. What kind of a God would do that to her?"

"And now, Peter? What do you believe now?"

He smiled. "Only a God could have brought me you and Benny."

Kim kissed him. "We'll put it behind us," she whispered. "We'll put it behind us and move forward. We'll do it together, Peter, whatever it takes—counseling, anything."

Donley felt his emotions overcome him, and he choked out the words. "I wouldn't have made it without you, Kim. I'm sorry. I'm so sorry."

They held each other, hearing the sounds of the hospital and low hum of a basketball-game broadcast coming from somewhere down the hall.

Finally, Donley said, "I'd like to go home. I'd like to see our son."

Chapter 24

Kim and Donley managed to avoid the cameras and the crowd gathered outside the hospital by sneaking out a doctor's entrance at the back of the building. The hospital staff brought Kim's car. Unfortunately, there was no separate entrance to their home.

The television reporters had camped out across the street, illuminated in the glow of lights that formed a pocket of daylight in the onset of night. A stiff breeze blew fog up the street and wreaked havoc on the reporters' hair and clothing as they stood holding microphones and waited to go live on the six o'clock evening news. There was a lot to cover, and Peter Donley would be a featured story. Anchors in newsroom studios continued to report on the bizarre series of events that had led to a massive manhunt for a decorated San Francisco police officer. The police chief had gone live earlier that evening and confirmed that Dixon Connor was a fugitive suspect in the murder of Andrew Bennet and should be considered armed and dangerous. The chief would not comment on the rampant rumors that Bennet had been blackmailing prominent businessmen, but like the swirling fog, the rumors grew thicker with each passing hour. The media wanted to know the contents of the videotapes and the sordid sexual activity they might reveal. They smelled headlines.

As Kim and Donley approached their driveway, Kim suggested they hole up in a hotel for a day, but Donley dismissed it. This was his house, his home. He would not go into seclusion again. He would not hide his past.

The crowd surged, overwhelming the two officers who tried in vain to part a path to the driveway. Faces pressed against the glass, shouting questions through the closed windows. Kim inched the car forward, allowing it to part the masses. One of the officers moved a barricade, and the car descended their sloped driveway into the sanctity of the garage, but even as the garage door lowered, the reporters continued to shout their questions.

"That explains why Anne has the phone off the hook," Kim said.

"And why the amazing sleeping dog is barking hysterically out back," Donley said.

Kim opened the passenger door and retrieved Peter's crutches from the backseat. They were awkward to use, but with his strength returning, Donley would manage.

"The back steps will be a problem," she said. They were narrow and steep.

"Well, I'm not going back out front," he said. "I'll go around the side to the back, take care of the ferocious watchdog, and come through the kitchen."

"OK, just let me help you."

He waved her off. "You're going to be taking care of me for the next six weeks; don't be too anxious to get started. I'm fine. It's only three steps up to the deck. Take care of Benny, and see about getting Anne home."

Kim walked around the front of the car. "You're sure?"

"I have to learn how to use these things sometime."

Kim disappeared up the back staircase. Donley hobbled out the side door to the dog run, a six-foot-tall redwood fence down the side of the property. He flipped a light switch on the side of the house, illuminating the deck in a powerful floodlight. Bo struggled at the end of a leash tethered to a stake in the ground. With effort, Donley managed to bend down and unhook him. When he did, the dog took off like a shot across the deck, leash trailing him through the dog door and into the house.

Donley shook his head. "Glad to see you, too, pal." He retrieved the tin dog bowl and placed it beneath the outdoor spigot. As it filled with water, Donley looked over the top of the fence at the glowing white light. A stiff breeze blew a hanging wire past him. He followed it to the side of the house and up to where it hung from a telephone pole.

Anne wasn't answering the phone.

Donley dropped the water bowl and noticed the shattered windowpane in the basement door. Inside the house, Bo continued to growl and bark.

Heart pounding, Donley hobbled as quickly as the pain allowed, struggling up the three wooden porch steps. He reached over the top of the fence for the latch, shoved the gate open, and hurried across the back porch. The door into the kitchen was unlocked.

"Kim?" he called out, hobbling across the linoleum.

She did not answer.

Shadows flickered from the fire in the living-room fireplace.

"Kim?"

He crossed to the hall. The light in the bathroom illuminated a wedge on the parquet floor. Donley used his crutch to push open the door. Water filled the bathtub. Steam had fogged the mirror, but the room was empty. Bo barked from the back bedroom.

Donley retreated and approached, and slowly opened the door.

Anne sat on the edge of the bed holding Benny, who was wrapped in a canary-yellow bath towel. Kim stood close by, gripping Bo by the leash and collar. Standing by the rocking chair in the corner of the room, Dixon Connor held the .44 Magnum in a bloodied, heavily bandaged hand.

"Looks like the guest of honor has arrived," Connor said in a raspy voice. "Good of you to join us, Counselor." Connor's face was an ashen gray. "I thought maybe you wouldn't make it."

Benny reached for Kim, crying and calling for her.

Donley could not swallow. For a moment, he could not breathe. "It's OK, Ben," he said softly. "It's all right."

"Sure, it is," Connor said. "It's a regular fucking tea party."

"Let them go, Connor. This is between me and you."

"Just as soon as I get what I came for."

"Whatever you want. Just let everyone else go."

Connor grimaced, and the barrel of the gun lowered. Bo lunged. Connor raised the gun.

"No!" Donley yelled.

"If you release that dog, I'll shoot it, then you, in that order," Connor said to Kim.

"Calm down," Donley said. "She's not going to release the dog, Connor. You're not going to shoot anybody. Just let them go."

"I want the videotape."

"OK, but I don't have it."

"Well, then, I guess you have nothing I want." Connor pulled back the hammer on the gun.

"No! I don't have it here, but I know where it is."

Connor's eyebrows arched.

"I left it in the wrecking yard. I hid it. We can go get it."

He hoped the tape and Father Martin's black book remained in the pocket of his jacket stuck in the barbed wire atop the fence.

"I told you, you're a shitty liar. You should really think about another profession."

"We'll get the video," Donley said. "And Father Martin's Bible. You and me."

"You and me and the Chinawoman here will go together. If anyone calls the police, I'll kill you both."

Donley wanted Connor out of the room. He wanted him away from Kim and Benny and Anne.

"You'll have me and the tape. You said yourself, you can bargain for anything you want with the tape."

Connor grimaced in pain, shuffling along the side of the bed. "Move that dog out of my way."

Kim stepped back, pulling Bo with her. He continued to growl. Benny reached out to Kim as she passed. Connor pointed the gun at the back of her head. "Tie the dog up." Kim tied Bo's leash to the bed frame. Once she had, Connor spoke to Donley and Kim, motioning with the gun. "Move."

They stepped from the room. Connor shut the door behind them, muffling the sound of Bo's barking.

Donley said, "My car keys are in the other room."

"Get 'em."

He hopped on his good leg, crutches in hand, into Benny's room. Kim and Connor followed. The desk was in the corner. Donley looked to Benny's bed. Unmade, the covers had been thrown to the side. Simeon was gone.

"Hold it," Connor said as Donley reached for the drawer handle. Connor walked into the room and stood by the side of the desk. He pressed the gun to Kim's head.

Donley pulled open the desk drawer and picked up a set of keys. "OK?"

"The Chinawoman will drive. Give her the keys."

Donley handed Kim the keys.

"Now move."

Donley couldn't let Connor get them into the car. If he did, they'd be trapped, and any chance of escape or fighting back would be severely reduced. He worried about Kim getting hurt.

Out of the corner of his eye, he saw the closet door start to swing open.

"Connor," he said, drawing his attention.

"What—"

Danny Simeon burst from the closet, switchblade in hand. Connor swung the gun toward Simeon. Donley lunged and fell into him, getting his hands on the barrel and shoving it upward. It discharged into the ceiling. Donley and Connor fell backward, crashing into the onrushing Simeon.

Connor screamed in pain, the knife embedded in his back. Donley yanked the gun from his hand and turned to tell Kim to run, but she was already on the move, out of the room to the back of the house.

By the time Donley had redirected his attention, Connor was on his knees, with Danny Simeon standing over him, holding the bloodied knife to Connor's throat.

"No!" Donley yelled.

Anger had contorted Simeon's face into a sickening mask.

Donley put out his hand. "Danny, give me the knife."

Simeon shook his head.

"Danny, put the knife down. You don't want to do this."

"I do. He deserves to die for what he did."

"If you kill him, you'll never be rid of him. You'll never be able to get that face out of your mind."

Simeon seethed.

"It will haunt you for the rest of your life, Danny. He isn't worth it. Give me the knife."

Simeon's chest heaved.

"Let him go, Danny. Father Tom needs you. Those boys need you."

Simeon released his grip and stepped back, his body shaking.

Donley managed to pull himself onto his good leg and gently eased the knife from Simeon's hand.

Chapter 25

Donley waited patiently in the modest reception area outside what the polls were predicting would not be Gil Ramsey's office for much longer. Donley had dressed casually in a blue shirt and his leather jacket, which he and Ross had retrieved from atop the fence at the junkyard. He'd had to slice the seam of one leg of his blue jeans to accommodate his cast.

The telephone rang at the receptionist's console. The woman took the call, then stood and advised Donley that Mr. Ramsey would see him. Donley fit his crutches under his arms and followed her down the hallway to Ramsey's open door. Ramsey came out from behind his desk and greeted Donley with a smile.

Donley declined coffee, and the two men forsook the handshake, given the crutches.

"I'm sorry to have kept you waiting."

"No rush," Donley said.

"I understand you've filed a civil action?"

In the two weeks that had passed since the night of Dixon Connor's arrest, Donley had filed a civil action against the city and county of San Francisco and the San Francisco Sheriff's Office for the "mistake" that had caused Father Martin to be placed in general population and nearly killed. The city, now eager to wash its hands of the entire sordid affair, wanted to resolve the matter quietly. Before coming to Ramsey's office, Donley had been down the hall, listening to a six-figure settlement offer.

"I'm glad to hear you're doing better," Ramsey said. "I'll tell you now, from the moment I met you, I admired your courage and your poise under some pretty heavy fire."

Donley didn't respond.

"Have a seat," Ramsey said, walking behind his desk.

Donley remained standing. "Thanks, but I don't intend to be long."

"However I can accommodate you," Ramsey said. "I assume you're here about Father Martin's criminal matter?"

"No. I assume that case is closed."

"Based upon your statement, Frank Ross's statement, and the statements of the other witnesses, there was more than enough evidence to convict Dixon Connor of all three deaths, if he had lived."

Dixon Connor had remained in intensive care for three days. He had lost a considerable amount of blood, and his body was riddled with infection from the piece of steel that had pierced his back and ruptured his liver. The doctors said Connor never regained consciousness, never put up a struggle. Connor's fight was over.

That hadn't stopped the families of the three boys from suing the city and the county in civil actions.

"I came to ask about the prosecution of the men Bennet was blackmailing," Donley said.

Ramsey shook his head. "Well, that's a problem, of course. Unfortunately, it appears that if other videos existed, they were either destroyed or they're hidden someplace."

Gil Ramsey was partially correct. At Donley's suggestion to Aileen O'Malley, the police department had issued a statement that they'd found a key to a storage locker in Dixon Connor's home and were working to locate that locker. Donley had hoped the fear of the tapes being revealed would cause some of the men on them to come forward.

A few had.

"I understand from Lieutenant O'Malley that two more came forward last week," Donley said. "Will they be prosecuted?"

Ramsey shook his head. "The fact that these men are coming forward shows they are remorseful. Besides, as you indicated, there is no hard evidence to prosecute them and the statute of limitations is a problem. We're recommending community service and counseling."

"Maybe the threat of being exposed will at least make some of the others who don't come forward consider what they've done."

"One would hope," Ramsey agreed.

"I wonder," Donley said, "whether any of this would have happened if Jack Devine had been prosecuted."

Ramsey went pale.

"You see, Mr. Ramsey, I have a theory. I learned it from a judge. I don't believe men like Jack Devine are sorry for what they do. I think they're only sorry they get caught."

Ramsey did not respond.

"If Jack Devine had been prosecuted, the existence of the tapes might have been revealed then, before Connor found out about them, and those three boys would still be alive. Perhaps the men on those tapes would have been prosecuted."

"Hindsight is always twenty-twenty," Ramsey said.

"Devine said it was because his father was a personal friend of the governor, your father. He said your father convinced you not to prosecute him."

"Did he?"

"Why would your father be so intent on convincing you not to prosecute a scumbag pedophile like Jack Devine?"

Ramsey's jaw tightened. "Mr. Devine isn't exactly credible, Mr. Donley. It never happened that way."

"No? Devine is convinced it did."

"He's mistaken."

"I guess it's like those tapes, huh? Without them, nothing can be proven."

"I'm afraid not."

"What did you say to me the first time we met in this office?" Donley lowered his head, as if thinking, but he remembered Ramsey's words well. "Justice isn't always about right or wrong. It's all about what we can and can't prove."

Ramsey nodded.

"I found Father Martin's Bible and the log-in sheet for that night."

Ramsey paused. "Did you?"

Donley pulled folded papers from his pocket. He'd given the original copy to Aileen O'Malley. "Connor took it when he broke into the office. He was worried it would reveal that Bennet had brought a tape to the shelter."

Ramsey cleared his throat. "Does it?"

"No, unfortunately."

"Well," he said, "I guess we'll never know if a tape ever existed then, or if Connor was just bluffing."

"Bluffing?"

"Whether he made it up."

Donley looked around the spartan furnishings. "It looks like everything worked out for you, didn't it?"

"I'm eager to win and to get to Sacramento and get started."

Donley turned as if to leave, then turned back. "You have no remorse, do you?" When Ramsey did not immediately answer, Donley said, "You could have put a stop to it. You could have done the right thing. I just gave you another chance to do the right thing, but you have no interest in that, do you?"

"I have no idea what you're talking about."

"Sure you do. Dixon Connor told me all about it that night, about your father on the videotape, and the money you were going to pay Connor to get it back. He told me everything."

Ramsey raised his chin, defiant to the end. "And as I said, Mr. Donley, justice isn't always about right and wrong. It's about what can and can't be proven. And you can't prove anything. Not now, anyway. Not with Dixon Connor dead."

Donley smiled. "I've always wondered why it is that men like you and your father end up landing on your feet while people like Andrew Bennet get trampled."

"People get trampled every day," Ramsey said. "It takes strength to survive. It takes great strength."

"Dixon Connor said something similar to me. He called it survival of the fittest."

"Perhaps," Ramsey said, "though I wouldn't want to be linked in any way to Dixon Connor."

Donley locked eyes with him, reached inside his jacket, and removed a copy of the videotape. Ramsey went white. Donley placed the copy on Ramsey's desk.

After a moment, he said, "And yet you are."

EPILOGUE

The ceremony to reopen the Tenderloin boys' shelter was short and simple. Archbishop Donatello Parnisi gave a brief speech from the steps of the building to a crowd of about fifteen who had braved a cold March morning to celebrate. Then, he and Father Martin cut a red ribbon stretched across the entrance, and Parnisi extended to his full height to pull down a piece of brown paper covering a bronze plaque above the shelter's entrance.

THE FATHER THOMAS MARTIN BOYS' SHELTER
OF THE ARCHDIOCESE OF SAN FRANCISCO

Frank Ross popped a cork on a bottle, drawing everyone's attention.

"Sparkling cider," he said, filling Mike and Rochelle Harris's outstretched paper cups.

"I'll take one with alcohol," Lou Giantelli said.

"No, you won't." Sarah said. She looked to Peter. "I have to watch his diet like a hawk."

Ruth-Bell held out her glass. "I'll take his and mine. He's more ornery than before he had the heart attack."

Lou had cut back work to two days a week and retired completely from any trial work or court appearances, though he still ventured into the office every day "just to check on things." It was Donley's practice now. He'd turned down the offer to work for Max Seager.

Danny Simeon released colorful balloons into a clear blue sky, which thrilled Benny, who was bundled in Kim's arms. Then Simeon handed Father Martin a computer mouse. "You got one kick-ass computer, Father T. I'm just sorry I won't get to teach you how to use it."

Simeon was moving on. He'd received a job offer with a computer company in Daly City.

"I'm happy you won't," Father Martin said.

"I'll be back, though," Simeon said. "You can count on it."

Father Martin approached Donley and Kim, who was starting to show. The two men stared at each other for a moment. Then Father Tom pulled Donley close, embracing him. "Thank you," he said. "For believing in me."

"Thank you for believing in me," Donley said.

Father Tom released his hug, and Parnisi put a meaty hand on Donley's shoulder. "As the new attorney for the archdiocese, I'll expect to see you in church tomorrow," he said. "That's my only requirement of church counsel."

"Is it a deal breaker?" Donley asked.

Kim slapped his shoulder.

"I'll be there," he said. "With Lou's clients, I can't afford to lose one who can actually pay its bills."

They laughed.

"Shall we see inside?" Father Martin said to those assembled.

Parnisi and Father Martin walked up the ramp to the entrance to the shelter. Kim handed Benny to Uncle Lou, and the others followed inside. With the money from the settlement of the civil action, and significant donations spurred by the media coverage of the events, the inside had been remodeled and updated, including Father Martin's own bedroom and private bathroom. He also now had a staff.

Frank Ross lingered behind with Kim and Donley. "Aileen O'Malley tells me Gil Ramsey is squealing like a pig."

Ramsey had little choice. The videotape clearly revealed his father, Augustus, with Andrew Bennet.

"His lawyers are trying to work out a plea deal," Donley said, "but the new district attorney isn't interested. She's pushing an obstruction of justice charge, among others. Apparently, she has political ambitions and sees this as an opportunity for advancement."

Ross chuckled at the irony. "What about Augustus?"

"So far, he's not saying a thing, but they're also focusing on him for what happened to Father Tom the night he got his blood drawn."

"Will they prosecute him as a pedophile?"

"I don't know. There are statute-of-limitations issues, but whether they prosecute him or not, he's done. Nobody wants anything to do with him."

Ross smiled at Kim. "Congratulations, by the way. When's the baby due?"

"September," she said.

"Summer. That's good," Ross said.

"Have you heard anything?" Donley asked. Frank Ross and his wife had filed to adopt twin boys.

"If all goes well, we'll have our new sons in six months."

"Congratulations," Peter and Kim said.

"I'm going to head in," Ross said. "You coming?"

"In a minute," Kim said, gripping Donley's hand and holding him back.

After Ross had departed, she reached into her purse and handed Donley a red envelope.

"What's this?"

"Your Christmas present."

Donley opened it and pulled out a sonogram. He stared at it, feeling the same glow he'd felt when they'd first seen Benny's sonogram. It felt good. It felt like a family. Lou had been right. Donley had needed to climb one more mountain, and now that he had, standing atop it, he could see their future. He liked what he saw.

He looked at Kim. "Are you going to hold me in suspense, Doctor?"

Kim smiled. "Say hello to your daughter, Peter."

ACKNOWLEDGMENTS

I wrote the first draft of this book in 1996. In 2003, when my agent went out with my first three novels, we received an offer of publication but decided to go a different direction with the first two David Sloane novels. This book got put in the proverbial writer's desk drawer. More than a decade later, after several more reiterations—OK, about ten rewrites—I'm pleased that it will be published.

I'm pleased because this book includes so many people who meant so much to me. Sam Goldman was, for seventy-three of his eighty-five years on this planet, a newspaperman, selling the *San Francisco Call-Bulletin* on San Francisco streets when he was not yet a teenager. I don't think Sam stopped for a minute from that point forward. He became a high school teacher, then a college journalism instructor and adviser, and that's where he came into and changed my life. Sam's enthusiasm and energy were boundless. I never saw him tire. He'd work all day in the journalism room, then jump in the car with his wife, Adele, and drive down to a Giants or 49ers or a Stanford game, and work in the press box. He called everyone hero, chief, and friend, even President Jimmy Carter. I know. I was there. When I mentioned it to him, he said, "He puts his pants on one leg at a time, just like me and you, chief."

He was one of a kind. He passed a couple of years ago, but I think of him almost every day. He's with me when I teach and when I write. He's with me every time I put on a tie—one of his ties, given to me by his daughter, Ruth. Usually I wear Mickey Mouse, but sometimes it is a tie with dozens of books on bookshelves. I keep smiling, Sam, for you. I keep smiling.

Bo the Rhodesian ridgeback also passed before this book was published. After twelve years, he developed Alzheimer's or dementia, and it was painful to watch our dog—our children's first dog—deteriorate. We were grief-stricken when the time came to say good-bye, but Bo, being such a great dog, made the decision easy. He looked at my wife, whom he loved most of all, lay down on the veterinarian's table, and just closed his eyes. He never regained consciousness. He just slipped away. We buried him with Nick, our first Rhodesian and his buddy.

Archbishop Donatello Parnisi was based on my cousin, Monsignor Charles Durkin. "Cuz," as I called him, was a bear of a man, more than six foot six and 250 pounds with a voice that made an organ envious. He smoked a pipe, and I recall the smell of it and the way he held it in his mouth, though I now wish he'd never smoked. Stomach cancer took him just short of his eightieth birthday. Charlie was the historian for the Branick, Mullins, and Durkin families. I loved him like he was my uncle. At his funeral, his nephew relayed Charlie's battle with the then-archbishop of San Francisco. I, too, was aware of it. So I decided to make Charlie the archbishop of San Francisco as Donatello Parnisi. I hope you're up there in heaven having a good laugh, Charlie.

Lou Giantelli is loosely based upon my uncle Lou, who for many years was counsel to the Archdiocese of Sacramento and an incredibly formidable lawyer. Back in the day, he was also a celebrated football player. Lou used to come to our house and balance us on the soles of his feet, then drop us, but he always managed to catch us. He was great fun. He, too, has passed, along with his wife, Auntie Gerry. They were good to our entire family, always hosting us for Easter in Sacramento, where they had a pool and a big backyard. I loved them both.

All other characters in this book are fictional.

Let me also say that while Peter Donley's father was a monster, my father, William Dugoni, was the best man I've ever known. I lost "Pops" in June 2008, but I was blessed to be there when he went. He taught me many life lessons. In death, he taught me perhaps the most important. As I sat at his desk the morning he died, I was looking at all his watches and rings. My dad liked to go to New York and collect them. Some weren't worth much, but some he'd picked up on his and my mother's travels, and they were worth some money. And yet, as I sat at his desk that morning, he spoke to me. He said, "It's just stuff, Bobby. It's just stuff." And he's right. I've never again worried about the stuff in life, and I've never felt so unencumbered.

Because the novel was first written two decades ago, much of the settings have changed. At the time, I relied on my knowledge of San Francisco, having lived and worked there for fifteen years, as well as on research. The city has changed, however, and I'm well aware of that. So I kept the story set in 1987, when the Superior Courts remained in city hall, the Hall of Justice was on Bryant Street, the new jail hadn't been built, and we didn't have cell phones or e-mail. I love San Francisco. I know it isn't perfect, but to me, it remains the greatest city on the planet.

I'm blessed to have so many who have helped my career from the day I took a leap of faith and left the practice of law to write novels.

Thank you to super agent Meg Ruley and her team at the Jane Rotrosen Agency, including Rebecca Scherer, who offers terrific suggestions for my manuscripts and is an absolute wiz on everything to do with e-books. From the day I wrote *The 7th Canon*, Meg said it would be published, and she was right, as she is with just about everything that has to do with my career. Thank you all.

Thanks to Thomas & Mercer for believing in this manuscript. This is the fourth novel with the T&M team, and I couldn't be happier with everything you've done for me and my career. Special thanks to Charlotte Herscher, developmental editor. She's edited all my novels. This one was challenging, and she patiently allowed me to work some things through. Thanks also to Elizabeth Johnson, copy editor. I asked for the best, grammar and punctuation not being my strength, and they immediately recommended Elizabeth. She pushes me on just about every sentence and word choice, and the books are infinitely more accurate.

Thanks to Jacque BenZekry, then in marketing, who is a true force of nature and does an incredible job promoting my novels. Your efforts pushed me to number one, and I hope we can light that number again. Thanks to Tiffany Pokorny and Sarah Shaw in author relations for always going the extra step to make me feel appreciated. My family has become a big fan of Thomas & Mercer for all the terrific gifts and little acknowledgments you send. You are the best. Thanks to my publicist, Dennelle Catlett, for promoting me and my work. Thanks to my former publicist and new editor, Gracie Doyle. She works tirelessly to help me improve my work and find the next great story. Thanks to Kjersti Egerdahl, acquisitions editor, and Sean Baker, production manager. Sean, your covers are the bomb! Thanks to publisher Mikyla Bruder, associate publisher Hai-Yen Mura, and Jeff Belle, vice president of Amazon Publishing. These people all walk the walk when it comes to their authors and their authors' work, and each has helped me quickly to feel at home.

Special thanks to Thomas & Mercer's former editorial director, Alan Turkus, for his guidance, spot-on editorial advice, and friendship. By the time *The 7th Canon* is published, Alan will be settled in Minnesota working on his own novels, and I sincerely hope you light the #1 sign at Thomas & Mercer.

Thanks to Tami Taylor, who runs my website, creates my foreign-language book covers, creates my newsletter, and otherwise does a fantastic job. Thanks to Sean McVeigh at 425 Media for his help with all my social-media needs. You're both a lot smarter than I am, and I'm glad to have you on my team. Thanks to Pam Binder and the Pacific Northwest Writers Association for their tremendous support of my work.

Thank you also to the loyal readers who write to tell me how much they enjoy my books and await the next. You are the reason I keep looking for the next great story.

Thanks to Joe and Catherine and to my wife, Cristina. After eleven novels, you know I couldn't do this without you three. You know how much I love you all and how proud I am of both our children.

Thanks to my mother, Patty Dugoni. You've always been my inspiration. When things get tough, I think of you, raising ten kids, going back to school at forty, starting your own accounting business, and forty-three years later still going to work at your own business. Remarkable. At eighty-three, my mother attends writers' conferences with me, and by the second day, everyone is talking about how wonderful she is. They're right. Love you, Ma.

ABOUT THE AUTHOR

Robert Dugoni is the author of the bestselling Tracy Crosswhite series (*My Sister's Grave, Her Final Breath*, and *In the Clearing*) as well as the critically acclaimed David Sloane series (*The Jury Master, Wrongful Death, Bodily Harm, Murder One*, and *The Conviction*). He's been ranked number one on Amazon's list of most popular authors in the United States, Great Britain, Germany, France, and Italy, and he has been a *New York Times, Wall Street Journal*, and Amazon bestseller multiple times. Dugoni was nominated twice for the Harper Lee Award for Legal Fiction and for the International Thriller Award. *My Sister's Grave* won the 2015 Nancy Pearl Award for Fiction and was named one of the best thrillers of 2014 by *Library Journal* and *Suspense Magazine*. Dugoni's nonfiction exposé, *The Cyanide Canary*, was a *Washington Post* Best Book of the Year, and the *Providence Journal* referred to him as "the undisputed king of the legal thriller" and "heir to Grisham's literary throne." Visit his website at www.robertdugoni.com, e-mail him at bob@robertdugoni.com, and follow him on Twitter at @robertdugoni and on Facebook at www.facebook.com/AuthorRobertDugoni.